# KRISTOFFERSON
## THE WILD AMERICAN

# KRISTOFFERSON

## THE WILD AMERICAN

**STEPHEN MILLER**

UNAUTHORISED

**OMNIBUS PRESS**

London / New York / Paris / Sydney / Copenhagen / Berlin / Madrid / Tokyo

**Exclusive Distributors**
Music Sales Limited,
14/15 Berners Street,
London, W1T 3LJ.

Music Sales Corporation,
257 Park Avenue South,
New York, NY 10010, USA.

Macmillan Distribution Services,
56 Parkwest Drive
Derrimut, Vic 3030,
Australia.

Every effort has been made to trace the copyright holders of the photographs
in this book but one or two were unreachable. We would be grateful if the
photographers concerned would contact us.

Typesetting by Galleon Typesetting.
Printed in the EU.

A catalogue record for this book is available from the British Library.

Visit Omnibus Press on the web at www.omnibuspress.com.

# Contents

*For Sasha*

# Acknowledgements

There was never any chance of Kris Kristofferson co-operating with this book. I knew before I contacted his wife Lisa – who manages a lot of Kris' business affairs – that Kristofferson had signed a deal with Hyperion to write his memoirs. There had been talk of some kind of autobiographical book for years. When challenged on the subject by a television interviewer in 1999, not long after his triple heart bypass operation, Kristofferson gave various reasons for not having got down to it. "Maybe I'm afraid to get started."

He said he had always thought he would begin work on such a book when he "slowed down a bit" but that this had not happened. Kristofferson conceded that he had some difficulty disciplining himself to undertake such a lengthy project – he has always worked best with shorter work, principally the kind of poetic lyrics which characterise so many of his songs.

A number of publication dates for his memoirs have been mentioned from time to time but as yet there is no sign of the book. Amazon's website currently carries a slightly misleading entry for an "untitled auto-biography" which it claims is, "Currently unavailable . . . we don't know when or if this item will be back in stock." This lack of definitive progress has caused some good-natured irritation among fans eagerly anticipating Kristofferson's own account of his remarkable life; "The best unpublished book I never read," joked one Amazon reviewer. "If you are not going to write the damn book," complained another, "just kill it and be done with it. At least put out a REAL publication date."

Kristofferson's memoirs will doubtless appear eventually but Lisa made it clear to me that he would not co-operate with anyone wanting to write his biography in the meantime. She also warned me about the World Wide Web saying that "much of what is on the Internet is factually incorrect." This may ring true, making cross-checking essential, but the Internet also allows writers to access vast amounts of information in a very short space of time, making it possible, for instance, to obtain details of albums, films or to check dates, a spelling, etc., etc. – and to do so in a very short space of time.

Furthermore, it enabled me to see many articles online; those from before World War II provided some fascinating glimpses into the bygone world of Kristofferson's early upbringing. I venture to suggest that the chapters on this period might contain some information of which the subject himself was unaware.

The Internet also helped me to carry out much detective work, sometimes successful, sometimes fruitless, but always stimulating – albeit with the major challenge of resisting the temptation to follow the countless digressional distractions on offer. Comparatively late in my research, I picked up the fact that Kris had been one of the artists performing for passengers on a QE2 cruise in 1992. After surfing about for a while, and nearly giving up, I managed to track down a musician who played on the same trip and who gave me a good story about Kristofferson's appearance in jeans and boots in front of a prosperous, formally dressed audience.

Similarly, I managed to locate Kristofferson's first wife, Fran. She refused an interview request but I did manage to find a tribute to her recently deceased companion of many years which provided interesting information on some aspects of the life Fran chose after her turbulent times with her first husband.

Since Kristofferson did not want any involvement, it was not surprising that his family and ex-family members did not want to co-operate either. This extended to some of the musicians who are most closely associated with Kristofferson. I was however surprised, not to say, frustrated, that some people with only a minor connection followed suit. Initially enthusiastic, a number of potential interviewees in this category backed off after receiving a negative response to the question, "Is it authorised?" I think the problem, particularly with musicians, is the fear of doing anything which might cause offence or be seen as some kind of betrayal; especially in the Nashville music scene where there is a small interdependent world. The fear is that careless talk might cost jobs, even careers.

However, I am indebted to the following people for their contributions:

Bill Black, Sandie Black, James Blundell, Bobbi Boyce, Chris Charlesworth, Jack Clement, Graeme Connors, Michael Creed,

Fred Foster, Donnie Fritts, Chris Gantry, Dave Gibbons, George Hamilton IV, Stacy Harris, Tony Hatch, Ronnie Hawkins, John Hedley, Byron House, Dave Johnston, Marilyn Sellars Kuipers, Spencer Leigh, Paul Lincoln, Barry McGuire, Mark McKinnon, Sue Marshall, Edward Miller, Fred Mollin, Andy Neill, Murdoch Nicolson, Beth Odel, Cynthia Peters, Dave Roe, Neil Ross, John Sayles, Chris Schofield, Hazel Smith, David Simons, David Sinclair, Professor Frederick Sontag, Jonny Steingold, John Tobler, United Nations Reference Team, Thalia Watmough, John Buck Wilkin, S. Brian Willson.

I must also mention a chance encounter at a cocktail party at the Edinburgh Festival last year which afforded me some valuable insights into one of Kristofferson's early inspirations. I found myself in conversation with Professor W H Stevenson, a leading Blake scholar, and I am most grateful to him for the picture he painted not just of William Blake, the polymath and his varied artistic endeavours, but also aspects of Blake's private domestic life.

As ever, my thanks go to Judy for her love, support and instinctive counselling skills.

*Stephen Miller*
*June 2008*

# Introduction

THE Playhouse, Edinburgh, April 1, 2007. As the house lights dim, an expectant murmur rises among the audience. For many, it will be their first, and quite possibly, last opportunity to experience an intimate communion with one of music's truly legendary figures. Suddenly, cheers and whistles rise up as a black-clad figure with a strapped-on acoustic guitar shuffles into the limelight. Is that really Kris Kristofferson?

Unlike some others in the business, Kristofferson is not obsessed with staying young and beautiful. His appearance and demeanour resemble that of a busker and at times, the stark lighting blurs the careworn facial features, the unkempt grey hair and beard, creating a white and ghostly apparitional effect akin to the one imprinted on the Turin Shroud.

Despite almost 40 years of performing in front of audiences both large and small, Kristofferson's well-documented stage nerves are still in evidence. Only after singing a few songs, making several mistakes and rapping with the audience does he seem to relax a little. He even injects some self-deprecating humour. "I just want you to know that if you're trying to clap along with me and we're not together, it's not your fault."

But Kristofferson does not reveal much of himself; a few self-conscious anecdotes of little consequence, a humble expression of gratitude or two, no more. The impression is of a reluctant entertainer striving to rise above a natural aversion to public displays. In some ways, Kristofferson has only made it harder for himself, having dispensed with the security of a live band with just a guitar, a couple of harmonicas and his voice – an acquired taste to put it mildly – to fall back on.

Like all performers Kristofferson appreciates the approval of an audience but he also feels a sense of duty – of the kind his father, a Major General in the American Air Force, instilled in him from an early age. Not content with merely being a popular entertainer, Kristofferson saw the importance in getting a message across – whether personal or political. For years his gifts as a writer enabled him to describe the human condition in an individualistic way and since the mid-Eighties, his ire has mostly been directed at his country's successive governments over their questionable foreign policy – as he sees it.

Predictably this can have a polarising effect on Kristofferson's audiences. In the Eighties, Ronald Reagan enjoyed considerable support and the views Kristofferson stuck his neck out to deliver were in the minority, resulting in people picketing his concerts. Nowadays more and more people have come to agree with his leftist opinions and at the Edinburgh show, many applaud his anti-establishment views – "I admire your spirit" he drawls with apparent sincerity.

However, Kristofferson's shows are not solely politically charged. Over the course of two hours, he delivers a diverse range of songs from a large back catalogue, including the four that brought him into prominence, namely 'Me And Bobby McGee', 'For The Good Times', 'Help Me Make It Through The Night' and 'Sunday Morning Coming Down'. Writer Jack Hurst described Kristofferson's best work as, "That of an educated and intelligent wanderer, an inveterate prowler into late evenings and deep bottles, an incorrigible hitch-hiker thumbing his erratic way across horizons both geographical and philosophical."

Kristofferson has indeed crammed a vast amount of experience into his 72 years. Born into a privileged world in Texas, he was a high achiever from an early age, in school, sport and other extracurricular activities. Initially he followed the conventional path his parents' high expectations held for him, becoming a Rhodes Scholar studying English literature at Oxford University's Merton College. His folks were a great deal less understanding of his love for Hank Williams – direct country music that addressed the concerns of those at the other end of the social scale. Kris started writing songs from an early age, some that aped the Williams style, and during his time at Oxford, he tried to kick-start a career in music. However, it proved a false start and as the Fifties became the Sixties, Kristofferson returned to America, a conventional marriage and career beckoning.

To his family and their social circle, everything looked to be going as planned. However, under the surface Kristofferson knew he was not following his heart. He served time in the army, but his penchant for carousing and performing improvised versions of country songs indicated that a traditional career was not for him. In 1965, he shocked his family by quitting the army and relocating to Nashville to follow his dream of being a songwriter. Several years of dues-paying followed with Kristofferson scraping a living from a variety of jobs. Despite the calibre of his educational background, Kristofferson sought jobs that required no qualifications at all, "that didn't take any kind of brains". He was determined to educate himself in all walks of life, as some of his literary influences had, to provide inspiration for his writing.

Although he placed an inevitable strain on his marriage by a lack of money or being absent in Music City's honky-tonks, he found Nashville in the Sixties exhilarating and has since said that going there "saved his life". Eventually, after sheer hard graft and a few lucky breaks, the rewards did come. "You have to believe in yourself," Kristofferson reflected. "If you don't, nobody else will." It was as one of his literary heroes, William Blake, had proposed: "If the fool would persist in his folly he would become wise."

Kristofferson's most enduring songs became hits for some of the top male and female artists of the early Seventies, achieving massive sales and a slew of top awards. Janis Joplin's 'Me And Bobby McGee', Ray Price's 'For The Good Times', Johnny Cash's 'Sunday Morning Coming Down' and Sammi Smith's 'Help Me Make It Through The Night' clearly demonstrated that Kristofferson's remarkable gift enabled him to reach all areas of popular music including rock, soul, easy listening and folk as well as country.

Reflecting on Kristofferson's sudden emergence, one commentator said he possessed "that particular, indefinable power that every straightforward and sentimental artist needs to elevate naive clichés into native myths".

Many became fans of Kristofferson's music even though most could not put a face to the name. His best songs were simple, well-written and catered to wide interpretation, as exemplified by some of those who have covered 'Me And Bobby McGee': Bill Haley and The Comets, The Grateful Dead, Jerry Lee Lewis, Lonnie Donegan, Roger Miller, LeAnn Rimes, The Platters, Arlo Guthrie, Joan Baez, Dolly Parton, Olivia Newton-John, etc.

Only a handful of songwriters have the ability to transform a random collection of ideas, observations and images, combining personal experience and human emotion, into an accessible three-minute hit record and Kristofferson was one of them. Kristofferson's early classics adhered to legendary writer Harlan Howard's maxim about good country songs: "they don't mystify you." In a relatively short space of time, he had done what so many others could only dream of on his own terms. As his friend Willie Nelson confirmed, "Kris made his own rules, did it his own way."

Kristofferson also gave Nashville a much needed shot in the arm, transforming the way country songs were written in much the same way Bob Dylan altered rock songcraft – although, as Bobby Bare pointed out, Kristofferson's songs "are basic country but the way he puts them across, the way he puts his words together, is much deeper than the average song". George Hamilton IV described Kristofferson's music as "very sophisticated thinking man's country", while Waylon Jennings said he was like nothing Nashville had heard before, bringing "a new maturity and sophistication to country lyrics, and explicitness to the verse". There is no doubt that Kristofferson was also responsible for bringing more overt references to sex into country in particular and pop in general.

For his own part Kristofferson modestly claimed that his songs didn't exactly break new ground but were finding new ways to talk of people and their relationships in ways that reflected the changing times. He avoided judging personal failings, preferring to empathise with the subject; he knew from personal experience that life involved difficult choices and a distinct lack of easy answers. For him, loneliness and isolation were no abstract notions in view of his estrangement from his family, the failure of his first marriage and the fact that his children lived far away from Nashville.

The concepts of living for the moment and the pursuit of freedom also featured regularly in his songs. Sometimes idealised, but often imbued with doom and foreboding, there was a sense that freedom was the ultimate human goal but one that was often not achieved because it was so hard to attain. Though usually described in personal terms, there is little doubt that ruminations on freedom in Kris' songs chimed with some of the important movements of social liberation of the Sixties and Seventies such as civil rights and feminism.

By the time he achieved his breakthrough Kristofferson was approaching his mid-thirties – a decade or so older than many of the struggling Nashville writers he hung out with and only a few years younger than established stars like Johnny Cash, Merle Haggard or George Jones. While he was excited to find himself in this company, he was not overawed.

When success came he was able to function as an equal, respectful but not unduly deferential.

Kristofferson never again came close to matching the spectacular success of his early Seventies period in terms of creative and commercial achievement. As his record sales dwindled, he became increasingly drawn to the world of cinema and starred in some of the best-known films of the Seventies including *Pat Garrett And Billy The Kid*, *A Star Is Born*, *Alice Doesn't Live Here Anymore* and the notorious *Heaven's Gate*, which set his acting aspirations back with a jolt. For a time, Kristofferson was not offered serious leading roles and when the roles did start to come in again, they were for television films and cinema of limited artistic merit. Nonetheless he persevered, more out of financial necessity, and in recent years, Kristofferson has secured smaller parts in films, some of which have garnered favourable critical comment.

Kristofferson's vocal criticisms of American foreign policy helped to ensure that his musical output remained commercially redundant for a time. However, he enjoyed a taste of renewed mainstream success in 1985 after hooking up with Johnny Cash, Waylon Jennings and Willie Nelson in The Highwaymen, which ended up stretching over a 10-year period in the studio and on the road. For Kristofferson, it was always the greatest pleasure to spend time with artists who started out as his heroes and ended up close friends.

In the course of an extraordinary career, Kristofferson has had to struggle with a major drink problem and depression; he got the better of the former but continues to battle with the latter. His second wife, the popular singer Rita Coolidge, fell for his magnetic and seductive charms and initially toured with her soon-to-be husband on his road shows in the early Seventies. But by the end of the decade, her star was outshining his and, while this contributed to the strain on their union, a decade of Kris' hard living and womanising spelt the end of their relationship.

Divorced and estranged from his children, he was fortunate to get another chance at turning his life around with a woman 20 years his junior. He has come to value and cherish the joys of a rich family life as the father of eight children – some young enough to be his grandchildren – on the Hawaiian island of Maui.

On a personal level he has regrets about the many upsets he caused those closest to him. However, he tries not to cast such regrets aside because his

actions were part of the journey that brought him to the feeling of fulfilment, of a life well lived, that he enjoys today.

As this biography sets out to show, Kris Kristofferson has enriched and
been enriched by the lives of a vast number of people and the human
events and circumstances that have shaped, affected and in some cases
destroyed them. To a great many fellow artists, aspiring and established, he
is simply the songwriter's songwriter.

While it would be no exaggeration to describe him as a polymath, the
key to Kristofferson's importance as an artist remains his affecting ability as
a lyricist – the one creative outlet that he will pursue to the last. In doing
so, he will assuredly endeavour to follow his own lessons on life: "Tell the
truth. Sing with passion. Work with laughter. Love with heart."

As he said, "I feel luckier every day with just what I've had in my life.
It's been such a full one."

*Stephen Miller,*
*June 2008*

# Chapter 1

KRIS Kristofferson's ancestry can be traced back to Dalarna, an ancient province of central Sweden covering approximately 30,000 square kilometres. Among the district's outstanding natural features is the freshwater Lake Siljan, one of countless lakes dotted around the landscape, situated in the centre of the province with a surface area of 290 square kilometres. The northern part lies within the Scandinavian mountain range, while the southern region is characterised by large plains that have historically provided many of the crops grown to support the country's population.

Records going back to the 16th century show that the Kristoffersons, along with their relations and ancestors, were predominantly farmers although some other occupations – filer, permanent juryman, soldier, church warden – were registered. A few were members of the Swedish Riksdag (parliament). In the second half of the 17th century, Dalarna's northern area was among a number of provinces in Sweden to experience a rash of witch hunts. Women were denounced for practising sorcery and associating with the devil, sometimes by young children, sometimes by relatives or neighbours nursing a grudge.

Though some cases were unproven, an atmosphere of near-hysteria took hold, often whipped up by priests who sensed the devil's ubiquitous presence, and who cast around for luckless victims (mainly, though not exclusively, women) to blame. Eventually King Karl XI and his advisors, concerned at the number of executions (which often involved burning at the stake), instructed commissions to carry out investigations into the situation.

They looked at the nature of the charges that were being brought and the quality of the evidence. Some sentences were upheld though only in the cases of those 'witches' who had confessed and were regarded as recidivists. Within a few years the witch hunts started to die out, but during the following century the Swedish king was once more concerned at the significant numbers of young women being executed, as he was required to sign warrants giving authority for the penalties to be carried out.

Illegitimacy carried with it such a powerful stigma that some mothers felt driven to kill their babies rather than live with the inevitable shame and ostracism. Those found guilty were usually sentenced to death. After considering the matter with his advisors, the king resolved the matter by decreeing that women giving birth no longer had to reveal their names.

The Swedes, along with the English and the Dutch, were among the first to attempt colonisation of America in the 17th century. The settlement of New Sweden was founded on the west bank of the Delaware River in 1638 on land acquired from the indigenous population, their arrival occurring just 18 years after the Mayflower had transported the Pilgrim Fathers to Plymouth, Massachusetts. The original New Sweden community consisted of approximately 50 pioneering souls who named Fort Christina, the fortified building at the heart of their small settlement, in honour of Sweden's young queen.

Early immigrants became involved in the fur and tobacco trades, which brought them into conflict with Dutch and English settlers. Peter Stuyvesant, the governor of the New Netherland colony, arrived in 1655 with a formidable armada and took the Swedish settlement by force. Though it was a short-lived undertaking, some of the colonists stayed on, thus marking the first significant instance of Swedish emigration to America. Many of the descendants of the Delaware Swedes fought with distinction in the American War of Independence against Great Britain in 1776. However, it was not until the middle of the 19th century that circumstances conspired to produce the first substantial influx of Swedish immigrants to America.

One of the principal reasons for those leaving Sweden in significant numbers was economic hardship. The country suffered from a limited amount of fertile and productive agricultural land and it was estimated that about 40 per cent of the soil was unproductive. It was also managed by means of an archaic, fragmented system, which came under even greater pressure as the population rose by about a million in the space of 30 years or so, to three-and-a-half million by 1850.

America was seen as a country overflowing with opportunity. While an urgent longing for economic betterment was undoubtedly the main factor towards large-scale emigration, conscription and religious considerations also played a part. With the Lutheran church being dominant in Sweden, people could be fined, exiled, or arrested for conducting non-sanctioned religious services. In 1858, all faiths were officially declared equal, but non-Lutherans still found themselves under pressure from the established church.

In 1846, Erik Jansson and a small number of fellow emigres founded the Bishop Hill settlement. Jansson's belief in religious simplicity and the Bible being the only true book of God angered the Lutheran Church and he was imprisoned on several occasions prior to fleeing Sweden with his family via Norway. Once reaching America, Jansson and his followers were allowed freedom to practise their religion in the manner they wished. The resultant colony in Illinois gained over 1,000 immigrants within a year and became a destination for future expatriate Swedes. The Lutherans contributed to the new settlement in one other significant way by helping to educate the population and, crucially, taught literacy skills.

Early in the 20th century, newspaper reports and "American letters" from friends and relatives who had already moved to this new land told of the availability of well-paid work and cheap land for those who were fit and prepared to work hard to earn a decent living. A coal miner, Oskar Andersson, wrote back to caution that while the prospects were indeed very promising, there was very little support for people who became ill and were unable to work. However the overriding message was that America was a far better prospect than Sweden, despite the distance separating emigrants from their loved ones.

According to some accounts, by the early part of the 20th century, Swedes owned over 12,000,000 acres of land in the United States – a much higher figure than most other immigrant groups. Some settlements sprang up in close proximity to the rapidly expanding network of railroads on cheap land sold by the railroad companies, thus affording hard-up immigrants the possibility of combining farm work with jobs associated with the iron horse. Evidently the Swedes were valued for their hard work ethic. As the 19th-century railroad tycoon James J. Hill said, "Give me snuff, whiskey and Swedes, and I will build a railroad to hell."

Some prospective emigrants were fired up by breathless reports of the California gold rush and the lure of an easy fortune; they joined tens of thousands of hopefuls from America and abroad in what often turned out to be a vain quest. Further incentives came from shipping companies, who saw great opportunities for generating revenue from the thousands of emigrants whose only way of getting to the Promised Land was in their boats; thus assisted passage schemes were offered.

Lars Kristofferson, a 25-year-old soldier, based latterly at Tolsbo, decided to emigrate to the United States with his pregnant wife, 29-year-old Elin Karolina Kristofferson (nee Johansson). It seems likely they had already planned a new life abroad when they exchanged vows in the fortress town of Karslborg on October 8, 1903.

On June 9, 1905, the couple sailed from Gothenburg on board the 300-foot-long steamship *Ariosto*, which had been built in 1880 for the Wilson Line of Hull. The ship had a cruising speed of 14.5 knots and accommodation for 53 first, 24 second and 1,000 emigrant-class passengers. Though conditions for most passengers were fairly cramped, the *Ariosto* was technically advanced for its day, benefiting as it did from refrigerating machinery and electric lighting throughout – conveniences that Lars and Elin were unlikely to have been accustomed to in the homes they were now leaving for good.

The voyage to Hull was only the first leg of a gruelling journey. From the north eastern port, the pair travelled by train, most likely to Liverpool, from where they sailed across the Atlantic. After a sea journey lasting about a week, the sight of the Statue of Liberty and the forest of masts in New York harbour must have come as an overwhelming relief. However, a lengthy train journey followed that took them across America, almost to the West Coast, before they finally reached their destination: Tacoma, Pierce County, Washington; a particularly popular destination for Swedish immigrants, along with Seattle. The whole experience must have been particularly exhausting for soon after she and Lars arrived at their new home, the heavily pregnant Elin gave birth to her son, Kris' father, Lars Henry Kristoffer Kristofferson, on August 16, 1905.

While the authorities recognised that hard-working, motivated people constituted the best guarantee of future prosperity, immigration to the United States was by no means an open-door policy. The Naturalisation Act of 1790 had stipulated that "any alien, being a free white person, may be admitted to become a citizen of the United States". Candidates also had to be "of good moral character". It followed that indentured servants, slaves and coloured people were excluded.

Immigrants could apply for naturalisation after two years of residence, which involved swearing an oath of allegiance to the Constitution of the United States. It seems Swedish immigrants were among those who had little difficulty in complying with all aspects of the legal requirements of making America their permanent home. In 1910, approximately 150,000 Swedish-Americans resided in Chicago – which meant that getting on for 10 per cent of all Swedish immigrants lived there; only Stockholm had more Swedish inhabitants – and some said that it was possible to live and die in Chicago without speaking any language other than Swedish.

A statue of the 18th-century botanist Carl Linnaeus became a rallying point for local Swedes. Though many of the original settlers used their agricultural skills to set up their own farms in rural areas, the majority of new arrivals headed for the cities. They were prepared to work hard but many of the first wave found that the reality of their new home did not live up to the seductive dreams that had led them there in the first place; many men ended up as low-level labourers while the womenfolk took poorly paid jobs as housemaids.

From the start of the 20th century the term *Svenskamerika*, or Swedish America, came to be applied to the settlers as a whole; it was an epithet that aimed to encapsulate the cultural and religious traditions the Swedish immigrants brought to their new homeland. These traditions were both preserved and changed through interaction with American society, and formed the basis for the Swedish-American identity that developed among many of the immigrants and their descendants. Many newcomers were drawn to organisations created by a variety of Swedish religions, the largest being the Lutheran Augustana Synod. Apart from ministering to the spiritual needs of their members, such organisations also founded benevolent and educational institutions such as colleges, hospitals, old people's homes and orphanages.

A number of American colleges and universities, including Bethel College in St Paul, Minnesota, the "Swede State of America", and the California Lutheran University in Thousand Oaks, California, can trace their origins to Swedish immigrants. Many other smaller organisations such as choirs, political groups and mutual aid societies such as the Scandinavian Fraternity of America also developed. Such bodies provided a general network of social and cultural support for Swedes, who could meet fellow countrymen and speak, sing or put on plays in their mother tongue.

Politically, the Swedes who came over at the start of the mass emigration tended to be socially conservative though strongly opposed to slavery. Initially, emigration was predominantly to the northern states of America and not to the "slave states" in the south. The great majority of Swedes voted Republican and it is believed by many commentators that but for their support (and that of immigrants from other northern European countries such as Great Britain, where slavery had been abolished in 1833), the election of Abraham Lincoln as the 16th president of the United States in 1860 would have been an impossibility.

Had Lincoln not been elected it is possible that slavery (there were nearly four million slaves recorded in the 1860 census) might not have been abolished as early as it was, in 1865. In general, Swedish integration into American life seems to have been achieved without significant hostility or resentment.

By 1950 it was estimated that some 50 million Europeans had emigrated to America, of whom approximately 1.3 million were Swedes. Many of their descendants went on to make significant contributions to the life of their new homeland. Buzz Aldrin became the second man in history to set foot on the moon. Ann-Margret Olsson (better known simply as Ann-Margret), who made the move to America after the Second World War, is a distinguished singer and actor. Charles Lindbergh, one of the most renowned figures in aviation, was the first man to fly solo across the Atlantic Ocean, in the "Spirit of St Louis". William Rehnquist became the 16th Chief Justice of the United States of America. Melanie Griffith (daughter of Tippi Hedren) starred in such films as *Night Moves* and *Working Girl*. Mamie Eisenhower achieved the distinction of becoming America's First Lady between 1953 and 1961. Candice Bergen followed a successful career in films with another in photojournalism. Ray Bradbury, a prolific and acclaimed writer in many genres, received the National Medal of Arts award from President Bush in 2004.

In the 2000 census some four million people answered "Swedish" to the question about their ancestry. In proportion to the population of their home countries, only the British Isles and Norway surpassed Sweden in the number of people who emigrated to America.

Not everybody who made the pilgrimage to America stayed. Dan Andersson, a distant relative of Kris Kristofferson, was born into a working-class family in 1888. He travelled around from an early age as a result of his father's quest for work. After leaving home, Andersson moved from place to place, restlessly seeking new experiences and adventures as well as a means of financial support while he tried to pursue his first love, writing. He took a wide variety of jobs, woodsman, temperance lecturer, factory worker and travelling salesman among others, not all of which were commensurate with his talents. These experiences did, however, provide Andersson with a rich store of characters and experiences that would enrich his later writings. He also served time in the armed forces.

In a brief American sojourn at the age of 14, he worked on a farm belonging to an aunt and uncle but soon returned to Sweden having achieved little apart from blisters and precious little money. Andersson died young in 1920 as a result of accidental poisoning in a hotel in Stockholm – cyanide had been used to rid his room of insects and the room had not been properly aired. His work, which often concerned themes of religion and feelings and issues relating to sin and guilt, as well as sympathy and empathy for those at the bottom of the social heap, only achieved significant recognition after his death.

While Kris Kristofferson would not meet an early demise, it's uncanny how his distant ancestor's wide variety of experiences would parallel his own life journey.

# Chapter 2

L ARS and Elin Kristofferson soon adjusted to their new surroundings. In what appears to have been a deliberate move towards assimilation, they became known as Louis and Ellen, the anglicised versions of their names helping them, perhaps, to ease their way into American society. Their son's name was also modified – "Lars" was dropped and he was usually referred to as "H. C. Kristofferson" or "Henry C. Kristofferson".

Henry was passionate about flying from an early age. Following studies at the University of Washington and Washington State College, he became a successful airline pilot at a time when the industry was still in its infancy. By the mid-Thirties he had transferred to duties in Christobal, Panama Canal Zone as a senior pilot with Pan American World Airways (originally Pan American Airways when it was founded in 1927).

He married Mary Ann Ashbrook, roughly six years his junior, who was born in Columbus, Franklin County, Ohio. Given her husband's career, it was perhaps appropriate that she should hail from the "Birthplace of Aviation" as licence plates in Ohio proudly proclaim. Though the Wright brothers achieved the first powered flight from Kitty Hawk in North Carolina, they made their plans and constructed their aircraft in their bicycle shop in Dayton, Ohio.

Among Mary Ann's ancestors were people imbued with military and religious traditions. Her father, Roy Wilson Ashbrook, saw service in the short-lived Spanish-American War in 1898, which came about over Cuba's desire for independence from Spain but in the course of which America targeted Spain's other remaining overseas territories. In the course of the conflict he had one of his eyes put out by a spear during the Philippine Insurrection.*

Her paternal grandfather, Aaron Pence Ashbrook, who died in 1919, fought on the Union side in the American Civil War. In the 18th century

---

* It is said that Kris Kristofferson still has the spear to this day.

her ancestor Levi Ashbrook was a Baptist minister who saw service in the American War of Independence. Mary Ann's earlier ancestors had hailed from Scotland and Ireland, thus introducing a Celtic connection into Kris Kristofferson's already rich heritage.

Despite the subtle alterations made to his own name, when Henry Kristofferson's first child, a son, was born on June 22, 1936, he was given the Swedish name Kristoffer. This represented the continuation of a widely observed Kristofferson family tradition for first sons going back centuries.

People born under Kris' star sign, Cancer, the crab, are said to be sensitive, moody, emotional, thoughtful, concerned for other people's feelings, naturally empathic, appreciative of family structure, prone to sulkiness when their desires are not met, romantic, sentimental, with a good memory for slights inflicted and favours bestowed. Regardless of what credibility one attributes to astrology, Kris' personality has come to embrace all of these elements over the years.

During his childhood years the name Kristoffer was shortened to Kristy and also to Kris; by the time he was into his teens Kris was the name he was most commonly known by. In 1936, approximately six months after his birth, it was reported that his maternal aunt and her husband, Mr and Mrs N Searles, had arrived in Brownsville at about the time Kris' mother had left for Panama. She was presumably going to join her husband though it is not clear whether Kris accompanied her or stayed behind to be looked after by his aunt and uncle. The family was completed with the arrival of Karen in 1938 and Kraigher (later usually known as Kraig) in 1943. When Kris was born the family was living in Brownsville, Texas, on the border with Mexico. This would be home for the greater part of his early childhood up until the Kristoffersons moved to California, although in order to further his career, Kris' father moved his family on a regular basis.

Brownsville, whose motto is, "On the border by the sea", was founded in 1849, the largest city in the Rio Grande Valley in terms of population and size. An attractive, semi-tropical part of the world with majestic palm trees, constantly blooming bougainvilleas, exotic birds and warm Gulf breezes, the city lies in territory that has been fought over by Spain, Mexico and America. The dramatic events of the 19th (the Mexican-American land war 1846 to 1848) and early 20th centuries (the 'Fort

Brown incident' of 1906) had a considerable impact on the border country, with a significant degree of anti-Mexican sentiment on the part of some in Brownsville and surrounding areas.

By the time Kris Kristofferson was born, such feelings may have diminished, partly as a result of attempts at progressive legislation, partly as a result of the passage of time, but many of the attitudes they engendered were still present.

Although Kris' father was the son of an immigrant, Henry was white, successful and married to a woman who came from a traditional American family with military associations. During the years Kris spent in Brownsville, up until about the age of 11, he inhabited the privileged sector of this border world. His general consciousness of the underlying tensions and latent and overt hostility evinced towards particular ethnic groups came later as he started to reflect on, evaluate and make sense of his early surroundings. However, Kris believes that his mother may well have contributed to the earliest stirrings of an awareness of what prejudice and social injustice really meant.

When Kris was around eight, the distinguished Mexican World War II hero, Jose Lopez, a native of Brownsville, returned from Europe with a Medal of Honour, and a parade was arranged in his honour. The youngster joined the crowds who greeted him but was struck by the fact that none of the other "Anglos" turned out. "It was an atmosphere that my mother, God bless her, taught me was wrong . . ." he later said. "I think that probably planted the seed." She also helped to inspire in him a sense of social justice that would be a common theme in much of his later work.

That said, Mary Ann also spent a great deal of her time engaged in a whirl of upper-class social events for whose organisers the most serious problem requiring attention might be finding flowers that did not clash with the dining room curtains. Her name (and those of her husband and children) appeared regularly in the society pages of local newspaper *The Brownsville Herald*; though she was invariably described in terms of her husband's name: "Mrs H. C. Kristofferson" or "Mrs Henry C. Kristofferson".

Sometimes as a means of fundraising for good causes, other times for pleasure and an early version of social networking, Kris' mother threw herself into events such as bridge club evenings, often as the hostess, sometimes as a contributing organiser.

In 1939, on the eve of war in Europe, *The Brownsville Herald* reported Mrs H. C. Kristofferson was in charge of the bridge club's annual Christmas party, which was evidently a colourful occasion. "A white and red theme was developed through the use of poinsettias and white carnations and red tapers in silver candelabra." At one coffee morning, which attracted nearly a hundred guests, the importance of colour and presentation was once more illustrated.

"The coffee table was pretty with its centrepiece of three large red hearts on which were set small bowls of red sweet peas. Elsewhere about the home were red and white carnations, godetias and other flowers carrying out the red and white motif."

The language used by the respectful journalists who recorded such events was at times unfathomable to the modern ear. In 1940 the society page reported that, "In the (bridge) games of the Wednesday tournament club this week at the home of Mrs Phil K. McNair, Mrs H. C. Kristofferson was high. The floating prize went to Mrs James L. Rentfro." On another occasion, in 1942, it was recorded that Mrs H. C. Kristofferson was one of the guests when Mrs Harold Rammer was "honoured with pretty luncheon and bridge . . . luncheon was served at small tables centred with nasturtiums, while nasturtiums were used throughout the reception rooms."

With the start of the Second World War many society women became involved in work aimed at providing support for some of the victims of the burgeoning conflict. "They're knitting and crocheting and sewing against time in preparing sweaters, garments etc for refugees for the Red Cross," according to one article in the local press. It was noted that Kris' mother was "one of those turning in completed dresses".

For the right people almost any event, no matter how minor, was deemed worthy of mention, and this fawning attention was also accorded to their children. As an example, in 1942 it was reported that Karen Kristofferson had been "returned to her home from Mercy Hospital" having undergone a tonsillectomy earlier in the day. In the same year Karen and Kristy attended a party that "complimented" Denis Randolph on his third birthday. It was noted that, "A patriotic theme of red, white and blue was used throughout in all decorations for the event. Favours and refreshments carried out the chosen colours."

In 1945 young Kristy attended a watermelon party given by Mrs

Andrew J. Chapman for her son Richard. It was noted in the report that Kristy won a musical chair contest and also that, "Favours of victory guns were given to the guests. Later in the afternoon tiny decorated birthday cup cakes and punch were served to the youngsters." Other early attempts at activities of a musical nature were less successful. It was probably while Kris was at kindergarten that he first appeared on stage. He sang a song but was so shy that he did so with his back turned to the audience. His mother described his performance as "horrible".

Henry Kristofferson pursued his aviation career just as assiduously as his mother engaged in her social whirl. Throughout his early years, right up until the time he went to college, Kris, together with his mother and siblings, moved around in accordance with the dictates of his father's vocation, but even when they had settled in some new locale the nature of his work often meant that they didn't see him for long spells.

In 1942, under the heading, "Brief Items About People You Know", *The Brownsville Herald* announced that "HC Kristofferson has returned to his home after a trip to Miami, Florida and New York – he will spend a vacation here of 2/3 weeks with Mrs Kristofferson and their children." It is perhaps ironic that in later life Kris himself pursued a peripatetic existence albeit in a manner his parents could not and did not identify with.

In 1946, under the heading "City Briefs", the paper intimated that "Mrs H. C. Kristofferson has returned to Brownsville following a three week plane trip to points in Mexico, Merida, Yucatan, Havana and Miami." For this particular trip she was accompanied by Henry but no reference was made to the children, who were presumably left in the care of domestic staff with whom they inevitably spent a great deal of time – their services came cheap and most middle-class families employed them. Indeed, Kris was able to speak some Spanish words before he could speak English.

In 1941 Henry had been appointed operations chief for Pan Am in Africa, charged with carrying out a detailed survey of the trans-Africa route, a post he held for a year prior to beginning active duty with the US Army, first as a captain, then lieutenant colonel. He was promoted to full colonel in 1944 and was initially stationed in Accra on the Gold Coast. Colonel Kristofferson was subsequently awarded the Legion of Merit (later enhanced by the addition of an oak leaf cluster to mark a second award) for outstanding service in connection with the establishment of air transportation across Africa (he was chief pilot for the first survey of the trans-African route), the Middle East and China. Other honours to come his way included the Distinguished Flying Cross and the Air Medal.

Although he ended active duty in 1942 he continued to act as a consultant and adviser to the military authorities. He came to the China-Burma-India theatre towards the end of 1943 to serve as operations officer for the India-China wing of air transport command – an Army Air Force unit later cited by President Roosevelt for its exceptionally meritorious performance. Kris' father personally flew some of the early missions necessary to determine the best routes to follow. Their planes succeeded in delivering large quantities of vital materials to China including gasoline, ammunition and small arms. The Burma Road had been lost as a supply line following the invasion of Burma by Japan, and Chinese seaports were blockaded. Deliveries were achieved by means of "flying the hump" over the rugged Himalaya mountains of North Burma and the vital supplies helped the Allies to stave off enemy attacks.

"The hump" was a high altitude military aerial supply route that went from the Assam Valley in north-eastern India, across northern Burma, to Yunnan province in south-western China. It was the first long-range, 24-hour, all-weather, aerial supply line in military history. There were no precedents to call on so courage and a pioneering spirit were essentials for those involved. The routes that Colonel Kristofferson and his colleagues helped to create went on to become crucial components in an aid supply network for the United Nations after the war.

Visits home were of necessity infrequent and when they did occur were occasions for celebration, not just for the family but for the local press. In 1945, in what appears to have been a pre-planned photo-opportunity, a picture appeared in a number of newspapers that showed Colonel Kristofferson, Mary Ann Kristofferson and all three children standing in front of the B25 bomber he had just flown to Rio Grande International Airport, Brownsville from Washington. A cactus and a wooden "Brownsville" sign are emblazoned on the side of the plane along with a cartoon picture of Colonel Kristofferson astride a rocket flying from Karachi to Brownsville.

Though the circumstances were somewhat different, Kris would later find that the attraction and pull of his work, and his driven desire to immerse himself in it, meant that he was also an absent family man for much of the time. "He was the shining best at everything he did," Kris later sang of his father in song, but for a considerable part of his childhood he was simply not present in his life. Kris also said his father gave him "a sense of living up to who I should be".

The trouble was that once Kris reached adulthood, his ideas of who he should be were very different from those of his father.

# Chapter 3

FROM an early age Kris was something of an outsider, with what he subsequently referred to as a sense of separateness. One way in which this separateness manifested itself was in his musical taste. The artists of choice for most of the young teenagers he mixed with were purveyors of sentimental lightweight pop such as Patti Page and Johnnie Ray ("The Prince of Wails") for whom Kris had little time.*

When he was about 11, the family having now moved to San Mateo, near San Francisco, Kris heard Hank Williams singing an early hit, 'Lovesick Blues', on Nashville's Grand Ole Opry radio show and was smitten. Kris was not deterred by the fact that many of his acquaintances branded him a "total weirdo" due to his bizarre musical passion. He did his best to acquire all the 78 rpm records Williams made. Williams' brand of country music would later be described by legendary writer Harlan Howard as "three chords and the truth"; the epitome of the direct, plaintiff expression of raw human emotions and the very heart and soul of country music.

Kris was particularly struck by the Luke the Drifter recitations in which Williams reflected on and empathised with the people whose lives had turned out badly, who found themselves at the bottom of the social and economic pile; underdogs whom he referred to as "men with broken hearts". It's not hard to see how Williams came to be such an important influence on Kris' own music but also why he was considered too un-sophisticated for mainstream radio in America, not to mention the elite world occupied by the Kristofferson family.

Kris may have appreciated Hank's empathy for the underdog but the music got to him on a personal level too. "I'd never seen a robin weep, but

---

* Ironically, one of the artists Kris later came to admire most, Bob Dylan, cited Ray as an early influence, claiming that he was the first singer whose voice and style he "totally fell in love with".

could imagine it, and it made me sad." While at high school in San Mateo in 1953, one of Kris' schoolfriends shocked him with the news that his hero had died. He later found out that Williams had expired in the back of his car as a result of an unfathomable cocktail of drink, drugs and exhaustion.

"It was like a great tree had fallen," recalled Kristofferson. "Hearing about Hank's death caught me squarely on the shoulder. The silence of outer space never seemed so loud. Intuitively I knew, though, that his voice would never drop out of sight or fade away – a voice like a beautiful horn."

By the time the youngster heard 'Lovesick Blues' he had already been writing his own rudimentary songs for several years. He has said one of the first complete songs he ever wrote, around 1947, was a Hank Williams pastiche called 'I Hate Your Ugly Face' – an early indication perhaps of Kristofferson using the writing medium to express strong underlying personal emotions. Kris also appreciated other country artists such as Gene Autry and was a fan of Buddy Holly and the close backup harmonies on his records, which were provided by a vocal group called the Picks.\* Nearer to home he drank in the exuberant Tex-Mex music, with its simple melodies and vibrant harmonies, which were part of the local environment.

There is no indication that his parents had any particular musical gift and indeed, in a 1974 interview, Kris indicated that there was little parental encouragement in that direction in the household. He recalled singing with his brother and sister in the Fifties, "against their will . . . they'd been told they couldn't sing, and while my sister managed to fake it pretty well, it turned out my brother could carry a tune, so we harmonised on some Everly Brothers things."

Being a so-called army brat, the young Kris was exposed to an eclectic variety of music and did not become strongly attached to one particular regional style. His preference was invariably for music with the simplicity and lyrical directness of genres such as country and blues.

During the time that his musical direction, alongside a burgeoning but unexpressed social conscience, was starting to take shape in his mind, Kris'

---

\* Many years later, in 1988, Kris acted as MC for the film *Buddy Holly and the Crickets: A Tribute.*

father's career – switching between civilian and military duties – continued to flourish but, as before, it was not one that was conducive to spending a lot of time with his children.

The Kristofferson family moved to California around 1947 after Henry was named director of operations, with the rank of master ocean pilot, for the Pacific-Alaska division of Pan Am. In San Francisco, Colonel Kristofferson was presented with the Order of the British Empire at a ceremony at the residence of the British Consul General, Cyril H. Cane. The honour was bestowed in recognition of his substantial achievements during World War II and his work inaugurating a pilot training programme, which ensured the maintenance of a regular schedule of operations from Casablanca to Karachi.

In a letter to friends, Mary Ann revealed that while the family liked their new home in San Mateo, she and the children would trade it for a return to Texas any day. She accepted her role as supportive wife with all that this entailed, but must surely have become weary of constantly having to uproot the family and begin again in new places – these included Guatemala, New York, Florida and Virginia.

In 1950 Colonel Kristofferson accepted a post with the Air Force, which resulted in him eventually rising to the rank of major general. He was in charge of the transportation task force of the military air transport service at the Fairfield-Suisun Air Force base, and was responsible for airlift activities from all West Coast bases including Fairfield, March, Castle, Moffett and McChord; this being a particularly hectic time because of the Korean War.

By this time the family were living in Dorchester Drive – in an upmarket peninsular area of San Mateo – in a spacious house set in large grounds that today would sell for around $3 million. Mary Ann worked for a time as staff assistant to the Red Cross Speakers Bureau and also undertook a range of voluntary work.

Kris was enrolled at the private San Mateo High School along with his brother and sister. Although Kris' parents were not hands-on parents in the modern sense they certainly had his life mapped out for him. When asked years later what his father envisaged for him, Kris laconically replied, "Well both my parents probably thought that I would do something a little more respectable than songwriting." It was a given that from an early age he was to be groomed for a military career, followed by a high-status profession in, for example, law or politics. There was little prospect of Kris' future being mulled over by a concerned careers adviser.

As it turned out the Kristoffersons stayed in San Mateo long enough to enable Kris to complete his high-school career. Contrary to a later disingenuous claim that his only interest at school was listening to Hank Williams records, Kris threw himself into school and his local community with gusto.

In 1950, under the rubric "Boy Scout News", the local press reported that the scouts of San Mateo Parks Troop 1 had achieved a number of merit badges including two for Kris Kristofferson for first-aid safety and public health. In the same year he participated in a musical evening put on by his school. The following January Kris was one of 15 scouts to visit Yosemite National Park on a skiing and tobogganing trip. Another scout excursion involved Kris visiting Mount Diablo, in the San Francisco Bay area, for a hiking holiday.

He also won honours for his contributions to the school's football team and was one of 35 San Mateo High football players to be awarded block letters and special sweaters at a banquet in 1952. The culmination of Kris' high-school football career came in 1953 with the match between the San Mateo team, known as "The Bearcats", and long-time rivals Burlingame High School. In the build up to the match there were profiles and photographs of the teams. Kris' vital statistics were given as – position: E, weight: 150 pounds, height: 5' 9", class: senior. The Bearcats were said to be blessed with a very accurate quarterback and Kris was one of the attacking players, an end, he targeted with his throws.

The result of the match, the "Little-Big game" as the press dubbed it, must have been wildly satisfying for Kris as, for the first time since 1945, the Bearcats came out on top: 14–0. Kris was among several players to receive a special mention for quality play; it was however decided later by the coaches and players that no individuals should be singled out for special praise – all were described as heroes and all were included in the week's prep honour roll.

By nature an introvert, the young sportsman was shy when it came to speaking in public. Despite this, throughout his high-school years he chose, probably with some robust encouragement from his mother, to put himself forward for a number of positions on committees and the like and his candidature was often successful. San Mateo High School had a sophisticated administrative structure that allotted functions and responsibilities to the pupils themselves for carrying out a variety of activities.

In 1953 Kris was a member of the San Mateo High School committee that organised a fun night at the gym, the culmination of the year's social events. The evening featured swimming and volleyball and was rounded off with dancing and refreshments. Kris' sister Karen was one of those furnishing entertainment for the evening. As with other such activities that Kris participated in, the adjectives "wholesome" and "all-American" seemed naturally to go along with them.

Kris was elected president of a committee ("Block SM") whose main function was to organise football games as well as publicity for various other events that took place in the school. One of the committee's tasks was to decide on the system of bestowing sporting awards known as "letters". (Although Kris was prominent as a football player he was also a letterman in athletics.) There was also an organisation within the school called the Bearcat Booster Boys, which was put together for the purpose of stimulating "pep and spirit" among San Mateo supporters at basketball games.

In 1953 Kris was elected to the position of vice president of the student cabinet body, having had to undergo the ordeal of making a speech in support of his candidature to the assembled student body. Late on in his high-school career he served on the Fresh Boys Commission. Not all of the roles he undertook were arduous. To publicise the annual San Mateo High School carnival, a photograph of Kris and two friends perfecting their "balloon shaving" (to lather up a balloon and then shave it without the balloon bursting) technique appeared in the local press.

Kris had a knack not just of getting himself elected to official positions but also of being chosen when it came to events involving publicity for the school and beyond. In 1954 a photo of the fresh-faced, short-haired and clean-shaven 18-year-old appeared in the *San Mateo Times*. Along with 33 other invited pupils from his school and Serra High School he attended the City Offices as a guest of San Mateo's mayor, as part of celebrations to mark the city's annual youth day. Kris and four other pupils, all office holders at their schools, appeared in the photograph along with their civic counterparts.

The impression that emerges from Kris' high-school years is of a talented young man with a competitive streak, trying to live up to ambitious, some would say unattainable, ideals set by his parents. Yet at the same time as Kris appeared to be participating fully in the life of the school, his underlying feelings of estrangement from the mainstream came out in his observations of life around him; observations that at the time he kept to himself. As he later told one journalist, "Driving into San Francisco when I was a kid used to scare the devil out of me . . . all those boxy houses squeezed against one another. If you was really bad you got stuck into one of those places."

Kris later admitted that he was "no scholar", but he did well enough at San Mateo High School to be eligible for a place at a college of further education, having graduated in 1954. Inevitably it was Mary Ann who persuaded her son to consider Pomona College in southern California where she herself had graduated in 1933 (she also studied at the University of Kansas). For Kris the most important factor was the quality of the football team and whether he could get a place in it. At this stage he was more interested in being a football star than a songwriter. "The closest I've come to knowing myself is in losing myself," Kris later reflected. "That's why I loved football before I loved music. I could lose myself in it."

Kris unsuccessfully tried to gain football scholarships to Yale, Dartmouth and Harvard (where, he later complained, it was a condition that candidates had to weigh at least 250 pounds). Deep down he knew he was probably not good enough to make the top level ("I wasn't very big and I wasn't very fast") but he had the desire and was looking to punch above his weight. The only coach who said he thought Kris would make the team was Jesse Cone at Pomona College, who actually made the effort to write to him.

Pomona was established in 1887 and claims to be one of the leading liberal arts colleges in America. Located in Claremont, a city full of character situated approximately 35 miles east of Los Angeles, historically, the town has absorbed a variety of influences, from a thriving citrus industry and a Spanish architectural heritage to a strong academic presence. The appearance of Claremont has been greatly enhanced by a policy of tree planting over many years, which contributed to the city's epithet, "Trees and PhDs".

In the autumn of 1954, Kris quickly settled in at Pomona where he majored in English; the individual courses he studied included creative writing and literature. As well as sport (in his first season he was one of 15 freshmen to earn numerals in football, once more playing as an end), he again threw himself into a variety of extracurricular activities. In 1956 photographs of Kris and about 20 other youngsters were selected to appear in pamphlets produced by Peninsula YMCA for use in its club programme and for distribution across America. Titles of the pamphlets included For This We Work (explaining the YMCA's objectives) and Partners In Growth (which was aimed at young people's parents). Presumably Kris was among those chosen because he was regarded as a good example of early American manhood.

Kris made a powerful impression on one of his teachers, Professor Fred Sontag. In sport and athletics Sontag recalls that Kristofferson was well known by the coaches as a very strong athlete. However in academic subjects the professor was struck by the youth's reserved nature. "He took a philosophy course with a few others I knew and they had encouraged him to do it. He spoke very little but when he did speak he made a great deal of sense so you were aware of him. I talked to him, took him to lunch; he was clearly an interesting person but not very outspoken about it. It was never in his character to dominate a group. We put somebody next to him in class and I said, 'When Kris has something he wants to say will you raise your hand', and everything Kris had to say was rather intelligent but he never made the big splash himself."

Pomona prided itself on having small classes and Sontag recalls that other students listened closely when Kris spoke. He also felt that whether in sport or academic pursuits Kris had a preference for working with people like himself, quiet but expressive. He was generally well liked and was certainly not a loner but neither did he relish the limelight. As Professor Sontag puts it, "Being a frontman was quite hard for him.

"His mother was remarkable . . . he wouldn't have done some of the things if she hadn't urged him to and yet she was not nasty or difficult about it; she just made good sense when she spoke and she spoke when she thought she ought to."

Sontag did not detect any musical talent or inclination, though he did feel there was something of the poet in Kristofferson. "He spoke in symbolic terms, always well, but didn't try to startle or dominate the class." He did not detect any early signs of Kristofferson's later political activism – at this stage it appears that Kris kept such thoughts to himself. Sontag did notice one particular aspect of Kristofferson's college life that would be a constant – he was always "popular with the ladies". Sometimes when the professor wanted to know more about problems a male student might be experiencing, he would find that speaking to the boy's girlfriend might be productive but this did not work in Kris' case. Kris later admitted that his shyness ensured he "never got laid" as early as some of his more confident friends.

As was the case at San Mateo High School, Kristofferson's list of achievements at Pomona was most impressive. As a freshman he won the Jennings English contest at the college, was sports editor of the Metate College Year Book and of the Student Life college newspaper, became a member of the Ghosts men's honour society and was elected to the highly regarded Phi Beta Kappa, an academic honour society dating back to 1776, whose mission is to foster and recognise excellence in the undergraduate liberal arts and sciences. The society's motto is "Love of learning is the guide of life". At Pomona, the award was made annually to an outstanding, all-round senior man who ranked in the top third of all the men in his class. According to Sontag, Kris was quite blasé about the accolade.

His view was that over the course of his time at Pomona, Kris' strengths lay more in the academic field, though people respected him because of his positive attitude and the decent and determined way he conducted himself in his sporting activities. Kris became a letterman in football, played rugby and was a member of the boxing team, making quite a splash in his final year when he gained a technical knockout in the first round of a Golden Gloves competition in Los Angeles against his hapless opponent, Howard Schultz. One report announced that the face of welterweight Schultz "slipped out of gear under pressure of a direct hit by Kris Kristofferson in this novice Golden Gloves action . . . Schultz was already on the way down from a previous punch when the blow landed." A photograph of the loser appeared in several newspapers a split second after the victor had landed the ferocious blow.

Unfortunately Kris was hammered in the next bout, later admitting his personal disgust for putting up such feeble resistance against his opponent. He had fallen below the high standards he invariably pushed himself towards. Kris' involvement with sport generally led to a number of injuries including cartilage damage and a small scar on his forehead. According to some reports, the droop over his left eye is attributable to some of the blows he received in the boxing ring.

Kris' exploits were regularly chronicled in a section of *Sports Illustrated* entitled 'Faces in the Crowd'. Among other sporting figures deemed worthy of inclusion in this section of this Fifties magazine were Jack Nicklaus and Bobby Fischer. Not for the last time Kris found himself in the company of extremely famous and talented people, uncertain of how he got there and whether he really deserved such an accolade.

In 1958 the local press prominently featured a photograph of Kris standing in front of a group of uniformed military students who were holding an American flag. Kris was a member of the Reserve Officers' Training Corps (ROTC) and the ceremony was held to give him a superior cadet award. He was a battalion commander and had been designated a distinguished military student. Kris' parents doubtless approved of the fact that his military activities were going so well at Pomona. Kristofferson has subsequently hinted that he joined the ROTC to appease his parents, who assumed and expected that he would excel in it. "I was the worst ROTC platoon commander in the history of the school – never could give a guy a demerit."

Kris could have been forgiven for thinking there were not enough hours in the day for his diverse interests – modern psychological jargon might label him a human doing rather than a human being. However in addition to everything else, he was finding time to write fiction and, as it seemed with most other things he turned his hand to, was achieving results. He submitted four short stories to *Atlantic Monthly* (now simply known as *Atlantic*), a literary and cultural magazine founded in Boston in 1857 by a group of eminent writers including Ralph Waldo Emerson and Henry Wadsworth Longfellow. Each year the magazine held a creative writing competition for college and university students with 20 prizes available.

Kristofferson sent in four entries, which took first and third place along with two honourable mentions.* The stories displayed remarkable maturity for a young man just out of his teenage years. Skills, themes and insights which would later become Kristofferson trademarks – strong and engaging narrative, economical dialogue, simple but powerful descriptions and a

---

* Kris claims *Atlantic* told him his stories were the best they received but that they felt it would not be right to give one person the four top awards. Nonetheless he felt "pretty stoked".

sense of outrage at and contempt for prejudice, injustice and religious and all pomposity – were in evidence, along with a wicked sense of humour. It's of note too that one so young, who had always moved in elevated social and educational circles, had managed to acquire so much knowledge and insight into the lives of people living in wholly different circumstances.

In 'Gone Are The Days' Kris tells the story of a young man, Chet, who, having arrived home from a stint in the army, learns that his father and other local men are planning to attack a local negro, Johnny Willis, and his family, and set fire to their house. In what was evidently a heartfelt piece of writing, Kris articulates the dilemma faced by a young man who finds himself at odds with the values and attitudes of his family and friends and has no one to turn to.

Chet drives out to the Willis house and attempts to persuade the family to escape but it is too late. Kris contrasts the baying mob of rednecks fired up on booze with the quiet dignity and bravery displayed by Willis, who confronts his attackers unarmed, with his wife standing behind him. Realising there is nothing he can do to stop the gang, who beat Willis unconscious and torch his home, Chet disconsolately leaves the scene. He encounters Willis' 18-year-old daughter, Alma, surrounded by a similar gang of townsmen intent on molesting her. Chet intervenes but the mob turn on him, beating him into unconsciousness. By the time he comes round he is alone and nearby is one of Alma's shoes. Realising that the place he grew up in no longer holds anything for him, Chet thumbs down a truck and is resigned to go wherever the driver is heading for.

Chet's unhappy conclusion – that it was necessary to cut himself loose from the world he knew – would uncannily foreshadow Kristofferson's own experiences.

# Chapter 4

WITH his short stories, the young Kristofferson was showing early signs of a rich artistic palette. While 'Gone Are The Days' told a grim morality tale, 'The Rock', another of his entries for the *Atlantic Monthly* competition, was a lighter piece – albeit one that again showcased mature insights. The story revealed deep-rooted fears and prejudice as well as gleeful fascination with the forbidden, cleverly using an object as a metaphor for something that did not comply with society's norms.

Following a flood, a man named Harve Ginn, of Wheatonsville, finds that a large rock has been uncovered on his land. The problem is that the rock is a "freak of nature" – about 40 feet high and in the shape of a woman in a sexually explicit and provocative position. The story is told through the innocent but inquisitive eyes of Harve's son. After Harve decides to inform the local *Wheatonsville Herald*, crowds of people gather around the rock, its unorthodox design bringing out extreme reactions from the townsfolk.

In the ensuing moral panic, a meeting is arranged regarding the "leering strumpet". As the conference progresses Harve tries to keep things in perspective, pointing out the rock was a natural phenomenon and that if people didn't like it, they should simply ignore it. Events move quickly amid growing controversy: some "crackpots" try to use the figure to start a new religion; nudists claim it is proof God is on their side; while none other than Billy Graham says it shows that everybody is going to hell. Matters turn nasty when one group take matters into their own hands by covering the figure with a giant tarpaulin.

Eventually the state council decides the only way to deal with the problem is to dynamite the stone sculpture, thus eliminating a symbol that dares to be anti-establishment. The point was made all the more effectively thanks to Kristofferson's use of dry humour.

On the face of it, Kris was making the most of the opportunities that his privileged background had given him; he was naturally gifted in many areas and Pomona provided the impetus he needed to capitalise on these attributes. However, it was also a time of great pressure. Kris was essentially following the path staked out for him by his socially elevated, high-achieving parents, a plan that was largely taken for granted by most of his college mates and their families.

It was a path in contrast with his passion for Hank Williams: a man who was at best misunderstood, at worst despised by Kris' social milieu. This only contributed to his feelings of being isolated. For Kris, loneliness was a fact of life he first encountered in a childhood that beneath the surface was far from happy – a reason perhaps why songs like Williams' 'I'm So Lonesome I Could Cry' meant so much to him.

But these growing doubts, Kristofferson largely kept to himself. Around the time he won the *Atlantic Monthly* prizes he became, in his own words, "a model student . . . straight as an arrow", and indeed "straight arrow" was his nickname for a time.

In 1956 Henry Kristofferson became air operations manager for the Arabian American Oil Company (Aramco), requiring yet another move, to Dhahran, in Saudi Arabia. Being in charge of a private service from New York to Dhahran, which began in 1947 and continued until 1961 when the advent of scheduled jet flights (Aramco operated DC4s and DC6s) rendered the service unnecessary, Henry could doubtless take credit for the company's impeccable safety record. Approximately 80,000 passengers – personnel working in the oil industry and their families – flew the 7,500 mile route without mishap.

When Kris was an usher at the society wedding of a friend and fellow graduate from Pomona in 1958, he was described as "Kris Kristofferson of Saudi Arabia", though he of course lived principally on campus. Despite residing so far from California, the Kristofferson family were still well-regarded figures on the Peninsula, as the following report, which appeared in the *San Mateo Times'* Partygoer's December 1957 diary, indicates: "Christmas is customarily an occasion for covering great distances to be with friends and family during the joyous season . . . and to follow the custom of 'Christmas at home' the Henry C. Kristoffersons have travelled half way round the world . . . they have taken Mrs Alvin Schramm's Popper Avenue house in Burlingame for two weeks before returning to Saudi Arabia which [sic] is their new headquarters . . . General Kristofferson stopped en route in the east on business and joins his family here today . . . all in the one room for the first time in months . . .

"Mary Ann Kristofferson has been regaling envious friends with reports of 'lots of household help' to staff their Arabian place . . . otherwise their home halfway round the globe is typically American – part of an Aramco housing development for a colony of 3,000 American employees and their families . . . among parties for the popular former Peninsulans is the cocktail and dinner session which [sic] the Robert Rudds will host for close friends of the Kristoffersons on Saturday."

Such reports painted a rosy picture of success and fulfilment but for Kris, the reality was somewhat different. In a frank *Country Style* interview in 1981, Kristofferson stated that his parents were at times very strict and that he had sometimes been disciplined with a strap. He also asserted that though his father was highly respected, Henry was in fact a closet alcoholic. "In those days you couldn't talk about it because it would ruin your career." He said his father used to sneak drinks. "I had been covering up for him since I was in fourth grade. We never talked about it . . ."

Kris evidently felt justified in resenting many aspects of his upbringing despite the numerous advantages it offered him. Initially at least, all three children fitted in with their parents' expectations.*

After the success of the *Atlantic Monthly* articles, and given his continuing academic and sporting success, while in his senior year at Pomona, Kris was mentioned as a possible candidate for a Rhodes Scholarship – the highly prestigious international award, open to only about 30 American students per annum, to study at Oxford University for two to three years.

In the late Fifties, Rhodes scholars received significant financial benefits; all university fees were paid, as were travelling expenses. In addition students received an allowance to cover their living expenses. Professor Fred Sontag had no doubts that Kris should apply for the scholarship. "He had undeveloped talent, great ability, so really he was capable of

---

* Karen married an army officer who eventually rose to the rank of colonel and as in her own childhood, she and her three children followed him where his career took him. Later in life Karen made a major change when she embarked on what became a moderately successful television and film career with parts in *The Exorcist III* and *Sommersby* among others. She also did a television commercial for the unsuccessful presidential candidate John Kerry in 2004 not long before her death in 2005 at the age of 66. Kraigher pursued the sort of career his parents had in mind for him; he became a navy jet pilot and saw action during the Vietnam War. He currently holds a senior position in a major firm of commercial estate agents in San Diego.

anything." However, he and Dr Edward Weismiller, who taught creative writing, Kris' favourite class (in which he was the only footballer), had some persuading to do.

"Kris told me he didn't think he would be good enough, that there were other good candidates from Pomona," Sontag remembered, "but I told him he should try . . . in fact if you asked Kris I think he would say I told him he *had* to do it." Naturally, Henry and Mary Ann were strongly in favour of their son attaining such a prestigious award. Overcoming his instinctive reticence, Kris obtained letters of recommendation from his teachers that were uniformly excellent.

Before writing his own recommendation, Professor Sontag talked to Jesse Cone, the football coach, for ideas on what to say about his pupil, who responded, "Kris is a football player by the will of Kris Kristofferson, not by the will of God."

Sontag recalls that Kris nearly changed his mind after the initial round of interviews had not gone particularly well. Kris was also not convinced he really wanted the award, feeling he had been a student long enough and that what he needed now was to get out into the world. "I was going upstairs for a meeting and I happened to meet him. He said he was not going through with it. I said, 'What do you mean?' I took him out into the courtyard. He said, 'I'll never get it.' I said, 'The heck you won't, I want you at that meeting tomorrow.'"

Kristofferson himself recalled that Sontag told him, "You know, years from now, nobody's going to say, 'Well, you *could* have made it into Oxford.' But if you do it, and you get it, it's something you'll have forever. And I've been grateful to him ever since. It was one of the best things that ever happened to me."

Sontag was not surprised that Kris was successful.[*] "When he presents himself, he makes good sense though he does not present himself as if he thinks he *ought* to be famous. I think the scholarship was given on the strength of the interviews."

The professor also believes that Kristofferson going to England to further his academic career was not necessarily uppermost in his mind; he realised that part of Kris' motivation was to broaden his general life

---

[*] News of Kris' achievement was announced not only in California but also in Brownsville where the Kristoffersons remained well-regarded – and Kris was still referred to as Kristy.

experience. Sontag claims credit for Kristofferson's chosen specialist subject at Oxford. "William Blake was his major subject and I'm the one who put him onto him. I had been reading Blake and I told him that Blake was a person who used philosophy and was called a philosopher and yet he was a well-known literary person."

A former student of Pomona, who spoke to rock manager Peter Rachtman in the early Seventies after overhearing him talking about Kristofferson in a restaurant, later reflected, "We always thought he'd do something big; he was president of his freshman class, sophomore class, every class . . . debating team, writing club, football team, baseball . . . he was the most respected, best liked guy the school ever had. He could have been president of the country if he'd run but there was always something else about him, nice as he was . . . a sadness. In a funny way I wasn't surprised we didn't hear from him again."

Kristofferson began studying at Oxford's Merton College in the autumn of 1958. Among the dreaming spires, he found himself in an environment that bore little or no resemblance to anything he had known before. As was his wont, he threw himself into university life but inevitably, he was once more an outsider looking in as some of the intellectual scholars at Oxford quickly brought him down to earth.

"I went off to Oxford a star – ha! – and quickly found out what a fucked up little wimp I was . . . Those British, they peel off layers of bullshit instantly. I'd organised a rugby team at Pomona but at Oxford they wouldn't even let me try out for the team [he later did get to play some rugby]. They maintained an American couldn't know shit from rugby. Nothing much is going to impress those British. I never did want to pick up any British accent. They all called me Yank so I just kept on talking more like I always had.

"I got on OK with some of the English athletes, it was the sherry party guys who drove me bananas; they truly gave me to understand I had shit on my boots."

He did however have the satisfaction of achieving good grades in many of his subjects, particularly philosophy. Interviewed in the early Seventies, Kristofferson triumphantly sneered, "I wiped them cats out." He described himself as an "oral schizophrenic" – talking like a hick but saying things that revealed good insight.

While at Oxford, Kristofferson purchased a 1932 Austin 7 for around £10, which repeatedly broke down, much to its owner's frustration. On one occasion a wheel came off, rolled along the street and ended up at the feet of a policeman who advised Kris to sell the car before it killed him. Being naturally keen for new experiences Kristofferson used his time in England to see other parts of the British Isles, making his first visits to Scotland and Ireland.

Kristofferson's main ambition was to embark on a serious writing career; indeed at this stage, he regarded music merely as a sideline. He worked on various ideas and completed and submitted a novel, around the end of his second year at Oxford, to Houghton Mifflin, and came close to despair when it was rejected. He did, however, receive some encouragement – the publisher said it would be interested in looking at anything he wrote "after I'd lived a while". Of one of his Oxford writing projects, he enigmatically stated, "It was a sort of complicated thing, in which I look at the same episode through five different points of view."

Writer Peter Doggett contrasted Kristofferson's wide-ranging ambitions with those of his musical hero. "Hank Williams made it to Oxford, Mississippi, but he never wanted to be F. Scott Fitzgerald."

For all the changes and rebuffs Kris had to confront in England, there was much to relish. Asked in 1995 about this period of his life, a gleam of excitement lit up Kris' eyes at the memory of the freedom he had at his disposal. "I was in a wonderful position at the time. I was boxing[*] and playing rugby and seeing places I'd never seen before and reading people I'd never read before. William Blake was an explosion in my mind, and Shakespeare – I fell in love with literature and reading.

"American education at the time didn't allow you to specialise enough, especially for someone as lazy as I am, to really do the reading. You had to do economics and philosophy and if you did extracurricular activities such as football you didn't have enough time. At Oxford I had to go to two tutorials a week but I didn't have to go to lectures – I could live in libraries."

Though there was one aspect of his studies he did not appreciate. "The only downside was having to learn Anglo Saxon; you'll never speak it and you'll never read it unless you want to read something shitty."

[*] He won a blue, though also suffered the humiliation of losing a key bout to a boxer from Cambridge University.

Kristofferson evidently made a favourable impression on some of the academics he met at Oxford. One Merton College tutor, Hugo Dyson, reportedly remarked, "He is one of the most favourable specimens of Rhodes Scholarship . . . the kind of man you can trust to pick his own career."

Kristofferson proposed to write his major dissertation on the 18th and 19th-century prophet, poet, composer, painter and engraver, William Blake. In a description that bears more than a passing resemblance to Kristofferson's later achievements, Dr Kathleen Raine wrote, "Blake's unique greatness lies in no single achievement, but in the whole of what he was, which is more than the sum of all that he did." As Kris succinctly commented, "He opened doors for me."

Blake had also displayed many characteristics similar to Kristofferson and his emerging beliefs. The artist was appalled at the injustices suffered by many underprivileged people, although he was not overtly political and would never have considered standing for parliament. He definitely had a religious faith, a belief in God and the afterlife, but he did not adhere to any particular group and was not a regular church attendee in any conventional or blind way and had no time for organised religion. Despite his radical views, Blake actually lived an ordinary bourgeois life with his family.

Among Blake's many works (which were little understood or appreciated in his own lifetime), Kristofferson was particularly impressed by *The Marriage Of Heaven And Hell*, a collection of texts that paralleled prophetic biblical works but expressed Blake's own romantic and revolutionary beliefs. As with his other books it appeared as a set of printed sheets from etched plates containing prose, poetry and illustrations, which were coloured by Blake and his wife, Catherine. Included were the *Proverbs of Hell*, some of which Kris subsequently often quoted in interviews, as an explanation, if not a justification, for his extremes of behaviour. Kristofferson said that Blake helped set him on the right spiritual path and was the perfect inspiration for a young man with dreams of becoming an artist. Indeed Blake saw it in terms of duty, as he wrote:

"If he who is organised by the divine for spiritual communion, refuse and bury his talent in the earth, even though he should want natural bread, sorrow and desperation will pursue him throughout life, and after death, shame and confusion are faced to eternity."

Explaining his admiration for Blake as a free spirit, Kristofferson later said, "I studied his commitment to being an artist, to not being enslaved to another man's system."

It would be quite wrong, however, to suggest that Kris' involvement with the high arts was all he was concerned with during his time at Oxford. During a visit to London he wound up at the legendary 2I's Coffee Bar at 59 Old Compton Street, Soho. There was live music, recently imported Italian coffee machines, and hordes of young people only recently relieved of the ominous prospect of conscription. As record producer Tony Hatch put it, "There was a real buzz about the place," despite the fact that no alcoholic drinks were available. Several stars were discovered or performed at the 2I's in the early stages of their career, including Tommy Steele, Cliff Richard, Screaming Lord Sutch and Paul Gadd, later known as Paul Raven and who eventually found fame in the early Seventies as glam-rock star Gary Glitter. The venue was then owned by Australian Paul Lincoln, a wrestler, self-made promoter and manager, whose stage name was Doctor Death and who was sometimes known as The President.

"I had a friend, Pat Doncaster, who was entertainments editor of the *Daily Mirror*," Lincoln recalled. "He gave me information on anyone new and coming up. We decided to run a talent competition and call it 'Just Dial Fame'. The idea was that people had to phone up to apply for an audition. We actually blocked the Gerrard telephone exchange for three days. We tried to pick a winner but it was very difficult. We kept coming back to a tape sent in by an American boy called Kris Kristofferson. He'd written and sung everything on the tape. He did an audition, a couple of songs I seem to remember, and we decided to select him as our winner – from a great many entrants I might say."

For a time, according to Lincoln, Kristofferson played well-received solo spots with an acoustic guitar at the 2I's (though recently Kristofferson has claimed that Lincoln would not always allow him to perform because his singing wasn't good enough). Kris claimed to be completely naïve about the music business but he had nonetheless succeeded in getting himself a slot at one of the seminal music spots in London – even if the house style was more gutsy rock'n'roll than folksy singer-songwriter.

Lincoln quickly saw that Kristofferson had great potential, partly because of his obvious talent but also, in the days before American culture readily travelled across the Atlantic, he was so different from the British artists playing the 2I's, so there was a strong novelty factor. "I signed Kris up to a management contract. We were over the moon about him. He was an athletic young American boy from Oxford, the complete opposite of most of the rockers we had around the place, some of whom were pretty rough and quite unreliable. He was a breath of fresh air, a very nice guy; always a straight guy to deal with. I also liked the whole Yank at Oxford angle."

Lincoln was keen to exploit the talents of his new find, and before long arrangements were put in hand for Kristofferson to go into a recording studio to see if he could equal the kind of success he had attained in so many other areas of his life to date.

# Chapter 5

AS a result of his association with Paul Lincoln, Kris signed a contract with Top Rank Records (there was also talk of a tie-up with the American subsidy, Rank Records, which never materialised). His recordings were produced by Tony Hatch, who later wrote and produced 'Downtown', an international hit for Petula Clark in 1964, and went on to a successful writing-recording partnership with wife Jackie Trent.

As with most pop singers of the day, Lincoln decided that Kris would have to change his name, thinking that a surname like Kristofferson, despite the neat alliteration with the artist's first name, wouldn't catch on. For the purposes of his short-lived recording career in England, Kris Kristofferson became Kris ("Chris" according to some contemporaneous reports) Carson – a moniker bearing a close resemblance to Kit Carson, the legendary American frontiersman, immortalised and fictionalised in films and comic books (it's unlikely that this was a coincidence).

Hatch remembers the young Kristofferson well. "He was terribly clean-cut, quite short hair, not crew cut but carefully groomed. The general impression was of a clean-living graduate; the sweater, the Bobby Rydell look. He was very nice, courteous but quite firm on what he wanted to do. Fair enough. I've always been one to let the artist have their say on what they want to do on a session. I was handling the actual arrangements in the studio; in those days we had to 'routine' a record, set keys, get some arrangements done. Kris was able to play guitar but I'm pretty sure we just used session men."

When later interviewed, Kristofferson thought the songs he wrote and recorded at the time were "probably imitation Buddy Holly". He also said some resembled the music of The Kingston Trio (whose career was launched with the 1958 hit, 'Tom Dooley'). "They were not good. I thought they were at the time, I guess, or I wouldn't have tried to sell 'em."

Kristofferson's musical exploits helped to bring him to the attention of a journalist from *Time* magazine – a Yank at Oxford studying Blake by day and trying to become a "teenager's guitar-thwonking singing idol" by night was too good a story to miss.

The article, entitled 'The Old Oxonian Blues', appeared in April 1959. The jocular tone was set early on. "Blond Kristoffer Kristofferson is a modest, husky youth, and had he stuck quietly to his study of English literature, chances are that few of his Oxford friends would have discovered what an uncommon sort was swallowing their tea." The article featured an extract from one of Kris' songs described as "pleasant, blues-tinged lyrics [his songs neither rock nor roll]", which were said to be "suggested by the summers he spent working on Wake Island, labouring with railroad crews and fire-fighting gangs in Alaska."

"I can't remember individual songs," says Hatch, "but the style of music was what I would call pop-folk music. Not pop-rock. I'm sure all the songs we recorded were his own compositions. I don't remember if they were good or bad, but I think we felt that we had discovered quite an interesting singer and character. We were always on the lookout for something different and he was certainly different to anything we had at the time. Top Rank was a recent creation and there was considerable shareholder pressure to come up with successful acts. In the event it folded after about two years. The fact that Kris was American was of some interest too. Top Rank had already had a Top 20 hit with US singer Freddie Cannon's 'Tallahassee Lassie' and that was probably in [Kris'] favour."

When assessing Kristofferson's vocal ability – something that would become a recurring theme throughout his career – Hatch commented: "I recall thinking, 'This isn't fantastic,' but he certainly had something about him and the songs had a distinctiveness about them."

However, problems intervened that scuppered Kris' budding career – problems that stemmed from the *Time* article. Lincoln's recollection is that things were looking promising; a publicity photograph of Kris signing autographs for fans even appeared in the *New Musical Express* in 1959. "The record company were right behind him. They made an LP with him I believe [Kristofferson later said that only four tracks were actually recorded], laid out quite a lot of money; he was going to take off. Then the journalist from *Time* magazine came to see me – I was over the moon – thought we could maybe get into the American market."

The article in question was spotted by a man in Los Angeles with whom

Kris had previously signed a speculative recording agreement.

"Kris said it meant nothing," Lincoln ruefully recalls. "Some lawyer took up Kris' case – there was a proposal to pay the man in America some top level royalties on the record but the man would not play ball. The record company didn't want any litigation and that was the end of it, the recordings were never released. I was bloody devastated . . . lost another one."

Lincoln claims that he made other attempts to exploit Kris' talent, although what he came up with is hard to reconcile with Kristofferson's later public image. "The head of Decca Records wined and dined me and asked if I could find someone to compete with Pat Boone. They wanted a clean-cut type. I was told I would get all the help I needed. I thought of Kris: college boy, very athletic and all that. It was just my thought but it never came to anything." Lincoln later joked that if he could not launch Kristofferson on a musical career he could always turn him into a professional wrestler.*

Kristofferson has no regrets. "Kris Carson was someone who did not know what the hell was going on. None of the songs have survived in my brain as something I'd want to do." Musing on what course his life might have taken had the recordings been successful he told one interviewer, "God knows who I would have been now – probably one of those Fifties or Sixties casualties."

One of the reasons Kris hoped his music career would take off was for it to enable him to finance a career writing novels. He did receive a little money for his efforts with Top Rank, which he used to visit Switzerland with some fellow students. After his embryonic recording career petered out, Kristofferson decided to abandon his musical ambitions for a while.

As already seen, Kris never had much time for the kind of academic snobs he ran into at social functions. He later recalled one particular social event, around 1960, as his time at Oxford was drawing to a close, at which he got into a discussion with the late Nevill Coghill, one of the world's foremost translators of Chaucer. Kristofferson brashly expressed his opinion on how Blake's *The Mental Traveller* ought to be read. "[Coghill] was like

---

* The Top Rank tapes were transferred to EMI some time later. However, a recent search of their archives revealed no trace of any recordings by Kris Carson and so it appears that they most likely no longer exist.

this big expert . . . they'd given me another year on my dissertation but after that I was officially taken off Blake."

Kris was in two minds about his academic career. He came to feel he had conned himself into believing that he wanted to gain another degree and the more he thought about it, the more he wondered what he was doing at Oxford at all. He feared he was simply doing what somebody else wanted him to do. His parents were blissfully unaware of these feelings and assumed things were going well.

A boxing trip to France had been arranged towards the end of 1960 but when it fell through, Kris decided to get away from Oxford and return home to America. "I went to California for Christmas and I never did go back."

Kristofferson valued many aspects of his time in England; not many Fifties American students could boast of being able to simultaneously pursue sport, William Blake and a burgeoning pop career. He felt less constricted than had been the case during his time at Pomona but, despite the intoxicating spell of the great English writers, Kristofferson felt apart from the academic world. While he loved and admired the spirit of Blake and Shakespeare, he was no academic. Years later Kris had a sly dig at his years at Oxford when commenting, "I think between us, Bill Clinton and I have settled any lingering myths about the brilliance of Rhodes Scholars."

Once back in America, Kris appeared to accept the inevitability of a conventional life by preparing for the kind of military career his father had programmed him for. He had in fact received his commission for the American Army after graduating but got it deferred to allow him to go to Oxford. He also re-connected with fellow Pomona graduate, Frances Mavia Beer, known as Fran, who had also attended San Mateo High School where she had been one of the pom-pom girls assisting the cheerleaders, later moving up to head cheerleader. Fran had also worked alongside Karen Kristofferson as a member of the junior prom committee at San Mateo responsible for organising refreshments at various school events. Fran's family inhabited the same elevated social environment as the Kristoffersons; her father had been a senior captain with Pan Am.

In 1960, Fran graduated from the University of Nevada with a BSc in education. Like Kris she was a member of a Greek letter fraternity – in her case Kappa Alpha Theta, a sorority whose aim is to encourage personal excellence, friendship, sisterhood, scholarship, service and leadership. As a 19-year-old freshman she had made something of a splash when she was crowned "blackfoot-whitefoot princess" at an annual dance, "which followed an Indian theme". The occasion was intended to foster better relations between two other Greek letter fraternities, Sigma Nu and Alpha Tau Omega.

Karen went to Pomona but she and Fran remained close friends and, in 1960, Fran was Karen's maid of honour (indeed the sole attendant; Kris was at Oxford) at her wedding. Karen and her new husband, Gary (whose parents were also based in Dhahran), went to Laguna Beach during the Christmas holidays where Kris joined them. It was presumably around this time that Kris and Fran's relationship started to develop.

Kris and Fran's engagement was announced in February 1961. Under the heading "Romance report", *The San Mateo Times* breathlessly revealed that Fran Beer was to be a spring bride, her engagement having been announced by her parents, Mr and Mrs Kenneth Beer of Hillsborough. It was clear that the wedding would be a traditional affair. Shortly after the announcement, there were reports of Fran being honoured with "luncheons given by Mrs F. S. K. Lewis and Mrs Horace O'Keefe and her daughter Maryellen."

It was also reported that "many of the bride-elect's former classmates at the University of Nevada will be on the Peninsula for the ceremony . . . Mrs Gary Hendrix [Kris' sister Karen] and Mrs Raymond Von Gunten of Menlo Park will be sharing honour attendant roles." Kris and Fran were said to be "avid skiers" who would "honeymoon at Squaw Valley before the future benedict [newly married man] reports for army duty as a second lieutenant."

Kris and Fran were duly married on Saturday, February 11, at a candlelit ceremony held in St Paul's Episcopal Church in Burlingame. Kris' parents had flown in from Dhahran, as they had for Karen's graduation in 1960. The local press faithfully reported: "Given in marriage by her father, the bride wore a waltz length gown of Chantilly lace with a fingertip veil held in place by a crown of pearls. She carried lilies of the valley and sweetheart roses. The honour attendants . . . were gowned alike in bouffant teal blue taffeta accented with delphinium blue. They carried bouquets of white carnations and red roses . . . Kraigher Kristofferson was his brother's best man." The reception was held at the Beer residence.

Henry Kristofferson imbued in his son a sense of duty and responsibility. Kris' educational and sporting achievements had helped bolster his self-confidence and on one level he was well-equipped to take on the challenges he was being "programmed for" in life. However, there was a gnawing dissatisfaction with how things had planed out thus far. It was ironic that the very lessons Kris had learnt at home, school and university contributed to the abrupt shift away from the path he was expected to follow.

However, for the time being, he was prepared to go through the motions, with an army career beginning in the spring of 1961. Given his background, most observers would have said the 25-year-old was en route to a distinguished military career. However, Kristofferson has since said that even though it was inevitable that he would do an army stint, his ambitions as a writer ensured it would not be for long. With the probable benefit of hindsight, Kris later said that his father did not really expect him to progress in the military. Starting out with the rank of second lieutenant, Kris' mood was black. As he later said, "Shit, I remember driving onto the military base the first day. It was like driving into hell."

As well as serving in the 8th Infantry Division, Kris was a member of the Army Air Corps, which was renowned for special skills including flying in support of hazardous missions. He received some of his helicopter flight training at Fort Rucker in Alabama. "You had to be controlling the rotor disc with the right hand, the RPM and pitch of the blades with your left hand, and countering every change with the foot pedals . . . your foot pedals controlled the tail rotor. It was very difficult."

He hated the many behind-the-scenes routine jobs, such as a supply officer, "my notion of some sort of Kafka hell". He also instinctively resented the mindless deference to people in power. "You have to submit to authority that may not be wise; there are a lot of dumb people you have to say 'Sir' to." In addition, getting up early in the morning was not to his liking.

Kristofferson did take to flying and as a young army officer, he became a member of the elite Airborne Rangers and earned the right to wear "Jump Wings", a military badge awarded to soldiers who complete parachute training and accomplish the requisite number of jumps. Once more, given a range of opportunities, Kris showed himself to be a high-achieving participator. As he put it rather modestly, "I did a little more than was required." For much of his time in the army he was assigned to American bases in West Germany, as Elvis Presley and Johnny Cash had been during the previous decade. At one point Kris was stationed at Bad Kreuznach in a unit known by the soldiers as the Buffaloes; the company motto being, "The thundering herd, to the sound of the guns."

In a pattern that had started at school and university, Kris was perfectly capable of mucking in with his colleagues and fellow soldiers, while at the same time experiencing a degree of separateness. It was hard on him moving around from one faceless furnished military house to another when, as he conceded later, "You're not doing what you think you should in life." He felt under pressure; not just because he was trying to do a demanding job that felt wrong, but also because he was having to face up to the responsibilities of being a husband and father. Fran had given birth to the couple's first child, Tracy, on January 9, 1962.

The situation was no easier for Fran, uprooted as she had been from a comfortable civilian life in America and now living with a man who felt trapped and frustrated. To add to her woes, Kris was now drinking heavily – presumably when the disillusionment at his lack of direction frustrated him to the point that he felt he "touched bottom". He wanted to write, and to achieve the therapeutic release it offered, but in his darker moments Kris feared that the events of his life had conspired against him to make this an impossible goal.

Inevitably, Fran was on the receiving end of much of her husband's dissatisfaction. Away from home he took it out on inanimate objects, which led to him crashing a number of cars and motorbikes. He and some of his army buddies reportedly risked life and limb by flying their helicopters low into the hollows of the Rhine Valley, going dangerously close to the surface of picturesque lakes on occasion. It seems he relished the exhilaration that such deadly risk-taking provided.

Having initially signed up for a three-year stint, it was perhaps surprising that he stayed on for longer, but Kristofferson has always maintained that despite his internal frustrations, he did not regret his time in the army. It provided a form of security for Fran and Tracy and there were the exciting physical challenges to savour – from flying and parachuting to fighting through swamps. It also offered the opportunity to visit many interesting historical parts of Europe and on at least one occasion, he went on a hitch-hiking holiday as well as reconnecting with Paul Lincoln on a trip to London.

It was inevitable that Kristofferson would find outlets for his musical passion. He later recalled his appreciation of Johnny Cash and Willie Nelson, who was starting to attract attention with his idiosyncratic singing and phrasing styles. "There was a disc jockey who loved Willie – he had a programme that all the soldiers listened to in the afternoon and he would talk about Willie every day and play a lot of the songs that I guess weren't big hits because Willie wasn't a commercial singer. He phrased like a jazz singer, and that was a long way from Ernest Tubb."

Roughly halfway through his time in the army, Kristofferson hooked up with a few like-minded soldiers and formed a band referred to variously as The Boozers or The Losers. They played ad hoc gigs at servicemen's haunts, such as Rod and Gun clubs as well as *gasthauses* (roughly equivalent to local pubs) at the weekends. Their repertoire consisted mainly of country-oriented songs and X-rated parodies of contemporary pop songs reflecting their military experiences. Kris attracted the disapproval of some of his officer colleagues who looked down on the fact that he played at clubs for enlisted men and non-commissioned officers. The fact that he got drunk and pugnacious doubtless attracted their opprobrium too.

Though Kris' songwriting was generally limited to rewriting well-known songs for the amusement of his fellow soldiers, he was in fact carrying on a military tradition that stretched back many years. Such songs had been written by musically minded soldiers and passed on by word of mouth – part of an oral tradition that contributed to the upkeep of morale.

Kristofferson revamped the song 'Big Bad John', a massive hit for its writer, Jimmy Dean, in 1961.[*] His version, called 'Sky King', became a regular part of Kris' live repertoire in subsequent years though he never actually recorded it until 2003. Written and performed when he was in West Germany, 'Sky King' was subsequently sung by troops in Vietnam – a source of great pride for Kristofferson – and was probably taken there by some of the soldiers and airmen he knew or had entertained with his army band in the early Sixties.

Another song to receive the Kristofferson treatment was 'Itazuke

---

[*] After Kristofferson became famous, he sang it for Dean who "howled with laughter".

Tower', one of the most popular soldier songs during the Korean War. Kristofferson's version, 'Phan Rang Tower', was carried on to the Vietnam conflict by his friends in the 48th Assault Helicopter Company, and was subsequently reworked in Thailand by Phantom Jock Dick Jonas as 'Ubon Tower'. With particular reference to Vietnam, General Edward Lassdale said of such songs, "They belong to the Americans who served in Southeast Asia and express their own emotions about a war, a people, and a land far from home."

Although Kris might not have been able to pursue his ambitions as much as he would have liked, he did make one chance connection that would prove to be of crucial importance. When flying with his platoon commander, Donald "Donny" Kelsey, Kristofferson told him of his musical aspirations. Donny suggested that Kris send some of his songs to his aunt Marijohn Wilkin, a songwriter who lived and worked in Nashville.

Wilkin had achieved fame in the late Fifties with 'Waterloo' for Stonewall Jackson and 'Long Black Veil', a hit for Lefty Frizzell and a country standard ever since. Her songs were soon being recorded by many of the top artists of the day, including Patsy Cline, and by 1963 one of her songs was being recorded by someone every week. The following year, having become a significant figure on Nashville's Music Row, she set up her own music publishing company, Buckhorn Music.

A relationship of sorts developed before she and Kristofferson ever met; it seems that Wilkin understood both Kris' talent and his uneasy relationship with the army. His preference for hanging out with the ordinary soldiers and writing perceptive, poetic lyrics led her to refer to him as a "renegade". Speaking in 2003, Wilkin said the music Kristofferson gave her was "a mix of Shelley and Keats set to the tune of Hank Williams". The songs clearly made an impression and she informed Donny to tell Kris to stop by if he was ever in the Nashville area.

Towards the end of his time in the army (by which time he had risen to the rank of captain), Kris confided the turmoil over his future plans to a general he flew with. He was taken aback by the response he got. "I told him that I really thought I wanted to be a songwriter. I'm sure it sounded like I'd said I wanted to be Bozo the Clown. But he looked at me and he said, 'You know, follow your heart' . . . it was surprising advice to come from a military man. But he knew where my heart was."

Kristofferson had indicated a willingness to go to Vietnam but his superiors had overruled this, believing that his talents were better suited to a new assignment – teaching English literature to cadets at West Point (the United States Military Academy), about 50 miles north of New York City. He was due to take up this new role in 1965 once his current tour of duty in Europe was completed. Kris visited West Point and was briefed about his new job but he quickly realised that this august academic military institution, with its hierarchies, rules and traditions, was not for him. He was told the cadets would come into class and stand in a semi-rectangle around the teacher, waiting to be told to sit down. Teachers also had to turn in lesson plans 24 hours prior to each class.

Kristofferson later said he felt a "vague sense of despair" creeping over his body. "It sounded like hell to me." The position might well have offered the chance of a distinguished career in academia but it would certainly have put a block on his restless desire to step outside the confines of the establishment and express his thoughts and feelings in his own particular way. He did, however, give the proposition very serious consideration. "I would have been a major and on my way, and I thought heavily about doing it."

However, he had reached a point where he was able to summon up the resolve to move away from doing what was expected of him by his parents and peers. One army colleague, hearing of Kris' desire to write, missed the point entirely when he suggested that Kristofferson could write for the army if that was what he wanted – there was always a need for people to produce technical manuals and the like.

The gap between military assignments created the opening for what would be the major turning point in Kristofferson's life. He had some leave due him prior to starting at West Point. Instead of joining up with Fran and recuperating at home on the West Coast, Kris took it into his head – "I just went crazy" as he later said – to visit Marijohn Wilkin. Ever conscious of literary figures and their work, Kris said that going to Nashville was comparable to a case of "following your bliss", a reference to an idea of writer and philosopher Joseph Campbell, who opined that "if you follow your bliss you put yourself on a kind of track that has been there all the while, waiting for you, and the life that you ought to be living is the one you are living. When you can see that, you begin to meet people who are in your field of bliss, and they open doors to you."

Having found inspiration in the writings of Campbell and, of course, William Blake, who saw it as the duty of a creative person to devote his life to his art and not to "bury his talent in the earth" even at the expense of material comfort, such views merely fed Kristofferson's certainty of the new road he had to take. He was conscious, too, that by the age of 29 many successful artists already had a substantial body of work behind them. It's inconceivable that an acute observer like Kristofferson was unaware of, or unaffected by, the momentous goings on in the world of popular music that had exploded in Britain. The Beatles and The Rolling Stones were the figureheads of a cultural revolution that saw old ideas being questioned, traditional assumptions being challenged and a general attitude of irreverence permeating all areas of life from religion to politics to sex.

There was growing tension between the old guard and a new generation who wanted to bring change. Things were more constrained in the Fifties during Kristofferson's first visit to the British Isles but by 1965, the so-called permissive society was helping to cast aside many of the shackles that had held much of the population in deferential thrall to the establishment. The social upheavals of the mid-Sixties set the stage for a singer-songwriter with something to say, as Kristofferson confirmed: "I just figured that thanks to people like Dylan that I could do my own stuff, because a voice that doesn't fit into a groove can be accepted doing original material."

# Chapter 6

KRISTOFFERSON's introduction to a way of life radically different from anything he had ever known – and one that was misleadingly glamorous – came when Marijohn Wilkin's 19-year-old son Bucky picked him up from Nashville airport in a white Alfa Romeo Giulietta Veloce Spider roadster.

Bucky, who had bought the car on the back of his success with rock'n' roll group Ronny and the Daytonas, still remembers Kris' appearance. "He was wiry, clean-shaven, with short hair, in his army uniform. As we drove into town, my song 'Sandy' was playing on the radio, so I was in my prime and he seemed impressed and eager to achieve that status as soon as possible."

Kris was still in uniform at this stage – though he claims he disliked wearing it – with some people addressing him as "Captain Kris". With Marijohn generously showing him around Music City USA, one of his first visits was to producer Jack Clement's studio. The trio later went to the Professional Club together, a gathering place for songwriters and musicians with time to kill between sessions. Clements and Wilkin performed a song together called 'Too Used To Being With You', a hit for Bobby Bare and Skeeter Davis.

"It was a real nice harmony thing," Clement recalls. "[Kris] loved it – he wanted to hear it over and over again. He got kind of hooked on it and we ended up having a real big time. He just seemed to get drawn in."

The producer described his first impression of Kristofferson. "He was shy and well mannered, but not overly so; definitely not pushy, quite humble."

Wilkin introduced the newcomer to other writers, including Bobby Bare, who saw his talent right away.

However, one particular encounter at the Ryman Auditorium, then home of the Grand Ole Opry, the spiritual home of country music, put Kristofferson's decision to turn his back on a conventional life beyond doubt. After Wilkin had introduced Kris to the official who decided who could pass through to the backstage area at the Ryman, Kris had his first meeting with Johnny Cash.

Kris later said it was akin to shaking hands with Hank Williams. "His electric handshake was the final nail in the coffin of my army career . . . he looked like a panther pacing around backstage . . . he was so skinny and wired out . . . [he] was the most driven, gifted, exhilarating and self-destructive man I'd seen."

Kristofferson knew he wanted a shot at following in the footsteps of his heroes and was not deterred by the fact that Hank had killed himself with drug and alcohol abuse at the age of 29 – Kris' age at that time – and that Cash was doing his level best to emulate the feat. On the contrary, it imbued Kristofferson's quest with a sense of urgency. "If you didn't examine it too closely, there was something very attractive about burning brightly and dying young."

Kristofferson was also introduced to other important local figures such as singer-songwriter Merle Kilgore (who had recently had a massive hit with his co-write of 'Ring Of Fire' for Johnny Cash), with whom he and Jack Clement stayed up all night. Kristofferson's initiation into the Nashville scene continued the next day as he watched Rusty Kershaw unsuccessfully attempt to sell Clement the publishing rights to 'Louisiana Man'. Jack fired Kris' imagination when he told of how he sometimes rode trains all over America just writing songs.*

In the course of a two-week vacation, during which he rarely slept, Kristofferson had his moment of epiphany, albeit one that had been brewing for some time. He wanted to go out and "hustle like Hank Williams" and "to burn not to rust". He later talked of "crossing the Rubicon . . . I was totally infatuated with the whole life".

To the horror of his parents, Kris decided to resign his commission – he was on course to become a major in less than two years – to move to a small apartment in Nashville with Fran and Tracy. His parents were simply unable to comprehend their eldest son's lament that he was creatively stifled by army life, nor his later assertion that until he went to Nashville in 1965, "I was failing and didn't realise it."

---

* Kristofferson wrote several songs during his initial visit to Nashville, though he later said that none of them had any merit.

The Silver Tongued Devil.
(JACK ROBINSON/CONTRIBUTOR/GETTY IMAGES)

Kris's parents were quite often in the news during
his childhood, as on this occasion when his father
went back to work for Pan American after the war.

School yearbook, San Mateo High School,
California. 1954. (ROGER RESSMEYER/CORBIS)

After studying at Oxford, Kris appeared to be following the conventional
path his parents desired when he married Fran Beer in 1961.

At the 1968 BMI awards in Nashville with fellow writers Eddie Miller (centre) who wrote the country classic 'Release Me', and Chris Gantry. Chris was there to receive an award for his song 'Dreams Of The Everyday Housewife' and Kristofferson went along as his guest. (COURTESY OF CHRIS GANTRY)

Left to right: Nashville, late 60s. Shel Silverstein, music publisher Bob Beckham, Kris and Chris Gantry. Kristofferson co-wrote a number of songs with eccentric writer and *Playboy* cartoonist Silverstein including 'Once More With Feeling' which was brilliantly covered by Jerry Lee Lewis.

(COURTESY OF CHRIS GANTRY)

Roy Clark comforts a stunned and emotional Kristofferson after presenting him with the CMA award for Song Of The Year for 'Sunday Morning Coming Down' in 1970.

(JIMMY ELLIS/THE TENNESSEAN)

With Joan Baez at the last Big Sur Festival, October 3, 1970. (HERB WISE)

Poster for *A Star Is Born*, 1976. The 40-year-old Kristofferson was uncomfortable with his role as a sex symbol. (GETTY IMAGES)

With Jon Peters and Barbra Streisand at the New York premiere of *A Star Is Born*, December 23, 1976.
(RON GALELLA/WIREIMAGE.COM)

With Rita Coolidge, backstage at New York's Radio City Music Hall, September 23, 1977. They performed two sold-out nights at the venue.
(BETTMANN/CORBIS)

Singing with Rita Coolidge on *The Muppet Show*, 1978.
(DAVID DAGLEY/REX FEATURES)

In transit with Rita and their daughter, Casey. 1978. Kris was constantly on the move in the 1970s pursuing his music and film careers. (DANI GERRARD/REX FEATURES)

Andy Gibb, Kristofferson, Olivia Newton-John and Rod Stewart, rehearsing for the UNICEF benefit concert, A Gift Of Song, January 9, 1979. (RON GALELLA/WIREIMAGE.COM)

With Muhammad Ali, at a press conference promoting *Freedom Road*, 1979.
(LFI)

Joan Baez talks to Kris and his daughter Casey, backstage at 'Bread and Roses' concert, October 1980. (HENRY DILTZ/CORBIS)

Kris with the children from his first two marriages, Kris junior, Tracy and Casey.
(DOUGLAS KIRKLAND/CORBIS)

With daughter Casey, 1981.
(DOUGLAS KIRKLAND/CORBIS)

Kris with Isabelle Huppert, one of his co-stars in *Heaven's Gate* (1980).
Overlong and loathed by the critics, it was one of the worst financial catastrophes in cinema history.
Kristofferson found it hard to get work for a few years afterwards. (UNITED ARTISTS/THE KOBAL COLLECTION)

Kris relaxing in the studio.
(DOUGLAS KIRKLAND/CORBIS)

In order to cushion the blow for his wife, Kris told Fran he would be successful within a year. Fran was understandably apprehensive about moving to Nashville; all she knew of her husband's musical surroundings was his band in West Germany, which played in "the worst kind of dives". The couple rented a $50-a-month "cold water flat". Despite the calibre of his educational background, Kris sought jobs "that didn't take any kind of brains". Indeed he was keen to work alongside people from all walks of life – especially those near the bottom of the socio-economic ladder as such experiences supplied grist to his writing mill.

Kristofferson was employed as a bartender, a railway labourer, a construction worker and even did occasional labouring work for country singer Faron Young. Kris was able to romanticise these menial jobs by comparing them with the sort of work Ernest Hemingway and Jack London had taken on. Apart from benefiting his writing, the experience also enabled Kris to pick up the rhythms of the way different people spoke.

There was apparently some hope that he might use his English qualifications to try to get a job teaching at Nashville's Vanderbilt University but he was not prepared to do this. "I was afraid that if I got a job I was equipped for educationally I'd lose contact with the people I wanted to get to know."

After nearly five years in the stiflingly regulated world of higher education and the military, Kristofferson enjoyed an intense sense of freedom. While fully aware that the going would be tough, he knew that Nashville was the place to be if he wanted to make it. "Nashville was where the store was," as Willie Nelson put it, "you had to take your goods there if you wanted to sell them." Kris also comforted himself with the thought that by meeting so many fascinating people, even if he didn't make it as a writer, he would have amassed a wonderful collection of material for a whole shelf of novels.

Soon after his arrival, Marijohn Wilkin signed Kristofferson to her music publishing company, Buckhorn Music, paying him a modest weekly stipend that augmented his meagre and irregular earnings elsewhere. According to Bucky, there was much about this newcomer that impressed people like his mother. "Kris was the Man with the Right Stuff, like an astronaut; he brought the goods and the attitude to the job – Rhodes Scholar, Golden Gloves champ, army captain, hell of a writer, hell of a sense of humour."

Kristofferson quickly made contact with other aspiring writers. However, the competition in Nashville was fierce, with over 200 publishing houses, about 15 studios and around 2,000 songwriters – known as "bugs" because they were always bugging people to listen to their songs – longing for the big break. It was soon clear that success, if it came at all, would not be overnight. Apart from anything else, the more successful singers tended to use well-established writers and most of Nashville's music scene was contained in two streets – Music Row – making it easy to "hit all the spots where everybody was".

Kristofferson was invigorated by how he could find himself in a room with artists and writers he looked up to and who were all motivated by the desire to generate quality songs. He was in a hurry; at nearly 30 he was aware that he was older than most of the competition and had a wealth of experience they had not known, which gave him a certain confidence, but in his darker moments, he worried that he might have left it too late.

There was a lot of mutual support as well as inevitable competition and rivalry, as Willie Nelson recalled: "Whoever had a recording session that week had better watch out, because he was going to get swarmed by a lot of songwriters. We'd find out who his A&R man was, who his publisher was, where his house was. You could try any way you wanted to get your song to him." Kristofferson compared Nashville in the Sixties to the extraordinary creative energy of Paris in the Twenties, an energy that, as one writer put it, "illuminated the town".

The first Kristofferson song that Wilkin managed to place was 'Talkin' Vietnam Blues,' which he wrote en route from the army to Nashville. Kris witnessed an anti-war demonstration in Washington and was determined to write a song from a soldier's perspective. An American GI comes across some demonstrators in Washington who are trying to get signatures for a "telegram of sympathy". He assumes the sympathy is for the families of soldiers killed in Vietnam and is enraged when he discovers it's intended for Ho Chi Minh, leader of Communist North Vietnam. He recalls another telegram in which the wife of one of his buddies is told that he has been killed in action. He looks on at the protestors' anti-war stance with barely concealed disgust.

Years later, when an interviewer brought up the song's sentiments in an attempt at provocation in view of Kristofferson's leftist views, Kris conceded that he was concerned the song led to him being branded a right winger. He explained how the song came about, making the point that, at the time, he was inevitably influenced by what he read in *Stars And Stripes*, the official US Armed Forces newspaper, and that he was still thinking like a soldier. But as he pointed out, "I wasn't so much pro-war as pro-soldier." He then picked up his guitar and sang the song, virtually word perfect.

Even after he left the army and found that his views on Vietnam had turned "180 degrees", a lot of the soldiers he knew were over in Southeast Asia and inevitably much of his sympathy lay with them. His beef was with the leaders who sent the soldiers to fight – what someone of his persuasion might describe as "lions being led by donkeys".

After settling in Nashville, Kristofferson visited some of his old flying buddies at Fort Campbell just as some of them were preparing to fly off. He had been drinking and crashed his car near the entrance to the base, but managed to see some of them. It occurred to Kris that he should join them as he was not making progress in Music City ("I've got a great future behind me," he joked) and his relationship with Fran was in trouble. They assured him he would be out of his mind to go to Vietnam. Though the thought of going back into the army did cross Kristofferson's mind, it was never a serious possibility and, as he later reflected, if he had, he might well have done something in the name of duty he would have had a hard time living with later.

It was reports from his army buddies that helped to change Kristofferson's outlook on Vietnam. He complained of a warrant office programme that saw high-school graduates being rushed through flight school in preparation for front-line duties. He spoke, too, of terrified young recruits being forced to parachute out of helicopters. Like many others, his views were also influenced by the extensive and rapid television coverage the Vietnam War received – on a far greater scale than any previous war.

For all its patriotic sentiment, 'Talkin' Vietnam Blues' remains dear to Kristofferson. It was first recorded by award-winning DJ Jack Sanders and then briefly made the country Top 20 for Dave Dudley, who had achieved a major hit in 1963 with one of the great trucking anthems, 'Six Days On The Road'. Kristofferson's name came to the attention of top writer Harlan Howard and also Ralph Emery, host of *Nashville Now*, one of the city's most influential television programmes, who both loved the song – jingoism was common currency in Nashville in the Sixties. They were powerful allies to have and working friendships based on shared musical interests soon developed among the three.

Initially Kris kept his hair short – though not quite as short as it had been in the army; this was probably just as well since many Nashville traditionalists were not ready to embrace any kind of hippie culture. Bob Dylan's then producer, Bob Johnston, recalled that when he and musicians such as Robbie Robertson and Al Kooper showed up with hair over their faces and collars, "They nearly ran us out of town."

When not working Kris spent much of his time carousing in bars frequented by fellow writers and musicians, such as The Professional Club and the Tally Ho Tavern, where he tended bar for a spell. Given his excessive intake of liquor at the time, he later quipped, "That's kind of like putting the fox in charge of polishing glasses in a chicken coop."

Another popular haunt was the Boar's Nest, a favourite hang-out of Waylon Jennings and his band, run by Sue Brewer, who was somewhere between a barmaid and a loan company, and the inspiration for the Mac Wiseman song, 'On Susan's Floor'. Sue loved songwriters and their wild excesses and as she put it, "The only time I ever said no was if somebody asked me if I'd had enough."

It was a hard-working, hard-drinking culture. When talking music and boozing, Kristofferson could become argumentative – sometimes getting involved in fights. In one instance, he became embroiled in a fracas in some dive on Printer's Alley when trying to rescue Roger Miller from the aggressive attentions of an overly zealous fan.

For Kris, the most important part of the constant carousing was the chance to rap with such artists and writers as Webb Pierce, Little Jimmy Dickens, Hank Cochran and Willie Nelson (it was in such bars that the two probably met for the first time). He also hung out with others who were more interested in the contemporary rock scene – "the ones that were much hipper than me" – and listened to a wide variety of music; apart from country, rock and Dylan (he loved the inference that Hank Williams was as important as Norman Mailer in the sleeve notes to *Bringing It All Back Home*), Kristofferson took in such singers as Josh White, the black civil rights activist who sang folk, blues and gospel.

As well as drink, amphetamines played a big part in Nashville's nocturnal habits. Waylon Jennings said that pills were the "artificial energy on which Nashville ran around the clock . . . and then some." Tom T. Hall described the effect on a writer's cognitive state. "After they'd been around somebody's house for a while drinking, taking pills, writing songs, singing songs, somebody would say, 'What time is it?' and somebody else would say, 'Half past eight' and the next remark would be, 'Morning or night?'" Among the favoured stimulants were "speckled birds", "Johnny White Crosses" and the trucker's favourite, the "LA Turnaround".

What emerged from these honky-tonks was a kind of songwriting brotherhood, embracing new and established writers alike. Songs were tried out at all-night "guitar pulls" (where a guitar gets passed around to each artist, who plays one or two songs and then awaits the verdict of his peers. Willie Nelson described them as the "nitric acid test" for a songwriter where "the inferior materials dissolve to leave the gold"). Another reason for guitar pulls was simply that there were very few places for little-known artists to perform, though some established artists would allow an unknown or two a brief slot during his show with any payment coming from the tip jars.

When marathon guitar pulls were going extremely well, the participants were said to be "roaring". As Kristofferson later put it, "We used to take about a day and a night trying to sing up all the soul in sight." It was at some of these sessions that other writers and artists first started picking up on Kristofferson's songs.

Despite the highly social nature of such occasions, inevitably, there was intense competition, which Nelson compared to a "roomful of piranhas" or "a bunch of old Wild West gunfighters coming together to see who is best". Kris was just as competitive as the next hopeful and did his best to land a knockout blow with the night's best song.

Some insiders referred to this loose group of writers that Kris was now part of as the "Nashville Underground" and there was a steadfast belief among the individuals that some – though definitely not all – of their songs had real merit, and that their talents would be recognised sooner or later.

Kristofferson also got to understand the more prosaic side of the business – how to pitch songs and what sort of money he might expect to make. He had earned very little money from 'Talkin' Vietnam Blues', so his interest was piqued when Tom T. Hall mentioned he was earning about $10,000 per annum. This sounded reasonable until Kristofferson realised that Hall was one of the most successful writers around and how long it had taken him to get to that level.

Although Jack Clement did not actually work with Kristofferson, the two formed a mutually beneficial friendship, as Clement confirmed, "He would find these songwriters that nobody else wanted to listen to and bring them to me, such as Vince Matthews . . . I got some hits out of it . . ." Like others with experience in the business, Clement knew he was dealing with a rare talent but one in need of refinement. "To begin with his songs were long and poetical – not what I would consider songs, more like prose." Because most of Kristofferson's new-found friends were hard up and had come from genuinely poor backgrounds, he inevitably sought to play down his privileged background the better to merge with his new surroundings. Clement did not see this as a drawback. "He just came over as a regular guy."

One fellow aspiring writer with whom Kristofferson became friendly was Chris Gantry. "We all hung out together in the streets for a lot of years and saw each other every day," says Gantry. "We used to compare our songs and went through the whole camaraderie that exists between songwriters, like a very exclusive sort of lifestyle – it was like an apprenticeship, because we were around some very heavy writers and we all influenced each other because we were all different. The Nashville industry didn't go too much for it at first, and it took us a long time to be even accepted to the point where somebody would even consider recording one of our songs. Then when we did start getting some cuts, they jumped on us as being 'the new breed' though we'd actually been there for a long time."

However, not everybody saw Kris in a positive light. The writer Will Campbell had an office below his small apartment on 18th Avenue. For him Kristofferson was nobody then, "just one more drunk on the Row".

While Kris appreciated the honesty of country music and the fact that it was not afraid to talk about cheating and hurting and drinking – he agreed with the description of it as white man's blues – he had no time for the bland, pop-oriented form of country that many producers in Nashville turned out as fodder for the charts.

The country-music scene in the Sixties was still dominated by smooth, violin-softened recordings, generally referred to as "the Nashville Sound", associated with crooners like Jim Reeves and Eddy Arnold. Such artists had moved mainstream country away from a folk-based sound towards a lighter approach accessible to a wider audience. The charts also featured such lightweight offerings as 'May The Bird Of Paradise Fly Up Your Nose' by Little Jimmy Dickens and the religious ditty (with the glorious title), 'Drop Kick Me Jesus Through The Goalposts Of Life' by Bobby Bare.

Even Roger Miller's catchy hits like 'King Of The Road' and 'Dang Me' hadn't really anything new to say. With the advent of all the new pop sounds bursting out of Britain and America, along with a corresponding cornucopia of vivid colours and fashions, Nashville was looking staid and dated, as it had in the late Fifties. Although it was not yet obvious to Kristofferson and his contemporaries, there was a real opportunity to radically change the face of country music.

While it was encouraging that he was making headway so soon after arriving in Nashville, Kristofferson had yet to get into his stride as a writer. Marijohn Wilkin felt that having been an English student and a writer of fiction, his grammar was "too perfect" and that he should learn to write in a way that people actually talked. Initially Kristofferson tended to write as if he were an orthodox country songwriter, trying too much to sound like Hank Williams, rather than expressing his own voice. Though capable of writing clever lyrics and reasonable tunes, he had yet to make a distinctive personal mark. One writer working at the same time described Kristofferson's early songs as "long and rambling requiems to the good old girls and the good old times; others were strange Satan-conscious allusions to his head full of book learning."

One example of this, 'The Golden Idol', was produced by Nashville legend Billy Sherrill; Wilkin had persuaded him to take on the project, but the song was not a hit. At this stage, Kristofferson had no serious aspirations to be a singer and the recording was regarded as a one-off venture. Wilkin was one of many to find his singing voice unappealing, so when she set up demo sessions to try to sell his songs, she engaged singers such as Johnny Duncan and Mel Tillis (who wrote 'Ruby, Don't Take Your Love To Town'). It was only when she was unable to justify the cost of hiring other singers that Kristofferson got to sing on his own demos.

Marijohn and Kris shared things in common from their backgrounds. Like Kris, she had given up a conventional occupation (as a schoolteacher) and her family thought she was totally wrong to go to Nashville. At times Wilkin worried that her encouraging Kristofferson while he was in the army was in some way responsible for him throwing away a promising career. With this in mind, it was Marijohn who suggested he might try to use his qualifications to obtain some teaching work.

Their relationship could be fraught on occasion as Wilkin recalled. "I remember this one day I could hear his cowboy boots coming down this old wood floor hallway we had. I was not having a good day and neither was he. He came right up to my desk. 'You're doing more for Chris Gantry than you are for me,' he said; whine, whine, whine, typical writer. He said he wanted his contract back and it just really hit me wrong. I got the contract and gave it to him and said, 'Shove it up your ass and see if it fits.' He turned his heels, clicking back down the hall. He stopped in front of the door, turned round and came back. I looked up and those blue eyes were just twinkling. He slammed the contract down in front of me and said it didn't fit. Then he smiled and walked out. We never spoke of it again."

Marijohn sometimes poked gentle fun at Kris about his songs. When she was listening to some new effort she might say, "My God, were you out again last night?" Mystified, Kris would ask what she meant. "You just told me in your song; you even told me her name."

Wilkin's recollection confirms that Kristofferson's home life was far from settled. In West Germany, despite her husband's frustration and his heavy drinking, Fran had the company of other army wives at least. In Nashville, she had gone from being an officer's wife to living in a hovel in an unfamiliar part of America. She was in a situation she had not foreseen – being a penniless musician's wife with a young child.

While drunk, Kris had a number of accidents but miraculously escaped serious injury when riding his Honda motorbike and driving the Volkswagen Beetle he had shipped over from Europe. "I think God takes care of fools and songwriters . . . He was looking after me cos I wasn't."

However, despite the stresses and strains, Fran endeavoured to maintain what one visitor recalled as a peaceful, tasteful household, enhanced by modern Danish-style furniture. Kris later acknowledged the untenable position Fran was placed in by his desire to follow music. "It was OK for me to be starving and doing something that I loved to do, but it was hard on my wife and my kid . . ." The couple did attempt to make the marriage work but Fran thought the wild side of Kris was driving him to the devil. "It was like a dirty thing that was taking me out of the house."

The pair had to contend with family disapproval as well. Kristofferson said his parents thought he must be "an insane hippy or a communist or a dope addict". Mary Ann found her son's move to Nashville incomprehensible; in her eyes he had given up a wonderfully promising career in order to be a drop-out with no prospects. Working as a bartender or a labourer was an embarrassment to the family.

Kristofferson readily acknowledged that his departure from the army in order to write songs contradicted his parents' whole away of life. "My father's life was discipline – he ran his whole world by rules of behaviour that God knows I carried a long time, thinking that was the way people had to behave. Their idea was that being a writer was fine when you are young and single but after that forget it . . . I knew [he] pictured writers as wearing elbow patches and smoking pipes, not smoking funny stuff in Nashville."

# Chapter 7

ONE job that came Kristofferson's way, courtesy of his friend Billy Swan (who had written 'Lover Please', a hit for Clyde McPhatter in 1962), was that of gofer (or 'studio set-up man') at Columbia Studios. For $55 a week he found himself carrying out menial tasks, sweeping floors, positioning microphones, running errands, wiping tapes and emptying ashtrays – Kris sometimes said he was a "janitor-flunkey".

The studios were quite shambolic, cluttered with microphones and instruments; wires ran everywhere like spaghetti, there were coffee stains on the floor and ashtrays were always full to overflowing. However, the job took Kristofferson close to some of the major artists of the day. Kris might see three or four sessions in a day that could last up to nine hours, so it was a priceless education in the recording industry.

George Hamilton IV, whose first glimpse of Kristofferson was through a control room window, recalled Kris looking like "a clean-cut college kid". Hamilton, who was struck by the fact that this janitor was also a heavy smoker, recalls just what an impact Kris made even then. "He became sort of the talk of the town . . . there was a buzz going round that there was a great new songwriter who was a Rhodes Scholar who had come to Nashville to learn the country music business."

Kris also got to see his hero Johnny Cash at close quarters. Unlike their initial meeting at the Ryman, what he now witnessed was a much less glamorous figure. Cash was destroying himself with pills even though he still had the ability to impress. "It would be painful . . . John would come in and four hours would go by and nothing would happen. He was wasted, but electric to watch." Cash later recalled that Kristofferson would sometimes mop the same bit of floor 20 times – "because he was trying to get a real good look".

Kristofferson was nearly fired on one occasion because he failed to prevent a couple of songwriters getting into the studio; they cornered Cash and tried to pitch him some religious songs. Consequently, Kris was advised to stay away from the studio and was delegated the task of erasing tapes in the basement. To his surprise, Cash – ever sympathetic to the underdog – said he was not going to start the next session until Kristofferson came back up.

Kris also got to see Hank Williams' widow, Audrey Williams, who was regularly in the studio attempting to breathe new life into some of Hank's recordings by adding string arrangements and the like – a task that Kristofferson saw as "pretty hopeless".

Probably the most memorable sessions that Kristofferson witnessed came in February–March 1966 when Bob Dylan recorded *Blonde On Blonde* at Columbia. There was so much interest that the local police had to stand guard outside the studio to prevent unauthorised people getting in. Kris was fascinated by Dylan and his total dedication in the studio. "It was like watching Van Gogh go through different stages of his painting and his inspiration."

Kenny Buttrey, who played drums on *Blonde On Blonde*, recalled an incident involving Kristofferson when Dylan recorded *Nashville Skyline* at Music City.* It concerned the genesis of the introduction to 'Lay, Lady, Lay'. When asking Dylan and producer Bob Johnston what sounds they envisaged for the drum part, Buttrey was taken aback when they respectively told him bongos and a cowbell. The drummer regarded these suggestions as nonsensical and tried proving his point by asking Kristofferson to hold the bongos and cowbell next to his drum kit during the take. Buttrey improvised a distinctive tick-tock introduction using the instruments that blended perfectly with the shimmer of organ and steel guitar. Despite his misgivings, it became one of the more memorable aspects of the song.

With regard to the termination of Kristofferson's janitorial work, Glen Snoddy, the operations manager at Columbia, who took him on originally, said, "He spent about a year learning all he could and then we asked him to do something a little harder like compiling some data for us and he said he couldn't do that." According to other reports, he finally quit following a dispute over wages.

Kris' parents called in to Nashville on the way back from a stint in

---

* The album was recorded at Columbia in 1969, after Kris had quit the janitor's job, so it seems he continued to visit his old place of work from time to time.

Dhahran in the hope of talking some sense into their wayward son. The visit was not a success and they left after just one night. Mary Ann subsequently wrote him a letter in which she all but disowned him and expressed her amazement that Kris should idolise someone many regarded as a dope addict and felon (a reference to Cash). She also enclosed newspaper clippings detailing the successes achieved by some of his former friends and fellow students, saying he was an embarrassment to his family and their friends and warned him not to contact people the family knew. Although Mary Ann was the initiator, Henry went along with her sentiments.

Clement told Kristofferson to keep the letter about him and not long after, while doing a session at Columbia with Cash, he invited Kris to show Johnny the letter in the control room. "Johnny really guffawed and it warmed things up between them." Johnny teased Kris about the letter whenever he saw him in the studio. "It's always nice to get a letter from home, isn't it, son?"

Eventually, a degree of rapprochement was achieved between father and son. This came as a relief to Kris, as one of his friends said, "It was tearin' at him." Kris valued the fact that his father had given him a sense of duty and claimed that he had conversations with him after his death in 1971. "He said he couldn't really understand what it was I was doing," Kris said, "but he could understand my need to do it."

Despite their differences and the fact that he was a hard man to please, Henry Kristofferson "could light up a room". He was present at Pomona when Kris was presented with an honorary doctorate by Professor Sontag, who was not particularly impressed by his promising pupil's dramatic change of course, referring to what he got up to in Nashville, initially at least, as "not very meaningful". When making occasional visits home thereafter, Kris received a reasonably cordial welcome. His mother certainly relented to a degree as time went by; she and Kris' sister, Karen, phoned up radio stations asking them to play his songs. Having apparently been dazzled by the more glamorous aspects of showbiz.* What Mary Ann's attitude to her errant son would have been had he not become

---

* Despite having referred to Johnny Cash as a felon, Mary Ann was impressed by Cash's television show and his friendship with Billy Graham. Years later, she flung her arms round Johnny's neck when Kris introduced the pair backstage.

successful can only be a matter for speculation; she died in 1985.

Estranged from his own family, to add to Kris' personal woes, it had got to the stage where Kris and Fran found it hard to talk to each other. Their second child, Kris Junior, was born prematurely in 1968 with health problems, the treatment of which amassed around $10,000 worth of medical bills (which it seems his well-to-do parents and parents-in-law did not assist with – or perhaps pride prevented Kris from asking for help). Added to this, Tracy had a kidney ailment and while medical bills were met when Kris was in the army, he and Fran now had to come up with the money themselves. This was at a time when Kris was earning $200 per month as a janitor.*

At one point, Kraig Kristofferson flew to Nashville in another attempt to get his brother to see the error of his ways. He put it to Kris that he had surely given songwriting long enough and that it was now time to return to a more conventional existence. It was all to no avail. In reality Kris did not feel that he was failing in the way that he did in the army; he was "working towards good stuff". He believed his writing was improving and he was greatly bolstered by the support and encouragement of his fellow "bugs". He never seriously considered going home; hanging on to his dream meant being selfish.

To ease their financial burden, Kris fell back on his experience as a helicopter pilot to secure comparatively lucrative work with PHI (Petroleum Helicopters International) based in Lafayette, Louisiana, earning around $800 a month flying personnel and equipment to and from oil rigs in the Gulf of Mexico. He would spend a week in Nashville and then another going back and forth to the Gulf from Lafayette. The job required a lot of waiting around and ironically, it also offered him plenty of opportunities to write without any distractions; even in the air it was music that was on his mind.

"I was flying for hours without anything to think about except for the songs. I'm surprised they didn't all come out with that same rhythm of the blades."

The isolation enabled him to express his feelings – sometimes he came up with as many as three songs a day. Several years later, when his

---

* A few years later, when Kris was in a position to give something back, he played a benefit concert in support of the Kidney Foundation.

creativity dried up for a time, Kristofferson's music publishers joked that he should perhaps head back to the Gulf. From time to time he met up with other pilots socially, when a guitar would be passed around. Kris was delighted when one of the other pilots recognised a song he had written back in his army days, having heard it in Vietnam.

Unsurprisingly, Fran eventually reached the end of her tether; there had been frequent blow-ups and partings but this time there was no going back. She headed back to California with the children. Years later, reflecting on their relationship, Kris enigmatically told one journalist, "See there was this girl at home . . . I'd gone with her at high school, Fran, we thought we could solve each other's problems."

It seems there was a strong mutual affection between the couple that lived on and Kris was able to visit his kids without difficulty.* Interestingly, Fran still uses the surname Kristofferson and she subsequently became the long-time companion of a man who, like Kristofferson, had attended San Mateo High School. He was also a keen sportsman but when he had to decide between following his heart and pursuing a sporting career or getting a proper job, he took his father's advice and became a sales executive.

By the start of 1969, after several years with Buckhorn Music, Kristofferson had still not scored a major hit. A few of his songs had been recorded – most recently Billy Walker and the Tennessee Walker Band's version of 'From The Bottle To The Bottom' – which briefly made the country Top 20 early that year. Despite his gratitude to Marijohn Wilkin for giving him his initial entrée to the Nashville scene and much else, when his contract ran out he felt it was time to move on.†

He was keen to get a bigger "draw" and approached Bob Beckham at publishers Combine Music. Beckham was immediately interested and contacted his boss Fred Foster, a major mover in Nashville at the time. Apart from Combine Music, Foster had set up the Monument record label in 1958 and was responsible for most of Roy Orbison's major hits,

---

* The couple did not actually get divorced until the early Seventies, by which time Kristofferson had made a lot of money. He is on record as saying how much he appreciated the fact that she did not try to claim half of his assets.
† In the mid-Nineties Nashville's BMG music publishing office acquired Kristofferson's songs that had been published by Buckhorn Music. According to press reports the price was around $1 million.

including 'It's Over' and 'Oh, Pretty Woman'. He had also given a young Dolly Parton a recording contract at a time when few others showed any interest in her.

Beckham told Foster he thought Kristofferson had potential but that he was looking for more money than he could authorise. Foster told Beckham to bring Kris over to his office and at their meeting, he asked him to sing four of his best songs. Kris was apprehensive – he was not playing any proper gigs at this stage and by no stretch of the imagination could he have been described as a polished performer.

Foster recalls the day well: "He was real nervous; he didn't fancy himself as much of a singer. He was finding confidence in himself as a writer. I think he basically knew he was a great writer, but he hadn't proven it yet. The reason I asked him to sing four songs is any songwriter might luck up and write one great song, never more than two and certainly never four. If you write four great songs you're a great writer."

Foster knew immediately he was dealing with a rare talent. "I imagine by the time he was somewhere in the middle of his second song, I was almost in shock. I thought, 'My God, is this as great as I think it is? Maybe I'm hallucinating or something.'"

Kristofferson had approached Combine for a songwriting deal but Foster quickly saw other future possibilities opening up for the edgy young artist in front of him. He could tell he was educated to a high level and liked his literary turn of phrase, which set him apart from other writers, but he also liked the way he put the songs over. Foster told Kristofferson he would give him the financial deal he wanted – on condition that he also signed with Monument and recorded an album. This was a great opportunity – many organisations simply wanted to hire people to write songs for their artists – but Kris was taken aback.

"Man I can't sing," he protested. "I sing like a frog." "Yeah but a frog that can communicate," Foster shot back, "cos you just sold me."

The songs that Kris sang that day were 'To Beat The Devil', 'Duvalier's Dream', 'Jody And The Kid' and 'The Best Of All Possible Worlds'. The inspiration for 'Jody And The Kid' came from Critter, one of Kris' nicknames. Somebody saw him at the Tally Ho Tavern with his daughter Tracy and said, "Look, here comes Critter and the kid."* 'The Best Of

---

* 'Jody And The Kid' was recorded by Roy Drusky in 1968 and made the country Top 30.

All Possible Worlds' owed much to Kristofferson's literary background. The phrase had been coined by the German philosopher Leibniz in the 18th century as a way of explaining evil in a world with an omni-benevolent god; the notion was subsequently ridiculed by Voltaire in *Candide*.

The link-up with Foster would prove to be of critical importance to Kristofferson's future. As with all the artists he handled, Foster did not attempt to categorise his new signing. "If you put a label on anything you've limited it. I just thought he was a universal soldier, could do any-thing. I got to working with him and I saw how fast he mastered everything. His guitar playing improved enormously in a short time and he began singing harmonies and everything. He was an adept student of the game."

On a more personal level, Foster observed, "It was obvious that Kris was the kind of person who had his own thoughts about things, obviously a deep thinker, thought about things at the kind of level that many people didn't."

Foster attracted writers who thought outside the box. Dennis Linde, who wrote 'Burning Love' for Elvis Presley and, much later, 'Goodbye Earl' for the Dixie Chicks, used to set himself bizarre challenges like daring himself to write songs starting with every letter of the alphabet, which led to 'X Marks The Spot' and 'Zoot Suit Baby'.

Kristofferson was introduced to other promising writers at Combine including Shel Silverstein, who wrote 'A Boy Named Sue' for Johnny Cash and the lyrics for many of Dr Hook and the Medicine Show's songs, and Tony Joe White ('Polk Salad Annie', 'Rainy Night In Georgia'). He also became friendly with Mickey Newbury who had enjoyed early success with 'Just Dropped In (To See What Condition My Condition Was In)', a 1968 hit for the First Edition featuring Kenny Rogers – who claimed it was one of Jimi Hendrix's favourite songs. Newbury had been in the air force and, like Kris, had spent time in England. Kristofferson sometimes fetched up at Newbury's houseboat on the Cumberland River about 25 miles north of Nashville; Mickey would wake up in the morning and find Kris passed out on the deck. During one visit, Kris lent too far back in a chair and fell into the water.

Despite the general rivalry between songwriters, there was a lot of mutual support too, and Kristofferson and Newbury sometimes pitched each other's songs. Mickey became a kind of personal guide, showing Kris around Nashville; he got below what he described as Kristofferson's "gruff exterior" and discovered a "heart of glass" below. "He wants everyone to love him, at times to his detriment, and he is a fiercely loyal friend." Others observed that for all his networking, Kristofferson was something of a loner. "He was a clearly defined self-contained person . . ." opines writer Dave Hickey. "He exudes a kind of serene confidence . . . he keeps his feelings tightly under control."

Not long after Foster hired him, Kristofferson said his creative well had run dry. He even suggested that Foster should drop him – he was taking his money for nothing. However, Fred had faith and told Kris that other talented writers he'd known had hit barren spells. He told him that he just needed to persevere. Kris had ongoing financial problems at the time – principally because of the medical expenses incurred in the treatment of his son.

Fred Foster: "We addressed Kris' financial situation and it was soon after that I suggested the idea for 'Me And Bobby McGee' . . . that must have been like pulling the log out of the log jam . . . I guess there wouldn't have been a 'Me And Bobby McGee' if it hadn't been for me, but I can't take much writing credit.

"Boudleaux Bryant owned the building where the Monument Records offices were. He had a suite of two offices in the middle floor. He had just replaced a secretary he had had for quite a while with a new girl and he introduced her to me . . . I heard her name but it didn't register. Anyway one day I had to speak to him about a project we were working on; instead of calling him on the phone, I just walked a hundred feet down to his office. The girl's name was Bobby McKee, so I'm going down and about the fourth time I'm down there, he said, 'I don't think you're coming to see me at all, I think you're coming to see Bobby', and I had no idea what in the world he was talking about. 'You know, Bobby,' he said, and it came back to me. I said, 'Oh yeah, haven't you heard about me and Bobby McKee?'

"I know an idea when I hear one so I just flashed up the steps and called Kris. By the time I got up there basically the way you hear it had come to me. I gave him the title and said, 'You know, you bum around and so on and so forth and finally it's over' . . . I don't remember exactly what I said now but I did make the point that having Bobby as a woman was a good hook and so he wrote the song . . . he misheard the name as McGee not McKee. The lyrics and the music were really his . . . he put my name on it as co-writer, that was very generous of him and I appreciated it."

It was not uncommon in Nashville for someone to suggest an outlandish title and bet someone that they could not turn it into a song. However, initially, Kris could not see any way he could write to that title and for a time, he kept out of Foster's way to avoid being asked how the song was coming on. However, the title stuck in his mind and it became linked to the rhythm of a Mickey Newbury song called 'Why You Been Gone So Long'.

"One day I was driving between Morgan City and New Orleans. It was raining and the windshield wipers were going. I started coming out with Baton Rouge and the places I was flying around at the time. I took an old experience with an old girlfriend hitch-hiking in Europe. I had finished by the time I got to Nashville."

'Me And Bobby McGee', one of the first songs Kristofferson came up with as a staff writer for Combine Music, "turned over more audience to me than any song I ever had". The song's most famous line about freedom being another word for nothing left to lose surely had its origin in the recent upheavals in Kristofferson's life and his despairing feeling that he was on the bottom – broke, marriage in tatters, disowned by his loved ones.

"What I was thinking about most of all was a scene in the Fellini film *La Strada*." Starring Anthony Quinn and Giulietta Masina, in one scene, Quinn drives off leaving Masina behind – echoed in the line about letting Bobby slip away somewhere near Salinas. In another scene, towards the end of the film, when Quinn hears of Masina's death, he gets drunk, gets into a fight and then staggers to the beach where he rages impotently at the sky – he was free of Masina but, as in the words of the song, he would have "traded all his tomorrows for a single yesterday" with her.

"It definitely expressed the double-edged sword that freedom is . . ." Kristofferson explained, "you may be free but it can be painful to be that free. But maybe at the very end, when you leave, you will be free when you've nothing else to lose, you know, when you're gone." In a recent reassessment of the song, one journalist described it as, "A hobo hippy ballad as lean and literary as a great short story, and as honest and evocative as the best country song."

There is considerable disagreement as to who first cut 'Me And Bobby McGee'. Foster maintains it was Kristofferson himself when he and Billy Swan stayed up drinking into the night while laying down a demo using two mono machines. (Swan later described the heady excitement of creating this classic as a religious experience.) Another claim to have recorded the song first came from Jack Clement, who recalls producing versions by Mac Wiseman or possibly The Stoneman Family. Bucky Wilkin says he was the first and there are also claims on behalf of Gordon Lightfoot and Mickey Newbury.

The artist who first released an official recording of the song in early 1969 was Roger Miller. Though Kristofferson didn't know him that well during his time as a janitor, Miller was aware that there was a major new talent in Nashville. Kristofferson was about to start a construction job when out of the blue he got a call from Miller saying he was interested in 'Me And Bobby McGee'. Kris and Mickey Newbury had been trying to find Miller, thinking he was at the Ryman for the recording of Johnny Cash's ABC television show. He was in fact appearing in the *Daniel Boone* show in Los Angeles at the time and wanted Kristofferson and Newbury to fly out to California where it was being filmed.

Miller had heard about 'Me And Bobby McGee' ("Bobbie" in some early reports) and liked the sound of it, although at this stage it was not definite he would record the song. It seems likely it was Newbury who first mentioned it to Miller and who persuaded him that it might suit his singing style. Kris and Mickey were flown out to California first class in stark contrast to the way Kristofferson had been living in recent years. However, when they arrived, Miller was so busy with his television show that, by the time filming finished each evening, he was extremely tired, so there were few opportunities to pitch songs. Miller liked 'Me And Bobby McGee' and decided to record it after Kristofferson ended up teaching it to him on the plane back to Nashville.

When Miller came to record his version, it seems that Kristofferson had not quite finalised all the lyrics and he only gave Roger the final version of the second verse between takes. In view of the song's subsequent classic status, it was perhaps surprising that Miller's cover did not fare better (it made number 12 in the country charts in 1969), especially given his stature – but the interpretation was lightweight and lacklustre and did not draw out the earthy essence of the song. One journalist wrote of Miller's version, "It was quite like 'King Of The Road' but with a hippy slant."[*]

Paying tribute to the influence of Newbury, Kristofferson said, "Mickey is such a resolute artist; he is never going to compromise his vision of what the whole picture should be so you get this Newbury picture with sound effects and beautiful melodies . . . to me he was a songbird. I'm sure that I never would have written 'Me And Bobby McGee' if I had never known Mickey. God, I learned more about songwriting from Mickey than I did from any other single human being. He was my hero and still is."

They were nonetheless very different people. Kristofferson later recalled a time when the pair were working on a John Hartford television special. "Hell, I was a drunk . . . I went and hung out in the bars where the action was. Mickey was more of a stay at home. We were kind of an odd couple. He would stay at home and do that music over and over in his head. I'd come in all wasted from the Palomino . . . and I'd have about two hours' sleep before we went to work."

For his part Newbury recognised one of Kristofferson's key strengths as a singer, telling him, "You can communicate a song, you can sell a song." Newbury also claimed he knew Kristofferson would be a star the first time he met him and presciently foresaw a future in films – though Jack Clement claims to have been the first to spot Kris' movie potential. "He had a nice sculpture in his face . . . looked like Robert Stack."

George Hamilton IV remembers an incident around this time that demonstrated just what an impact Kristofferson and his songs had on his fellow artists, despite his natural diffidence. Joni Mitchell held a musical gathering when she was in Nashville to appear on Johnny Cash's TV show.

"She invited me to a little party she was having down at the Ramada Inn behind the state capital. I walked into the room and there was Mickey Newbury, Graham Nash, David Crosby, Mike Nesmith – Joni knew all these people from the California scene – the folk-rock movement. There sitting in the corner was a young man, Kris, looking like he did at Columbia studios – short hair, beardless, button-down collar shirt, Ivy League collegiate look.

---

[*] Roger Miller recorded two other Kristofferson songs, 'Darby's Castle' and 'The Best Of All Possible Worlds' – a considerable compliment since Miller mainly recorded his own compositions; indeed when Willie Nelson heard the latter at first he assumed Miller had written it.

"Joni was holding court, sitting in the middle of a bed with a guitar in her lap and passing it around and everybody was singing songs. Kris was not that well known. Everybody else had had a song or two and she said, 'Kris, why don't you sing us a song.' I'll never forget it, all these major talented singer-songwriters in the room, and this young fella picks up the guitar and opens a file folder notebook, sang the song all the time looking at the words – 'Me And Bobby McGee' – like electricity, the room just suddenly got deathly quiet and every face in the room was mesmerised.

"When he finished there was this hush and then suddenly everybody was going over and patting him on the back, shaking his hand and giving him their business card in LA, saying to call them if he was ever on the West Coast. Everyone had been singing songs and nobody had really noticed Kris, but once Joni turned the spotlight on him and gave him the floor, he took over. He just needed to be seen and heard, the talent was there in spades."

# Chapter 8

KRISTOFFERSON received an advance from Roger Miller's version of 'Me And Bobby McGee' that further helped to ease his precarious financial situation but, around this time (1969), he made one notoriously audacious attempt to advance his prospects that has since become the stuff of legend.

Even though an amicable acquaintanceship between Kristofferson and Johnny Cash had developed, Cash had not made any moves to listen to, let alone record, any of his songs. While employed at Columbia studios, it would have been unwise for Kristofferson to make a direct approach to the artists he observed but, after a while, he did start slipping demos of songs, including 'The Golden Idol', to June Carter (who married Cash in 1968) and also Cash's lead guitarist, Luther Perkins. Luther in particular had been very encouraging, telling Kristofferson that Cash really liked some of his songs and it was said that he carried some of the lyrics around with him. When June passed them on to her husband, he invariably threw them into Old Hickory Lake, next to their house; a pity, as a song of the calibre of 'The Best Of All Possible Worlds' would surely have been a major hit for the Man In Black.

With hindsight, Cash realised how genuinely passionate Kris was about his music. "I didn't know much about him but I surely knew that the fire burning in him was a hot one."

Kristofferson was well aware that Cash took prodigious quantities of pills and that his health was seriously compromised, so it crossed his mind that if he didn't get a song to him soon, it might be too late.

In what appears to have been a spur of the moment decision, Kristofferson decided to drop in unannounced – literally, as it transpired – to Johnny and June's lakeside home in Hendersonville, about 15 miles north-east of Nashville. He had just taken a weekend job flying helicopters for the Tennessee National Guard in Nashville and happened to be flying north of Nashville.

"I figured I would impress him one way or another if I flew into his backyard, and I did . . . in fact I almost landed on his house. They were pretty old helicopters . . . I'm lucky he didn't drop me out of the sky with a shotgun . . . I could have damaged the house or the helicopter, and I could have gotten into trouble with the guard . . . it could have gone real wrong."

It was certainly a high risk, reckless strategy. However, five years' experience in the army had given him the confidence he needed to pull off the stunt; determination to succeed in the music business did the rest. While it is undoubtedly true that Kristofferson flew onto Cash's property, eyewitness accounts from the principals involved differ.

"Kris was determined that I was gonna listen to his songs," said Cash, "so one Sunday afternoon he landed a helicopter in our yard. I was asleep. June came in and woke me up and says, 'Some fool has landed a helicopter in our yard!' We went out and it was Kris. He fell out of the helicopter with a cigarette and a tape in one hand and a beer in the other. I said, 'Anybody that would go this far, I'm gonna listen to your songs.'"

"I wouldn't have been able to fly while holding all that . . ." Kristofferson maintained, "it takes two hands and two feet to fly a helicopter and I've never flown with a beer in my life . . . John had kind of a creative memory. But he did me so much good I'm willing to go along with the story. It sounds so much better anyway."

Cash was, in fact, furious at the time and added the tape to the countless others he had previously thrown into the lake. Cash said the song Kristofferson tried to pitch was 'Sunday Morning Coming Down' whereas Kristofferson thinks it was 'It No Longer Matters' (which neither of them recorded).

Kristofferson subsequently regretted his actions as it gave other aspiring writers the idea that it was somehow acceptable to invade people's privacy in this way. However, his bold move paid off as, not long afterwards, he was invited to visit the Cash residence in a more conventional manner, taking part in some of the guitar pulls that were held regularly in front of a crackling log fire in the Cash family's rustic living room. One famous session in 1969 reputedly featured Bob Dylan singing 'Lay, Lady, Lay', Joni Mitchell ('Both Sides Now'), Graham Nash ('Marrakesh Express') and James Taylor ('Sweet Baby James').

In his autobiography, *Chronicles Volume I*, Dylan recalled an incident that caused Kristofferson some discomfiture. Bob had just played a song and was about to pass the guitar on when Joe Carter (June's cousin) said, "You don't eat pork, do you?" Dylan was momentarily taken aback. "Ah, no sir, I don't . . . Kristofferson almost swallowed his fork . . . he just shook his head."

That same year Cash provided what turned out to be easily the most important fillip for Kristofferson's career as a stage performer. Johnny was booked to play at the Newport Folk Festival in June and he suggested to Kris that he might like to join him as a performer in his own right. This was a daunting prospect for Kristofferson, as it would not be an exaggeration to say that when it came to performing live in small clubs – let alone major festivals – he was a novice. He had unsuccessfully sat in for a friend one night at Nero's Cactus Canyon, a diner in Nashville. "I got fired after about an hour. I was supposed to be playing my 12-string while they ate dinner, and I don't think anybody could eat. Nero came up to me and said, 'How long have you been playing that thing?' I said, 'Well, about an hour.' And he said, 'No, I mean in your life.'"

Kris hitched to Newport with his friend Vince Mathews and they slept in an old church that served as a kind of dosshouse for hippies. Cash had to deploy his considerable powers of persuasion to get the organisers to agree to let Kristofferson perform – there was insufficient time and they were no doubt concerned about giving such exposure to a totally unknown quantity. It was agreed that he could make a brief appearance during Cash's set, thus depriving Carl Perkins of his slot (Perkins was a close friend of Cash's and performed regularly in his troupe).

Kristofferson's lack of confidence was not alleviated by Cash's advice not long before going on. "You know, you don't sing very loud in my house. You'd better sing out so they can hear you past the first row." By the time he was due to take the stage, he was almost paralysed with nerves and legend has it that June Carter propelled him towards the stage with a kick up the butt. His Newport debut took place on July 18, three days before Neil Armstrong became the first man to set foot on the moon. However, it's likely that Kristofferson was the more nervous of the two.

Much to his evident relief, Kris' set, which included 'Me And Bobby McGee' and 'Sunday Morning Coming Down', was well-received and the organisers asked him to participate in afternoon workshops on the festival site with artists such as James Taylor, Joni Mitchell and Ramblin'

Jack Elliott. For someone who had been struggling to achieve success in his chosen field, the experience of appearing on the same stage as some of the top artists of the day – the kind whose ashtrays he had recently been emptying – was overwhelming.

"It was like heaven . . . took me from being a guy who sat on a chair at John's house to getting an invitation to appear at the Berkeley Folk Festival – I never looked back." He was even more enraptured when the press greeted his performance with enthusiastic praise.

At 33, Kristofferson later said that Newport "was responsible for my whole life as a performer . . . it might just have been the most important individual moment in my whole career". He felt that without this remarkable opportunity, he would simply have been too old to make a serious stab at launching a credible performing career. It was just as well that things were looking up. Kris' financial situation remained precarious; he had monthly child support payments to make and was only just making ends meet. Worse still, he lost his job flying helicopters for Petroleum Helicopters International for "not letting 24 hours go between the bottle and the throttle". According to one report, he was found asleep in the cockpit with the rotors whirling above him. He suffered great anguish and despaired at how he had allowed his life to descend into such a sorry state, which exacerbated his tendency to dark moods and depression – a lifelong affliction.

However, such bleak moments were symptomatic of a previous existence, as soon after the loss of the helicopter job, with his growing success, Kristofferson was able to turn his back on the world of conventional employment for good. Thanks to Johnny Cash and other important figures in the business taking every opportunity to talk up his work, more and more artists started recording his songs. Late in 1969, Ray Stevens covered 'Sunday Morning Coming Down', which scored in both the country and pop charts.

'Sunday Morning Coming Down' (previously known as 'Sunday Mornin' Comin' Down') was one of a number of timeless classics Kristofferson wrote in a short space of time. Undoubtedly autobiographical, the words evoke an image of timeless poignancy, describing one man's experience of alcoholism, failure, loss of family and religion in a sharply poignant way that countless numbers of people could identify with. While Stevens' soulful take moved its writer to tears, the record was unsuccessful due to Monument being unsure how to market it (Stevens was generally associated with novelty records).

Faron Young's version of 'Your Time's Comin'' (which Kristofferson co-wrote with Shel Silverstein) reached the country top five and was one of the first significant Kristofferson-associated hits. Jerry Lee Lewis had a number two country hit with another Kristofferson-Silverstein co-write, 'Once More With Feeling', and also covered 'Me and Bobby McGee' in a boisterous, piano-driven interpretation. Of the hundreds of artists to cover his songs, Kristofferson holds a special affection for Jerry Lee Lewis. "The first time I ever really heard a song of mine transformed was Jerry Lee singing 'Once More With Feeling' . . . it was so good, and I was used to performances not being quite up to what I hoped for."

Bobby Bare had two Top 10 country hits with 'Come Sundown' and 'Please Don't Tell Me How The Story Ends'. "Kris got to be so hot as a writer that the DJs would say, 'Well here's another Kris Kristofferson song,' and play my record," Bare jokingly complained. "They didn't say, 'Here's Bobby Bare's latest hit.'" Even the traditionally mainstream Patti Page had a 1971 hit with 'I'd Rather Be Sorry'.

Ray Price gifted Kristofferson his first number one country hit with 'For The Good Times' in 1970. The song also crossed over to the pop charts where it reached number 11.* Price's lazily crooned version – laden with strings and redolent of the much derided Nashville Sound (some used the epithet "countrypolitan") demonstrated that Kristofferson's songs could sit comfortably alongside mainstream pop. There was some irony in the fact that Price, a staunch traditionalist, had a hit with a song written by an individual some of Nashville's traditional stalwarts regarded as a seditious hippy.

Kristofferson often wrote a song as a complete package, and sometimes, as in this instance, inspiration came in a flash but the song was not actually completed until later, when other pieces of the jigsaw fell into place. One of several Kristofferson standards that regularly draws spontaneous audience applause after a few introductory bars, 'For The Good Times' was written in the late spring of 1968 as Kristofferson recollected: "I was dividing my time between making nothing as a Nashville songwriter and earning around $900 a month flying helicopters for offshore oil rigs in the

---

* A follow up, 'I Won't Mention It Again', was also a major crossover hit for Price.

Gulf of Mexico. I'd always wait till the last possible moment to leave to go down there from Nashville, because I'd really have to fight the drive all the way down there in this Opel I had. There was a lot of expressway between here and Birmingham, but from there on across Mississippi just seemed endless.

"One of those drives from Nashville to the Gulf I began a song about making love to a woman for the last time. After a while the melody really got to me. I couldn't wait to get to a guitar. I was riding along thinking that part where it says, 'Hear the whisper of the raindrops blowin' soft against the window,' and I wondered what the chords were. Hell, I wondered if I could play it. I wrote only the first part of the lyrics then. A while went by before I finished it, I can't remember how long." Enigmatically he added, ". . . but I do remember who I wrote it about."

Some have suggested that the inspiration for the song came during the dying days of his relationship with Fran. For a time, some radio stations would not play the original recording by Bill Nash because of its overtly sexual content; indeed for a brief time, Kris could not find anyone who wanted to record the song, despite the fact that even in country music, sexual mores were being relaxed in line with pervasive trends in that direction throughout most of the western world. (Of course for the artists, especially when on the road, sexual morals had always been lax in the extreme – but that was a world with its own rules.)

It is perhaps hard to appreciate that such eloquent, allusive lyrics, so tame by present-day standards, could have aroused heartfelt opposition, as, despite the clearly sexual theme of the song, Kristofferson's simple poetry still left something to the imagination.

A spokesman for Buckhorn Music, which published the song shortly before Kris switched to Combine Music, said later, "It's recorded by pretty much everyone who comes into town to do an album, Englebert Humperdinck, Dean Martin, Andy Williams, Chet Atkins, Loretta Lynn and many more."[*]

In 1969, actor Dennis Hopper scored an unexpected hit with *Easy Rider*, an iconic piece of counter-culture cinema, which he directed, co-wrote

---

[*] As result of the success of this song in particular, Marijohn Wilkin was able to buy a boat that she sailed on Old Hickory Lake – she named it "The Good Times".

and starred in alongside Peter Fonda. Hopper and Kristofferson had met at a weekend-long party in Fort Worth, Texas, when *Easy Rider* was pulling in big audiences and Kris was starting to get his songs recorded on a regular basis. With a high credit rating in the film industry and having heard and liked 'Me And Bobby McGee', Hopper invited Kristofferson down to Peru, where he was directing *The Last Movie,* to contribute to the soundtrack, in exchange for his travelling expenses and accommodation.

The movie, with an impenetrable plot about a film company making a western, was said by some to be an allegory of the implosion of the kind of future hopes generated by the cultural upheavals and new directions the Sixties had brought. It was a commercial flop when released in 1971 despite winning Critic's Choice at the Venice Film Festival.*

Kris enthusiastically threw himself into the marathon drinking on the set, which was on a wilder scale than anything he'd yet encountered. "It was my first time near anything that bizarre. Hell, I was straight out of Nashville with shit on my boots . . . Dennis even got a priest defrocked in one town where we were filming."

It's interesting that Kristofferson should describe himself as he did; within a few short years he was happy to acknowledge he had "shit on his boots", a hick accusation that had irritated him in his Oxford days. By 1970 part of Kris' image was the language of the new young culture; he took to it like a duck to water and quickly started dropping gs from the end of participles, sprinkling his language with "chick", "cat" and the ubiquitous "man".

Kristofferson got a small part in the film – along with Bucky Wilkin, he played a "minstrel wrangler". It could be said that he fell into acting by accident; when one of the stunt men was injured, Kris got the nod because he could ride a horse. However, when grabbing the bridle of a mare that panicked on the set, he injured his hand in the process.

Kristofferson's searching openness to new experiences meant that he had taken the initial steps on what would become a lengthy career in films. His cause was helped by some kind of innate confidence and self-belief, however superficial it might have been at times, which enabled him to relate to everyone, from directors and producers to extras, as an equal.

---

* Not all assessments were so favourable; the film was also included in the 1978 book, *The Fifty Worst Films of All Time.*

Taken along with his openness and honesty, he became a popular figure who gained the respect of many people he came into contact with. His penchant for partying helped too.

One writer, Tom Burke, who spent time on the set, felt that Kristofferson's "pleasantness and goodness" marked him out from many of the other participants. It was clear to Burke however that Kris was regularly under the influence. "He appears to sleepwalk hungover through some good dream."

Another of Kristofferson's early associations with the world of cinema came at around the same time when he was asked to contribute to the soundtrack for Tony Richardson's *Ned Kelly*, starring Mick Jagger in the title role. Waylon Jennings and Shel Silverstein were principally responsible for the music, but the former apparently fell out with the film's production team thus creating an opportunity for Kristofferson's involvement. He sang three songs on the soundtrack including 'The Kellys Are Coming'.

While in Peru, Kristofferson received a telegram from Johnny Cash saying he wanted him to appear on his show when he returned to Nashville. Cash had made it clear that his weekly ABC television variety show, which had started transmission in June 1969, would not just be a vehicle for the usual suspects who appeared on traditional country programmes like *The Porter Wagoner Show*. Kris and many other writers knew that it attracted an eclectic mix of artists to Nashville to whom the "bugs" all wanted to pitch songs.

In the course of two years, Cash's guests included Bob Dylan, Neil Young, Joni Mitchell, Ray Charles, The Monkees, and Mama Cass Elliot (who nicknamed Kris 'no eyes') among many others.

Kristofferson was in pole position to receive exposure on the show; he had paid his dues and his name was well-known to insiders. On top of this he had, through his own idiosyncratic efforts, joined Cash's large circle of friends and acquaintances – beginning a firm friendship that endured up until Cash's death in 2003 – although Kris always found it hard to believe that he had become best friends with someone he looked up to as a hero.

Cash included 'To Beat The Devil' on *Hello, I'm Johnny Cash* released at the start of 1970. However, Kristofferson's real breakthrough came in April that year when Cash performed 'Sunday Morning Coming Down' on the show, introducing it by telling the audience not to forget the name

Kristofferson, "You're gonna hear it a lot . . . He's the finest young song-writer today."

For Nashville, some of the lyrics were controversial, but Cash was not interested in the idea of softening them in order to avoid the risk of offending members of his audience. One of the television producers wanted to replace the line, "Wishing Lord that I was stoned" with, "Wishing Lord that I was home." Indeed they suggested it might not be possible to air the song at all if the offending word was left in. During discussions on the subject Kristofferson complained that the essence of the song would be compromised if the words were changed.

As show time arrived, Kristofferson, sitting up in the gallery of the Ryman, did not know what would happen. "When it came to the bit Johnny looked up at me and sang the original words . . . to me that saved the song. I don't think it ever would have been that big if it had not had that word in it. He preserved the integrity of the song. And he won." However, Kristofferson later admitted that if the change had been made, he would have gone along with it – at that stage he did not feel in a position of strength vis-à-vis the entertainment establishment.*

When released as a single, the live recording quickly rose to the top of the country charts. Although Ray Stevens' version was a worthy attempt, it took Cash to really bring 'Sunday Morning Coming Down' to life and put over its grim message in the starkest way. He had struggled with addiction for years and, like Kristofferson, had caused sorrow and heartbreak to his loved ones by single-mindedly pursuing his artistic ambitions. When Cash sang the song, he was publicly confessing his failings and anyone who had a heart could not fail to be moved.

It also conveyed the message to those who had experienced similar problems in their lives that they were not alone and that somebody understood what they were going through. Others just marvelled at the brilliance of the lyrics and the obvious sincerity of the delivery. Cash later said 'Sunday Morning Coming Down' was so "close to him" he felt as if he had written it himself.

The narrative simply represented a slight embellishment of what many Sundays were like for Kristofferson before he made his name. Music Row

---

* For the TV show, Cash did have to make one minor change – amending the words "cussin' at a can" to "playin' with a can".

was closed down, many people were away with their families, and he had little money. "About all you can do is walk around wishing Monday would hurry up and come." On one occasion, his apartment was broken into. He called the police, one of whom expressed horror at the way the place had been trashed. Kris was embarrassed because in fact the burglars had hardly touched the place – it always looked that way.

It was Kristofferson's good fortune that a lot of money was being pumped into country music by 1970. Showcases like *The Johnny Cash Show* and a number of radio shows were being broadcast to a wider area than Nashville and its environs; there was a push on to spread the country music brand far and wide from which he could only benefit.[*]

Fred Foster was alarmed at the cavalier way his charge had given some of his best songs to other artists to record – as Kris' manager, these were really decisions for him to make. Foster wanted to hold some of these gems back for Kris' own album, a project he'd had in mind since first discovering his protégé.

"Lots of people sing my songs but not necessarily the way I intended," Kris explained. The *Kristofferson* album allowed him to deliver his own versions of songs others were making famous such as 'Sunday Morning Coming Down', 'Darby's Castle', 'The Best Of All Possible Worlds', 'For The Good Times', 'Me And Bobby McGee' and 'Help Me Make It Through The Night'.

Kristofferson did not have an established band at this stage and it was necessary to round up a few musicians in a hurry, including Billy Swan. Therefore the production and instrumental work were unsophisticated, rough around the edges with little attention paid to fancy introductions or virtuoso lead breaks.

The album was also something of a mishmash musically; Kristofferson might have been a simple singer-songwriter but the album was beefed up with a melange of rock, country and folk sounds. While blues and soul music were dear to him, Kris conceded he was not vocally equipped to perform either. By way of introduction to 'Me And Bobby McGee', Kristofferson delivered an enigmatic barb at those who endlessly agonised

---

[*] On April 29, 1970, Kristofferson himself appeared on *The Johnny Cash Show* singing 'The Pilgrim'. Also on the show were Rick Nelson and Doug Kershaw.

over the meaning of real country music and fretted about its dilution. "If it sounds country, man, that's what it is, a country song."

*Kristofferson* was eagerly anticipated by Nashville's artist community, who foresaw a class collection of demos that might well provide a hit. Two tracks revealed the extent of Kristofferson's rejection of his earlier life and his increasingly hostile attitude towards the establishment. The irony-laden 'Blame It On The Stones' used The Rolling Stones' position as so-called moral corrupters to highlight the generation gap — there was even a reference to the Stones' 1966 song 'Mother's Little Helper', which is spoofed by a reference to mother telling the ladies at the bridge club about "the rising price of tranquillisers".

As well as the contemptuous reference to the bridge club, which surely had personal resonance, another subtle dig at Kris' genteel background was the chorus being delivered in the manner of a Salvation Army band. The equally sarcastic 'The Law Is For Protection Of The People' took a pot-shot at redneck police harassing an innocent hippie — supposedly in the interests of the common good.

'The Best Of All Possible Worlds' resulted in a conflict with the record company over the use of "black" in the original lyrics. Despite Kristofferson's protests, the word was replaced by "low-down". (He invariably sings the original version in concert.)

In a spoken, half-mumbled introduction, Kristofferson dedicated 'To Beat The Devil' to Johnny and June Carter Cash. By way of thanks, Johnny contributed the album's liner notes in the form of a plain, down-home poem of 13 verses based on Kristofferson's experiences.

The song, in which Kris' character strikes up a conversation with an old man — the Devil — at the bar, owed much to Kristofferson's early struggles in Nashville and his eventual triumph. The message is positive — the writer rejects the Devil's negative message and sticks to his guns because it is the right thing to do. Bearing in mind that Kristofferson wrote the song before his success was assured, the song betrayed an underlying combination of determination and optimism on his part.

The songs on *Kristofferson* amounted to a statement of where the artist had come from and where he was going. Though not lacking a sentimental streak, Kris preferred to focus on deeper aspects of the human condition — inner turmoil and emotional passions, freedom, failure and loss as well as issues of relevance to wider society as they affected, in particular, ordinary people, especially those at the bottom of the social ladder or those who chose to be outcasts.

The theme of personal freedom was one he would return to again and again in the way that painters repeatedly return to the same subject in an effort to glean some insight that brings new enlightenment. A friend once said to Kris, "Take freedom out of your songs and you'd be speechless." In one interview, Kristofferson said that his own desire for freedom was what convinced him to leave the army and it just grew from there as an element of his writing.

"I value the freedom to be what I want to be and I suppose I just expected that such freedom should be universal and that everybody should have it if they can . . . I was in love with the expression, 'The creation of the products of my imagination,' and living up to the standards of the people who inspired me."

# Chapter 9

DESPITE containing a wealth of classic songs, *Kristofferson* did not fare well commercially, selling just over 30,000 copies and only briefly showing up in the country charts. The cover shot featured the artist staring intently out of the darkness with only half his face visible. Also prominent in one hand – the fingers stained orange with nicotine – was a cigarette; Kristofferson was rarely seen without the embellishment of a Bull Durham, his particular favourite and about the strongest cigarette that money could buy.

"He sings simple songs that speak eloquently of experiences . . ." *Rolling Stone* wrote. "He is always totally believable." Other reviews were less affirmative with Kristofferson's singing voice, unsurprisingly, attracting the most opprobrium. "It is not an especially interesting album even though I seem to see this guy hyped here and there," an unnamed reviewer sniped. "Basically he's just another adequate singer – sometimes barely that – with a handful of ideas that wear thin before the end of the album."

Another charged, "He's the worst singer I've ever heard. It's not that he's off key – he has no relation to key. He also has no phrasing, no dynamics, no energy, no dramatic ability and no control of the top two thirds of his note range."

While enjoying a high reputation as a writer, it seemed the public were not quite ready to embrace Kristofferson the singer. One artist who memorably transformed a Kristofferson song – much as Johnny Cash had done for 'Sunday Morning Coming Down' – was Janis Joplin. She reworked 'Me And Bobby McGee' into a characteristically raw blues-rock treatment that succeeded brilliantly and helped to considerably broaden Kristofferson's appeal by introducing him to a rock audience. As with many of his songs, 'Me And Bobby McGee' was strong enough to be taken in any number of musical directions – though Kristofferson had not envisaged the song being sung by a woman.

In the wake of his Newport Festival triumph, gig offers had come Kris' way. He performed in Greenwich Village at The Bitter End, where he played, jammed and partied with, among others, Mickey Newbury, actor Michael J. Pollard (who played C. W. Moss in *Bonnie And Clyde*) and Bobby Neuwirth, a well-connected artist, best known for his friendship with Bob Dylan. Neuwirth introduced Kristofferson to other music people of note and, at a typically hedonistic Manhattan party, he suggested that Kris might like to meet Joplin.

It's most likely that Neuwirth first let her hear 'Me And Bobby McGee' in New York, before either he or she had ever met Kristofferson. Ever spontaneous, Kris used most of his dwindling resources to fly out to Larkspur, California, to meet Janis in the early summer of 1970. Given her established status as one of the top female rock singers, Kristofferson entertained high hopes that she might record one of his songs.

Janis was always ready to party and the arrival of Neuwirth and Kristofferson triggered the start of what some dubbed "the Great Tequila Bash". The revelry was fuelled by excessive quantities of booze; pina coladas for breakfast, screwdrivers for lunch, cocktail hour at the Trident (a local bar) and then a late-night party at Joplin's arty, colourfully decorated house.

"I'd get up intending to get out," Kris recalled, "and in she comes with the early morning drinks and pretty soon you're wasted enough and you don't care about leaving . . . she had people she'd bring into the house and then she'd bitch because she was giving them bed and board."

The scene fitted in with the stereotypical hedonistic excesses of the late Sixties; one visitor noted that you might open a door and find a couple – in the fashionable argot of the day – balling. It has been widely reported that Joplin and Kristofferson had an intense fling in the course of a month of "high boogeyin", though Kris' initial interest in Janis reportedly cooled off as her ardour grew. As he said, "I dug her, but I had itchy feet."

Apart from an eclectic taste in music, the pair both came from well-to-do backgrounds against which they'd rebelled. They also had problems controlling their intake of alcohol and drugs. As with his time in Peru, Kristofferson gained entrée to new territory – Joplin was like nobody he had ever known before. It's likely that one of his infamous aphorisms – "Never sleep with anyone crazier than yourself" – emanated from his experiences. He qualified this by saying, "Assuming you are not in the middle of a drought with no choice," adding the payoff, "You'll break that rule and regret it."

Kristofferson was also aware that Joplin was insecure. "Nobody in this business is very stable," he said, "or else we wouldn't all be up onstage making asses of ourselves." In Janis' case, beneath her exotic and flamboyant exterior, the problems appeared to run deep. She constantly sought approval and feared that people would take advantage and then abandon her. She shared her suicidal thoughts with Kris and talked of resorting again to heroin. While Kris was sympathetic and genuinely surprised given the degree of adulation Janis commanded from colleagues and fans alike, he had his own demons.

Kristofferson never heard Joplin's version of 'Me And Bobby McGee' until several months after her premature death from an overdose in October 1970. While he loved the interpretation, he had reservations about her changing the lyrics – namely from Bobby clapping his hands in time to "holding his hand in mine". Kris put a great deal of thought into the inner rhyme of his words and, as with 'Sunday Morning Coming Down', to change things round, in his view, was to lose some of the essence of the song.

In January 1971, her interpretation posthumously reached number one in the *Billboard* pop charts and it remains for many the song for which she is best remembered. Many say she made it her own – then again similar claims are made about certain Kristofferson songs that have a wider resonance.

Joplin's death was a harsh and upsetting blow for Kristofferson, and it momentarily made him think about the life he was pursuing and the price to be paid by many in the business whose lifestyle was similar to his own. However, Kris did not change his ways as a result – Janis probably had no real death wish, he reasoned, and was just unlucky. Pushing himself to the limit had resulted in a four-month bout of "walking pneumonia", which necessitated an enforced period of rest. During his lay up, Kristofferson found it hard to shave and so he grew a beard, something which, along with his rapidly lengthening hair, was destined to become a trademark much commented on by the Nashville press for years to come.

Although events were moving at breakneck speed, he somehow

managed to take it in his stride. Looking back, he commented, "I'm amazed now that I wasn't more amazed."

Among the singers clamouring to record his songs, a little-known artist called Sammi Smith — with whom Kristofferson had sung some demos at Combine — released a winsome version of 'Help Me Make It Through The Night' in 1970.

The idea for the song, written on top of an oil rig in "one of those little bubble helicopters", had been sparked by remarks made during an interview by Frank Sinatra, who said that he would use religion, a broad or the bottle — "or anything else that would help a man make it through the night". Kristofferson said that he probably started writing the song "because I liked Dylan's 'I'll Be Your Baby Tonight' so much."

The song's theme was one Kris was well-familiar with. "Anyone who has ever been alone knows that the idea behind the song is right. Loneliness is probably a bigger killer today than cancer — but you don't hear of any loneliness foundations."

Despite the theme of solitariness, it is also part of the song's great strength that it can also be read in a totally different way — as a joyous celebration of the intimate union of a man and a woman. For some, the apparently guileless sexual candour of the lyrics went against traditional mores in country music, which had little to do with physical love other than in most indirect terms. Dottie West, a traditional country singer, who had had a hit with 'Mommy, Can I Still Call Him Daddy?' (featuring her four-year-old son, Dale) refused to record the song because of its "immoral connotations".

"Before 'Help Me Make It Through The Night'," said Bobby Bare, "one would be hard pressed to figure out what a honky-tonk angel did when you got her out of the honky-tonk."

Smith's version, which brought out the smouldering desire in the song, had all the more impact on the country scene (where it reached pole position) because the lyrics were delivered by a woman; some were shocked at the brazen notion of a woman's sexual desires. "I never did see anything scandalous about that song . . ." Smith insisted, "for me it was just very tender."

Reaching number eight in the pop charts (and also becoming a lesser hit for Joe Simon), 'Help Me Make It Through The Night' became Sammi Smith's career song. She compared attempting to find a follow-up with "like trying to follow a Rembrandt with a kindergarten sketch."*

In the wake of Kristofferson's commercial breakthrough, there was much comment on his particular contribution in changing the face of Nashville's country music scene, with him being seen as a key element in the cultural shift on Music Row that sounded the death knell for much of the product that had been turned out there by the late Sixties. "Records were put out and people didn't care if they were good or bad . . ." said Bobby Bare. "The writers before Kris were mostly making up the crap as they went along."

While many experts and insiders were in awe of his writing skills, others were uneasy that in the rush to praise Kristofferson, traditional values – both social and musical – were being eroded. These same people would have despaired at Bare's assertion that Kris made "the hippies and the long-haired funky people acceptable."

While most comment centred on his lyrics, the outstanding quality of some of Kristofferson's melodies was often overlooked – 'Help Me Make It Through The Night' and 'For The Good Times' being good examples. "It's the simplest ones that are hardest to write and Kris had that ability," as Fred Foster pointed out. Some songs had a subdued raunchiness redolent of soul music, others had the intellectual urgency of Dylan and many owed something to Kristofferson's love of the Romantic poets. One writer recently said that Kris created a "new-Romantic prototype for Nashville tunesmiths".

"Before 'Help Me Make It Through The Night', with its mention of hair, body and skin, writers couldn't really say what they felt," said Billy Sherrill. "Kris said what you'd always wanted to say and know. The sky's the limit in writing and recording."

Tom T. Hall was greatly impressed by the fact that Kris could "tell a story in one line that most of us can in five", while an unnamed commentator saw Kristofferson as a force for good because he "turned country music around on its nose by singing about sex and drugs and all the things a person could see on the six o'clock news any night of the week".

By 1970, Kristofferson's name was a contender when various music

---

* In 2006 Smith's version was placed at number one in country music authorities David Cantwell and Bill Friskics-Warren's book, *Heartaches By The Number: Country Music's 500 Greatest Singles.*

organisations in Nashville – and America – decided which artists should be honoured for their work. Although he was nominated in a number of categories at the prestigious annual Country Music Association Awards, the organisers demonstrated their view of his chances of winning anything by placing him at the back of the Opry House. To the surprise of most people, not least Kristofferson himself, 'Sunday Morning Coming Down' won Song of the Year. When his name was announced, Kris snapped his head back so sharply that he cracked it on the wooden pews at the back of the Ryman and nearly knocked himself out. Marty Robbins, sitting nearby, urged Kristofferson to get moving.

Dazed and unsure of exactly how to get to the stage, he took quite some time to make his way up there to receive his award from Roy Clark (who won the award for Comedian of the Year). Outraged traditionalists charged that Kristofferson showed great disrespect for such a grand occasion by his appearance. In the midst of a sea of tuxedos, under the watchful eye of the immaculately attired but visibly shaken MC Tennessee Ernie Ford (who had scored one of country's biggest-ever hits with 'Sixteen Tons'), Kris headed stagewards wearing a pair of jeans and a crumpled suede jacket without a tie. By now his hair was long, trailing well over his collar. (A few inaccurate reports described him as "bearded" though on this occasion he was clean shaven.)

During his brief acceptance speech, Kristofferson made sure to acknowledge the debt owed to Johnny Cash, seated near the front of the auditorium, for giving his career such a massive boost. The previous year, Cash had won a record five awards but then again he had started having hits approximately 13 years before; Kristofferson had come from nowhere in the space of little over a year.

'For The Good Times' was named as the Academy of Country Music's Song of the Year (and Single Record of the Year) in 1970 – the first time a writer had won Song of the Year awards from the Country Music Association and the Academy for different songs in the same year. 'For The Good Times' won Ray Price a Grammy for Best Country Vocal Performance, Male, in 1970, while Sammi Smith took the female equivalent award for 'Help Me Make It Through the Night' the following year. Kristofferson songs received five other nominations in two categories so that his stiffest competition was himself. He was named Songwriter of the Year by the Nashville Songwriter's Association in 1970 – not in recognition of any one song but rather his output in the course of the year. The host for the evening, Biff Collie, said that Kris had received the largest majority of votes cast since the inception of the awards.

When he received his Nashville Songwriter's Association award it was reported in the local press that, "While his fellow songwriters gave him a standing ovation, Kristofferson showed them only the shaggy back of his head. He was crying." Evidently sensitive to stinging comments made about his demeanour at the CMA Awards the previous year he said, "I'm not stoned."

There were suggestions – credible given his demeanour and heavy drinking habit – that Kristofferson was either soused or stoned when he went up to receive his CMA award. He stumbled slightly and was also rather awkward in his manner and speech when accepting the award. Kristofferson rejected such claims. "There wasn't anything wrong with me except that I couldn't believe it." He was particularly incensed by one out-of-town journalist who reported that Kris openly smoked marijuana at the ceremony. "Hell, I don't even closedly smoke marijuana," he retorted, somewhat disingenuously.*

It was clear that Kristofferson was making some kind of statement. Somebody of Kris' background knew about dressing "appropriately" as he had done for his wedding and other special occasions. Many of the old guard had fervently hoped that the counter-culture and all that was associated with it would somehow bypass Nashville. His casual appearance put an end to such wishes. Some spoke darkly of a lack of morals, while others murmured that they would never vote for him again.

Historian Bill C. Malone saw much significance in the award and the image Kristofferson projected, describing it as a turning point in country music history. "It seemed to be living proof that the new breed had not only arrived in Nashville but were beginning to compete favourably with the city's music establishment."

Kris had gradually been influenced by hippy culture and his appearance and demeanour encouraged many of his contemporaries to break free from the restraints that so many younger people had already rejected in the

---

* Kristofferson's case was not helped when, soon afterwards, he appeared on a local television talk show – in part to deny that he had been stoned at the CMA Awards. He tripped over a cable and dragged some microphones off desks onto the studio floor.

world outside Nashville. This shift in culture would take a few years to be absorbed by the country establishment. An important step came in 1971 when the Nitty Gritty Dirt Band's album, *Will The Circle Be Unbroken*, featured some of the most upright traditional artists alongside rising stars who wore their hair long and their clothes casual while still sharing and displaying the utmost respect for musical traditions.

Another observer who understood where Kristofferson was coming from was Willie Nelson. "If they liked a mangy freak maybe they would love a mangy cowboy as well." From this time on, Nelson's trademark appearance – long hair, beard, jeans and T-shirt – became an indelible part of his image and helped to widen his own appeal.

It was ironic that in the same year Kristofferson received his CMA Award, Merle Haggard won just about every other major accolade going, including Single Of The Year, for 'Okie From Muskogee', a patriotic assault on hippies and anti-war protestors similar in nature to 'Talkin' Vietnam Blues'. While a great admirer of Haggard's, Kristofferson said that country music had too much to offer to be limited to the kind of mentality expressed in such a song.

Kris was disappointed to note that some of those who complained about the way he comported himself were people he had worked with, and indeed, whose ashtrays he had once emptied. He felt their actions smacked of hypocrisy; whatever his demeanour and habits, he was usually unfailingly polite. It was ironic that such conservatives should carp at his unkempt appearance when he had actually done his best to work conventional jobs to earn money to support himself and his family. Indeed some of his fellow writers criticised him for this, asserting that he should devote all his time to his muse.

Older, established artists were not generally described as "clean-shaven," "smartly dressed" or "well-groomed" and Kristofferson was by no means alone in his taste for strong liquor. The many one-sided press reports that appeared over the next few years would invariably describe him as "bearded", "shaggy haired", having a "hippy-pacifist" look or similar; there were also references to his "hophead image". This doubtless reinforced his view that he was "an outsider in a town full of insiders".

If still not a household name, thanks to the CMA Awards, Kristofferson was now a recognised player in the music business. The fact that his songs had crossover appeal contributed to a process of cross-fertilisation that helped blur the lines between country and other genres. Artists of the calibre of Waylon Jennings and Johnny Cash acknowledged a debt, stating that Kristofferson's songs helped them to write more thoughtfully and poetically. They saw beyond the mindlessly repetitive cheating lyrics and empty expressions of love and longing, and, in effect, started the process of widening country music's appeal.

"To many observers," said Bill C. Malone, "Kris Kristofferson seemed the embodiment of country music's liberation from its conservative puritan rural southern past." Thanks to his example, along with other writers like Tom T. Hall ('The Year That Clayton Delaney Died', 'Harper Valley PTA') and John Hartford ('Gentle On My Mind' – a song that Kris later described as "revolutionary"), other struggling writers in the vanguard of the so-called New Breed, such as Billy Joe Shaver and Mickey Newbury, gained a greater degree of acceptance for their intelligent and sensitive songs, while established stars felt able to break free from Music Row's incessant demand for formulaic hits.

At the time, Kristofferson did not see himself as a mould-breaker – he was just trying to write the best songs he could. He later modestly put it the other way, acknowledging his debt to country music, maintaining he was simply part of a historical continuum: "It's not like I came into Nashville and changed their thinking. It's more like I was a product of Nashville's songwriter training."

By making clear his admiration for greats from Hank Williams to George Jones, Kristofferson – whom one Nashville journalist went so far as to describe as "Nashville's Hank Williams of Now" – lent the music a credibility in the wider music world that had previously eluded it. People from outside the country-music sphere were now prepared to listen to such artists as Waylon Jennings and take them seriously. "Kris had a lot to do with showing that . . . roots didn't have to trap you in the ground," Jennings acknowledged.

In the past, if not wearing ornate Nudie suits, country singers were often seen in stereotypical situations; wearing dungarees, sitting on bales of hay while singing their songs. This kind of presentation gradually became less prevalent, so much so that in the early Seventies, the magazine *Look* produced a major feature entitled *Country Music – Hillbilly No More.*

Kristofferson had numerous ideas swirling around in his head at any one time but claimed he was not motivated by commercial success – he simply got an idea and did his best to turn it into a quality song. However, he was infuriated when others tried to take credit for his creations, as did a man from Albuquerque, who threatened to sue, claiming that Kristofferson had lifted 'Help Me Make It Through The Night' from one of his own songs. The man claimed that he had recorded the song in 1970 before it became a hit for Sammi Smith. Kristofferson had in fact made a recording in 1969 so was quickly able to crush such claims.

While this was nothing new for a successful songwriter, there was an amusing irony in the spurious attempts of people craving a piece of the action when Kristofferson himself was prepared to overlook the similarities between 'Help Me Make it Through The Night' and the George Jones classic, 'He Stopped Loving Her Today'. Though his publishers told Kristofferson he might have a case, he said he could never contemplate any kind of legal action against a country great like Jones.

He was more annoyed when one of his supposed writing buddies, whom Kris had helped to get bail, announced that he was now working under the name Kristofferson.

Feeling a debt of gratitude to Nashville – believing that success had come to him more readily there than it might have done in New York or Los Angeles – Kristofferson accepted an invitation to take part in a course at the University of Tennessee, entitled 'The Fundamentals of Song-Writing', along with other writers including Harlan Howard, Eddie Miller and Clarence Selman, the president of the Nashville Songwriters Association. Miller (who wrote 'Release Me') confidently claimed, "I think we can take five years off the street for anybody interested in becoming a commercial songwriter."

Addressing the 55 aspirants who came from as far away as Chicago and Florida, Kristofferson was much less upbeat. "Don't expect to ever be anything but poor. Mickey [Newbury] and I have been lucky, but there are people just as good as we are who are still bumming drinks." He also said that they should write for an audience "outside themselves" and not to be swayed by discouraging comments when "something inside you tells you that what you are writing is good".

The course certainly gave the students differing philosophies. Miller told the students that writing popular songs was not literary work: "Literary work feeds the mind, songwriting feeds the heart." With the references to great writers in his oeuvre, this was not a proposition Kristofferson could have wholeheartedly endorsed, no matter how much he appreciated all popular music forms on a gut level.

Nonetheless, Kris liked the idea that he might have benefited the music business in some way. With his knowledge of literature, he was able to bring another rich ingredient to the mix. Harlan Howard said, "Kris was much more of a poet than I am. I admire his imagery. You can make anything you want of his songs." More modestly, Kristofferson simply saw himself as continuing the singer-songwriter tradition of heroes such as Jimmie Rodgers and Hank Williams, though he would never have compared himself to those particular giants.

Asked about his songwriting style, Kris stressed the importance of mentally logging personal experience, "the things you see and feel", especially those inducing strong feelings that are often easier to explore in song than discuss openly. "All of us have a dark side we might not be particularly proud of." While regarding it as unnecessary that a writer should have lived every detail, Kris said, "You have to at least feel the emotion that is called up by the experience."

Asked which of his songs he rated best, he replied the ones that "just wrote themselves".

# Chapter 10

HAVING little performing experience but with important support coming from high places, Kristofferson officially launched his live career with a remarkably prestigious string of gigs. With the help of a production-team member of Johnny Cash's television show, he secured a gig at the Troubadour in Los Angeles in June 1970, opening for Linda Ronstadt. When asked if he wanted to do the gig, Kris responded, "Is that a trick question?" Right from the start of his performing career, promoters were not sure where to place him. The memory of being fired from his solo restaurant gig was still fresh in his memory, so Kris and his band, including Billy Swan and Donnie Fritts, had to hone their instrumental skills speedily in order to come together as an efficiently functioning live unit.

The Troubadour, "a rock'n'roll folk club", as Kris described it, was not a typical venue for a country singer. However, Johnny and June Carter Cash and their children attended the gig and Johnny even went up on stage to sing with him. Kris went down well – helped by a favourable review of the show in the *Los Angeles Times* – and more bookings followed. One night after playing the Troubadour, he was pulled over by a police car. "I had this little bottle of Binaca [breath spray]. The cop asked me what it was. I said, 'Oh, I shoot up Binaca.' Bang! Hands behind my back, handcuffed. I spent the night in jail."

Bert Block booked his client into rock venues – an uncommon move as managers of country artists, and Kris, nominally at least, fitted this description – were generally reluctant to do this since the rock crowd were reluctant to turn out for their country cousins. Some sought to categorise Kris with artists such as The Byrds, Michael Nesmith (& The First National Band) and Gram Parsons (who had just left The Flying Burrito Brothers), who came from pop or rock backgrounds but were fusing country and rock.

Quite the most remarkable coup that Block pulled off was securing two slots for Kristofferson at the Isle of Wight Festival in August 1970; approximately 600,000 attended – roughly the same number of people who had flooded to Woodstock the previous year. Unlike the major artists who appeared – The Doors, The Who, Ten Years After, Joni Mitchell, Jimi Hendrix and many others – Kris and his fledgling band were not afforded five-star treatment, being allotted rooms in a small bed and breakfast establishment near the festival site – and received no payment for their services.

Despite the massive exposure, the experience was not a happy one for Kristofferson, as evidenced by the film footage shot by Murray Lerner for his IOW festival documentary (belatedly released in 1997), *Message To Love*. During his main appearance, which was beefed up for the occasion with the inclusion of ex-Lovin' Spoonful guitarist, Zal Yanovsky, there was a constant undertow of hostile noise, though Kris was initially defiant. "Can you hear me out there? I can't sing real loud." Billy Swan thinks they might have misunderstood the lyrical subtleties behind 'Blame It On The Stones'. "The sound was bad so what happened was partly misinterpretation, I think," says Swan. "Maybe the kids couldn't fully hear what Kris was singing. I think some people took it wrong."*

However, the crowd was also unsettled as a result of events offstage. Many thousands of people who had not bought tickets were watching from a nearby hillside and the organisers were under pressure from radical and anarchist elements to turn the event into a free festival. Kris appeared genuinely frightened as the end of his set neared – as he walked offstage after delivering 'Me And Bobby McGee', he remarked, "I think they're gonna shoot us."

Some protestors were creating an ominous din by pounding on the fencing. "They were throwing shit at me, but I kept singing . . . I told 'em, 'I brought this band over here at my own expense. They told me to do an hour, and I'm going to do an hour, in spite of anything but rifle fire.'" Swan said the other artists were largely unsympathetic. Nobody congratulated them when they came offstage and he had to break a window in the band's locked trailer to get his guitar case.

---

* 'Blame It On The Stones' and 'The Pilgrim – Chapter 33' were featured on the triple album, *The First Great Rock Festivals Of The Seventies: Isle Of Wight/Atlanta Pop Festival*.

For the next 18 months, Kristofferson and his group were like a band of wandering minstrels, playing their way around a variety of clubs and venues in America, generally living a high (and low) life of music and debauchery, fuelled by large quantities of stimulants. One journalist described them as, "Four tranquil clear-eyed country or mountain boys with faces like old pictures of rebel soldiers."

Speaking in 1971, Kris said that he was in "a kind of a gypsy state" and that he was "hard to be around for a long time . . . I'm so much freer now that I don't have to work and I don't have to think about money. I have some cat who does that for me. All my money goes straight to him. They tell me I got money."

Away from the stage, touring entailed a seemingly endless round of cities and hotels indistinguishable from each other. Donnie Fritts said the easy part was the performing. "It's the other 22 hours you gotta watch out for . . . we were all doing all kinds of stuff."

"[Kris] dressed weird, his band dressed weird and they all acted weird," remembered Willie Nelson. "They drank and did other taboo things and they sang about drinking and taking drugs like it was fun. They sang about men and women the way men and women really were and nobody booed them off the stage or threw brickbats or even beer bottles."

By his own admission an introvert, Kristofferson regarded the act of performing as one of the most frightening things anybody could do. "That's when you're really naked, especially when you're doin' all your own songs." Alcohol helped to deaden the nerves he invariably felt before a performance, doubtless contributing to his trademark hazy drawl. "People used to ask me, 'How can you drink so much and perform?' I said, 'I couldn't perform if I didn't drink so much.' You rarely feel like singing when you're sober."

There were times when Kris was so drunk he was incapable of giving anything like a professional performance and at times he behaved abominably – leering at people in the audience or making faces at his current flame or just simply staring at his feet. He later conceded that there were times when he somehow saw the audience as his enemy, as some kind of threat. "What I had done was turn a good thing – the opportunity to go out and do what you like to do for a living – into a torture thing."

There were times in the early Seventies when stage performances became so stressful that the broad smiles at the end of shows were simply a sign of immense relief that the ordeal was over. Kristofferson was typically honest when speaking to Jack Hurst of *The Tennessean* in 1972. "The other night we gave what I thought was a crappy performance in Washington, but it got great reviews." It would be hard to imagine any fresh-faced, production line country singer speaking in such blunt terms.*

Kris had a similar outlook to performing as his friend Mickey Newbury – keep it simple. Neither had much in the way of stage props; "no fancy stage show, tight pants or thrusting hips". Reviews from this time continued to focus on Kristofferson's voice. Some felt his limited vocal ability almost worked in his favour, à la Bob Dylan, because the writer was able to put over the message in his own work more effectively than anyone else. One of the lessons Kris learned from Dylan was that a voice didn't have to fit into a particular groove to be acceptable.

"[Kristofferson] growls at the bottom and roughly slides up the scale to scraping baritone," one writer described. "His cadence is imprecise and he sometimes talks the melody as well as the lyrics. The style is honed, a perfect reflection [in his performing context] of remarkably sincere writing."

The constant touring took its toll on Kristofferson's voice but despite his stage fright, he felt that performing helped his writing. "My band, they're so good musically, it stretches me; when I get home I can write better because of them."

In 1971, Kris was back in the studio to record *The Silver Tongued Devil And I*. The album featured songs that had already been covered by other artists such as 'Jody And The Kid' and 'The Taker' – the title track of a Waylon Jennings album (released the same year) that also included three other Kristofferson songs. Both 'The Taker' and the title track explored similar themes, painting a cynical picture of the ways men treated women.

In his liner notes, Kristofferson revealed that the songs were auto-biographical and so it can only be assumed that the lyrics reflected his guilt

---

* Journalists who interviewed Kristofferson in the early Seventies often found him to be a breath of fresh air; natural and devoid of the usual clichéd platitudes. Describing the contradictory aspects of his personality – partly inherent, partly put on – one writer described him as, "Totally open and completely inaccessible, he's shy and gregarious, honest and devious, rude and polite, smart and dumb."

about the numerous one-off couplings he'd experienced. No doubt his ex-wife, Fran, could have identified with some of the sentiments from her own perspective.

Quite a few of his early songs sought to explore the female mind. Despite the obvious hedonistic benefits, part of him recoiled at the way so many women made themselves available. In one early Seventies interview, he attempted to distance himself from the stereotypical rock star. "I'm no male chauvinist pig; hell, the only people I ever got hung up on are women. They're different. I'm more likely to get closer to a girl than I am to a man. A friend of mine once remarked that he had never heard me say a bad thing about a woman."

*The Silver Tongued Devil And I* also included 'Good Christian Soldier' (which touches on the conflict facing a soldier who aspires to be a good Christian), written by Bobby Bare and Billy Joe Shaver – not for the last time would Kristofferson show a willingness to help fellow writers, in particular those who had paid their dues alongside him.

With its beautiful imagery and enigmatic narrative, 'Loving Her Was Easier (Than Anything I'll Ever Do Again)' was one of the album's stand-out tracks – an obvious benefit from Kristofferson's studies of great poets. Music critic Dave Hickey marvelled at "the long, perfectly metrical tightly structured quarter note lines of 12 and 16 syllables, double the standard country-line length. They are so tight and clear that it is like having another rhythm instrument in the band . . ."

Probably the most memorable song on the album was 'The Pilgrim – Chapter 33' – a title that Kristofferson initially thought was unwieldy and would have to be simplified. The song contains some of his most incisive and analytical lyrics, which brilliantly nail the flawed and contradictory natures of the artists he had mixed with. By way of introduction, Kris lists a number of people who provided inspiration including Chris Gantry, Ramblin' Jack Elliott, Dennis Hopper, Jerry Jeff Walker, Billy Swan, Bob Neuwirth – and Johnny Cash.

"There were a lot of people the pilgrim stood for," Kristofferson said. "Most were people who were serious about songwriting – but an awful lot of us just looked like we were out of work."

If the pilgrim of the song could be said to be a composite, the true inspiration was the artist himself. Virtually every line reflects Kristofferson's own experience; he spares himself nothing and only the poetic use of generalised imagery softens the realities of the events he describes. Yet despite all the implied despair, the concluding "the going up was worth the coming down" is tinged with optimism.

'Epitaph (Black And Blue)' ended the album – a brief, mournful remembrance of Janis Joplin, in which Kristofferson expressed feelings of guilt that her friends were unable to save her.

Musically, *The Silver Tongued Devil And I* veered between a pop-country and a soft-rock sound, featuring a mix of understated acoustic and electric backing delivered with a loose feel. Occasional string accompaniment sweetened some of the more sentimental numbers and, despite the intellectual bias of the lyrics, some of the songs merited the epithet easy listening. A laconic, world-weary air pervades Kristofferson's vocals – resembling a croaking frog at times – but his racked voice imbued the songs with a sincere, at times despairing feeling of one who has actually lived the experiences described.

With Monument having been sold to CBS, of which it was now a subsidiary, the album received major label distribution and made the Top Five in the country charts (reaching the *Billboard* Top 20), eventually gaining gold status. Released as a single, 'Loving Her Was Easier (Than Anything I'll Ever Do Again)' was only a minor hit, probably as a result of the acquired taste that was Kristofferson's voice, and his controversial status among the more conservative elements of his potential market.*

After the spectacular success of Janis Joplin's 'Me And Bobby McGee' and the healthy performance of *The Silver Tongued Devil And I*, Kristofferson was re-released as *Me And Bobby McGee*. This time around, it made a much greater commercial impact, showing up in both the country and pop charts and soon achieving gold status. The tide of artists having hits with Kristofferson songs continued unabated. O.C. Smith made the pop charts with his reading of 'Help Me Make It Through The Night' while Gladys Knight's molten soul version of the track became a hit on both the pop and R&B charts in 1972.

The sheer breadth of Kristofferson's activities during this time was striking. He was the subject of *Boboquivari,* a Public Broadcast Service

---

* The potential of 'Loving Her Was Easier . . .' was quickly spotted by Roger Miller, though his version was also only a minor hit. It took until 1981 for Tompall and the Glaser Brothers to have a Top Three hit with the song.

programme on pop and rock music, as well as a local news report that followed him round Nashville for a day. He played in a summer cabaret that featured a selection of songs from the musical *Hair*, and co-produced an album with Joan Baez. He and Baez were also on the bill of the Big Sur Folk Festival in California alongside a diverse mix of artists including Blood, Sweat & Tears, Taj Mahal, Mickey Newbury, Big Sur Choir, and Lily Tomlin & Larry Manson. (The event was recorded and Kristofferson appeared on the subsequent album, *One Hand Clapping*.)

At the BMI (Broadcast Music Inc) awards, Kristofferson shared the Songwriter of the Year award in the country music category with writer and producer Billy Sherrill in 1971 and 1972 (and in 1974 with Sherrill and Norro Wilson). As an indication of Kristofferson's prolific output, no less than five of his songs contributed to his award. In 1972, he shared the equivalent award in the popular music category with Paul McCartney and George Harrison.

That same year, Kristofferson was also the recipient of the Robert J. Burton award for the most performed country song – 'Help Me Make It Through The Night'. On February 24, he appeared performing his Grammy winner on *The David Frost Show*, precluding an appearance to collect his second Songwriter of the Year award from the Nashville Song-writer's Association. After the taping, Kristofferson was mobbed by autograph hunters, which unnerved him. He found it hard to identify with the mindset of such people, many of whom, he was sure, did not know who he was, merely that he'd appeared on television.[*]

Around this time, Kristofferson was offered the possibility of work in a Las Vegas hotel "if I got into some schmucky rock star gear". While he was able to work largely on his own terms, he certainly did a lot of smiling for the cameras on highly rated TV shows in order to boost his career, including those of Roger Miller, Gordon Lightfoot, Ramblin' Jack Elliott and Billy Edd Wheeler.[†]

---

[*] His comment, "I can't imagine what a grown adult would want with an autograph," was disingenuous to a degree. He had asked a host of friends and heroes to scratch their autographs onto his old acoustic guitar including Bob Dylan, Janis Joplin, Roger Miller, Odetta and Peter Fonda among others.

[†] When Kristofferson was still working as a janitor, he met Wheeler in a bar and was able to pass on the news that Johnny Cash had just recorded his song 'Jackson', a duet with June Carter, which went on to become one of the high points of Cash's live concerts.

Some people were now grandly referring to Kristofferson as the first superstar of the new country music.

There was also a new and serious love interest in Kristofferson's life, as evidenced by the mysterious note – "Special thanks to The Lady for her help on The Taker" – that appeared on the sleeve of *The Silver Tongued Devil And I*.

In the course of his peripatetic existence, on a journey to Nashville from the West Coast for a major magazine interview in the autumn of 1971, Kris met manager Ron Rainey at the airline ticket counter. Rainey wanted to introduce Kristofferson to his client, Rita Coolidge. Kris was not keen; he had just ended a relationship and was focused on his upcoming interview. However, when the pair were introduced, for Coolidge, 10 years Kristofferson's junior, the attraction was immediate. "I couldn't get over his face, those incredible deep-set blue eyes . . . I couldn't help staring at him." She said he was "sort of fumbly-warm".

They later disagreed about which one of them saved a seat for the other but in the course of the flight to Memphis – where Coolidge was due to rehearse with her band, the Dixie Flyers – she and Kris sat next to each other and a passionate relationship formed. Kristofferson forgot about the interview and disembarked at Memphis where he stayed with Rita for a few days, his spontaneity fitting with his assertion that he gave up planning ahead when he quit the army. Thereafter, Coolidge became, as Kristofferson told an interviewer early in 1972, his "steady lady".

The daughter of a Southern Baptist minister, the Reverend Raymond Coolidge, Rita was born in Lafayette on May 1, 1944. Her father was Cherokee and her mother had Cherokee and Scottish ancestors; according to one report she was a direct descendant of Mary Queen of Scots. Rita sang in church from the age of two and learned to harmonise with her musically gifted sisters. Alongside classmate Brenda Lee, she was a high-school cheerleader in Nashville, where she had moved when still young. Over the years her love of music grew and as time went by, she was increasingly drawn to modern popular forms such as soul and rhythm and blues.

The family later moved to Florida where Rita obtained a degree in art from Florida State University. She considered a career as an art teacher but decided to pursue her interest in singing. Having moved to Memphis, she soon found work doing jingles with her sister Priscilla and, more importantly, singing backing vocals for southern soul revue Delaney & Bonnie and Friends (who, on a late-1969 European tour, included Eric Clapton and George Harrison). They also had a cameo in the 1971 cult film *Vanishing Point*. Soon in great demand, Coolidge also toured with Joe Cocker's Mad Dogs And Englishmen troupe, featuring Leon Russell, before striking out on a solo career.

Unlike his marriage to Fran, Kris' relationship with Rita was musical as well as personal. For a time they criss-crossed America to meet and make music but as Coolidge said, "It all got a bit ridiculous." They soon decided that it would make sense to amalgamate their lives and their bands. Such commitment suggests an exceptionally strong mutual attraction for people who had little difficulty in attracting companions. Each had been briefly involved with a string of well-known artists – Kristofferson had wooed Carly Simon and Joan Baez, while Coolidge had been involved with Stephen Stills and Graham Nash.*

Kristofferson's irresistibility to women once he became famous was the stuff of legend. Not long after joining Monument, he spent time with Canadian singer Ronnie Hawkins, for whom he opened some shows earning a welcome $250 per night. "Kris was a lady's man beyond belief," confirms Hawkins. "He didn't hustle them or hit on them. Women made fools of themselves around Kris – he was spoilt."

Hawkins recalls an occasion when he invited some people to his farm for the weekend. "There was this big-time girl from New York who asked me if she could get with Kris. They checked in to the cabin Friday night and I didn't see them all day Saturday, then Sunday, the door opens and here comes Kris, yawning and stretching and hungry and wanting a cigarette, and then she comes out and she looks like she'd been attacked by a school of piranhas."

Rita quickly slotted into Kris' live shows. They would each do a solo segment and then come together for duets at the end. However, it was understood that Kristofferson was the main star. The fact that they spent so much time together was, for a time, a stabilising influence for Kris; he

---

* It has been suggested that her decision to leave Stills for Nash was a contributory factor in the first break up of Crosby, Stills, Nash & Young. By way of a tribute, Leon Russell wrote 'Delta Lady' for Coolidge.

now had an excuse not to party after the shows. Live performances became much less of an ordeal because he was able to share the limelight. Coolidge has subsequently claimed that thanks to her supportive presence, Kristofferson was able to resist the countless demands placed on his time – to do shows, interviews, attend functions and so on.

Constantly touring and with one eye on continuing his movie career, he was under considerable pressure to follow up the commercial success of *The Silver Tongued Devil And I* and had no alternative but to write under the pressure of deadlines. In an interview from this time, he let it be known just how concerned he was by the thought that his muse could desert him.

"Now that I have felt the elation of writing things that are good, wow! There is no other feeling like that and to think you would never be able to do that, to feel that any more, frightens you . . . you know, Hemingway obviously did himself in because he recognised that it was all over – he was dry."

Canadian singer Ronnie Hawkins said of Kristofferson, "He was a lady's man beyond belief... women made fools of themselves around Kris." (DOUGLAS KIRKLAND/CORBIS)

With Jerry Lee Lewis at the Performing Arts Center, Nashville, 1982.
Kris particularly liked Jerry Lee's versions of his songs. (TIME & LIFE PICTURES/GETTY IMAGES)

Performing at the Country Music Festival, Wembley, London 1982.
(RICHARD YOUNG/REX FEATURES)

With close friend Willie Nelson on the set of
*Songwriter*, 1983. Working with Willie has
always been a great pleasure for Kris, not
least because of his wicked sense of humour.
(TIME & LIFE PICTURES/GETTY IMAGES)

Kris on stage at Ontario Place, Toronto, Canada,
June 6, 1983. (TS/KEYSTONE USA/REX FEATURES)

With Rita at the 'Welcome Home
Festival For America's Vietnam
Veterans', February 24, 1986
at the Forum, Los Angeles.
(RON GALELLA/WIREIMAGE.COM)

With Johnny Cash at Terry Wogan's talk show in 1987. Kris
could never quite get used to the fact that one of the people
he admired most in the world became his close friend.
(CLIVE DIXON/REX FEATURES)

Sitting next to peace activist Brian S Willson in Nicaragua 1988. Willson's delegation observed historic ceasefire discussions between the Nicaraguan government and the rebel Contras.

(PHOTO BY MARK BIRNBAUM, COURTESY OF BRIAN S WILLSON)

With third wife Lisa Meyers, 20 years his junior. They have had five children and live on the idyllic Hawaiian island of Maui.

(TIME & LIFE PICTURES/GETTY IMAGES)

Country supergroup The Highwaymen. Waylon Jennings, Willie Nelson, Kristofferson and Johnny Cash. Promotional shot for second album, 1990. (EVERETT COLLECTION/REX FEATURES)

Kris with son Kris Jr and daughter Tracy, 1992.
(TIME & LIFE PICTURES/GETTY IMAGES)

With Tracy, 1992. Tracy has worked as an assistant producer on several of her father's films.
(McCOY COX/REX FEATURES)

The Highwaymen live at Central Park's Summerstage, New York, May 23, 1993.
(AP/PA PHOTOS)

As the vicious Sheriff Charley Wade in the critically acclaimed 1996 film *Lone Star*,
directed by John Sayles.
(GETTY IMAGES)

With Leelee Sobieski at the premiere of
*A Soldier's Daughter Never Cries*,
September 15, 1998.
(STEVE AZZARA/CORBIS)

As Abraham Whistler, mentor to Blade, played
by Wesley Snipes. His role in the *Blade* trilogy
introduced Kristofferson to many new fans who
were unaware that he had written some of
the best popular music of the 1970s.
(NEW LINE/THE KOBAL COLLECTION)

With Willie Nelson, June Carter-Cash, Johnny Cash, Sheryl Crow and Wyclef Jean at
TNT's all-star tribute to Johnny Cash, April 1999. (LEO SOREL/RETNA)

With Michael Clarke Duncan collecting a Lifetime Achievement Award at The Diversity Awards, November 17, 2001. (REUTERS/CORBIS)

# Chapter 11

KRISTOFFERSON's recordings to date had benefited from long periods of gestation. Now in 1972, he had just a matter of months to put together material for two albums. *Border Lord* contained familiar Kristofferson themes and was particularly striking in that six of the songs, including 'Josie' and 'Little Girl Lost', concerned women who had become debased in some way, for which the narrator seemed to feel some vicarious or personal guilt.

While Kris produced some of his affecting poetry with characteristic cleverness, the melodies were unremarkable and with his limited vocal range, a number of the songs suffered from a dirgeful quality. The topics were less appealing to a mass audience as evidenced by 'Josie' only being a minor hit when released as a single. The album also included four songs that dated back to the late Sixties, which indicated that Kristofferson was forced to revisit his back pages to come up with sufficient quality material. It was disappointing but not surprising that *Border Lord* failed to achieve the kind of commercial success its two predecessors enjoyed.

Most reviews were lukewarm, though *Rolling Stone*'s Ben Gerson's criticism was contemptuous and, at times, personal. In his opinion, the lyrics were characterised by confusion, inanity, hyperbole, and "pseudo-poeticizing". Gerson described Kristofferson as "a fast-livin', hard lovin' dude who has just enough time between ballin' and brawlin' to jot down a tune or two. He's a cracker-barrel philosopher, able to spout truisms grown from a life rooted in unadorned reality."

Gerson took exception to the structure of the songs – Kristofferson's strength in the eyes of other commentators. "His sentences are very long, clauses and prepositional phrases Latinately balanced, and they betray this country and western singer's Oxford education."

He also highlighted an inherent contradiction. "By appealing to the more cosmopolitan urges among C&W listeners, as well as the more provincial yearnings among the rock audience, Kris has won a sizable following in both camps. But what makes him commercial condemns him artistically. He has neither the intensity and originality of vision of the solo artist, nor the simple integrity and force of personality of the more restricted country and western artist. What is left is a strange hybrid: a C&W Jim Morrison, or a Bobby Goldsboro with sex appeal."

Kristofferson was well aware of the dichotomy between the worlds he inhabited; complaining that he spent half his time living down a redneck image in the urban jungles of Los Angeles and New York and the other half "getting killed" for his cosmopolitan ways when going back to Nashville and the south. "I really have the feeling I'm an outsider, every place I go. I've never been a part of any group or any party or hung around with any one cat. The women I know today won't be the ones I'll know tomorrow."

Reading between the lines, Gerson's barbs might well have overstated the inevitable disappointment felt when the album failed to live up to expectations. While Kristofferson had by no means run out of ideas, there was little indication that he was going to be able to maintain the high standard he'd achieved over the previous three years – he had set his own quality threshold so high. Acknowledging that he was neither a great singer nor musician, he reacted defensively but truthfully with, "I think I'm making the most of what I've got."

The criticisms rankled though and Kristofferson used the title track of his other 1972 album, *Jesus Was A Capricorn*, to hit back at some of his detractors. As with *Border Lord*, Rita guested on several songs and appeared on the sleeve, albeit well-disguised behind large dark glasses, next to her lover and collaborator. While the album was once again devoid of any classics, the quality of the instrumental work and production was generally ahead of Kristofferson's first two albums. The presence of an incredible 47 musicians and backing singers including three vocal groups, The Bergenaires, The Jordanaires, and The Joint Venture, doubtless contributed.

However, such excessive quantity was unnecessary, with the un-intended consequence of emphasising his vocal inadequacies. Though it would take many years for the penny to drop with producers, in the studio and in concert, Kristofferson benefited from a "less is more" principle.

A common criticism directed at *Jesus Was A Capricorn* was that it was overproduced and moved Kristofferson's songs too far away from the rough-hewn charm of his earlier work. Despite being put together in haste, the album had quite a mellow feel and featured some reflective love songs, although anger at his parents' rejection was very much evident in 'Jesse Younger', which bore more than a passing resemblance to the sarcastic aggressiveness of 'Blame It On The Stones'.

Once more the theme of sympathy for the fallen woman was prevalent, for instance, the junkie prostitute who ODs in 'Sugar Man'. For someone who attracted the epithet of "womaniser", it was perhaps a surprising fixation, though no doubt his philandering ways had provided him with valuable insights.

With an album bearing the word Jesus in the title, naturally there was some speculation as to Kristofferson's religious beliefs. It was reported in the Nashville press that he had undergone some kind of religious experience at the Reverend Jimmie Snow's Evangel Temple in Nashville, which had become known as "the Church of Country Music Stars" because so many celebrities, including Johnny Cash, attended. Kris had been persuaded to attend by singer Connie Smith when the pair had played a recent benefit concert and it may well have been Kristofferson's first church attendance since his wedding to Fran, though he had previously gone to the Episcopalians rather than the Southern Baptists. At the service, Larry Gatlin – who had also worked as a janitor – performed 'Help Me', a pleading prayer-ballad to the Lord that inexplicably moved Kristofferson.

He walked down the aisle in response to Snow's altar call. "It was what I guess you would call a religious experience. I'd never had one before. To this day I don't know why I did it. I think Jimmie sensed that I didn't know what I was doing because he asked me if I was ready to be saved and I told him that I didn't know. He put his hand on my shoulder and told me to get down on my knees. There were a number of us kneeling and I don't remember what he was saying. It was something about freedom from guilt. All I can remember is that I broke into tears. I was weeping and when it was over I felt like I'd been purged. I was carrying a lot of guilt at that time. I felt that I'd disappointed my family, my friends, my ancestors and everybody that knew me so I wrote that song ['Why Me', from *Jesus Was A Capricorn*] – wrote it later that day in the back of Connie Smith's car."

Kristofferson agreed to appear on WSM's *Friday Night Grand Ole Gospel Time*, which took place after the *Grand Ole Opry* show. 2,000 people listened in rapt silence as he sang 'Why Me', 'Burden Of Freedom' and 'Pilgrim's Prayer' (a duet with Gatlin). Kris revealed it was the first wholly sober performance he had given for a long time. He was likely troubled by his persistent heavy drinking and hoped that whatever experience he had gone through might help him to address the issue.

Soon after, when arriving at a studio to record an interview, Kristofferson remarked that he was very tired, "because he had stayed up till 6 a.m. reading the bible." When asked he said he was not sure if he would become a regular churchgoer but hoped that he could "hold on to the feeling when I go back on the road".

As a free-spirited, middle-class intellectual, Kristofferson had difficulty in giving himself up to the requirements of a believer's church; his faith was more individual. The Southern Baptists accepted some discussion so long as this did not lead to any serious questioning of their faith. However, 'Why Me' went down so well with Nashville's religious community – the straightforward lyrics lacking any intellectual casuistry – that it suggested Kristofferson was, or was prepared to become, one of them. What's more, his despairing vocal delivery made his submissive message all the more credible, even though in reality Kris' tortured intellectual uncertainties and questionings would have found little sympathy among mainstream believers.

'Why Me' was not originally intended for release as a single. However, after the track was played on an Atlanta radio station, the switchboard lit up like a Christmas tree and record stores tried to place orders for it. The song eventually made number one in the country charts – Kristofferson's first as an artist in his own right – and was also a Top 20 pop hit eventually gaining gold status. It turned out to be his most successful country hit and the initially sluggish sales for *Jesus Was A Capricorn* took off in the wake of the single's success, resulting in gold status.[*]

In 1973, 'Why Me' won the Dove award for the Gospel Song of the Year, beating off nine other nominees. When the song was announced at the ceremony, it was said to have been written "for personal reasons". In a subsequent interview, Kristofferson said, "I went to a church and a weird thing happened to me that I really don't feel like talking about. I'm not a

---

[*] For a time, Elvis Presley featured 'Why Me' in his live concerts, and the song was eventually inducted into the Christian Music Hall of Fame (as 'Why Me Lord') in 2007.

Jesus freak. I *would* like to be a Christian. I'm lookin' for that answer and I come pretty close to it. But I ain't goin' around preachin'. It's a private thing."

The "feeling" stayed with Kristofferson long enough for him to agree to participate in Explo '72, a week-long evangelical jamboree in Dallas sponsored by Campus Crusade For Christ. The event – the absolute zenith of the "Jesus Movement", attracting over 100,000 people from America and from about 70 foreign countries – aimed to engender personal evangelism in young people who would then seek some form of Christian service career.

During the day, there were classes on evangelism and bible study work-shops while in the evening, participants came together for concerts, which, in keeping with the times, featured long hair and rock music – though the songs' messages were strictly chaste. Billy Graham, keen to demonstrate that non-believers didn't hold a monopoly on love, peace and music, described it as "a religious Woodstock".

The week culminated in an eight-hour concert of music and preaching at the Cotton Bowl on June 17 – the night of the Watergate break-in. The main stage had a quasi-psychedelic backdrop featuring garish orange, red and turquoise lines and stripes, with the word "Jesus" prominent in what was a rather tacky-looking arrangement. Graham personally appeared as did Johnny Cash, Children of the Day, Kristofferson and Coolidge among others.*

Some conservative Christian groups criticised Explo '72 for its ecumen-ical involvement with both Protestant and Roman Catholic ministries, and for its use of rock music: "strange fire from the pagan altar . . . they have clothed the demonic spirit of this satanic force in the holy and blood-stained garments of the sinless son of God". However, a survey found that more than 60 per cent of those who had participated entered the ordained ministry, were engaged in theological training, or had become missionaries. The future Pope John Paul II was said to have been heavily encouraged towards his evangelistic efforts by a Polish-American student who had attended the event.

---

* Some of the music from the event was recorded and released on a mail-order only album called *Jesus Sound Explosion*, which was only available from the Campus Crusade for Christ. Kristofferson was not featured on the album.

Although Kristofferson was an active participant, he was not comfortable with the brand of zealous fundamentalism expressed. He had hardly any religious songs in his repertoire and whereas his form of faith was nebulous, the Explo '72 majority were looking for religious certainty and a message that related specifically to Jesus. When Cash approached Kristofferson about the possibility of participating in other events he declined, saying that he would follow his own path in a more personal way; he felt it hypocritical to appear at such public outpourings of conventional religiosity.

Despite such reservations, Kristofferson accepted Cash's invitation to contribute to *The Gospel Road*, Johnny's personally financed, low-budget labour of love about the life of Jesus that was filmed on location in Israel. Given his hirsute good looks and burgeoning interest in films, Kristofferson would have been better suited to play the role of Christ than the film's director, the very blond Robert Elfstrom. More likely, it was not the sort of film Kris wanted to be seen in. Cash delivered Kristofferson's offering, 'Burden Of Freedom', in the film, while Kris and Rita, along with Larry Gatlin, sang on 'Why Me'.* The soundtrack double album made number 12 on the country charts – the fact that a lengthy religious album was so successful was a tribute to Cash's considerable commercial cachet.

Kristofferson was making the most of the many offers that came his way, not least the opportunity to appear in films. His appearances at venues such as the Troubadour, often attended by important movie people, had greatly helped his cause. As Johnny Cash amiably warned him, "You're shitting in pretty tall cotton now." Kris modestly said he was fortunate because producers happened to be on the lookout for new faces and his just happened to fit.

In 1971, a stoned Kristofferson was at a party in LA when a producer who had also known Janis Joplin asked if he wanted to audition for a film entitled *Two Lane Blacktop*. The next day, he could only remember that he had an appointment with Columbia and, thinking it was Columbia Records, Kristofferson initially went to the wrong office. He ultimately

---

* Cash himself later recorded 'Why Me'. He jokingly told the players in his band that Jesus wrote a song called 'Why Me, Kris'.

rejected the film, which ended up starring fellow musicians (and kindred spirits) James Taylor and Dennis Wilson and whose existential plot involved a car race across America, although he did allow the producers to use his version of 'Me And Bobby McGee' on the soundtrack.

His first starring part came in the title role of *Cisco Pike*, a fairly low-budget film released in 1972, after his friend, Harry Dean Stanton, supposedly put in a good word. The movie's opening credits – "and introducing Kris Kristofferson" – revealed his rookie status.

Before starting work, an old college friend, Anthony Zerbe, sent Kris a telegram: "Have a good time. Ignore the camera." "That was the extent of my training," Kristofferson later recalled. The only theory he adhered to was trying to understand the character and being as honest as possible.

Starring alongside Kristofferson were familiar leads, Gene Hackman, who played a corrupt cop, and Karen Black as Cisco's girlfriend. Cisco, an ex-rock star, is blackmailed by the cop, who had previously busted him, into selling a large quantity of drugs in a short space of time, which he endeavours to do while keeping it secret from his girlfriend. In one scene, he eats a whole stash to prevent it being found by the police. Some Kristofferson songs were featured: 'The Pilgrim-Chapter 33' was used as a *leitmotif* for Cisco and 'Loving Her Was Easier (Than Anything I'll Ever Do Again)' played over the credits.

Although the film had the feel of an insubstantial made-for-television movie and a less than coherent plot, Kristofferson ambled through convincingly enough. The language of rock culture – for instance "man" after every utterance – slipped easily from his tongue but was perhaps a little overdone. Kris' take on the part bore more than a passing resemblance to aspects of his own life, not least the effects of habitual indulgence in drink, drugs and chain smoking. Kristofferson's performance was amateurish in comparison with that of Hackman in particular, and he found it hard to inject real feeling into scenes where it was needed, as, for instance, when he made a truly limp attempt to help an overdose casualty.

Kristofferson was well aware of his limitations. "I sure as hell ain't no Laurence Olivier . . . these guys who really study for it, they must figure, who the fuck is this, some shit-kicker they hauled off the Troubadour stage." However, one *Playboy* critic saw a great cinematic future for the novice, suggesting that he could be "the answer to filmdom's prayers for a folk rock hero to replace the legendary James Dean". He was evidently not put off by the fact that Kristofferson was then 12 years older than Dean was when he died.

Kris was surprised that some actors simply learnt their lines without having much idea of what the film was really about; though no great actor himself, this struck him as short-changing the audience and was something he could not contemplate. Though taken with acting, he was somewhat surprised to find that, like touring, it was not a soft option. "Everything I made I spent on the road being miserable. *Cisco Pike* looked like it would be a day at the beach – it wasn't."

Kristofferson was not to be deterred, accepting an offer to appear in *Blume In Love* – "A love story for guys who cheat on their wives" as the film's tagline put it – with George Segal, Susan Anspach and Shelley Winters. It was not a mainstream Hollywood film and as with *Cisco Pike*, a key element of the plot was the way a stereotypical graduate of the hippy-rock alternative culture interacts with and threatens the conservative world of middle-class values and aspirations.

Kris played Elmo Cole, a "groovy, out of work musician" – also referred to as a "musician-vagabond" – living in a Volkswagen van. He becomes involved with the ex-wife (Anspach) of a man (Segal) who is still wildly in love with her, despite his propensity for taking advantage of the era's availability of casual sex. Set in contemporary Los Angeles, where, in certain circles, well-to-do lawyers rubbed shoulders with stoned dropouts at trendy parties, free love and swinging collided head on with more traditional values, leading to much questioning on both sides. One issue thrown up by the film was gender inequality, and behaviour that amounted to stalking and non-consensual sex was treated lightly in a way that would be wholly unacceptable in today's climate.

To emphasise his character's credentials, Kristofferson wore his hair and beard very long (with streaks of grey serving to remind that while he was new to films, he was long in the tooth) and he was required, uncharacteristically, to smile vacantly without saying much in many scenes, i.e. acting stoned. Director Paul Mazursky told him to be himself – "he even had me wearing my own clothes".

For his part, Kris merely had to make a few sanitising adjustments to his life on the road in order to deliver a convincing performance. At one point, he managed to inject a piece of autobiographical relevance into his part when saying, "The best place I ever lived in was Brownsville, Texas."

As one critic put it, "Kristofferson steps into this role as if it is a snug pair of jeans." Generally the reviews were positive, concentrating more on Kristofferson's onscreen sex appeal than acting ability. "He projects a strong old fashioned blend of sexuality and niceness rather as Gable did," was a view expressed by one pundit, while another earthier verdict found that Kris exuded "so much folky hippy sex appeal with his shirt unbuttoned to the navel".

*Blume In Love* was a contender for an award at the Cannes Film Festival. In one interview, Kris mispronounced Cannes as "Cans" – was this a display of feigned ignorance, another instance of his rejection of his cultured origins? Kris and Rita used the publicity junket as an excuse for a break in the French Riviera. As a couple, they were now inseparable and were soon making beautiful music together professionally as well as personally.

# Chapter 12

KRISTOFFERSON had made numerous invaluable contacts during his Nashville years, one of which led to an invitation from Willie Nelson to appear at his Dripping Springs Reunion Festival near Austin, Texas, in 1972. The event brought together a whole range of country music styles performed by stars both old and new. Kris performed with Merle Haggard, inspiring one journalist to describe the pairing as, "The bearded prince of pacifism and the hawkish little ex-con."

The behaviour of the attendees owed more to Woodstock than the Grand Ole Opry, with widespread drinking and general revelry continuing well into the night. Kris and Rita felt at home among such a rowdy ambience but some of the older stars disapproved of Kristofferson's behaviour, such as the "Texas Troubadour", Ernest Tubb, who said in 1973: "As a songwriter, I can't take anything away from him, but as a person – well, that's something else. I just don't like the way he conducts himself. I heard some pretty bad things about him at the Dripping Springs Festival. Standing up on stage – supposed to be representing country music – with a beard and using four letter words in front of children . . . it's just a shame. I didn't know a Rhodes Scholar could be so dumb."

The following year Kristofferson and Coolidge appeared at Nelson's Fourth of July Picnic – an event that has since become a Texas institution. One journalist said the huge crowds who spent hours in a traffic tailback in stiflingly hot weather were going to "the biggest honky-tonk of their lives". The event attracted a varied bunch of musicians including several traditional figures, but most were drawn from the country, rock and soul genres or as Kristofferson later put it, "people who had a lot in common but didn't know it before that". With 'Why Me' in the charts at the time, Kris performed it with Rita and Larry Gatlin providing backing vocals.

While a wild time was had by all the performers, it seems that Nelson had manipulated them into participating, as Kristofferson later claimed, "I think he said, 'Let's just you and me and Waylon and Loretta Lynn have a

Fourth of July picnic. We'll just split up the money . . . but nobody split up that money.'"

With Kristofferson's songs being picked up on beyond America, in 1972, he and his backing band, the Band of Thieves, consisting of Terry Paul (bass), Stephen Bruton (guitar) and Donnie Fritts (piano), visited some major European cities including a concert at London's prestigious Royal Albert Hall. As with a number of shows on the tour, though many took place in smaller venues, there were quite a few empty seats in the auditorium. Despite some shaky musical passages, Kris managed to invigorate the initially lukewarm crowd (among them, his former landlady from his time in Oxford).* By the end, they were calling for more encores.

Tony Byworth, who reviewed the concert for *Country Music People*, felt that Kris and Rita were too caught up in each other to deliver a "wholly professional performance". The couple certainly appeared caught up on *The Old Grey Whistle Test*, the BBC's flagship rock programme. During a rendition of 'Help Me Make It Through The Night', Kris seemed intent on consummating their passion on the studio floor, only just managing to hold himself back while he got the business of singing out of the way. It was as if the audience didn't exist.

Back in the States, Kristofferson continued to guest on various television shows, often insisting on appearing with Coolidge, as, for instance, on *The Flip Wilson Show*, despite resistance from producers who had never heard of her. Despite Kristofferson's increasing commercial acceptance, some country traditionalists in Nashville continued to be uncomfortable with his "intellectual middle-class hippy pacifist ways." There were artists who shared Kristofferson's left-leaning views but they tended to publically toe the line for fear of alienating any potential area of their audience. Even when Kristofferson appeared in support of a good cause, tensions could surface. When he agreed to be a celebrity guest at the United Cerebral Palsy Telethon, he was heckled by a member of the audience who expressed disapproval of his mores. "Screw you," Kris flashed back before giving a more measured response about people with the least to say making the most noise.

Yet even some of country's more conservative figures were able to

* Kris included Oxford in his tour itinerary, which enabled him to reunite with friends from his student days.

see that Kris had made a vital contribution. Before he died in 1974, Tex Ritter, who was no social progressive, said, "The work of Kris Kristofferson, Tom T. Hall and Shel Silverstein," liberals all, was "the healthiest thing going on in country music today." Apart from his musical impact, Kris hoped that his forward-thinking societal approach might help to bring about a situation in the south where people were more tolerant of unfamiliar lifestyles.

Having seen Kristofferson perform at the Troubadour and his appearance in *Cisco Pike*, Sam Peckinpah selected Kris to co-star as Billy in his upcoming film for MGM, *Pat Garrett And Billy The Kid*; the lead role of Garrett was played with distinguished coolness by James Coburn.* The fact that, at 37, Kristofferson was about 16 years older than Billy the Kid when he died did not deter the celebrated director. With many films having been made on the subject, when asked why he was doing it again, Peckinpah boomed, "Because *I* have never done it before."

Filming took place in Durango in Mexico over roughly three months in 1972. Rita accompanied Kris and was offered a non-speaking part as Billy's girlfriend at the time of his death. Another companion, Donnie Fritts, was also given a small part – but since his character was not originally in the script, he mainly just repeated the lines of other characters when they spoke to him. Peckinpah brought a gritty, tense reality to the story, creating a tough, pressure-cooker atmosphere with the unwashed-looking characters edgy and sweating in hot, arid conditions. The cinematography captured the unrelenting sunlight so well that it was hard not to avoid squinting at times.

There was little in the way of a plot – Sheriff Pat Garrett tracks down and eventually kills Billy – comprising a series of unconnected, often unfathomable, interminably laboured scenes. The popularity of method acting had contributed to a philosophy that held that it was acceptable to mumble indistinctly, literally in the case of Bob Dylan's character, Alias. One critic tried to excuse this practice on the basis that the story was so well-known that the dialogue was less important than the underlying

* At various stages of the film's gestation, there was talk of Marlon Brando and Jon Voight, Robert Redford and Sam Shepard, and Jack Nicholson and John Denver playing the lead roles.

emotions of the characters, while the uninitiated simply found it annoying. Fans spoke favourably of a "slow and ritualistic explosion" and a "folk tale, overhung by imminent death", while critics dismissed this notion, peppering their reviews with words like "dull", "inept" and "poorly made".

Kristofferson was as guilty of a lack of diction as the other actors (with the exception of Coburn) but when he was comprehensible, he brought a distinctive timbre to his lines, what Jackson Browne described as a "western way of speaking – saying things simply and powerfully in the manner of Gary Cooper and John Wayne and also Native Americans." One of the Duke's mantras – to which Kris adhered – was "talk low, talk slow and don't say too much". One reviewer went as far as saying Kristofferson's portrayal of Billy the Kid was more credible than, for example, Sean Connery as James Bond because, as a personality, "he was nearer the soul of the part".

Peckinpah, an alcoholic, was, to say the least, a challenging person to work with. Though he had successfully directed such excellent films as *The Wild Bunch* and *Straw Dogs*, he could be argumentative and unpredictable. Coolidge later recalled that sometimes he was so drunk he didn't know what scene was going to be shot. "The words that came out of his mouth more often than 'cut' and 'roll' were 'more vodka' and 'more blood'." Kristofferson recalled having to relieve Peckinpah of a gun that he was firing into a ceiling – he might just as easily have hit some of the actors standing nearby. On one occasion Kristofferson and Dylan were watching rushes when Peckinpah urinated all over the screen because the picture was out-of-focus. As Kristofferson recalled, "I remember Bob turning and looking at me with the most perfect reaction, you know, 'What the hell have we gotten ourselves into?'"

For one scene, Coolidge was told to wear a lot of make-up, in part to disguise a small facial scar. Kristofferson, who felt it shouldn't be covered up, went straight to Peckinpah and after remonstrating with him, a compromise was reached. According to Kristofferson, the belligerent director was wary of a confrontation – perhaps because of Kristofferson's military background. "He once told me, 'I'm afraid if I do it to you, you'll step right up and kill me.' 'You know, you're right,' I said."

Despite such bizarre incidents, Kristofferson said he felt an affinity with the director. "We made the same kinds of mistakes, irrational anger, hitting the wrong targets, and we were trying to live up to what we believed we should be, should do."

Kristofferson also respected Peckinpah's stand-off with the film's financiers. "He feels the actors are involved in the creative team and he's fighting the business team. It's us against them." As was increasingly the case, he identified with the little guy at odds with the establishment.

It was Kristofferson who helped persuade Dylan to appear in the film – not an easy task since Peckinpah was genuinely unaware of Bob's status. "'But if I do it, then they *got* me on *film*,' Dylan complained. I said, 'Hell, Bobby, they already got you on records, come on, we'll have a ball.'" Though some critics tried to find good things to say about his appearance – Dylan biographer Robert Shelton talked of his "wistful humour" – to most, Dylan appeared self-conscious and pretentious.*

Kristofferson was ambivalent. "I dunno what goes on in Dylan's head; he might have been trying to be Charlie Chaplin." Though the pair spent quite a lot of time together, they did not bond. "Hell, nobody knows Bobby all that well," said Kristofferson. "He's a dozen different people."

Dylan's one positive contribution to the project was the film's music – in particular, the mighty 'Knocking On Heaven's Door' – which was released as a soundtrack. Some of the music – mainly countrified doodlings – was recorded in Mexico City, and Kristofferson's basic knowledge of Spanish came in useful for negotiations on some of the Mexican Musician's Union's arcane rules. Kristofferson and members of his band got to play with Dylan, with Coolidge and Coburn contributing some backing vocals. They found Dylan to be demanding and abrasive at times; he played by his own idiosyncratic rules and by the middle of the night, when everybody else started to wilt, he would still be going strong.

Violence being a Peckinpah trademark, the British Board of Film Censors nearly refused to give *Pat Garrett And Billy The Kid* a certificate because of its "30 motiveless killings". MGM insisted on radical cuts and the final version was not what Peckinpah intended, nor indeed the kind of work he hoped to be judged by. A commercial flop when originally

---

* Dylan received a nomination in the Worst Performance by a Popular Singer category in *The Golden Turkey Awards*. He later complained, "I was just one of Peckinpah's pawns . . . there wasn't any dimension to my part and I was uncomfortable in this non-role . . ." Apparently uncertain about Dylan's role, Peckinpah cut a number of his scenes. Bob continually complained to Kris, "Well at least you're in the script."

released, more recently it has gained a certain cult status and a restored and reassembled version in line with Peckinpah's original vision is regularly featured at art-house cinemas around the world.

In a 1973 interview, Kristofferson elaborated on his rudimentary drama skills. To achieve a degree of honesty in portraying a role, he liked to research his character – doing a lot of background reading in the case of Billy the Kid. Kris acknowledged that his range was limited and that he was unable to turn his hand to a wide variety of roles in the way that a consummately skilled actor like James Coburn could. He made it clear that he was first and foremost a writer and would rather write a screenplay than appear in a film.

Kristofferson felt that his first two cinematic outings put him in danger of being typecast and that the role of Billy helped to avoid this – though in reality he played a similar part but in a different context. He also revealed, with his usual candour, that on medical advice he had quit drinking for a spell during the making of the film, though he had no intention of giving up altogether. "The doctor says I can drink again by the weekend. Boy, you're gonna see one drunk cowboy."

Kristofferson's involvement with cinematic rough diamonds like Dennis Hopper and Sam Peckinpah proved beneficial to his music career because it increased his standing with the rock audience; if he was cool enough to work with these people, they were prepared to overlook the country origins they usually sneered at. The fact that Kristofferson publicly associated himself with organisations dedicated to the legalisation of marijuana helped his street cred too.

Kristofferson was faced with constant demands on his time during the making of Pat *Garrett And Billy The Kid*. Quite apart from the day-to-day challenges of dealing with Sam Peckinpah, he was also required to attend meetings – with his music publisher for instance – relating to his recording and performing work. However, he did find the time to get hitched.

Kris and Rita's wedding was held at Rita's parent's house to the north of Malibu Beach, with her father conducting the ceremony, on August 19, 1973. Among the approximately 50 guests were Fred Foster, James Coburn and Sam Peckinpah. The bride wore a lacy dress and flowers in her hair while in keeping with Seventies male chic, the groom wore a ruffled shirt to go with his wide-lapelled suit. Rita's grandmother, then in her nineties, entertained the assembled guests with jokes and poetry.

The marriage cemented Kris and Rita's status as a power couple in Nashville and beyond. The demands of work were never ending and according to Fred Foster, the pair postponed their honeymoon to allow for an appearance on Dean Martin's television show. This was part of a strategy targeting the highly lucrative mainstream market – an easier nut for Kris to crack with a glamorous wife with a great voice by his side. Other guests on Martin's show included Ronald Reagan (then governor of California), comedienne Phyllis Diller and Olympic swimmer Mark Spitz. Kristofferson sported western gear for the occasion and in one scene, he and Martin stood amid a hokey country-style set with their arms round each other – Kris looking distinctly uncomfortable.

Commercially, it was both logical and inevitable that the newlyweds should record together. An agreement was reached between their respective record companies, Monument and A&M, that they would take it in turns to release an album – with A&M going first. The first collaboration, *Full Moon*, was released a month after the wedding. Musically, it moved Kristofferson closer to pop and rock music – with a folksy streak – of the easy listening variety. Lyrically there was a marked degree of dumbing down by the standards of his solo albums. Gone were the literary allusions, deep imagery and social conscience. In their place was a collection of mainly laid-back songs about love and relationships, a reflection of the singers' main passions at the time.

Only four of the songs were written or co-written by Kristofferson. A lightweight ditty like 'A Song I'd Like To Sing' set to a jaunty beat lacked the gravitas of much of his previous material, though the line on how a relationship "don't need to last forever" would prove prophetic. The song was released as a single and made a good showing in both the country and pop charts, as did 'Loving Arms', written by Tom Jans, which resonated with Kristofferson's experiences over the years and expressed his feelings about the importance of his relationship.

Among the happy/sad lyrics of love gone wrong, such as 'It's All Over (All Over Again)', a Kristofferson-Coolidge co-write, Kristofferson still managed to slip in some lyrics about an archetypal drunken loser in 'From The Bottle To The Bottom'.

One reviewer quipped the album was "light on message and heavy on massage", while another spoke for many when saying that Kristofferson had taken a wrong turn in his musical journey, "towards the more sobby modern country style . . . it is a trend I strongly hope he reverses".

The jarring contrast between Kristofferson and Coolidge's voices was one of the album's most striking features. The songs appeared to be aimed more towards Rita's high, smooth and gentle delivery and this was probably due to the album's producer, David Anderle, also being her producer. For much of the album, Kristofferson croons along, attempting, though not succeeding, to soften his gruff style. It was like a musical mismatch of beauty and the beast.

Coolidge was not overly concerned by Kristofferson's vocal limitations as she felt that the powerful emotion he put over meant that they complemented each other and that the whole was greater than the sum of the parts. Kristofferson, however, got frustrated by their disparity, telling Rita it was "like working with Aretha Franklin – we don't have the same talent". Of course, the overall sound was more important than the lyrics – the opposite of what he was used to.

With the added boost of the publicity surrounding their wedding, *Full Moon* topped the country charts and reached the *Billboard* Top 40, eventually going gold. At the time, both Kristofferson and Coolidge's solo albums were selling strongly and it was reported in some quarters that for a time, Kristofferson was outselling Bob Dylan – although for all his impact it was the gentler pop country of Glen Campbell that achieved the greater commercial success. Although he didn't know it at the time, by 1973, Kristofferson had reached his peak as a recording artist; it would last for another year or so before sales tapered off, never again attaining anything like the same levels.

For the past decade, Kristofferson had been living in run-down apartments (he had never bothered to terminate the lease of his last place in Nashville), in friends' spare rooms, on the road and, latterly, with Rita in California. In the wake of his marriage, he felt the time was right to create a more solid base. He and Rita considered the possibility of buying in Nashville and, at one point, they had their eye on a piece of land near Music City that some friends found for them. In the end, Kristofferson's film career proved the deciding factor and they eventually bought a large house in Malibu.

The Kristoffersons avoided a house right on the beach because, as Kris put it, "We didn't want people looking in at us when we were having dinner." He compared buying a house to acquiring a ball and chain, "but you can't bring up children in motel rooms". One visitor described the ambience in the house: "The living area around them reflects a harmless haphazardness about life. Guitars and cases litter the floor, Indian weavings serve as rugs and wall hangings, and the book shelves contain everything from Magritte to Summerhill to *The Bhagavad Gita*."

Soon enough, Rita found she was pregnant and in preparation for the event, she and Kris attended natural childbirth classes, as he recalled with amusement, "I felt it was all like the television show with Dick van Dyke and Mary Tyler Moore where you get all these representative couples – one black, one Jewish, one Chicano, one straight and us, the freaks."

Their daughter, Casey, was born in 1974. Kristofferson had told a journalist that he hoped it was a girl who would be as pretty as Rita, which tended to consolidate an impression of him settling down into married domesticity. The reality was somewhat different. Kris continued his rollercoaster life of rock'n'roll excess with barely a pause. Though now following his own rather than his parents' chosen course, he still had deep-rooted personal insecurities, a dark side that continued to haunt him. By drinking to excess, maintaining a 60-a-day nicotine habit and constantly throwing himself into work, he was doing his best to escape from reality and on the face of it, he was having a frenetically wonderful time.

Unlike some stars, Kristofferson did not complain about the stresses of a busy life. Regardless of his own concerns, he was, broadly speaking, doing what he wanted to do – and his anxieties would have been with him whether he was a labourer or a successful artist. He had little time for successful personalities who complained about never having enough time off, constantly living under pressure or having to pay too much tax.*

"The time I really felt put upon was when I was a janitor. Now I can rent a car or go wherever I want on just a few songs . . . you cannot tell me I'm in worse shape because I got big taxes and responsibility."

Kristofferson had little interest in material possessions and even when he was earning significant amounts of money, his accountant was surprised at how little Kris spent on himself, and much of what he did spend was on

* Kristofferson told one journalist that he paid $250,000 in taxes in 1974.

presents, especially Christmas gifts, for other people.

Kristofferson's manic schedule meant he was unable to see many of his real friends as often as he would have liked. In 1974, he ruefully said that he had not spoken to Johnny Cash for two years and complained that "you end up spending lots of time with people you don't give a shit for".

For a time, he was better able to stand up to the stresses and strains of his lifestyle with Rita there to support him and share the load. She was prepared to overlook the problem areas – drink, drugs, other women – because she, too, was having fun and like many newly married people was full of optimistic love. Some observers believe she had a stabilising effect on Kris; Larry Gatlin opined that Rita "kind of shielded him from all of us rowdies in Nashville".

However, it would be wrong to suggest that theirs was an idyllic partnership. From early on, they had their "falling outs". Leaving aside Kristofferson's hedonistic excesses, there was an inevitable degree of professional competition and good sales or reviews for one might be taken as some kind of slight by the other or arouse feelings of jealousy. Various reports emerged in the press of tensions between them; one suggested that Kristofferson was unhappy because journalists were more interested in interviewing her than him. On another occasion, Coolidge was said to be unhappy because journalists pushed right past her in order to get to her husband. They were professional artists keen to pursue and develop their respective careers – the most important single aspect of their individual lives if they were honest.

# Chapter 13

IT was inevitable and not a little ironic that Kristofferson – who had spent years trying to hustle songs – was bombarded by aspiring writers. Now that the boot was on the other foot, he realised that to preserve his sanity he had to become selfish to a degree and turn people away. This did not, however, prevent him from looking out for new talent at times and he was a contributor to the emergence of outstanding singer-songwriters such as John Prine and Steve Goodman (who wrote the hit, 'City Of New Orleans').

Goodman supported Kristofferson at a show in New York City* and during his set, the former performed 'Donald And Lydia', an outstanding Prine composition. Goodman mentioned to Kristofferson that Prine, still largely unknown, was playing across town, so they all took a cab over to see him. Jerry Wexler was present too and within a day or so, Prine had a recording contract. Kristofferson later contributed the liner notes for Prine's debut album, based on his first impressions of hearing him in that late-night New York club.

Graeme Connors is another artist particularly grateful for Kristofferson's encouragement and "generosity of spirit". Connors, then 18, supported Kristofferson and Coolidge when they were trying to crack the Australian market in the early Seventies, and was thrilled to be allowed to join them onstage for the final number of their set ('Rock And Roll Time'). Kristofferson even delayed his departure to Japan by a day so that he could produce four tracks for Connors with backing provided by Coolidge and the touring band.

"The tracks became the cornerstone of my first record and obviously gave the record company quite a hook for the media," Connors recalls. "He didn't need to do it, in fact he was pretty wrecked at the time;

---

* Paul Anka, who featured 'For The Good Times' in his Las Vegas show, was among the audience.

it was just another example of his generous soul. He is a permanent inspiration to every serious songwriter."

It seems Kristofferson had not forgotten the career boost Johnny Cash had given him with a few kind acts. Mark McKinnon, now one of America's top media advisers, recalls with affection his involvement with Kristofferson, even though he describes himself as "a mere gnat" by comparison. Despite outstanding success in his subsequent career – McKinnon has worked with President George W. Bush, Senator John McCain and Governor Ann Richards to mention a few – the early Seventies period remains "one of the favourite chapters in my life. [Kris] was very generous to me, as he was to so many others; he encouraged me, tried to get me a record deal [unsuccessfully, which is not surprising if you have heard the demos], gave me his old apartment and let me hang around his publishing company."

Kristofferson was also able to help out an old friend who had become stuck when trying to compose a new song. Marijohn Wilkin, by now in her early fifties and intermittently plagued by alcoholism, had taken to writing gospel tunes. The story most often told is that she was frustrated because she had come up with part of the song – a prayer – that she knew, with her Nashville publisher's hat on, was a hit, but the rest would not come.

Aware of the success of 'Why Me' and with Kris and Rita, by coincidence, in town, Wilkin phoned Kristofferson and explained she had the second verse and the chorus of a new song but could not come up with a suitable opening. "When I showed him how I started the song, 'I'm just a mortal . . .' he looked at me and said, 'Why don't you say, "I'm only human, I'm just a man . . ."' I said, 'That's good! That's what I need.' We finished the first verse in about 20 minutes. The lines just flew out from each of us."

The song, 'One Day At A Time', was initially a major hit for the little-known Marilyn Sellars. Hailing from Minneapolis, Sellars could sing most forms of popular music but decided to try her luck with country. A friend hooked her up with Wilkin's producer husband, Clarence Selman, who started to gather songs for an album. Marijohn told Marilyn she had one song in particular she wanted her to hear and played 'One Day At A Time', accompanying herself on a small electric piano, while they were out on Old Hickory Lake, near Nashville. Wilkin got the idea for 'One

Day At A Time' from the language of Alcoholics Anonymous meetings.

"In those days," says Sellars, "the treatment centres were just starting to come out of the closet so to speak, people were starting to talk about alcoholism openly – Lord knows there was plenty of it going on in Nashville."

The song suffered an identity crisis at the start – radio stations were not sure if it was country, gospel or pop, and some wouldn't play it because of the inclusion of the Jesus reference. However, public demand soon ensured it was played on most stations and Sellars believes that many people identified with the message, which is why the song became such a big hit.

Sellars has an interesting insight into the presence of Kristofferson's name as co-writer. "When the sheet music came out, I noticed Kris' name – I thought Marijohn had written the song. I asked her why his name was on it. She said she was stuck on one line of the song – don't ask me which one – she never said. She called him, he went round, helped her, and the song was complete. I expressed astonishment that she had given him half of the writing credit for just one line. 'It's very simple,' she said. 'When they send a new single out to all those countless radio stations – and there might be 50 new songs a week coming out – nobody will know who Marilyn Sellars is and they never remember my name, but if they see *his* name, because he's so hot, they'll pick it up and play it.'

"Later on I met Kris at a gig he had in Minnesota. I went in and introduced myself to him backstage. He said, 'Thanks for the song.' I said, 'Well, thank *you*,' and he said, 'Hey, I didn't do anything.'"*

'One Day At A Time' has subsequently been covered by many artists. Cristy Lane scored a major hit with the song in 1980 and cashed in thereafter with her life story, while Gloria Sherry's version remained in the Irish Top 30 for a record 86 weeks.

Kristofferson and Coolidge continued to pursue successful joint and solo careers in the mid-Seventies. Famous they may have become, but Kris was a little taken aback when he went to buy some guitar strings near his

---

* Kristofferson, along with Buckhorn Music, was later threatened with a multi-million dollar lawsuit by a woman who claimed that she had written the song. The case never proceeded.

Malibu home and the shop assistant asked which band he was with. Against that, there was some speculation that it was Kristofferson who was the subject of Carly Simon's 1973 smash hit, 'You're So Vain', rather than the much touted Warren Beatty. Kris might have enjoyed the fact that his sexy good looks and notoriety with women had put him in the frame for such an honour but denied he was the one. "Can't have been me. I don't own a Lear jet like the guy in the song."

Kristofferson's fourth solo outing for Monument, *Spooky Lady's Sideshow*, released in 1974, was recorded at Hollywood's Sunset Sound studios – the first album he recorded outside Nashville. Stung by reactions to some of his earlier albums and what he saw as the critics' intrusive methods – particularly when it came to his private life – Kristofferson subtly took ironic revenge on the album's sleeve. He is pictured smiling broadly while sitting in front of the mirror in a changing room, looking untroubled and healthy (despite the presence of the ever-present cigarette). Stuck around the mirror are several fictitious press clippings, which left no doubt as to the intended target; clearly, Ben Gerson's scathingly articulate 1972 *Rolling Stone* review had left a scar.

Producer David Anderle spoke of the album's impressive range, "from pure country to a totally new sound", claiming that Kristofferson had gone in a whole new direction. The album once again utilised top session players, who enabled Kristofferson and Anderle to try out an assortment of styles and inject the kind of variety that Kristofferson's vocal delivery fought against. Mike Utley's brilliant organ playing contributed a loose Dylanesque sound and, on occasion, an infectious jazzy-bluesy groove, as on 'Late Again'. Horns added to the rowdy atmosphere of 'I May Smoke Too Much', while steel guitar on 'Stairway To The Bottom' contributed to its honky-tonk feel.

Generally, the subject matter of the album was downbeat – in 'Stairway To The Bottom', Kristofferson revisited the character of a philandering soak, while in 'Same Old Song', he played the part of the jaded success story who finds out being at the top of the heap brings a new set of problems, something also similarly addressed in 'Shandy (The Perfect Disguise)'. Even though the lyrics are imbued with an enigmatic wisdom, there is a sense that Kristofferson was trying too hard, failing to recreate the kind of seemingly effortless results he achieved with songs like 'Me And Bobby McGee'.

Not all of the tracks were Kristofferson compositions. A cover of Larry

Murray's 'Lights Of Magdala' – a poetic ballad with religious overtones – worked well, indicating that Kristofferson's mid-Seventies albums might have turned out better if he'd chosen not to rely so heavily on his own songs. He also co-wrote two songs with Roger McGuinn and Bobby Neuwirth, including the partly autobiographical 'Rock And Roll Time'. In a similar vein, Kris defiantly spoke up for his rock'n'roll lifestyle in 'I May Smoke Too Much'.

In comparison with the previous two Kristofferson albums, *Spooky Lady's Sideshow* turned out to be a commercial disappointment; though it made the country charts' Top 10, it only just scraped into the *Billboard* Top 100 chart.

A second duets album with Coolidge, *Breakaway*, was also released in 1974. As with *Full Moon*, the cover shot depicted the couple in natural poses – this time in the company of horses – with little attention paid to glamorising their appearance. As per the agreement between their respective record companies, the album was released on Monument with Fred Foster producing.

As with *Full Moon* the emphasis was on an easy listening MOR sound aimed mainly at Rita's lustrous vocal prowess, and while Kristofferson's voice could be characterised as expressive on his solo albums, with Coolidge, its off-key sourness again tended to grate. In order to broaden the album's range and commercial potential, songs by a number of established writers (performed by crack session musicians) were featured, including Melba Montgomery's 'We Must Have Been Out Of Our Minds', Larry Gatlin's 'Rain', Larry Murray's 'Dakota (The Dancing Bear)' and the opening track, Billy Swan's 'Lover Please'. Two of Kristofferson's featured songs had already been hits for other artists, namely, 'I've Got To Have You' for Sammi Smith in 1972, and 'I'd Rather Be Sorry' for Ray Price in 1971, the latter track serving as a reminder of Kris' early days attempting to knock out mainstream hits on Music Row.

The album proved less of a commercial success than *Full Moon*, making the country Top Five but only scraping into the *Billboard* Top 100, while both 'Lover Please' and 'Rain' were minor hits in the country and easy listening charts. This was probably due to there being too much material by Kris and Rita on the market; since the start of the Seventies, aside from the two duet collaborations, they had amassed 10 solo albums between them. In addition, their professional partnership ran counter to their personal relationship. It had a built-in obsolescence given the inherent differences between their chosen musical styles that were always going to be better realised in a solo context.

However artistically unsatisfying, the pairing provided a commercial boost to both of their careers and gained them several awards. 'From The Bottle To The Bottom' won the 1973 Grammy for Best Country Vocal Performance by a Duo or Group ('Loving Arms' was nominated in the same category the following year), while 'Lover Please' won the Grammy for Best Country Vocal Performance by a Duo or Group for 1975. These awards followed earlier Grammy nominations for Kris for Best Country Song and Best Country Vocal Performance, Male, for 'Why Me'. In 1974, Ronnie Milsap won the Grammy for Best Country Vocal Performance (Male) with Kristofferson's 'Please Don't Tell Me How The Story Ends'.

Despite the demands of their hectic recording and performing schedules, the couple found time to get involved with issues of importance to them. In 1974, they appeared at a Nashville benefit for NORML (The National Organisation for the Reform of Marijuana Laws) at Vanderbilt's Neely Auditorium.

Kristofferson also participated in a long-running public service announcement campaign on behalf of NORML (as did friend and fellow aficionado, Willie Nelson). Though this did not endear either to the Nashville traditionalists, it was a sign of how much things had changed that a country star could do such things and still enjoy widespread acceptance – indeed Kristofferson attended that year's Country Music Awards as an honoured guest.

He also popped up regularly as a guest on television shows, appearing in a 1974 children's special entitled *Free To Be . . . You And Me*, hosted by Marlo Thomas. The programme grew out of Thomas' original idea of a record accompanied by an illustrated songbook aimed at helping children find their way through the challenges of growing up in the modern world. It was a saccharine affair, featuring songs and stories from many famous artists including Harry Belafonte, Alan Alda, Mel Brooks (playing a baby), a teenage Michael Jackson, Roberta Flack and Cicely Tyson, alongside Kristofferson and Coolidge who sang a song called 'Circle Of Friends'.*

\* \* \*

* The soundtrack album is still available and a sequel, *Free To Be . . . A Family*, was produced in 1987.

In 1974, Kristofferson once more hooked up with Sam Peckinpah, for a minor role in the commercial flop *Bring Me The Head Of Alfredo Garcia* – a dark and violent variation on the road movie theme. The patriarch of a wealthy Mexican family issues the edict that is the film's title on discovering that Senor Garcia has impregnated his daughter and a substantial reward is offered. In the deranged adventure that follows, having cut off Garcia's head, a bounty hunter talks to it all wrapped up in cloth on the back seat of the car, decomposing and covered in flies, while driving around Mexico.

The heat, sweat and grittiness of the landscape pervading the film, adds to the feeling of oppression that affects the characters, along with the ever-present threat of random violence. Kristofferson acquitted himself well without making a memorable impression, playing the part of a drifter on a motorbike who encounters the bounty hunter and his girl at night in a field. After a time he takes the woman off, apparently with the intention of raping her, but the boyfriend appears and shoots him.

At the time, critics were almost universal in their contempt for the film's incoherent plot, mumbled lines and extreme violence; the whole ambience had something in common with a pornographic film. With the passage of time, some now view it as an overlooked classic, prefiguring the macabre work of David Lynch and Quentin Tarantino and, like *Pat Garrett And Billy The Kid,* it has become something of a cult movie.

For all its artistic and physical demands, filming sometimes provided a welcome respite. Unlike some fellow Nashville stars, such as Dolly Parton, who became extremely frustrated with the interminable wait between takes, Kristofferson understood how this was an unavoidable element of the movie-making process. If the filming location was near a town, he was quite happy to wander about incognito for an afternoon, soaking up the atmosphere.

His other role that year was in *Alice Doesn't Live Here Anymore*, starring Ellen Burstyn (who had received acclaim for her performance in *The Exorcist* in 1973) and directed by Martin Scorsese. His fourth major feature, the film was something of a departure for Scorsese, who had come to be associated with gritty films such as *Mean Streets*. Unusually for the time, it was a woman's story – Scorsese said he took the job because he wanted to dispel the notion that he was only suited to directing male leads.

Not for the last time, Kristofferson was cast in a film that owed only a little to his abilities; other actors could have played his part as convincingly if not better than he did. However, he was popular with directors because he had an eye-catching appearance that gave good screen presence; the fact that he was a credible singing star – something that would have appealed to the rock buff in Scorsese – helped too.

The plot's main character, Alice Hyatt, is unexpectedly liberated from a loveless marriage by her husband's sudden death in a road accident. Alice now has the freedom to choose the course of her life and decides to follow an unfulfilled passion by pursuing a career in singing. She drifts into a brief relationship with a violent and unpredictable married man named Ben, played with scary menace by Harvey Keitel.

Kristofferson was cast as David, a kind-hearted farmer who meets Alice at the manic diner in Tucson where she is forced to take work when her singing job provides insufficient income. He helps to get Alice back on her feet and provides support for her 12-year-old son, Tommy, whose difficult and provocative behaviour – understandable given his unsettled upbringing – places a strain on the relationship. In one scene, which presumably Kristofferson had a say in, David shows the boy how to play Hank Williams' 'I'm So Lonesome I Could Cry' on the guitar. Despite a successful career in music, Kris' voice was such that he was not usually asked to sing in front of the camera.

The fact that this was also true of *Alice Doesn't Live Here Anymore* made his character more interesting; he was not some one-dimensional clean-cut hero of whom the audience would automatically approve. It is a film about a woman – Alice – and David fits in with her needs rather than the other way around. That said, there were those among the women's liberation brigade who doubted if Burstyn could truly be described as liberated when her journey of self-discovery ends up with her falling for a hunk like Kristofferson. There is a degree of realism in the way they work out their relationship, which is ultimately touching rather than sentimental.

The film moves along languorously but with Scorsese at the helm, there are sudden changes of pace and outbursts of violence and emotion that help to maintain interest, and Burstyn's performance is convincing enough to make the viewer care about what happens to her character. As an actor, Kristofferson was credible if wooden. Unlike fellow country actors like Johnny Cash and Willie Nelson, his face was not immediately familiar so he was better equipped at becoming a character. However, even by this stage, it was clear that Kristofferson did not have what it took to carry a film, finding it hard to express emotion convincingly when the script demanded it. His ability was also affected by his awkward loping gait – something remarked upon over the years – which was perhaps the result of a sporting injury suffered in earlier years.

In the main, critics approved of *Alice Doesn't Live Here Anymore*, helped by Scorsese's strong direction and the presence of some good supporting performances, notably from Burstyn, Cheryl Ladd and 12-year-old Jodie Foster. Burstyn won an Oscar for Best Actress and Ladd received an Oscar nomination for Best Supporting Actress. Of Burstyn's performance, one critic said, "She pulls it off with different shells: a layer of self-confidence, a layer of aggressiveness, a layer of passivity and a layer of weakness. This . . . gives the film a huge emotional heft." Another observed that the film had been made with "much skill and intelligence".

*Alice Doesn't Live Here Anymore* was also an outstanding financial success when released in 1975. Made on a budget of around $2 million, it grossed more than $17 million nationwide.[*]

In 1975, Kris was back at Sunset Sound Studios to record a new album, *Who's To Bless And Who's To Blame*. Despite a hectic schedule, he found time to write all nine songs, which perhaps accounted for the sameness of much of the material, as always not helped by Kristofferson's kazoo-like vocal timbre. When not derivative – 'If It's All The Same To You' bore a strong resemblance to 'Once More With Feeling' – the melodies were generally unmemorable.

The title track, like other songs on the album, concerned itself with issues of morality; it offered no easy answers but rather asked questions making the essential point – without ever achieving great profundity – that there are no simple solutions to most moral conundrums. 'Easy, Come On' found Kris once again returning to the theme of women with a lack of self-respect – something that seemed to guiltily obsess him. However, the words lacked bite, while the elliptical 'Silver (The Hunger)' was over-laboured and at eight minutes plus, overlong. 'The Year 2000 Minus 25' revealed an interest in global political issues. However, in

---

[*] A successful spin-off television sitcom, *Alice*, based on the characters in the diner where Alice worked, was subsequently produced.

contrast to his later plain-spoken militancy, the political was also the personal as Kris confined himself to light-hearted jibes.

One unusual number was 'Rocket To Stardom', inspired by the practice of some aspirants who would sing at the security camera installed outside the Kristoffersons' Malibu home in the forlorn hope that Kris or Rita would be sold enough to record the songs. This gave Kristofferson the zany idea of visualising the entrance driveway to his house as a kind of vaudevillian audition stage. He set the song to carnival-type music, with a rowdy chorus including Warren Oates, the star of *Bring Me The Head Of Alfredo Garcia*, which brought some welcome energy and lightness to an otherwise unremarkable album.

For all his reputation as a serious writer, it was not unusual for Kristofferson to come up with novelty numbers – he had been doing so since his army days. He wrote the title track for Willie Nelson's 1973 album, *Shotgun Willie*, referring to the lyrics as "mindfarts" that he was inspired to write one day in the bathroom.

The musical style on *Who's To Bless And Who's To Blame* was hard to define; it included country, pop and elements of folk. Producer David Anderle cut the number of musicians so that there was a smaller palette of sounds. Mike Utley once more made a major contribution to the overall sound and feel, predominantly laid-back and down-tempo, as did Jerry McGee with some tasteful guitar and dobro. Fred Tackett, who had a long association with Little Feat before finally becoming an official member of that band in the Eighties, contributed to the loose shuffling sound. Rita, Billy Swan and Donnie Fritts* were demoted to backing singers.

The sunny front cover photograph captured Kristofferson smiling unguardedly, free of any moodiness, while the visible greyness in his beard was a reminder that he was fast approaching 40. The back cover shot was entirely different – changed lighting cast his deep-set eyes in shadow and gave him the appearance of a tough gangster who might just be related to the Incredible Hulk. The first image was bright and optimistic, the second much darker. Was this a message about the two extremes of human nature intended to chime with the title?

*Who's To Bless And Who's To Blame* was not a commercial success – although Johnny Duncan had a Top Five country hit with 'Stranger' – nor

---

* Kris had produced Fritts' 1974 album *Prone To Lean*.

was it particularly well received by the critics, one of whom rather unkindly referred to it as "crap-on-vinyl".

It was hard to avoid the reality that despite releasing several albums of largely new material, the Kristofferson songs that other artists were mainly covering in 1975 were those that had originally made his name at the start of the decade. It was doubly unfortunate for Kristofferson that Bob Dylan released *Blood On The Tracks* that same year. Rapidly acquiring the status of one of Dylan's greatest albums, it demonstrated the extraordinary heights that an established singer-songwriter could still reach.

For all the success he'd attained, Kristofferson continued to express feelings of insecurity. "I think of myself as a writer just getting away with a lot of fantasy," he said in 1974. "There's a lot of people who can do what I do in many fields better than I. I'm not any great shakes as a musician and performers are a dime a dozen. I think I'm making the most of what I've got." He said that if he had to, he would just "stick my thumb out and head off again."

# Chapter 14

IF Kristofferson's recording career had stalled, his concurrent celluloid activities continued to pile up. "This movie trip is weird," he told a journalist in the mid-Seventies. "Some day I'd like to be a director. I've got no ideas about being Ingmar Bergman tomorrow but hell, why not? Maybe I'm fakin' it, but a lot of other people are too."

One of the more unusual offers Kristofferson received came in 1975 with *The Sailor Who Fell From Grace With The Sea*, for which he also contributed to the soundtrack. The film was based on a short novel by the writer and fervent Japanese nationalist, Yukio Mishima, who had very publicly committed ritual suicide (*seppuku*), with the assistance of two followers, in Tokyo in 1970 – an incident that followed his failure to inspire a coup d'etat aimed at bringing about the restoration of the historical powers of the Japanese emperor. In the novel, Mishima considers the futility of the human condition through the shifting perspectives of the three main characters.

For the purposes of the film, the story was simplified and relocated to the port of Dartmouth on the south coast of England by writer and director Lewis John Carlino. Kristofferson played the part of a sailor, Jim Cameron, who meets widow Anne Osborne, played by Sarah Miles, after returning from a voyage, whereupon the pair have a torrid fling. Subsequently they develop a more serious relationship when Jim returns from his next excursion. Perhaps in an attempt to enable Kristofferson to identify more easily with his character, Jim was portrayed as an avid reader of works by writers such as Jack London and Joseph Conrad.

Anne's teenage son, Jonathan, who initially regards Jim as a hero, is under the influence of a group of anarchic boys (echoes of William Golding's *Lord Of The Flies*), with a bullying and fascistic leader who preaches about the perfection of the natural order and the wickedness of adults. When it becomes clear that Jim is planning to give up his nautical life in order to marry Anne, the gang feels badly betrayed – he has failed to live up to their idealised image of the traditional values they believe Jim represents and deserves no mercy.

Jonathan's feelings are amplified by his distress at the loss of his father and a repressed Oedipal longing for his mother. The edgy aggression of the storyline contrasted dramatically with the beautifully atmospheric photography, which captures the tranquil nature of Dartmouth and its surrounding countryside. The fact that for most of the film the weather is perfect adds an air of unreality. Given its controversial nature, it was amusingly ironic that Dartmouth's mayoress was quoted that she was gratified to find people at work on "a nice family picture".

There were a number of fairly graphic sex scenes (only slightly disguised by the use of soft focus) and much violence, including the notorious dissection of a drugged cat, though the acting of the youngsters was unconvincing, devoid of the serious menace meant to be conveyed. Critics at the time were divided; most agreed *The Sailor Who Fell From Grace . . .* was unusual and some were prepared to award some credit for the ambitiousness of the project. One described it as an "uneasy combination of a sex-starved widow and twisted kids making for, at the very least, a memorable experience, if not entirely for the right reasons". Another said, "There is a beguilement to *Sailor . . .* that of sitting through a movie in a state of irascible unconvincedness while being more than half seduced."

Others saw the film as a hopeless mess. Since Mishima's original novel concerned itself with deep-rooted Japanese mores and cultural assumptions, inevitably aspects of the story were lost in translation or as one critic described it, "A farcically misconceived attempt to transplant Yukio Mishima's engagingly perverse novel to an English setting, and to make its peculiarly Japanese psychology and motivations work with a set of improbable Anglo-American characters."

In typical fashion, Kristofferson's character ambles through the film with the appearance of someone possibly under the influence of a mind-altering substance, or slightly disconnected from events around him; a case of life and art coinciding. "Kris Kristofferson . . . looks good but doesn't convey much more than puzzled weakness," wrote a reviewer.

The steamy scenes featuring Kristofferson and Miles in *The Sailor Who Fell From Grace With The Sea* gave *Playboy* magazine the idea of an associated pictorial featuring the stars of the film. It was planned that the shots – some from the movie, others specially posed and shot by *Playboy* staff –

would appear when the film was still in theatrical circuit, thus generating interest among cinemagoers.

According to some reports, Kristofferson was talked into the idea by Miles, while in several later interviews he blamed his agreement on the booze, implying that he would have never agreed if sober. "That was just about the worst thing I ever have done." He was doubtless aware, though, that such sensational photographs would provide considerable publicity for the film and earn him a substantial fee.

The photoshoot was published in the July 1976 issue and the magazine's circulation for that month enjoyed a significant boost. The pair were photographed entirely naked with only Kristofferson's genitalia hidden – under the smouldering banner, "Kris and Sarah. In a scene of electrifying erotic intensity, Kristofferson and Miles make love for the movie cameras – and for *Playboy*." The images, particularly the ones shot specially for the magazine (of which four were published), were extraordinarily graphic.

Whether or not the pair actually had coitus, it was clear that they were very much comfortable in a variety of sexual positions that the prurient public were able to share. In one particularly notorious shot, Miles is seen standing on a bed with her back arched, hands pushed against the wall, her face lost in lustful joy; the cause of her delight is Kristofferson, lying underneath her, his head buried between her legs, performing oral sex.

If Rita was understandably upset and embarrassed, there can be little doubt that the incident, and the breathless tabloid coverage it generated, represented a nail in the coffin of their doomed marriage.

In 1976 Kristofferson starred in *Vigilante Force*, an action movie produced by Gene Corman, which Kris treated as something of a potboiler between more substantial works. It brought him into contact with some well-known screen actors of the day, including the now largely forgotten Jan-Michael Vincent and Victoria Principal, who later had a leading role in the American soap *Dallas*. The plot concerned Aaron Arnold, a Vietnam vet (played by Kristofferson) who, along with some army buddies, is hired to clean up a remote Californian town that has been taken over by a bunch of rowdy oil workers eager to cash in after black gold is found near the town.

The trouble is, once they have sorted out the workers, the town guardians quickly become corrupt, set up a protection racket and generally turn out to be worse than their predecessors. Aaron's good guy brother, Ben (played by Vincent), has to eject him in order to restore peace. Full of violent thrills and spills, Kristofferson made a reasonable fist of his first attempt at playing the bad guy – up until *Vigilante Force*, his parts had been fairly sympathetic.

The film is, however, largely forgettable, lacking any kind of serious point beyond getting over some of the difficulties an ex-soldier can experience when re-adjusting to everyday civilian life. As one critic charged, "This action-drama mishmash is wildly off-kilter, thoughtless and mean-spirited . . . truly unseemly, with redneck clichés and mindless violence making up most of director George Armitage's script . . . Kristofferson is gruff and rude throughout."

Though Kristofferson claimed that he was not ashamed of *Vigilante Force*, he attempted to distance himself from it by saying he had understood the film was going to be a black comedy about post-Vietnam America.

Kristofferson and Coolidge continued to maintain a busy touring schedule that was fitted around his movie schedule. Kris felt the tours were driven by commercial opportunism with little regard for the performers – though some of the stresses he experienced were undoubtedly self-inflicted. He said the requirement of performing two shows a day was particularly gruelling, "if you're into drinking heavy", which helps to explain why some reviewers described his singing voice at live performances from this time as "drowsy".

A major opportunity for Kristofferson to break into the movie major league came in 1976 with *A Star Is Born*. The film had undergone a troubled gestation period, with much negative advance publicity, and it was partly due to chance and good fortune that he was eventually offered one of the starring roles alongside Barbra Streisand. The pair, who had dated in the early Seventies, first met after one of Kristofferson's Troubadour gigs. Kris later recalled an early taste of her star quality when they went on a double date with a "big-shot Hollywood agent". The party drove up to a theatre and when they arrived, the agent charged out of the car and collared the manager, shouting, "Streisand's here, I don't want any fuss, just give us tickets."

The two nearly worked together previously – Streisand had considered the lead role in *Alice Doesn't Live Here Anymore* but turned it down because she felt she was too young for the part and also that people would find it hard to accept her as a failed singer.

Screenwriters John Gregory Dunne and Joan Gidion were aware that the basic story of *A Star Is Born* had a notable Hollywood provenance. They had also read a treatment by William Wellman and Robert Carson that updated the setting by moving it into the world of rock and pop music. The original screen version, which starred Janet Gaynor and Frederic March, was loosely based on the 1932 film *What Price Hollywood,* directed by George Cukor. It was remade in 1954 with Judy Garland and James Mason in the leading roles, this time with music added, and again with Cukor directing. Dunne and Gidion's idea was revamped by many top Hollywood screenwriters – at one stage it was to be called *Rainbow Road* – and passed through the hands of a number of potential directors and producers before reaching Streisand's then-boyfriend Jon Peters, a hairdresser with ambitions beyond the salon.

Peters was allegedly unaware of the previous film versions and had little or no experience of producing films, but he was Streisand's boyfriend and they came as a package. Prior to their involvement, a number of star pairings had been considered for the leading roles – Elvis Presley and Liza Minnelli, Cybill Shepherd and Peter Bogdanovich, Diana Ross and Alan Price, Carly Simon and James Taylor. Streisand and Peters, who saw the film largely as a vehicle for Streisand's singing and acting talents, wanted a bona fide rock star to play the part of the male lead, a formerly successful rock singer now on the skids. He meets and falls in love with Streisand's character, whereupon she shoots rapidly towards stardom with an initial and vital boost from their relationship.

Streisand's first choice for the part was Elvis Presley and she went to discuss the project with him after one of his concerts in 1975. However, she had not reckoned on the venal tendencies of Presley's manager, "Colonel" Tom Parker. Annoyed at not having been consulted first, and showing a characteristic lack of pragmatism, he demanded an astronomical fee along with star billing for his charge. Presley had not been in a film for six years and was overweight and in poor health. Then again, part of his appeal to Streisand was that he really was a star in decline and might therefore be truly convincing in the role – another reason why Parker was against the idea.

Others in the frame for the male lead at various times included Mick Jagger, Neil Diamond and Marlon Brando. There was even a suggestion that Bob Dylan might be a contender. All had reasons for not wanting or not being able to accept the part – Diamond said he could not identify with a loser with a destructive personality.

Kristofferson was regarded as preferable to Jagger because director Frank Pierson considered him more romantic. In what was surely a case of revisionism, Streisand later said that Kris was probably the best person for the part; though she and Peters originally wanted to position his billing well below that of hers. One weak area of the film was its leads' ages. At 33, kitted out in expensive designer clothes and looking every inch the superstar she already was, Streisand was hardly convincing as a young singer desperate for a break, and Kristofferson, pushing 40, was already on the old side to portray a fading rock star. However, it was too rare an opportunity for him to turn down; the budget of approximately $6 million was more than any of his previous films.

Kristofferson did not have to do too much background research into the part of John Norman Howard – an impulsive, irresponsible drunk with a penchant for getting into fights, and whose life and career are falling apart. He is oblivious to the attempts made to help him by some of his loyal colleagues and is past caring about his fans – forgetting lyrics and falling about drunk on stage – and they are rapidly losing interest in him. Kristofferson's portrayal contained more than a few references to Jim Morrison; The Doors' charismatic frontman, who died in 1971, was already seen as the prototype doomed rock icon.

Howard chances into a nightclub where he comes across lowly singer, Esther Hoffman. For reasons that are not really made clear – why her and not the many other attractive girls he has met? – he falls madly in love and in due course, these feelings are reciprocated. He invites Esther up on stage with him one night and she becomes an instant hit. As her star rapidly rises, his decline continues apace towards an inevitable and dramatic final curtain à la James Dean in the form of a high-speed car crash in a Ferrari GTS/4 Daytona Spyder.

The impression is that Kristofferson was being directorially pushed more than in his previous films, which had mainly allowed him to turn up and be himself. Though Kristofferson looked the part, Pierson was said to have bowed to pressure from the producers to "make it tougher", so Kris' pumped-up antics, though based on rock-star realities, often seemed clunky and exaggerated.

He was reasonably convincing strutting the stage during the set-piece gigs early in the film – and the large audience (around 40–50,000 people) at the stadium gig provided more authentic passion than mere extras ever could (they were watching a specially laid-on free concert in Phoenix, Arizona, featuring artists such as Peter Frampton and Santana). The scene where Kristofferson rode a motorbike onto the stage might have been a great deal more spectacular, since there was talk of hiring Evel Knievel to deliver a far more sophisticated stunt.

Kristofferson delivers his short lines in a druggy drawl bearing a passing resemblance to John Wayne. Near the start of the film, when his limousine driver asks him where he wants to go, he says, "Back about 10 years." To Kristofferson's consternation, Streisand insisted on live vocals in all close-up singing scenes in order to avoid the pitfalls of dodgy lip synching. He put a lot of obvious effort into rising above his laid-back, rough-round-the-edges style in an attempt to sound like a fully fledged gutsy rock singer – with partial success.

While Streisand acted and sang with great skill in the scene when the film's signature song, 'Evergreen', was being recorded in the studio, Kristofferson's feeble additions as he fawns over her are an embarrassment, and the contrast makes the whole scene unrealistic. Similarly, towards the end of the film, after his character dies, it's hard for the viewer to be convinced by Streisand's tears as she listens to a tape of Kristofferson's rudimentary singing.

When John Norman provides that eureka moment when Esther tries unsuccessfully to find the inspiration for a new song, Kristofferson must surely have smiled inwardly at the irony of the situation. A few little musical suggestions and in seconds, a classic song, backed by sophisticated musical accompaniment emerges out of the ether. Pure Hollywood. What a contrast to the cold, hard realities of Tootsie's Orchid Lounge and the guitar pulls with Mickey Newbury and other hard-up songwriters, when they spent hours trying to tease out a few good melodies and lyrics from the dross.

There were considerable tensions on the set during the making of the film. As "executive producer", Streisand frequently clashed with Pierson and for some scenes, she effectively appointed herself *de facto* director with the heavy support of Peters. In a magazine piece published shortly before the film was released, Pierson did not mince his words about what a horrible experience it was working on *A Star Is Born* and that he had not felt so tired since WWII. He painted Streisand as egocentric, manipulative, argumentative and controlling, constantly dissatisfied with numerous aspects of the film, demanding numerous rewrites, and having no hesitation in getting rid of bit part actors without consulting him. Obsessive concerns over her appearance meant that she was anxious to be filmed on the "right side", but Pierson was unable to see any difference between either of her profiles, reckoning it was all in her mind.

Streisand considered Pierson's article a betrayal and attempted to play it down by saying that there were invariably tensions on film sets. Not surprisingly they never worked together again.

Although much of the vitriol in Pierson's article was directed at Streisand and Peters, his comments about Kristofferson were also barbed. "It's the old story – a short-haired, clean-thinking patriotic helicopter pilot, split open by booze, sex and music to release a free spirit." He recalled listening to one of Kristofferson's songs, in which he was "croaking like a man living on too much whisky and not enough self-assurance." During one heated exchange, Kris complained that he thought they would be making some true indictment about the rock music world but instead, "We're making a Barbra Streisand lollipop extravaganza."

The director was aware of how much Kristofferson identified with aspects of the character because he kept on saying, "Somebody's been reading my mail," reprising a line from 'To Beat The Devil' on his debut album. Pierson angrily referred to Kristofferson as, "An asshole who crawls into a bottle."

There was also aggravation between Kristofferson and Peters, which may have owed something to the former's previous relationship with Streisand. It was reported that Kristofferson had to wear flesh-coloured shorts for the scene where he and Streisand take a bath together, as she was worried about Peters' reaction if Kris was totally naked. A bitter exchange between Kristofferson and Peters was accidentally captured when Streisand forgot that she was miked up. Peters threatened "to beat the shit" out of Kristofferson, who responded, "Listen if I want any shit out of you, I'll squeeze your head."

Peters complained about Kristofferson and his band; he was looking for something nearer the harder-edged sound of Bruce Springsteen and The E Street Band. Kris was furious. "Who shall I say says my music isn't rock –

Barbra Streisand's hairdresser?" Peters screamed back, "It's shit, I don't care who says it." Pierson believed that Kristofferson disliked the music he was required to perform and worried what someone like Bob Dylan would think of it.

The starring actors also had their difficulties, with Streisand feeling that Kristofferson did not behave in a professional manner consistent with his star status. In order to act drunk, he got drunk. She was unimpressed at the way his band talked back to him like an equal in a way that she saw as rude. Characteristically, Kristofferson put her straight. "They ain't sidemen, that's my band."

On another occasion, the two were heard having a heated argument because one of her rehearsals overran leaving little time for him to rehearse. Sometimes when scenes featuring the two did not go well, he would blame himself and apologise for not giving her what she needed. Streisand saw this as a kind of arrogance and expressed astonishment to Pierson that Kristofferson somehow felt that what he did was capable of affecting her performance. When it came to making final cuts to the film, Streisand removed quite a few of Kristofferson's scenes – which were, to his chagrin, the ones that helped to explain and develop his character.

Kristofferson's guitarist, Stephen Bruton, described the scene on the set as "a new crisis every day". Interviewed some years later, he particularly recalled the heavy drinking culture with nightly visits to a bar called Mr Luck's. On one occasion, when he and actor Gary Busey were watching television in a hotel room, Kristofferson was lying between two beds completely out of it. People were looking for him and the phone kept on ringing. Eventually Peters called personally – but neither Bruton nor Busey let on that Kristofferson was with them. The next day, Streisand was really annoyed that she had not been able to get hold of Kristofferson, saying she wished she had security as effective as his.

There were lighter moments among the angry spats. In one scene, the two sat on a piano stool as a romantic interlude developed. Kristofferson was supposed to pick Streisand up and spirit her away to the bedroom. In a shot the public never saw, as he struggled to hoist her while sitting down, he accidentally scraped her feet along the top of the piano, sending ashtrays, glasses and other objects flying.

After the film was completed, Kristofferson later said that making *A Star*

*Is Born* "was the hardest thing I'd been through since Ranger School". In general though, his public comments about working with Streisand have been diplomatic. He conceded she was one of the hardest people to work with he had ever known, but "I'd say she's a mighty good sport to sing with somebody that sings like me . . . it's such a mixed feeling. It was definitely a challenge . . . the results were the way that she wanted them and I came out of it with a great deal of respect for her creative abilities . . . she believed in me more than I did."

Streisand brushed aside suggestions of strains between them, saying coyly that he was cuter than Elvis and had a wonderful face. She also said, "He's very honest, you can't fake it with him. He's frightened a lot of the time but it works for the role. There is a gentle craziness to him." The pair did not work together again nor indeed get together socially. Barbra moved in the most elevated of West Coast society circles while Kristofferson was generally happiest being around music people.

It was astonishing that Kristofferson was able to work with his heavy drinking habit – excessive for 20 years but which had gradually moved to new and dangerous levels. He appeared to be oblivious to the dangers to his health – or was perhaps burying his head in the sand. As he told *Woman* magazine, "I don't know how I didn't kill myself driving home every day stone drunk. We started at 6 a.m. and I'd have a pint of tequila first. By the end of the day, I'd usually got through a bottle and a half and maybe a case or two of beer . . . and I thought I was doing fine."

He drank more than ever during the making of *A Star Is Born* – it was reportedly written into his contract that a plentiful supply of alcohol be on hand at all times. "I had a half-gallon of Jose Cuervo in my trailer and they never let it empty," he told the *Guardian* in March 2008. "They just kept coming back in and filling it up, same half-gallon bottle." For all that, Kristofferson recognised that his drinking made him a liability and that complaints made about him by Peters and others were often legitimate. "I'd have fired myself," he later told a journalist. The trouble was alcohol helped him to overcome his inhibitions about performing and also to deal with the stresses and strains of constantly being on public show.

Even though he was still able to function as an actor he was a nightmare as a husband. Rita had a small part in the film, presenting Esther with a Grammy award where events are overshadowed by John Norman's drunken shenanigans. It was a case of art imitating life that must have been upsetting and poignant for her. By this stage the marriage was in real trouble, with fatherhood having done little to persuade Kristofferson to rein back on the wild side of life.

Kris knew that if he did not get his drinking under control his life expectancy might be measurable in years rather than decades.

# Chapter 15

A *Star Is Born* opened to a predominantly poor critical reception – several reviewers complained that quite apart from its dubious quality, it was, at 140 minutes, too long. "70 mm screens have been filled with some vacuous stuff in their time," said one reviewer, "but this monstrous remake takes the biscuit. It's set in the rock world, but the kind of rock these people peddle is the softest thing next to jelly . . . Pierson just lets it hang out, uncoordinated and ridiculous."

Kristofferson received mixed notices for his portrayal of John Norman's chaotic and inexorable decline – "He has a nice, unaffected looseness," said one, while another described his acting as "cringe-making".

The most fervent criticism was reserved for Streisand – "A Bore Is Starred" trumpeted the *Village Voice* – with a widespread view that the film was simply a misguided ego trip – "a filmed Streisand concert set against a soggy soap opera" as one journalist described it.

Despite the critical panning, the film was a box-office hit, ultimately grossing around $70 million worldwide. 'Evergreen' became one of the biggest hits of Streisand's career, holding the top spot in the *Billboard* chart for three weeks. The soundtrack topped the *Billboard* pop chart and held its own commercially against the most successful rock albums of the day including *Rumours* by Fleetwood Mac, *Hotel California* by the Eagles and *Animals* by Pink Floyd. Kristofferson was not called upon to make any contribution; the producers played safe by using a range of commercial writers including Kenny Loggins, Leon Russell, Donna Weiss, Paul Williams, Kenny Ascher and Streisand herself. The choices reflected her taste and left no room for Kristofferson's brand of intellectually crafted material. Even the harder-edged rock music was loaded with clichés.

The immense effort, financial and otherwise, that went into making *A Star Is Born* reaped recognition in the form of a number of awards. However, though nominated for four Oscars, it took only one – Best Original Song for 'Evergreen' (aka 'Love Theme From *A Star Is Born*').

The song also took two Grammies. The film fared better at the Golden Globes where it won Best Motion Picture – Musical or Comedy, Best Actress – Motion Picture Musical or Comedy, Best Original Score and Best Original Song (for 'Evergreen'); and in what would prove to be a rare accolade in his movie career, Kristofferson won Best Actor – Motion Picture Musical or Comedy. When subsequently given the job of co-hosting the *Billboard* Number One Music Awards along with The Bee Gees, one of the duties that fell to him was to accept on Streisand's behalf the award for top easy-listening artist.

*A Star Is Born* provided Kristofferson with a spectacular opening in the film industry. It was clear that he was no De Niro or Pacino and that while he'd established an acting brand of sorts, which would allow him to carve out a durable niche and bring a moderately powerful screen presence to a number of character roles, his limitations as an actor meant that he would not find himself in serious contention for any major awards.

Taken together, his appearances in *Playboy* and *A Star Is Born* meant that Kristofferson had become something of a sex symbol – an accolade he was not comfortable with, though it amused him that at 40, he should be able to attract the lust of teenage girls. In December 1976, following a poll of its 2,000 members, Kris made it onto Man Watcher Inc's annual list of the world's "most watchable" men for his "beautiful eyes and body". Other contenders included O. J. Simpson, James Garner and Nick Nolte.

During this time, Kristofferson went to see his doctor and was told that "my liver was the size of a football and that if I didn't quit, I was gonna kill myself". It seems that he was eventually shocked into taking decisive action at some point during, or shortly after, the completion of *A Star Is Born*. When he watched the film back, he found he had no recollection of making some scenes and that his timing and co-ordination were off. He felt too that the similarity between John Norman Howard's decline and his own problems were too close for comfort. Kristofferson was also horri-fied by his appearance on Geraldo Rivera's television talk show. "I saw it stone sober and I saw [*A Star Is Born*] at the same time. I realised it was my life I was seeing on the screen, a rock'n'roll star ruining himself drinking. I quit in September and I'll never touch it again."

Kris concluded that his drinking and drugging exacerbated the depression he was prone to, as he told one interviewer, "You need to get over some bad feeling to try to get to feel better." In several interviews around this time, Kristofferson stopped lightly referring to his heavy drinking and started describing himself as someone with a serious drink problem who, using the language of Alcoholics Anonymous, took one day at a time – which may have been indicative of a turning point. "I felt I was seeing myself through Rita's eyes for the first time . . . it was as if I was getting a second chance."

For years, he had deluded himself into thinking that he was coping – never thinking it would get to the point where having to quit would become an issue. It was fortunate that Kristofferson called a halt when he did; there really was a risk that he might have joined a long list of musical casualties. It was good luck as much as anything else that saved him from joining their ranks.

Apart from his grossly excessive consumption of alcohol, Kristofferson also confirmed that he'd experimented with LSD. On the other hand he claimed that in the mid-Seventies he was the only actor in Hollywood who didn't know how to roll a joint and that he was totally against heroin; taking it, he said, was a "death trip". This inconsistency allowed him to have strong views about the dangers of a particular substance while, at the same time, indulging in others.

Speaking later about going "cold turkey", he said, "It was probably harder on the people around me than on myself."

Once *A Star Is Born* was completed, Kristofferson went back out on the road for a 30-plus city tour accompanied by Coolidge, who had taken a six-month break after Casey was born before returning to the stage. Rarely able to spend any concentrated time at home as a result of his increased fame, Kristofferson said in 1977, "I knew I'd made it when I had a stranger training my dog for eight months."

While Kris' mainstream status helped to fill the large venues he was now regularly booked into, the tour got off to an inauspicious start. During opening night at Los Angeles' Universal Amphitheatre, there were problems with the sound and some of the instruments. Reviewers spoke of Kristofferson's lethargy onstage but the problems were ironed out and subsequent dates earned generally favourable comment.

Kristofferson continued to get his face onto various late-Seventies television variety shows. Rita joined him on Donny and Marie Osmond's primetime showcase; Kris duetted with Marie on 'You'll Never Find Another Love Like This' while fellow guests included the robots from *Star*

*Wars.* The couple were also the hosts for an episode each of *The Muppet Show* and *Saturday Night Live*. For the latter, they spoofed 'Help Me Make It Through The Night'. As Kris sang the song, Rita and Chevy Chase started to act out the lyrics but Rita couldn't take the ribbon from her hair.*

A further indication of Kristofferson's standing and the value of his song catalogue came when he met Frances Preston, president of royalty collection agent BMI (Broadcast Music Inc) in Chicago along with his music publisher and manager. The meeting had been arranged to discuss the renewal of Kristofferson's contract. Right at the start of the meeting, Preston played her card, stating that she would be prepared to offer a million dollars for him to stay with BMI. Kristofferson was overwhelmed by the offer, agreed the deal and asked where he should sign. His advisors were less than happy; they believed they might have been able to secure an even better deal if they had been given the opportunity to negotiate. Then again for Kristofferson, money was never the prime motivator.

In 1976, the so-called outlaw movement in country music emerged into national prominence, finding the most obvious manifestation in that year's *Wanted: The Outlaws* by Willie Nelson, Waylon Jennings, Tompall Glaser and Jessi Colter – the first country album to sell a million copies. The "movement" had actually been gaining momentum for some time at grass-roots level with increasing numbers abandoning the soft "Nashville Sound", which had emasculated the raw honky-tonk of earlier country music from, and inspired by, the likes of Hank Williams and George Jones. In a broader sense, it could be regarded as applying to any artist who did not go along with the Music Row establishment. As Jennings put it, "We were rebels but we did not want to dismantle the system – we just wanted our own patch."

In 1973, Hazel Smith was helping to promote Jennings and Glaser, whose music was becoming increasingly popular – though was still resisted by some country stations for being too "progressive". DJs who did play the music wanted a handle for it. Smith was aware of the song 'Ladies

---

* A similar idea was used by Ray Stevens' parody in 1992 – after the opening line, "Take the ribbon from your hair", there were the exaggerated sounds of material ripping and a woman screaming.

Love Outlaws', written by Lee Clayton and performed by Jennings in 1972. "We were trying to figure out what to call it, we thought of a lot of names. One day I reached under my desk and pulled out a dictionary. I looked up the word outlaw and it said, 'living on the outside of the written law', and I thought that was the closest thing I was ever going to find. They wanted their music on the records to sound like it did in concert. The name caught on. Chet Flippo at *Rolling Stone* helped to spread the word."

The writer Aaron Fox sought to put the Seventies outlaw movement into historical context, making the point that something similar had always existed in popular music in the southern USA. It was concerned with the fundamental tension between law and order authoritarianism and the image of "outlaw" authenticity that had structured country's presentation of masculinity since the days of Jimmie Rodgers in the Thirties.

There has been much debate as to who the true founder was. The truth is that no one artist can claim to have been the sole initiator – the loose, rough-edged music evolved over several years with artists trying out new sounds and new sartorial trends with a lot of cross-fertilisation along the way. Kristofferson believes that Willie Nelson can take most of the credit though Bob Dylan, too, could claim to have had some guiding influence.

Nelson's music moved closer to the rock ethos and his appearance – long hair, beard and jeans ("like a country boy who had not been to town", as Hazel Smith put it) was far away from the traditional appearance of country stars in their Nudie suits and smart bouffants, and of course, he enjoyed a high profile due to his commercial success.

However, there can be little doubt that Kristofferson (and the spirit of Johnny Cash) helped to influence its course. Kristofferson's appearance at the 1970 CMA awards had sent shock waves through the establishment.

As his hair and beard grew longer, his clothes more casual, his onstage demeanour less respectful and more rebellious, his chemical ingestion more intense, it could have been the prototype for the outlaw manifesto, as one commentator put it: "Kris Kristofferson led the charge; he was perfect for the role a half decade before the movement officially began. He was a long-haired dishevelled guy in jeans and scruffy work shirts writing groundbreaking lyrics that related to old and young, rich and poor, to diehard country conservatives and shaggy headed rock'n'roll liberals . . . by his actions, and the flak he took, he paved the way for later artists drawn to the same course."

A self-effacing Kristofferson tended to play down his role. "We could have a whole bunch of discussions as to whether I instigated it . . . who came first. I was a fan of Willie Nelson's long before anybody had ever heard of me . . . I didn't feel that I started the outlaw movement or anything."*

One of the ironies was that as the outlaw movement suddenly became popular, its leading artists won a number of awards from mainstream establishment organisations, prompting Waylon Jennings' deflating 'Don't You Think This Outlaw Bit's Done Got Out Of Hand.'

*A Star Is Born* not only mirrored some of the less savoury aspects of Kristofferson's personal life but it also uncannily reflected his and Coolidge's respective fortunes in terms of record sales. Although Kris was still a considerable draw for live shows, his albums were not selling at all well – due, in his view, to them not gaining radio play, more likely because they were not good enough. Rita's smooth MOR-oriented albums on the other hand were hitting the commercial heights – her 1977 album of covers, *Anytime . . . Anywhere*, eventually gained platinum status.

Being divergent in several directions, Kristofferson's career was hard to categorise, as writer Bill Friskics-Warren observed in 2006, "Kris Kristofferson had become a strange mélange of Hollywood beefcake/millionaire, hipster Renaissance man, and poet laureate of country music."

Though record sales had declined dramatically, Monument and Columbia continued to support the release of Kristofferson's albums. 1976 saw the release of *Surreal Thing*, a collection of Kristofferson originals. The number of backing musicians was stripped down to a quorum of four – guitars, keyboards, drums and bass. Mike Utley once more enriched proceedings with colour and variety while bassist Lee Sklar anchored the sound with simple solidity. In contrast, the album featured no less than 12 backing singers including Coolidge, Billy Swan and Gary Busey. Evidently this posse of fellow travellers helped to ensure a non-stop party atmosphere

---

* Kristofferson had lent support to Billy Joe Shaver – a musician who could certainly claim outlaw status, even though he did not enjoy commercial success – producing his critically acclaimed *Old Five And Dimers Like Me* album in 1973.

in the studio, which failed to transfer to the listener as the album was a fairly undistinguished affair. It wasn't that the songs were substandard, rather that they were, in the main, competent and ultimately forgettable with uninspired melodies.

The most probable explanation was that Kristofferson was again being asked to churn out too many songs in too short a time – it was under a year since his last album and a great deal of his time and creative effort was being expended on his movie career. Kris had expressed concern that his writing might suffer as a result of his involvement in the film industry as had happened in the case of Roger Miller. He worried that his melodies were all starting to sound similar and that his well of inspiration might run dry, as he admitted, "When I try to force it I get myself in such binds."

For *Surreal Thing*, he even resorted to re-recording new versions of 'The Golden Idol' and 'Killing Time' – each getting on for a decade old – rather than searching for good material by other writers, although the album contained a couple of agreeable country ballads, 'It's Never Gonna Be The Same Again' and 'Bad Love Story'.

Kristofferson was in jocular mood when describing the joys of a new relationship in the album's risqué opener, 'You Show Me Yours (And I'll Show You Mine)'. For the throwaway 'If You Don't Like Hank Williams', he reeled off the names of an eclectic bunch of artists who'd inspired him, making the point that, unlike some of his more conservative critics, he could appreciate a wide range of popular music and still have the utmost respect for country's most famous son. As with so much of Kristofferson's catalogue, it was another artist who brought out the best in the song – in this case, appropriately enough, Hank Williams Jr with his rollicking, reworked interpretation.

Kris' mood turned bitter for 'Eddie The Eunuch', a diatribe against certain snide elements in the press who he believed had it in for him.

Kris gave this and several other songs, including 'The Golden Idol,' a rock'n'roll treatment, but his vocals sounded more like a stressed foghorn than ever. While it was common knowledge that his voice was secondary to his songwriting, this album again confirmed the point, though of course when the songs were great, much was forgiven. The reality was that his newer material, however worthy, was simply nowhere near as good as his earlier classics and reviewers and punters could tell the difference.

*Surreal Thing* briefly made the country Top 10 but failed to enter the pop charts. 'It's Never Gonna Be The Same Again' was released as a single but disappeared without trace. In the face of negative reviews, Kristofferson complained that critics wanted him to keep turning out songs like 'For The Good Times' and 'Help Me Make It Through The Night' whereas he wanted to develop new directions.

The production of his Seventies albums suggested that those in control were not quite sure what to do with this unusual and idiosyncratic talent, and continually filled tracks up with new sounds – vocal and instrumental – in an attempt to inject life into the project. It was a similar story in record outlets where retailers were unsure as to where to rack his albums. Kristofferson's producer seemed to overlook the fact that Kris was at his strongest when simply putting his songs over solo, accompanied by his own unpolished guitar playing and minimal backing. Though things were moving in this direction, it would be years before the lesson would eventually be learnt – to telling effect.

It was ironic that at a time when Kristofferson's recording career was at a nadir, he received a major honour in recognition of his earlier outstanding work. In October 1977, he, along with Woody Guthrie, Merle Haggard and Johnny Cash, were inducted into the Nashville Songwriters Association International's Hall of Fame. Each artist received a "Manny" (short for "manuscript"), a bronze cast of a hand holding a quill pen. Though Cash and Haggard were present to receive their awards, Bob Beckham accepted the award on Kristofferson's behalf as he was out-of-town in New Orleans for the premiere of yet another movie: *Semi-Tough*, a light-hearted affair, in which he starred alongside Burt Reynolds and Jill Clayburgh.

The film contained a mixture of romance, comedy and sport while also satirising new religions, self-improvement gurus and quackish health remedies. Kristofferson (Marvin "Shake" Tiller) and Reynolds (Billy Clyde "BC" Puckett) play American football players who fall for the same woman – their coach's daughter, Barbara Jane (Clayburgh). Shake falls under the influence of cult leader Friedrich Bismark (played by Bert Convy) and his B.E.A.T self-help movement.* Shake attends one of

---

* This was a thinly disguised reference to Werner Erhard and his creation, est (Erhard Seminars Training), one of many "personal growth" organisations springing up in the Seventies, and which, depending on one's view, was part of a new age of enlightenment or a vacuous money-making scheme.

Bismark's courses; his personal confidence grows and he makes romantic progress with Barbara Jane, who enrols with B.E.A.T in a vain attempt to get on Shake's level. BC also takes the training in order to impress her. He eventually exposes the practice when Barbara Jane is about to marry Shake, and they admit their feelings for each other.

As part of their preparation for the film, Kristofferson and Reynolds trained together in order to look the part – not a problem for Kristofferson given his past sporting success. Filming was interrupted briefly when he cracked three ribs and broke a finger after an accident during one of the action scenes.

*Semi-Tough* was a moderate commercial success, attracting divided reviews though most singled out the satirical element for approval; one reviewer describing it as "without a doubt the year's most socially useful film". Kristofferson was reasonably convincing in his sporting and romantic role; one critic said he was good as a comic foil and another that his performance was "excellent". As with *The Sailor Who Fell From Grace With The Sea*, Kris demonstrated that he was prepared to take on roles far removed from stereotypical cowboys and hippy musicians.


Towards the end of 1977, Kris and Rita visited Nashville in a blaze of publicity – the first time they had spent any significant time there for four years. Kristofferson was now treated as a returning hero, with the press bandying around such words as "superstar", "old friend", "musical favourite son" and a "new Nashville legend". Success had a way of spurring selective memory.

There was much comment on Kristofferson's improved appearance, though some local reporters still felt the need to describe him as "bearded". He revealed that he'd lost 20 pounds in three months as a result of "exercise, hard work and no booze". Kris and Rita attended a reception at Monument Records thrown by Fred Foster. Kristofferson, whom many described as friendly but quiet, denied that being in the company of so many people drinking cocktails was a problem for him, though he did remark it felt "weird". Johnny Cash was not present but sent a message of support. "It ain't as much fun [not drinking] but you feel a lot better at the end of the day."

The couple's visit culminated in a three-hour concert at the Grand Ole Opry House attended by many fans and music professionals, with guest appearances from Willie Nelson and rising star Johnny Rodriguez. During a break, Kris was presented with a certificate that proclaimed him an "Honorary Citizen of Tennessee".

Security around the pair at the concert was extremely tight – even more so than when Frank Sinatra had appeared at the same venue 18 months previously. "Our privacy has been minimised," Rita told the press. "We can't move around freely like we once did. We want to meet our friends and fans but most of the time that is impossible."

According to some reports, security at their Malibu house included barbed wire fences and patrolling guard dogs. One article went as far as to suggest that limousine drivers were chosen for their ability to make fast getaways.

Before a 1978 show in Atlanta, various managers, musicians and secretaries converged on the city in advance of the couple's arrival. At the airport, the Kristofferson family unit was surrounded by a heavy cordon of security as they supervised the collection of about 40 pieces of personal and professional luggage. Without such measures, there would have been a constant risk of the pair being mobbed by fans. In Tallahassee, Florida, Kris and Rita and their entourage took over the entire 16th floor of the Hilton Hotel, where the management provided 24-hour guards at the exit doors and elevators. This kind of unreal existence was not to Kristofferson's liking but he came to regard it as necessary.

Rita's mother, Charlotte, who regularly travelled on tour as babysitter for Casey, admired her daughter's ability to juggle the roles of wife, mother and performer. She felt that Rita's resilience and serenity had helped to keep the family together in the face of Kris' self-destructive qualities. In some ways, Kris and Rita's marital relationship was quite conventional, as he confirmed in an interview, "Rita is very much a mother much like her own mother – she does all the real work, all the work around the house, all the cooking and anything that takes any responsibility or organisation." This extended to Casey; Kris was an indulgent father and left discipline issues for Rita to deal with.

People continued to try to pitch songs, sometimes showing little courtesy. On one occasion, a backstage interloper insisted on singing a song about his dying mother when Kristofferson was feeling unwell and about to throw up.

The media could also be trying. Although Kris was generous with his time, he was irritated when they homed in on personal areas. On a visit to London in the late Seventies, he did his best to politely respond to intrusive probing about his private life and his drink intake. He said he still allowed himself the odd beer – what he really wanted to cut out was the hard stuff and he felt he'd succeeded. "I wasn't doing anyone any good, least of all me."

Despite the negative impact on his life, he did not see his years of heavy drinking as wasted; he had been highly creative and developed a successful career in music and films – at the very least this could be set against the upset he'd caused in his personal relationships. He conceded that he'd not yet "licked" his drink problem and alluded to a deeper malaise. "I'm not cured but I'm more in control. I'm still not together. I'm still self-destructive, still crazy."

# Chapter 16

AS 1977 ended, Kristofferson was due to play a World War II bomber pilot in *Hanover Street*, to be filmed on location in England. For reasons that remain unclear, he became unhappy and walked off the set – he may simply have been exhausted after working on so many projects – but his public comments displayed a surprising ambivalence to the industry that had already given him so much. "I probably won't ever make another movie and that won't break my heart." Harrison Ford took over while Kris and Rita headed off for a month-long tour of Europe.

Despite the growing disparity in their record sales, it was still understood that when it came to concerts, Kristofferson was the headliner, even though by 1978, Coolidge was probably the bigger draw and without her, it's doubtful they would have been booked into larger venues. The frequent tours – Kris spent about 30 days at home that year – became large and complex logistical operations that generated huge public and media interest. The couple's respective record companies could tell if the number of units sold in a particular city rose after a concert and based return visits on such information, so careful planning was a key element in making sure profits were maximised.

While Kris was well aware of commercially tailoring his set to meet substantial touring costs, he was nonetheless prepared to include material – what he described as his socially oriented songs – that might alienate some of his audience. That said, he was a great deal more sensitive to this than would be the case in later years. "If I can get away with singing some of those songs I'll do it but not at the expense of ruining a mood we [he and Rita] might have created."

Kristofferson's eighth album, *Easter Island*, was released early in 1978. Despite his assertion on the sleeve, "I'm proud of this one . . . I think we're getting there boys," it was another largely unmemorable piece of work, although a slight improvement on his last few efforts. The same nucleus of musicians provided a loose sound, resembling a live gig at times, and producer David Anderle was kept on a tight rein. However, the laid-back feel, dominated by Kristofferson's off-key hoarseness, tended to wear thin by about halfway through. Kristofferson shared writing duties on the album with Mike Utley and guitarist Stephen Bruton.

The eerie title track, inspired by the famous stone figures on Easter Island, certainly contained some powerfully evocative Kristofferson lyrics but the underlying meaning of the song was frustratingly obscure, reminiscent of 'Silver (The Hunger)' from *Who's To Bless, Who's To Blame*. 'Sabre And The Rose' returned to themes of escape and freedom but the lightness of touch in early Kristofferson songs was nowhere to be found.

Songs such as 'How Do You Feel (About Foolin' Around)' were pleasant but inconsequential. 'Forever In Your Love', a ballad with a catchy melody, found Kris musing on a love ending. As his marriage to Rita sailed closer to the rocks, the song probably provided a glimpse of what he was experiencing. Coolidge's most recent album, *Love Me Again*, had sold in large numbers while Kristofferson remained in the commercial doldrums.

Their last joint collaboration, *Natural Act*, also appeared in '78. If there was any doubt that the relationship was over, Annie Leibovitz's cover picture removed it. Gone were the carefree unkempt lovers pictured on the first two album sleeves and in their place were two separate individuals, wearing smart clothes and strained faces. The pair's expressions spoke of bitter experiences and the end of the affair. The cover shots were apparently taken at different times – Kristofferson has a beard on the front but is clean-shaven on the back. In neither can he raise a smile.

Despite the dour sleeve, the album turned out to be a rather pleasant affair. Leaning more to pop than rock, it featured relaxed southern boogie, nostalgic pop ballads and country-tinged numbers alongside more unusual choices such as a reworking of 'I Fought The Law', a hit for The Bobby Fuller Four in 1966, which found Kris and Rita sounding like The Everly Brothers. Other tracks were by a range of writers including band members Billy Swan and Donnie Fritts.

Two vintage Kristofferson songs were also revived: 'Please Don't Tell Me How The Story Ends' and 'Loving You Was Easier (Than Anything I'll Ever Do Again)' (the original title adapted with the substitution of "her" by "you" to make it suitable as a duet). Given the state of the couple's marriage, some of the tracks must surely have been hard to sing –

for instance, Kristofferson's downbeat 'Love Don't Live Here Anymore'.

*Natural Act* did not match the commercial success of the earlier duet collections, though it was the only one that made a showing in the British charts. Some critics felt that Kristofferson and Coolidge were going through the motions, fulfilling their final contractual obligations. While their singing did not always sparkle and the usual stage and studio musicians were augmented by slick strings and saxophones, the songs were reasonably strong. The album had the added appeal of delivering some kind of personal testimony; it could certainly hold its own against much of the lighter pop material in the charts in the late Seventies.

When assessing the affects of Kristofferson pursuing the Hollywood dream, Hazel Smith took a fairly jaundiced view. "He didn't write any more hit songs after he went to Hollywood; it sucked his songwriting talent right out of him because he became a movie star, a victim of his own dreams I suppose. . . . Sam Peckinpah got all the blood and guts."

In 1978, Kristofferson once again worked with the idiosyncratic director. Based on the worldwide 1976 hit song by C. W. McCall (a successful advertising executive whose real name was Bill Fries), *Convoy* was a light-weight romp whose surprising popularity was explained in part by the then popular CB (Citizen's Band) radio fad.

Both Kristofferson and Peckinpah knew the script was poor. However, the latter needed box-office success after a string of commercial flops and was aware that similarly themed novelty films had raked in large profits. For each, the experience was vastly different from the last occasion they'd shared a film set. Both were fighting to steer clear of drink and drugs and according to most reports, Peckinpah was failing. His poor physical shape meant that James Coburn had to be brought in to take over some direc-torial duties. Peckinpah disliked the screenplay to the extent of encourag-ing the cast to rewrite and even ad-lib their own dialogue. Unfortunately the characters they had to work with were flimsy and shallow, the scenes often contrived, and the actors' struggle to effect any improvement in the screenplay might have made things worse.

A macho male affair in which truckers are portrayed as modern-day cowboys, the plot involved a police posse chasing a convoy of truckers across Arizona and New Mexico after a truck-stop fight, leading to a final showdown at the Mexican border. Though hampered by a rambling and barely coherent storyline, Peckinpah tried to inject some depth in parts; there was a subplot with racial overtones and a broader theme of the extent to which the authorities should be able to interfere in people's lives – issues Kristofferson had strong feelings about.

From early on, the conflict is personal: Rubber Duck (Kristofferson) versus Dirty Lyle Wallace (aka "the Cottonmouth", played by Ernest Borgnine). Rubber Duck reluctantly takes on the leadership mantle and his David ultimately succeeds against the establishment Goliath. Though essentially light-hearted, the violence turns nasty at times, aided by Peckinpah's well-tried use of slow motion. However, set against mildly comedic events, it somehow looks out of place. For all the film's faults, the edge Kristofferson brought to the film was one of its few saving graces; convincing as the unflappable trucker who has built up a reputation for toughness and fairness over the years and now faces his ultimate test of character.

A strangely lifeless, short-haired Ali MacGraw made no impact apart from providing an underdeveloped romantic interest. As one critic remarked, "Kristofferson and MacGraw look like they'd be hard-pressed to strike a spark if they doused each other in lighter fluid and skipped hand-in-hand through a Zippo factory."

It was no surprise to those involved with the movie that the critics were unimpressed, some seeing it as evidence that Peckinpah was a spent force. Despite such verdicts as a "shapeless mess", *Convoy* turned out to be a financial success. While costing around $12 million to make, double the original budget, it earned more than $45 million at the box office – a substantial proportion coming from overseas returns. This, despite the fact that shooting overran by more than a week and the producers had to allow for a month's break while Kristofferson, by prior agreement, headed off on tour.*

For all of Peckinpah's faults, Kristofferson admired the director and during the making of *Convoy*, he did his best to support him in the face of criticism from some of the film company bosses. However, on one occasion this backfired. At a crisis meeting, where it seemed possible that Peckinpah might be fired, Kris promptly stood up and said that if Sam was fired, he would quit the film. "I guess I was hot enough then that they

---

* It was also written into Kristofferson's contract that he had every other weekend free to fulfill recording and performing commitments.

gave a shit. Afterwards I'm walking back to my truck and Peckinpah comes out and says, 'Goddamn you, you stupid sonofabitch – I was almost out of here and you dropped me back in this shit!' "*

In January 1979, Kristofferson and Coolidge appeared in the Music For UNICEF (United Nations Children's Fund) Concert: A Gift Of Song, which kicked off the International Year of the Child, at the UN's General Assembly Hall. Kris looked out of place among some of the leading mainstream stars of the day, including Rod Stewart, The Bee Gees, Abba, Donna Summer and Earth, Wind and Fire, who had been assembled for the occasion by David Frost and Robert Stigwood.

The concert was recorded and an album released – the artists agreed to donate their performance royalties and those from one song each – with Kris and Rita's contribution being 'Fallen Angel', a song from Kristofferson's upcoming album, *Shake Hands With The Devil*. The lyrics were presumably inspired by the terminal state of his marriage.

The UNICEF benefit marked Kristofferson and Coolidge's last concert together. "It was impossible," Kris said later of the paradoxical situation. "It was one of the strangest things in the world to be getting up and singing love songs with somebody who wants to blow your brains out." Despite this brusque observation, there was still a genuine bond of affection between the couple but it was nonetheless a great shock to him when Rita finally walked out. "I'll be honest with you, I didn't want it . . . I was pretty heavily surprised . . . it takes some getting over."

Later in the year, the press formally announced the couple's separation. Kristofferson blamed the break-up on the stress and strain caused by two careers in one marriage but avoided going into detail. He later denied that the 1976 *Playboy* photoshoot with Sarah Miles had been the reason for the marriage failing – saying that it had simply "run its course". This was probably true but only in the sense that the Miles episode was one of many incidents that led Coolidge to the realisation that Kristofferson was incapable of being a reliable husband at this time in his life. (She wrote and

---

* Sam Peckinpah made just one more film before his death in 1984 at the age of 59. At his funeral, Kristofferson spoke out against the film executives who failed to support the director during his career. In 2006, one of Peckinpah's classics, *The Wild Bunch*, was re-released as a double DVD set, which included an in-depth documentary that Kristofferson narrated.

recorded the self-explanatory 'I'd Rather Leave While I'm In Love' for her next album, *Satisfied*.)

The remarkable success Kristofferson achieved in the music and movie world ensured that temptation came his way on a regular basis. Marriage and fatherhood did little to curb his behaviour. As Willie Nelson said, "I can out-party Waylon, but Kris, he makes it a religion."

Interviewed recently, Coolidge said she walked away from the marriage for reasons of "self-survival . . . I felt I could raise my daughter in a better way". Though she and Kris now get on very well, and have done for years, Coolidge later provided a glimpse of what she endured during their brief marriage. "He was a very toxic human being with his drinking and his womanising. I couldn't keep him at home. I can't say enough about what a great man he is. It's just that he was a shitty husband."

If Kristofferson was determined to continue in the limelight, he also made a conscious decision to be more involved in the care and upbringing of his children. In November, he raised divorce proceedings in Los Angeles, seeking joint custody of five-year-old Casey, and it seems that an acceptable arrangement was arrived at whereby each parent made a substantial contribution to their daughter's care. "We're working it out," Kris told a reporter. "I can see her as much as I want to and so can Rita. I have a governess who gets along great with her so it works out when I'm on the road. Of course Rita's on the road too." For the next few years, Kristofferson delighted in telling interviewers that he was a "bachelor daddy" and that looking after Casey had helped to "ground" him.

His next film project – an NBC television mini-series called *Freedom Road* – offered him the chance to work with one of his heroes, Muhammad Ali. It was not long since Ali had defeated Leon Spinks to win the world heavyweight crown for an unprecedented third time. Based on a novel by Howard Fast set in the turbulent years following the end of the Civil War, *Freedom Road* told the story of Gideon Jackson, recently freed from slavery, who entered politics to pursue the goal of securing black civil rights and, against the odds, becomes a senator. Kristofferson played the part of Abner Lait, a poor sharecropper.

Hounded by fans at his hotel, Kristofferson accepted an offer to move into a secluded house that Ali was renting. By now an experienced actor with considerable knowledge of the movie-making process, Kris acted as an informal coach and mentor, as he explained, "The range [Ali's] covering goes from an illiterate slave to a senator who's dealing with Ulysses S. Grant. Also, he's going from playing to a huge audience down to a camera that doesn't miss anything. His acting method has always been exaggeration. Now he's got to learn a much subtler approach."

Kristofferson found himself on the receiving end of Ali's playful sense of humour. On one occasion, while Kris was having his hair cut outside his trailer, Ali surreptitiously gathered up the locks before handing them out, amid great fanfare, to a group of teenage fans – to Kristofferson's great embarrassment. On another occasion at the house, Ali dialled a number. "Kris! Kris! I got somebody here I want you to talk to." On the other end of the line was the renowned English actor Christopher Lee. Taken aback, Kristofferson mumbled a few pleasantries. "Hey, great to meet you, over the phone even." Ali grabbed the receiver back and said to Lee, "You've got Kris Kristofferson blushing!"

Though he received some praise for his sincerity, critics generally didn't rate Ali's acting ability – hardly surprising since he had only previously been in *The Greatest*, the celluloid version of his life story.

"Muhammad is an amazing man," said Kristofferson. "In some ways, he's as simple as a child. But in other ways he's inscrutable. Like a sphinx. It's funny, he'll sit out there lookin' like nothing's happening, like he's between rounds waiting for the bell. But once that camera starts to roll, he comes to life. And once he hears the rhythm of a line, he doesn't forget it." But even Kris was not convinced that acting was for the world heavy-weight – he hated the interminable waiting around and had countless other interests and offers more to his liking.

Kristofferson's latest effort, *Shake Hands With The Devil*, appeared in 1979. The advertising tag – "Lovin' always raises a little bit of Hell" – proved to be an empty promise. The overriding impression was of another lacklustre collection thrown together without a great deal of forethought or planning. From the opening title track, it was clear that even by his unorthodox standards, Kristofferson was on worse vocal form than usual; often well off-key and with poor phrasing and timing, he exhibited less ability than the average club singer or karaoke hopeful.

In the Seventies, there was an unusual degree of loyalty shown towards Kristofferson. (In the modern commercial climate, an artist will only receive continued support from a record company if ongoing sales are strong.) Of course, his movie-star status was helpful in persuading

Monument and Columbia to stick by a contract that called for 10 albums (*Shake Hands With The Devil* being the ninth). However, it's somewhat surprising that there was no insistence on trying out a different producer, the usual course when a formula has become stale and is producing unsatisfactory results.

With David Anderle once again behind the controls and the same nucleus of musicians, even though some different styles were tried out – a Caribbean feel here, some Tex-Mex there – the results were unremittingly monotonous. It was also obvious that most of the songs weren't fresh – another indication that Kristofferson's filming commitments left him insufficient time to write. 'Come Sundown', 'Once More With Feeling' and the title track were all from 1970; 'Michoacan' was featured in 1971's *Cisco Pike*; Tom Ghent's 'Whiskey, Whiskey' had featured in Kris' live shows since around 1972; 'Seadream' came from *The Sailor Who Fell From Grace With The Sea*, while several others were co-writes.

The only entirely new Kristofferson song was 'Prove It To You One More Time Again', a simple ballad that worked well enough, while 'Killer Barracuda' – which, if taken personally, seemed to express remorse for his heartbreaking ways – had an edgy rhythm and menacing feel.

*Shake Hands With The Devil* turned out to be the first of Kristofferson's albums that failed to make the charts, although 'Prove It To You One More Time Again' scraped into the lower reaches of the country singles charts. The same collection of songs in the hands of a great singer could have made for a perfectly adequate album. Indeed, in contrast to Kristofferson's version of 'Once More With Feeling', unnecessarily embellished with Dixieland-style brass, Jerry Lee Lewis's straightforward country version was a certified classic.

By the end of the Seventies, few would have predicted that Kristofferson's film career would turn out to be far more commercially rewarding than the increasingly leaden albums he was turning out. While by no means among the elite division, he had established himself as a character actor whose screen presence, though prone to woodenness, was capable of adding to a diverse range of movies. However, in 1979 Kris began work on a project that turned out to be a disaster on such a monumental scale that it threatened to derail his film career completely.

Michael Cimino had originally tried to persuade United Artists to accept his script for *The Johnson County War* in 1971 but a lack of interest from big name actors meant the project failed to get off the ground. Cimino had better luck after winning two Oscars (Best Director and Best Picture) for *The Deer Hunter* in 1978, by which time the title of his proposed film had changed to *Heaven's Gate*. Perhaps carried away by the plaudits that rained on *The Deer Hunter*, Cimino sought full and free rein on his pet project. United Artists gave him his head and pegged an initial budget of about $11 million.

Kristofferson was given the starring role (partly because at $850,000, plus 10 per cent of the profits, he was cheaper than other big names) in a cast including Christopher Walken, John Hurt, Isabelle Huppert, Jeff Bridges and Joseph Cotten – in his penultimate screen performance.

*Heaven's Gate* was loosely based on a range war in late-19th century Wyoming between wealthy land owners and small farmers (European immigrants in the film). In an introductory section lasting around 25 minutes that bears little relevance to the main story, Kristofferson's character, James Averill – one of a number of idealistic young men with hopes of civilising a nation – is introduced at a Harvard graduation ceremony in 1870. The action then moves forward by 20 years to where Averill is now a Wyoming lawman. He receives word of a government-supported plot by the wealthy Stock Grower's Association to hire gunmen to kill 125 immigrants they have labelled anarchists and criminals. The Association wants to get rid of them because of the threat they pose to their expansionist plans.

What then follows – for over five hours in the original cut – is the unfolding of the plot punctuated by scenes from the lives of the immigrants. There is also a bizarre love triangle involving Averill, Nate Champion, a mercenary hired by the Association (played by Walken), and Ella, the madame of the local bordello (Huppert in a remarkable piece of miscasting). The film culminated in an extremely lengthy battle between the gunmen and the immigrants with the former eventually being saved by the US Cavalry. The movie's final baffling scene set years later features an affluent-looking Averill on board a luxury steamboat with a beautiful woman; the only dialogue concerning the woman's desire for a cigarette.

Shot mainly in Montana, *Heaven's Gate* benefited from some stunning photography, lavish sets that impressively recreated the period, and a rich musical soundtrack. However, when eventually released – overlong, over schedule, and nearly $30 million over budget – most comment was reserved for its many faults. The dialogue was often inept and amateurish – when it could be heard; Cimino's fixation with creating a truly genuine experience of, for example, the noisy bustle of city life in *fin de siècle* Wyoming meant that some dialogue was virtually inaudible.

Characterisation lacked subtlety: the Association men were painted bad with no redeeming qualities, while the immigrant farmers were generally portrayed in a favourable light with a few easily overlooked faults. Some of the set pieces looked out of place and would have been more appropriate in a major musical. In one such scene, Kristofferson and Huppert ride around the centre of town in a pony and trap like Roman charioteers, to the delight of the assembled townsfolk.

Although the storyline was fairly obvious, the significance of many individual scenes was unclear – it was as if Cimino was intentionally trying to obfuscate. Long pauses, intended to be meaningful, perhaps in the style of Ingmar Bergman, were either self-conscious or simply annoying. The phrase that continually comes to mind when watching *Heaven's Gate* is self-indulgent.

Originally intended for release in December 1979, hold-ups in production meant *Heaven's Gate* was not released until almost a year later. The delays directly affected Kristofferson, who had to cancel a 44-date US tour. He had other difficulties during the production, as Ronnie Hawkins, who had a small part in the film, recalls, "Rita had lawyers up there suing him – so he had to have meetings regarding all that stuff as well as all the other stuff that was going wrong in his life."

The critics, anticipating something spectacular in view of the quality of *The Deer Hunter*, were unrelentingly scathing. *New York Times* critic Vincent Canby called the movie "an unqualified disaster", comparing it to "a forced four-hour walking tour of one's own living room . . . it fails so completely that you might suspect Mr Cimino sold his soul to obtain the success of *The Deer Hunter* and the Devil has just come around to collect."

Roger Ebert opined, "It is the most scandalous cinematic waste I have ever seen . . . a study in wretched excess," while James Kendrick considered the film "an uneven, elaborate, sprawling set piece that highlighted [Cimino's] obsession with detail and his tendency to go overboard . . . the movie flounders and eventually collapses under its own weight . . . a shapeless mess." He was also far from impressed by Cimino's technical skills. "He fills every available scene with huge clouds of steam and so much dust that it is almost impossible to decipher the action. This is at its worst during the supposedly climactic battle between the Association and the immigrants, a scene that is so ineptly directed, photographed, and edited that it is almost laughable."

Kristofferson's performance received some praise but mainly of the faint variety. "A solid if not terribly nuanced actor . . . as James Averill he is appropriately stoic, but lacks layers," said one reviewer. In a barb that was partly aimed at Cimino, another wrote, "Kris Kristofferson is never allowed to generate enough character for us to miss him, should he disappear."

The head of United Artists, Stephen Bach, tried to talk up the film and its star in particular, ludicrously claiming that at moments Kristofferson "recalled Gary Cooper". The reaction to the film was extreme enough for it to be withdrawn after a few days. After six months, it resurfaced with over an hour excised (the editing process alone was said to have cost $1 million). However, the severe cuts only highlighted the film's failings and had the unintended consequence of rendering the film even less comprehensible than before.

None of the cast turned up to the "re-premiere" of the film at Hollywood's Grauman's Chinese Theatre and let it be known that they would not be doing any promotion. Box-office receipts only amounted to about $3.5 million against total costs of around $40 million. In the wake of *Heaven's Gate*, the major studios ceded less control to directors and there was a significant move towards mainstream blockbuster-type films with guaranteed box-office appeal.

There were whispers that some high up in the industry were determined to clip the wings of auteurs such as Cimino and Francis Ford Coppola; it was also said that as part of a negative campaign, *Heaven's Gate* was dubbed *Apocalypse Next* before its completion. Kristofferson was infuriated when an executive said that unless control of films was taken away from those with creativity, the film industry was headed for disaster. He incredulously enquired did this mean that power should be handed to the uncreative?*

---

* Kristofferson later claimed that President Reagan's Secretary of State Alexander Haig had a meeting with studio heads during which he said there should be no more films giving a negative view of American history like *Heaven's Gate*.

Although the reviews were almost unanimous in their condemnation, the film has enjoyed a degree of rehabilitation in more recent times. Phil Hall, writing for *Film Threat*, an online cinema review site, believes the film was treated unfairly and makes the remarkable claim that "*Heaven's Gate* is one of the most impressive and original motion picture epics ever created"; its main problem merely being the unnecessarily lengthy opening sequence. He was also impressed by Kristofferson, asserting that he "gave a career peak performance as a man who seems perpetually out of his element. As the uneasy law enforcement agent of the territory, he is scorned by the moneyed elite but is also viewed uneasily by those he is trying to protect. He beautifully underplays the role, expressing his no-man's-land existence through stoic glances which betray hints of inner turmoil."

Hall admired Cimino's depiction of American class structures, which he believes remain largely unchanged to the present day. The clear-cut, some might say simplistic, division of the characters into good and bad in order to make a political point later found echoes in the work of Michael Moore.

While Hall's reappraisal represents a minority view, over the years, *Heaven's Gate* has played at art-house cinemas, winning appreciative comments – at least for particular aspects of the film.*

From a career point of view, it would have been better for Kristofferson not to have got involved with the project in the first place. However, he harboured no regrets and to the present day, he defiantly maintains that the film is one of the best he's made and remains a passionate defender of Cimino's directing skills.

"I think there were a lot of people out there that wrote vicious reviews finding the film unredeemed . . . I told Michael, 'You realise the guys that got you – and they got him – were the same guys the movie was about, who believed that money was more important than people; fact is it was a political assassination.'"

---

* It was screened to a sold-out Halloween audience at New York's Museum of Modern Art in 2005 with an in-person introduction by Isabelle Huppert.

Kris in 2001, wearing a 'Free Peltier' t-shirt. For years Kristofferson has been tireless in his support for human rights causes. Leonard Peltier is a Native American activist currently serving life for murder; his supporters believe he did not receive a fair trial and are not convinced of his guilt.

Kris at the Los Angeles premiere of
*The Transporter* with son Jesse and
daughter Tracy, October 2, 2002.

(STEWART COOK/REX FEATURES)

Kris in Glasgow, where he was filming
*The Jacket* in 2004. He enrolled some of his
children into a local school.

(TSPL/CAMERA PRESS)

Kris and Joan Baez, backstage at South by South West, Texas. March 21, 2004.

(EBET ROBERTS/REDFERNS)

Live on the McEnroe Talk Show, CNBC,
New York, August 29, 2004.
(MARION CURTIS/REX FEATURES)

With Faith Hill on stage at the Grand Ole Opry
House for the 38th Annual CMA Awards,
November 9, 2004.
(FRANK MICELOTTA/GETTY IMAGES)

Signing autographs at the Los Angeles premiere of *The Dreamer*, October 9, 2005.
(LFI)

Performing with Norah Jones at the *I Walk The Line: A Night For Johnny Cash* musical tribute, October 25, 2005.

(KEVIN WINTER/GETTY IMAGES)

With wife Lisa, at the 39th Annual CMA awards, Madison Square Garden, New York, November 15, 2005.

(DAVE ALLOCCA/REX FEATURES)

With Greg Kinnear in the movie *Fast Food Nation*, 2006.

(FOTOBLITZ/STILLS/GAMMA/CAMERA PRESS)

Receiving an award at the Songwriters Hall of Fame ceremony, June 15, 2006.
(LARRY BUSACCA/WIREIMAGE.COM)

On stage at South by South West, Texas,
March 16, 2006. (EBET ROBERTS/REDFERNS)

At the ceremony inducting Kristofferson and the
late Waylon Jennings into Hollywood's
Rockwalk, Los Angeles, July 6, 2006. (LFI)

Accepting the Johnny Cash visionary award from an emotional Rosanne Cash at the
CMT Music awards, April 2007. (KEVIN MAZUR/WIREIMAGE.COM)

In front of the crowds, live at the Inaugural Stagecoach Country Music festival, May 6, 2007.
(JOHN SHEARER/WIREIMAGE.COM)

With Harry Dean Stanton at the Los Angeles premiere of *The Wendell Baker Story*, May 10, 2007.

Live at the Royal Albert Hall, April 2, 2008. In recent years Kris has played sell out shows to large enthusiastic audiences backed only by his own rudimentary guitar and harmonica accompaniment.

With Willie Nelson at the BMI Country Music awards, Nashville, November 6, 2007.

"I feel luckier every day with just what I've had in my life. It's been such a full one."

# Chapter 17

KRISTOFFERSON's impassioned support for Cimino and *Heaven's Gate* was inextricably linked to his increasingly left-of-centre political views. In 1980, Ronald Reagan was about to start an eight-year presidency, enjoying considerable support throughout the Eighties, and those on the left swam against the prevailing tide of public opinion when attacking his administration.

Kristofferson's antipathy to American foreign policy had grown ever since hearing stories about the experiences of young soldiers in Vietnam. He originally believed that the men had volunteered for noble reasons; "They believed they were standing up for the underdog, believed that Vietnam was an underdog being bullied by big Communist China – some of the best people I know volunteered for Vietnam."

However, once reality hit home, Kris felt great sympathy for those asked to put themselves in the way of danger on behalf of their country for a cause he did not believe was worth fighting for. "As well as killing 56,000 Americans we did worse than that, we killed for a lot of Americans the notion that America stands for justice for everybody."

Kristofferson's views had not come out to any significant degree in his music, which had been concerned principally with the personal rather than the political.* In 1976, he had been spotted wearing a United Farm Worker's badge when attending a lavish New York party at the Tavern on the Green in Central Park. The UFW, founded by Cesar Chavez, adhered to principles of non-violence, promoting the rights of agricultural workers mainly of Mexican or Filipino extraction.

It was Joan Baez who first made Kristofferson aware of the UFW as she recalled, "Who the hell's that?" was his initial response. "Farm workers," she replied, "they're getting a bum deal." He said, "You mean Mexicans?"

---

* In an early political statement, he sported a badge supporting George McGovern, the Democrat candidate in the 1972 Presidential election.

I said, "Yeah, the Mexicans." He replied, "Oh shit yeah, I'll do it for the Mexicans." While feeling this was not a particularly encouraging level of political consciousness, Baez came to discover that unlike a lot of celebrities, Kristofferson was serious and steadfast in his views and in a later newspaper interview, he named the UFW as his favourite charity and the only cause he'd ever "gone all out for".

His views extended to other parts of the world – particularly Latin America – where he believed his country was exerting a malign influence in attacking or destabilising regimes of which it disapproved. In March 1979, Kristofferson was one of a number of musicians who travelled to Cuba to record a live album during three nights of performances of jazz, rock and Latin music at the Karl Marx Theatre in Havana. Rita Coolidge also appeared, as did other well-known names on the celebrity left including Stephen Stills and Bonnie Bramlett. Given the American government's long-standing opposition to the Castro regime – at a time when the Iron Curtain was still very much in place – an appearance at such an event amounted to a strong political statement.

The concerts were recorded by CBS and a double live album, *Havana Jam*, was released, featuring Kristofferson and Coolidge performing, respectively, 'Living Legend' and '(Your Love Has Lifted Me) Higher And Higher'. Kris tweaked the lyrics of 'Living Legend' to include "in the Sierra Maestra" where Fidel Castro and Che Guevara spent much of their time during the Cuban revolution. In October, he performed at the Bread and Roses Festival at the Greek Theatre in Berkeley, California. The annual fundraiser had been started by Joan Baez's sister, Mimi Fariña, with the stated aim of bringing "light and music" into prisons, hospitals and nursing homes.

By way of light relief, Kristofferson was invited to tour with Willie Nelson during the winter of 1979–80 in support of the chart album *Willie Nelson Sings Kris Kristofferson*. The tour was a sell-out and received rave reviews – though it was Nelson who received most of the plaudits. The tour did, however, help to raise Kristofferson's flagging artistic profile and probably attracted more people to his own concerts.

The album of covers – dating back to 'Me And Bobby McGee' – was a further example of other people having greater commercial success with Kristofferson songs than the artist was able to achieve himself. Both the album and single of 'Help Me Make It Through The Night' made the country Top Five. "Kris' songs were easy," said Nelson, "that's one of the reasons I did it. It didn't require a lot of teaching of the band. We'd known these songs for years."

At the start of 1980, Kristofferson participated in a pair of television events celebrating the life and work of two of his favourite artists. The poster advertising *Johnny Cash: The First 25 Years* demonstrated just how close Cash and Kristofferson had become; on either side of a beaming Cash, pride of place is given to pictures of Kris and June Carter while positioned below were photographs of the other guests appearing including Dolly Parton, Waylon Jennings, Jack Clement, Carl Perkins, Kirk Douglas, Don Williams and Anne Murray.

With so many artists together in one place, not to mention countless producers, technicians and cameramen, the atmosphere behind the scenes was frantic to say the least, yet one journalist was struck by Kristofferson's calmness. "The man has the patience of a saint; he was pushed and pulled all over the place yet he complied with all the last-minute demands on his time that he possibly could." After taping the show, Johnny and June held a party for about 200 friends.

The Cash tribute was followed by a two-hour television special, *Hank Williams: A Man And His Music*. Hosted by Hank Williams Jr and featuring members of the original Drifting Cowboys, Hank's backing group, Kristofferson sang 'I'm So Lonesome I Could Cry', the song that had provided so much of his early inspiration.

With one more album to deliver on the Monument deal, a new producer, Norbert Putnam, was brought in for 1980's *To The Bone*. Several changes in personnel saw old friends Donnie Fritts and Billy Swan back in more prominent positions among the backing musicians. On first listen, *To The Bone* sounded fairly typical of the albums Kristofferson had been turning out of late. However, Kristofferson used the record to express his feelings over his split from Coolidge with many of the lyrics imbued with passionate and very personal emotions; from angry to sentimental, it was writing as catharsis.

For 'Snakebit,' Kris cast aside his usual laconic, laid-back delivery in favour of a "hate myself for loving you"-type rant. In 'Daddy's Song', Kristofferson laid bare the pain separation brought his young daughter, while in 'The Last Time', Casey's longing was addressed towards Rita without rancour. 'Nobody Loves Anybody Anymore', co-written with

Swan, gently expressed the feelings of bitterness and sadness at the end of a failed relationship.

'Blessing In Disguise' began and ended with verses from 'The Wild Side Of Life', a number one hit for Hank Thompson in 1952 about a wife who abandons her husband in favour of the night life. Since much of the album was inspired by Kris and Rita's life together, this intriguingly suggested that he might not have been the only one who wandered, or was he simply viewing himself through Rita's eyes?

Kristofferson later said that making *To The Bone* was helpful in the process of coming to terms with and getting over his marriage collapse. Apparently keen to let the world know that he was now taking an active role in parenting, he put several posed photographs of his children on the album's back cover.

*To The Bone* achieved a degree of commercial success, making a brief appearance in the country album charts while 'Nobody Loves Anybody Anymore' made a minor impression on the country singles listings. Kristofferson felt little effort was made by Columbia to promote the album and while this was probably true to some extent, his following was now down to a hardcore of fans who bought his records regardless.

Other artists were still enjoying success with Kristofferson's songs – Tompall and the Glaser Brothers only just missed the top spot in the country charts in 1981 with their version of 'Loving Her Was Easier (Than Anything I've Ever Done)'. The prospect of higher sales for Kristofferson product was further dented by the fact that country radio – a key source of support for all artists – had largely given up on him since around 1973/4. They had a pretty firm idea of which artists their listeners wanted to hear and Kristofferson was no longer one of them.

The early Eighties weren't a good time to be Kris Kristofferson: his records failed to make the charts – the public preferring his earlier classics and then performed by other people; his manager, Bert Block, was terminally ill; his acting career had hit the buffers after the *Heaven's Gate* fiasco; and his marriage had fallen victim to the excesses that fame brought.

To add to his woes, Kristofferson found himself on the receiving end of a $250,000 paternity suit from a woman called Peggy Hansen, who claimed that he had fathered her son following their relationship in

Nashville in 1969, when she was a waitress and he was still a struggling songwriter. The summons was served at Opryland where Kristofferson was a guest at a dinner for Fred Foster. Kristofferson denied the claims but it took until 1987, after DNA tests backed his assertion that he was not the father, for the case to be finally thrown out of court.

Having radically cut back on his drink intake, making him, as he himself wryly put it, "boring as hell", his use of marijuana – or "laughing tobacco" as he described it – had increased. After interviewing Kristofferson in 1981, one journalist said, "I remain high just by breathing Kris' exhaust."

Kristofferson continued to tour with a staff of about 20 to support. Billy Swan appreciated the fact that Kris ensured that the musicians stayed in decent hotels without having to share a room, especially since he was aware that the venues they played were gradually getting smaller and generating less revenue.

Kristofferson's new-found soberness had a beneficial impact on his live performances. "One of the great advantages me and the band have is we've gotten to where we communicate real well. It used to be I wasn't aware of anybody on the stage but that poor sonofabitch in the spotlight and how horrible he had it . . . but it's not terror any more. You're still scared though, oh yeah, you're still scared going on stage."

Asked to explain his fear he said, "What would *you* be scared of if you were standing in front of all those people reading a poem that you wrote especially from your heart and it wasn't anybody else's work? Why, they might hate you."

Despite his sometimes erratic onstage behaviour in the past, Kristofferson was upset when people suggested he didn't care about his performances. "I sweat blood over them, always have."

In the summer of 1981, Kristofferson visited the bedside of Jerry Lee Lewis, who had been rushed to hospital following surgery for a life-threatening stomach rupture. Kris was allowed half an hour with Jerry Lee – twice the time normally allotted for visits to intensive care patients. Asked to comment on the Killer's condition, Kristofferson poetically observed, "He's going to have to make his body as strong as his spirit is. A lot of what got him in the condition he is in now is probably what is saving him." Kristofferson must have thought how easily it could have been him in that hospital bed.

Kristofferson's next movie, *Rollover*, was a surprising choice for him since the part required him to play a high-powered financier, Hub Smith – something that represented the polar opposite of his interests and was very different from the roles he'd played to date. He had been contracted to make the film before the full-scale debacle of *Heaven's Gate*.

*Rollover* was directed by Alan Pakula, who made the stylish 1971 thriller, *Klute*, which starred Kristofferson's co-star, Jane Fonda. Pakula had not considered Kristofferson for the part but following Fonda's advice, he went to see him in concert in Toronto and was impressed, saying there was "a deeply sophisticated urbane man under that down-home drawl".

Fonda played Lee Winters, a former film star, whose husband is murdered in mysterious circumstances. She inherits his chemical company, which receives financial backing arranged by Hub on behalf of a failing bank as part of a deal so enormous that the potential rewards will solve the bank's own financial problems. Hub and Lee spend time spouting technical financial jargon, discovering a secret slush fund enabling Arab investors to convert holdings into gold, while becoming romantically involved along the way. In the finale, the world economic order is threatened as wealthy Arabs withdraw billions of dollars from American banks, causing a worldwide chain reaction and widespread panic among the public.

The film received a general thumbs down when released in 1981. *The New York Times* wrote, "The cleverness and proficiency of Mr Pakula's other work are astonishingly absent here, as are the shrewdness of Miss Fonda's better performances and the easygoing charm of Mr Kristofferson's." Esteemed critic Janet Maslin considered it "incomprehensible . . . and badly bungled". Fonda defended it as another in a line of "cause" films: "The *Rollover* theme is the most critical issue of our time . . . far more complicated than the issue of nuclear energy." She was concerned that America was dependent for its energy supplies on Saudi Arabia, which she perceived to be an unstable regime, whereas for Kristofferson, the movie was simply "a thriller love story".*

His film career being at a low ebb, it would be some time before Kristofferson started to receive movie offers and even then, the days of

---

* *Rollover* only received one award nomination – Kristofferson was up for a Golden Raspberry in the Worst Actor category – as he had been for *Heaven's Gate*. On neither occasion did he "win".

him seriously being considered as one of Hollywood's leading men were all but over.

In April 1982, 20-year-old Tracy Kristofferson, then a second-year student at Stanford University, suffered life-threatening injuries in a road accident and was rushed to intensive care in the Antelope Valley Hospital in Lancaster, California. She had been on the back of a motorbike in the Mojave Desert driven by Eric Heiden – the winner of five gold medals in speed skating at the 1980 Winter Olympics – when a mobile home crashed into the back of the bike, launching Tracy backwards through the vehicle's windscreen.*

According to newspaper reports, she suffered serious injuries. Kris rushed back from a European tour to be at her bedside, praying fervently for "no paralysis and no brain damage". When he reached the hospital, Tracy was unconscious and, as Kris later described it, "all tied up on this table. In a matter of minutes, one of the doctors said, 'Her foot just moved.'"

As the medical team fought to save her, Kris maintained a round-the-clock vigil with Tracy's mother, Fran; his only respite being to run in the desert "to get my head straight". Visiting was strictly controlled and flowers were not allowed in case they carried anything that could cause an allergic reaction. Despite the seriousness of her injuries, Tracy recovered after a lengthy period of recuperation.

By 1982, Fred Foster's Monument label had been in financial difficulties for some years. According to Foster, the problems were attributable to bad financial investments, although the continuing commercial decline of artists like Kristofferson was a contributing factor. In an effort to reverse the label's fading fortunes, Kristofferson joined forces with former Monument artists Dolly Parton, Brenda Lee and Willie Nelson for a double album entitled *The Winning Hand*. Parton and Nelson were enjoying great commercial success at the time so Kristofferson could only benefit by his association. The album was an unusual hotchpotch of solos and duets, new recordings and revamped versions of old songs featuring previously recorded vocals.

Kristofferson sang on seven duets including 'Help Me Make It Through The Night' with Brenda Lee, 'Casey's Last Ride' with Willie Nelson and the lightweight 'Ping Pong' with Dolly Parton (whose vocals had been

---

* It was reported that Heiden had braked to avoid a dog.

laid down some years previously). One reviewer described it as a vehicle "in which Dolly Parton at her cutesiest is outdone by Kris Kristofferson at his klutziest".

Kristofferson contributed two solo tracks, 'The Bandits Of Beverly Hills' and 'Here Comes That Rainbow Again', an evocative song inspired by a scene from John Steinbeck's *The Grapes Of Wrath*, which fitted well with Kristofferson's increasingly urgent concern for the oppressed.

Johnny Cash contributed extensive liner notes in which he talked about Kristofferson's early days in Nashville, relating his apocryphal version of the helicopter landing. Cash also hosted a two-hour television special based on the album in early 1983 on which all four artists appeared. *The Winning Hand* was well-received and led to Kristofferson achieving a rare commercial success when it made the Country Top Five. However, it was not enough to save Monument, which folded soon afterwards.

Kristofferson was among the artists appearing in the 1983 video *The Other Side Of Nashville*, where he was shown in the company of Bob Johnston and Billy Swan. Though it was less than 20 years since he had arrived in Nashville, Kristofferson was already waxing nostalgically about what had been lost; how the whole business was now so commercial, with Opryland (which replaced the Ryman Auditorium as the venue for the Grand Ole Opry) having more in common with Disneyland than the spiritual home of country music. Kristofferson and Willie Nelson also reflected on the outlaw movement. Kris saw many of the artists in Nashville in the Sixties – especially Dylan – as possessing, and prefiguring, the qualities of the artists to whom the term was applied in the Seventies. For Nelson, the use of the word was purely a neat ploy to sell records.

A high point of 1983 came when Kristofferson returned to Nashville for a week of events celebrating his music. One journalist's observation that it was a case of "the restoration of the black sheep to the flock" betrayed a vestige of the previous animosity Kristofferson had encountered in Music City. Johnny Cash led a special tribute at the annual Country Music Awards Show, singing a medley of Kristofferson standards along with Anne Murray, Lee Greenwood and Larry Gatlin. At a party afterwards, Kristofferson got together with old friends Roger Miller, Willie Nelson, David Allan Coe and Mickey Newbury for a guitar pull. "It's been a long time since I stayed up all night playing music," he told a reporter, "especially straight, so you remember what you did."

Soon afterwards, Kristofferson was specially honoured at the BMI (Broadcast Music Inc) Awards banquet for five of his best-known songs that had accumulated over seven million airplays between them. Standing ovations were the order of the day wherever he went – and though the beard and hair were still long, they were no longer deemed worthy of comment. Perhaps his decision to wear a tuxedo lent a more respectable air.

Kristofferson made a point of telling local journalists that his life was in better shape than it had been for some time. "I've cleaned up my personal life . . . and I'm taking care of business now." This was partly in reference to his "bachelor daddy" role, which he took seriously. Looking after his daughter provided a source of stability and according to one possibly tongue-in-cheek report, Kris won a Mother Of The Year award in 1981 because he'd attended Casey's school so many times to hear the Pledge of Allegiance.

It was also suggested in some quarters that a rediscovery of his religious faith had helped to provide strength to withstand the personal storms he'd experienced in the late Seventies. Of greater importance was a new romance. In 1981, Kris met Lisa Meyers, a lawyer approximately 20 years his junior, at a gym in Malibu. A relationship blossomed and on February 19, 1983, the pair got married in the chapel at Pepperdine University (where Meyers had graduated), which boasted a stunning vista overlooking Malibu and the Pacific Ocean. The ceremony was attended by about 15 guests including Kris' three children from his previous marriages. (It was Meyer's second marriage.)

Lisa soon got a taste of the realities of life with a famous personality when their honeymoon was delayed to allow Kris to complete a recording schedule. A woman of strong religious faith, she made it clear that her new husband should mend his ways but he initially found the going hard. However, it seems that a combination of the ageing process and a desire to be a better father contributed to Kris' motivation to change. He came to value family life in a way he had not previously done and was eager to make up for previous misdemeanours.

Now that *Heaven's Gate* had greatly dented his marketability, Kristofferson was prepared to overlook the fact that many of the films he was being offered were not projects befitting a man of his intellectual calibre. He now looked upon acting as a nine-to-five job. "You just sit there and wait to be told what to do – if you want to know something they say, 'Don't worry about it, it's not your problem.'"

Accordingly, he was content to move into a new phase of his career that saw him take on large numbers of roles in low-budget potboilers for television as well as the big screen.

In 1984 came a CBS television movie, *The Lost Honor Of Kathryn Beck*, a remake of the 1975 German film *The Lost Honor Of Katharina Blum* (based on the novel by Heinrich Böll) co-starring Marlo Thomas (Kristofferson had appeared in her television special *Free To Be . . . You And Me*). Kristofferson played the part of Ben Cole, a charming man with a shady past. Thomas played the title role of a businesswoman who meets Cole at a party resulting in a one-night stand. The authorities become interested in Cole's activities and by extension, Beck, who is ruthlessly hunted by the police and an investigative journalist. The film raised issues about civil liberties and the role of the media.*

Much more satisfying was a 1984 cinema outing directed by William Tannen, *Flashpoint*, which also starred Rip Torn and quirky character actor Roberts Blossom. Kristofferson's lanky physique, tough guy demeanour and rasping drawl were well suited to the part of Bob Logan, a Texas border patrol officer. An old jeep containing a skeleton and money is found buried in the sand – having lain undiscovered for about 20 years. Some kind of grandiose conspiracy theory gradually emerges but thanks to a number of twists and turns in the plot, it is only at the conclusion that a JFK connection is revealed. Kristofferson was generally convincing in delivering Logan's pivotal role, contributing to the film's compulsively uneasy atmosphere.

Kristofferson was not involved in the soundtrack; the dark feel of the film required eerie mood music, which was provided by German electronic band Tangerine Dream. Completing a trio of 1984 films was *Songwriter*, which offered Kristofferson the welcome opportunity to star alongside Willie Nelson. Conflicting schedules often meant that they rarely got to see each other, but Kristofferson and Nelson's time together on set provided a perfect opportunity to catch up and have fun – "So much time was spent laughing," as Kris later said.

* When rerun years later, the original title was prefixed by the words *Act Of Passion*.

The idea for the film had been around for a while, casually arising out of conversations Willie had with writer Bud Shrake. "I was tellin' him a bunch of stories and he was writin' down some stuff, makin' up some stuff to go with it." Kristofferson's part was originally intended for Waylon Jennings, who eventually turned it down.

Nelson played singer Doc Jenkins, who enlists the help of Blackie Buck (Kristofferson) to turn the tables on an unscrupulous promoter (Rip Torn) who has signed Doc up to an unfair contract that gives him the rights to all of his songs. The film mixes some unpleasant aspects of the country music industry – the exploitation of naïve artists by commercially minded businessmen – with much horseplay and fairly lame wisecracks between the two male leads. A splash of romance completed the scene.

As with many of the films Kristofferson appeared in, he found himself in a paradoxical situation: a liberal intellectual with radical views providing unchallenging fodder for fans, many of whom were of the redneck variety. However, Kristofferson later said *Songwriter* was the most enjoyable experience he'd had in films, ranking it among his own movies he liked to revisit as a reminder of a good time.

It would be stretching it to describe what Kristofferson and Nelson did in front of the camera as acting; it was more a case of playing themselves in a variety of situations with guidance from director Alan Rudolph, who described the pair's on-screen chemistry, rather excessively, as being "somewhere between Redford and Newman and Laurel and Hardy". Roger Ebert praised the film's "undeniable charm, moments of transparent honesty, some off the wall humour and a lot of good music".

With some sections of *Songwriter* being filmed in Nashville, and a lot of country music on the soundtrack, the film's invitation-only premiere logically took place in Music City at the Belle Meade Theater, which upgraded its sound system especially for the occasion. Luminaries from all areas of the music business attended, including Chet Atkins, Tammy Wynette, Ray Charles and Roger Miller. Also present were political VIPs such as Nashville's governor and mayor and Tennessee's two senators.

Despite this auspicious start, the film was poorly supported by its distributor Tri-Star Films; when initially released it was given a mere two weeks' exposure in a limited number of southern US markets – hardly a vote of confidence for someone of Kristofferson's cinematic track record and Nelson's audience pulling power. The film was subsequently shown in about 60 cinemas in the Los Angeles area to coincide with Kristofferson and Nelson's four-night engagement at the Universal Amphitheater.

Columbia released an album, *Music From Songwriter*, not strictly a soundtrack, on which the pair sang solo and a couple of duets, which made the country Top 20.* Kristofferson's 'How Do You Feel About Foolin' Around' was released as a single and became a hit in the country singles charts. His solo contributions reflected issues he was becoming increasingly concerned with such as immigration ('Crossing The Border') and war ('Under The Gun'). However, the tracks bore little relationship to the film's subject matter and were delivered to a predominantly rock accompaniment. Also, to Kristofferson's chagrin, the critics generally preferred Nelson's contributions.

The cinematic pairing of two country stars developed into a minifranchise that produced two more films, *A Pair Of Aces* (1990) and *Another Pair Of Aces* (1991), a couple of good ol' boy romps with Kris and Willie trading banter as they solved crimes. The quality of both was mediocre, the acting stilted, but a sufficient number of television viewers tuned in to make them ratings successes.

The Kristofferson-Nelson double act found favour with the Country Music Association and the pair co-hosted the 1986 CMA awards show (Kris had co-hosted with Anne Murray the previous year). Executive producer Irving Waugh said, "Because this is the 20th anniversary of the telecast, it is especially fitting that entertainers of the calibre and stature of Willie and Kris will headline the show."

The two also put in an appearance on television's long-running *Hee Haw*. Though inspired by the groundbreaking late-Sixties comedy series, *Rowan And Martin's Laugh-In*, the programme was almost exclusively based around country music and country life – in a stereotypical way. The humour was corny, the women voluptuous and scantily clad and the sets, with hay bales and wicket fences, were redolent of exactly the kind of image Kristofferson helped country music to discard.

Though essentially harmless fluff, it was undoubtedly significant, not to mention ironic, that Kristofferson deemed it an appropriate career move to overcome his instinctive scepticism about such a show. His appearance

---

* *Music From Songwriter* earned an Academy Award nomination for Best Original Song Score, losing out on the night to Prince's *Purple Rain*.

did not sit easily with the warm accolade accorded him by Waylon Jennings in his autobiography. "Kris had a lot to do with showing that country music wasn't some *Hee Haw* backwoods character with a bottle of sour mash liquor and a corncob pipe, and that roots don't have to trap you in the ground."

# Chapter 18

KRISTOFFERSON had not released any new material since his Monument contract expired in 1980. He recorded a number of songs around 1983 for a proposed album, supposedly to be titled *From Here To Forever*, around the time Monument went bankrupt. A chance to revive his ailing music career unexpectedly came at the end of 1984 when he, Waylon Jennings, Willie Nelson and Johnny Cash got together in Montreux, Switzerland, to record Cash's annual Christmas television special. Following the taping, the four indulged in an informal guitar pull from which the idea emerged for a country supergroup.

Producer Chips Moman worked with Cash and Nelson in Nashville early in 1985. During one session, Jennings and Kristofferson dropped by the studio (Kris had been asked to pitch some songs by Willie) and the four laid down a few tracks, starting off with 'Highwayman', a Jimmy Webb song that all four had heard in Montreaux and liked. Before long, the idea of an album emerged. On one level it represented a change from each individual's usual record-tour routine and it would also offer the chance to hang out together.

Bringing together four uncompromising egos was potentially fraught with difficulties but the fact that all, apart from Nelson, were in the commercial doldrums provided a powerful enough incentive to unite. It was agreed from the outset that each would receive equal billing – something that appealed to Kristofferson, who currently had the lowest profile of the four. He was simply humbled at being associated with three men he had regarded as heroes before they became friends. "I always looked up to all of them and felt like I was kind of a little kid who had climbed up on Mount Rushmore and stuck his face out there." Out of the four, he was the little kid at the age of 49.

Against the odds, the personal chemistry gelled – particularly between Kristofferson and Cash – and The Highwaymen as they dubbed themselves (although The Real Outlaws might have been a more accurate title) would prove to be a fruitful collaboration over the next decade.

For live shows, the four artists stood at the front of the stage with guitars (a largely cosmetic touch except for Nelson), each taking turns singing lead, backed by a slick and well-rehearsed band (to which each individual contributed a member from their respective bands). For all the feeling of equality, the principals retained their own tour buses and entourages. The money was divided equally, which meant less potential earnings than each of them had previously realised, but this was not to be dismissed considering the potential commercial benefits. It was also understood that all four were free to fulfil other commitments.

The Highwaymen debuted at Nelson's annual Fourth of July picnic in front of 10,000 fans, providing great exposure for their debut *Highwayman* album, released on Columbia, which made a strong showing in the charts, soon gaining gold (500,000 sales) and eventually, platinum status (1,000,000 sales). The single that gave the album its title* made number one in the country charts while a follow-up, Guy Clark's 'Desperados Waiting For A Train', made the country Top 20.

Apart from the novelty of getting four country greats for the price of one, it was not surprising that the album was a commercial hit, although musically it was something of a mixed bag, with a reliance on outside writers including Cindy Walker ('Jim, I Wore A Tie Today') and John Prine and Steve Goodman (the witty sing-along, 'The Twentieth Century Is Almost Over').

At times *Highwayman* sounded over-produced, not least because of the occasional presence of synthesisers, and while it had a definite country feel, at times it leant towards an AOR style. 'Deportee (Plane Wreck At Los Gatos)', Woody Guthrie's complaint about attitudes to immigrants (which dovetailed neatly with Kristofferson's own radical views) would have been most effective with just one singer and an acoustic guitar; although

---

* Although generally referred to as The Highwaymen in the press and elsewhere, it was only on their third and final album, 1995's *The Road Goes On Forever*, that the quartet was officially given this title; on the cover of the first album, the artists' names simply appeared above the album title. One problem was the prior existence of a group with the same name – who had enjoyed a major hit with 'Michael (Row The Boat Ashore)' in 1961. In the face of possible legal action, the matter was amicably resolved when the original Highwaymen opened a show for their successors.

sympathetically produced, the sound of a powerhouse chorus detracted from the song's emotional impact.

Kristofferson's profile was fairly low key; he sang on five of the 10 tracks and always those on which all four men vocalised. Although making a concerted effort to trim his rougher edges, with only marginal success, he was easily the weakest link vocally. Despite his writing reputation that helped get him the gig in the first place, none of Kristofferson's compositions made it onto the album.

*Highwayman* was nominated for a Grammy in the category Best Vocal Performance by a Duo or Group with Vocal but lost out to 'Why Not Me' by mother and daughter sensation, The Judds. The Highwaymen did, however, secure the Academy of Country Music's Single of the Year award and a CMA nomination. Kristofferson's songwriting gained further recognition in 1985 when he was inducted into the Songwriters Hall of Fame, which honoured the people who "create the songs that serve as the soundtrack of our lives".

Kristofferson and band were asked to do a solo 20-minute spot at the US Live Aid concert in Philadelphia on July 13 but he found the prospect of appearing without other musicians too daunting and declined to perform, a shame since to appear would have given him plenty of publicity and, like many of the performers at this high-profile event, probably boosted his career.

During its early stages, it was not clear what future direction the Highwaymen project might take. One idea floated was a film in which each of the four role-played their allotted parts in 'Highwayman': Kristofferson a sailor, Jennings a dam builder and Nelson a highwayman. Their characters hailed from the past whereas Cash's character was introduced with the words, "I'll fly a starship across the universe divide," suggesting a mysterious figure from the future – not exactly typical Cash material.*

Following their enthusiastic reception at the Fourth of July picnic, it was inevitable that The Highwaymen would take to the road and in October, they played a show in support of Farm Aid. Although the omens were good, Jennings was troubled by the band's stiffness onstage – something he could not understand since they were so relaxed offstage. "We

---

* This particular idea came to nothing beyond a promotional video that won a gold medal in the Country & Western category at the International Film and Television Festival.

looked like four shy rednecks trying to be nice to each other," he complained. "It almost ruined it . . ."

Things improved dramatically when the men loosened up, ad-libbing jokes and harmonies and generally creating an atmosphere that came across like they were having a good time around each other. Kristofferson even surprised Cash by attempting to harmonise on 'Folsom Prison Blues' – something nobody else had dared to do before. The banter between the four was sharp. When Kristofferson remarked that he thought he might be losing his voice, Nelson snapped back, "How can you tell?" Referring to Nelson's recent well-publicised, multi-million dollar tax bill, Kristofferson introduced one of Willie's songs by quipping he was doing it on behalf of the IRS.

There was no disguising the fact that when it came to Kristofferson's spot, the audience response was less enthusiastic. Kris himself conceded in an interview that he was not really qualified to share a stage with the others – all of whom were consummately skilled live performers.

Kristofferson was generally reluctant to strongly associate himself with one political party. However, during the early Eighties he had supported Governor Jerry Brown in his efforts to be elected to the Senate. Brown was on the left of the Democrats, had strongly opposed the Vietnam War and was enthusiastic about expanding the use of solar power when such a notion was seen as cranky.

Kristofferson joined a colourful assortment of supporters, including comedian Andy Kaufman, for a 10-city whistle-stop bus trip across America aimed at encouraging the electorate to vote for Brown. The "political magical mystery tour", as one writer described it, would pull into a city and set up a stage, the guests, including Kristofferson (supported by Billy Swan), played a few songs or did a routine, then whooped up the crowd as Brown delivered his message.*

The first album that gave significant vent to Kristofferson's political views was *Repossessed*, released by Mercury in 1986. Historical reflection had helped him to conclude that current issues were really nothing new. Even looking back to when he was growing up in Brownsville, he became aware that people south of the border felt that America acted as if it had

---

* The tour did not deliver for Brown, who lost to Republican Pete Wilson.

the right to control their destiny and to exploit their natural assets. "I got to experience things that I hadn't necessarily learned in school or the army and I felt it was my obligation to express that. I suppose some people called them political songs but I don't see them like that. They are songs about what is going on in the world."

The title *Repossessed* was suggested by Stephen Bruton as a reflection of Kris' new-found fire. It also referred to the album that Kristofferson had intended to follow *To The Bone*. "The record got taken into the bankruptcy court . . . it never came out."

Produced by Chips Moman, the music had a loose, languid feel despite some synthesised sounds and superfluous echo on the vocals, performed by Kristofferson's backing group, The Borderlords, who included Bruton, Billy Swan, Donnie Fritts and Sammy Creason. It resembled a live recording without an audience – particularly when Kristofferson called out intros to lead breaks as he would in concert.

Carl Perkins put in a guest appearance to add twang to the opening track – the hard-rocking, lyrically enigmatic 'Mean Old Man'. 'Shipwrecked In The Eighties' (with a spoken dedication to the "Vietnam vets") was partly inspired by Kris' depressing experiences in the early part of the decade.

"My family had just fallen apart, the company I was recording for had sunk, my manager [Bert Block] died and my song agent died as well." There was also the *Heaven's Gate* fiasco. "I was a little adrift so I was writing autobiography there in the beginning."

The lyrics also owed their genesis to a chance meeting with a Vietnam veteran on the beach at Malibu. "He came up to tell me how much my music had meant to him at a tough time in his life. He gave me this old bible that was all underlined; he was pretty wasted looking, he had obviously been standing too close to the flame for a while, but it seemed to me symbolic of many people who were kind of adrift after their experience in Vietnam."

Like other tracks on the album, 'Shipwrecked In The Eighties' had a dirgeful quality, which only seemed to highlight the unmelodic quality of the vocals. However, it became one of Kristofferson's favourite compositions and he regularly opens concerts with the song.

'They Killed Him' was inspired by Kristofferson seeing the film *Gandhi*. "I was so depressed by the murdering of all the visionaries . . . whoever was promoting peace seemed to get killed." Who exactly "they" are is left undefined; the lingering implication is that dark and powerful forces of the type Kristofferson despised were at work in high places.

'They Killed Him' was one of two songs on the album later performed by The Highwaymen (and also by Bob Dylan on his 1986 album, *Knocked Out Loaded*, a particular delight for Kris); the other was 'Anthem 84', a direct address to an undisclosed recipient and clearly someone Kristofferson had previously been close to.

In 'What About Me', Kristofferson made direct reference to the civil war in El Salvador; fearing another Vietnam, his anger was directed at President Reagan, who was providing support for that country's military in their efforts to defeat the left-wing rebels. In what appears to be belated praise, indeed affection, for his father, Kristofferson acknowledged his debt in 'The Heart' for aspects of his philosophy on life – some of the most important lessons he'd learnt – which he reiterated in his sleeve notes for the album.

For all the anger that typified much of *Repossessed*, the final track, 'Love Is The Way', displayed Kristofferson's sentimental side and affirmed his belief in the redeeming power of love and spiritual faith – though not, apparently, organised religion. As if to emphasise that his ire was generally directed at the forces of authority rather than the foot soldiers themselves, backing vocals were provided by the Memphis Police Choir. The lyrics, like many on the album, had a certain power with several good turns of phrase, but at times they veered close to the platitudinous.*

*Repossessed* marked a significant change in Kristofferson's songwriting. Although he disliked the label "protest songs" – he felt he was only telling it as he saw it – many commentators used the term as a convenient handle to describe, even vilify, the album, which lingered in the country charts for six months.

Kristofferson was not content to only write songs against his country's foreign policies and throughout 1987, he supported various causes that ran alongside his own beliefs, as he stated, "There's a responsibility that comes with freedom to do what's morally right." In February, Kristofferson postponed a tour in support of *Repossessed* to attend "For a Nuclear-Free

---

* As if to underline this, 'Love Is The Way' was promoted with a candy-coated video that featured perfect landscapes, flawlessly beautiful babies (one black, one white), toddlers and puppies.

World and the Survival of Mankind", a three-day peace forum in Moscow, instigated under the more liberal regime of Mikhail Gorbachev in the days of *perestroika* and *glasnost*.

Kristofferson was part of an 11-member delegation of notables from the International Center for Development Policy, a liberal lobbying group based in Washington. Gorbachev claimed that the Soviet Union was looking for ways of securing world stability in order that it could concentrate on domestic concerns. Western diplomats expressed the hope that there might be a move away from the Marxist-Leninist doctrine about the inevitability of conflict between communism and capitalism.

Kristofferson had the honour of attending along with many distinguished guests including the dissident Andrei Sakharov (recently released from seven years of virtual house arrest), Norman Mailer, Gore Vidal and Gregory Peck (Kris was "awestruck" that Peck knew who he was). Once more Kristofferson found himself in tall cotton; many on the right were openly contemptuous of leading American intellectuals giving support and encouragement to a Communist regime – albeit one on its last legs.

Kristofferson was that rare example of a celebrity who was prepared to examine and question what was going on in his own back yard. He was particularly critical of the CIA – which he compared to the KGB – asserting that during its existence, it had contributed to the overthrow of more than 30 democratically elected governments. He was also highly suspicious of America's National Security Council, created in 1947, responsible for co-ordinating foreign and defence policy and advising the President. Kristofferson expressed the view that much of what he found least palatable about American foreign policy had its origins in the initiatives of this institution.

His activities also extended into areas related to the support of civil and human rights. On June 12, Kristofferson travelled to Memphis to mark the anniversary of black civil rights activist Medgar Evers' murder by a member of the Ku Klux Klan in 1963. Shortly after, a trivial incident, almost certainly an inadvertent mistake, was blown up in the press, much to Kristofferson's fury. Having performed a number of engagements to benefit the Albany Vietnam Veterans Memorial Committee, he was presented with a commemorative plaque that was later found in a rubbish bin in his backstage dressing room. Kristofferson denied that any offence was intended but was forced onto the back foot. Lisa, by now taking care of myriad administrative functions on her husband's behalf, explained to the press that the plaque "ended up in the garbage by mistake".

Kristofferson, who was booked to play at Willie Nelson's Fourth of July picnic the next day, was incandescent with anger as Nelson later recalled. "Kris was in an uproar; he said, 'For God's sake, I'm on these guys' side. I'm busting ass for these guys. I'm not going to do anything stupid and humiliating like throw away their plaque.'"

Kristofferson found himself in hot water again on October 27 when playing a benefit – along with Joni Mitchell, Jackson Browne, Willie Nelson and comedian Robin Williams – for Leonard Peltier, whom many believed had been wrongly convicted of the murder of two FBI agents. Kristofferson and Joni Mitchell were blacklisted from some radio stations in California as a result. Kristofferson said it made no real difference to him because generally, radio had not played his songs for years.

Kristofferson's political stand helped ensure that his name received a black mark within the show-business establishment, as he said, "Particularly in LA, I found a considerable lack of work after doing concerts for the Palestinian children and for a couple of gigs with Vanessa Redgrave and if that's the way it has to be, that's the way it has to be. If you support human rights, you gotta support them everywhere."

Throughout the Eighties, Kristofferson landed film roles that were neither artistically satisfying nor commercially successful but as "small movies that don't compromise my soul", they paid the bills. From the mid-Eighties onwards, he had roles in roughly three movies a year. Some in Nashville had reached the conclusion that Kristofferson abandoned country to "go Hollywood". In reality neither facet of his career was in great health and besides, he didn't regard himself as solely a country singer with a duty to appease Nashville's traditionalists.

For the futuristic thriller *Trouble In Mind* (released in 1985), Kristofferson played the lead role of Hawk, an ex-cop released from jail after serving a sentence for murder. He returns to Wanda (Genevieve Bujold), who runs a shabby, Fifties-style diner in Rain City (Seattle) that acts as a magnet for other waifs and strays. Hoping to make up for past sins, thereby redeeming himself in Wanda's eyes, Hawk endeavours to rescue newly arrived couple Coop (Keith Carradine) and Georgia (Lori Singer) from the evil designs of crooked Solo (Joe Morton).

One reviewer praised director Alan Rudolph for creating "urban land-scapes where losers and dreamers collide in their efforts to escape from loneliness and find quick success". This was not a universal view and the film now looks dated, burdened by lots of supposedly meaningful looks that fail to convince, and an impenetrable and barely graspable plot. The unrelentingly grim weather and Marianne Faithfull's ravaged vocals on 'El Gavilan (The Hawk)' (from *Repossessed*), used as the theme song for the film, help to complete joylessness of the characters' lives in this sub art-house movie.

Critic Roger Ebert described Kristofferson as "strong and silent except when he's uttering wisdom ["A little bit of everybody belongs in hell"]; he looks definitely hawklike". Kristofferson felt he acted as well in *Trouble In Mind* as he had in any of his other films, and Rudolph claimed to have always had Kris in mind for the part. "He has a terrific range but he doesn't have to do a lot to be effective . . . as the camera got closer the movie got better."

In 1986, Kristofferson teamed up with Johnny Cash for a made-for-television movie, *The Last Days Of Frank And Jesse James*. It was well known that Cash had struggled for years with his demons and in 1984, as part of his latest attempt to detox, he gave a "sobriety party" at which Kris sang a song he specially wrote for the occasion entitled 'Good Morning John'.* "I knew he was a dear friend already," Cash gushed to a journalist, "but he's like a brother now."

Shot on location in Tennessee on a budget of around $2.5 million – a far cry from some of Kristofferson's Seventies films, *The Last Days Of Frank And Jesse James* depicted the final three years of the infamous outlaws' lives. Back in the early Seventies, Sam Peckinpah had said that Kristofferson would be just right for the part of Jesse James. He was speaking when Kris was roughly the same age as Jesse; by 1986, Kristofferson was 50 – 14 years older than the Wild West character when he died. Kristofferson read a book about the James brothers and sent it on to Cash suggesting that they would be ideal in portraying the brothers. June Carter, Willie Nelson and David Allan Coe also had parts in the film, thus ensuring an agreeable opportunity for camaraderie. Unfortunately the results were largely

* On a previous occasion, Kristofferson wrote a song called 'Hall Of Angels' for singer Eddie Rabbit after his two-year-old son died following a liver transplant.

forgettable, with Cash's stilted acting making Kristofferson look a true pro by comparison.

Kristofferson was also one of the leads in a remake of *Stagecoach*, which gave all four Highwaymen the chance to play at being cowboys for the cameras. The original 1939 version, directed by John Ford and starring John Wayne as the Ringo Kid (Kristofferson's role), was a western classic; this 1986 version was anything but. The acting was generally poor and Kristofferson was in no doubt about the film's general quality. "He didn't like anything about the project except that me and Waylon and Johnny were in it with him," said Willie Nelson. "I would send reporters to interview Kris and he would tell them, 'Man what a piece of shit this is. I wouldn't watch this fucking movie if they strapped me in front of a TV set and sewed my eyelids open.'"

Kristofferson and the others were probably equally frustrated by sudden directorial changes to scenes that the cast had stayed up well into the night rehearsing. The film looked highly amateurish and it can only be imagined what the one quality actor, Tony Franciosa, made of it all. The gap in abilities between Franciosa and the rest of the cast was all too obvious. Despite this, the film was a surprise hit with audiences – the highest-rated television movie of the year. As one fan explained, "How could I not like something with those four country superstars in it?"

Kristofferson got a better chance to shine in *Blood And Orchids*, a 1986 television mini-series in which he played a detective, Captain Curt Maddox, in Thirties Hawaii investigating the case of four local youths accused of raping the daughter of a wealthy socialite. His character's tough exterior gradually reveals a softer side and a sense of justice, which eventually leads to him unravelling the truth behind the events. Filming on location was very much to Kris' taste; always keen on sporting activity, he discovered the thrill of riding the Waikiki surf. Once again, the mini-series clicked with television audiences with one reviewer describing Kristofferson as a "first rate actor . . . who could have carried the film by himself".

In 1987, Kristofferson took a leading role in an ambitious and controversial 14-hour ABC television series entitled *Amerika*, which fictionally depicted the United States 10 years after a bloodless coup by the USSR. Some Americans ended up in labour camps while others collaborated with their new rulers. Kristofferson played the part of right-leaning former presidential candidate Devin Milford, who leads a rebellion against the

Soviets, whose forces are kitted out in uniforms much like those of United Nations peacekeeping troops. The series managed to upset just about everybody; the Soviet Union threatened to shut down ABC's Moscow bureau, American conservatives felt that the Soviet brutality was understated, while left-wingers saw it as a case of right-wing paranoia that might threaten détente.

The United Nations strongly objected to any implication that it would be prepared to support such a totalitarian force and publicly stated concern that *Amerika* might erode its public image. It was also unhappy at the unauthorised use of the UN logo and flag, which resulted in negotiations between lawyers acting for the UN and ABC. It was eventually agreed that Kristofferson would appear in a brief public service announcement, made by the UN's Radio and Visual Services Division, in praise of UN peacekeepers.* Kris was filmed in the Security Council chamber and was available for a press call afterwards. While making no direct reference to *Amerika*, the advert was shown at around the same time as the series was screened.†

The critics were united in their loathing of *Amerika* as being overlong, unrealistic, badly acted and generally tedious. Even Kristofferson had his doubts. "I don't know if people will sit through the first two hours . . . it's like the beginning of a slow Russian novel." ABC invested around $40 million in the series but after initially strong viewing figures, the public voted by switching off in large numbers. The venture lost money on a grand scale – $20 million according to some reports.

Kristofferson came in for particularly vitriolic criticism from one critic who said he "barely can grunt his few lines and basically just stands there like a wasted sequoia tree . . . let us pray his stone-faced performance in *Amerika* proves once and for all to the entertainment industry the man's acting career is based on wholesale consumer fraud."

*Amerika* received some recognition but mainly in minimal categories including an Emmy nomination for Outstanding Achievement in Hair-styling for a Miniseries or a Special. Once the Berlin Wall came down in 1989, its intrinsic message was rendered obsolete.

---

* There were unconfirmed reports that Paul Newman had been asked to do the spot but had turned it down.

† In an unintentionally ironic case of timing, *Amerika* started its run at about the time Kristofferson travelled to Moscow for the peace forum arranged by Mikhail Gorbachev.

# Chapter 19

KRISTOFFERSON was so fired up by the righteousness of his beliefs that he was capable of making dramatic and often polarising statements. "To me there are two big forces on the planet, love and hate, and it's a question of whether one is going to beat the other," he told a journalist. "We've got our increasing ability to do each other in – to blow the planet up – that's in a race with our spiritual evolution. There seems to be a growing consciousness of a concern for one's brothers that is almost like a return to the Sixties. I feel it."

At a recent "human rights" concert in Mexico, Kristofferson spoke to members of a Nicaraguan band on the bill, one of whom suggested he go there himself to see what was happening. Kristofferson's involvement in *Amerika* had also helped to sharpen his thoughts on the subject and in tandem with his growing political activism he first visited the country in 1987. Kristofferson explained his reason for going was to show how it "means a lot to those people to know that not all Americans want to kill them".

He was particularly concerned at US financial support for the Contras (*contrarevolucionarios*) in their attempts to overthrow the Sandinistas who had forced out the dictator Somoza in 1979. Kristofferson, who described the coup that brought the Sandinistas to power as a "righteous revolution that was undermined by the United States", was angered by reports of campaigns by the Contras to destabilise the new regime by attacking soft targets such as schools, health facilities and agricultural co-operatives. He was also strongly opposed to America's economic embargo of Nicaragua. Although history has shown there were atrocities on both sides, it's clear that the Contras were guilty of much bloodthirsty violence in their campaign to undermine the Sandinistas.

Kristofferson was not dogmatic about his attitude to particular administrations; he judged them on their actions, though inevitably his approval was more likely to rest with the Democrats than Republicans. However, he admired President Dwight Eisenhower, particularly because of his warning about the potential dangers he foresaw flowing from the growing might of the military-industrial power base. In Kristofferson's view, it was "getting rich off our kids getting shot and killed – and killing people around the world".

In 1988, he appeared with Joan Baez in *Armageddon Express*, a tribute to peace activists comprising two short films, *The Arms Race Within*, a critique of nuclear weapons with the music of Bob Dylan as a backdrop, and *The Healing Of Brian Willson*, about activist S. Brian Willson, who lost both legs during a protest in Concord, California the previous year when he put himself in the path of a train carrying military weapons bound for Central America. Although the pair had yet to meet, Kristofferson con- tributed a sincere introduction to the film. "[Brian] put himself in the place of the people of Central America and in doing so he opened up the deepest truths of human existence. For the life and times of Brian Willson had turned him into a *satyagraha*, a practitioner of the non-violent resistance to evil, the path taken by Martin Luther King, Mahatma Gandhi and Archbishop Romero of El Salvador."

It was Kristofferson who initiated contact – evidently keen to be associ- ated with such a high-profile dissident. "I was surprised that someone wanted to be identified with someone like me who was way out of the American box," says Willson. In 1988, Kristofferson and Willson travelled to Nicaragua, being met at the airport by President Daniel Ortega along with thousands of jubilant Nicaraguans. Willson had hoped that other celebrities might lend support to his visit but Kristofferson was the only one prepared to. On the drive to their hotel – Ortega himself at the wheel – Kris sat incognito in the back with Nicaragua's foreign minister. Willson was surprised that Kristofferson wasn't the slightest bit bothered at not being the centre of attention. "It was just as well because when we landed in villages to meet some *campesinos* [rural villagers] all the signs of greeting had my name on them."

On a subsequent visit, Kristofferson and Willson travelled around the Nicaraguan countryside in a Soviet-built helicopter. Willson recalled one anxious moment. "We couldn't see an opening in the clouds and Kris was nervous – he was a helicopter pilot of course. He said we had to tell the pilot to find a hole in the clouds and get back to the ground and wait for the cloud to lift. Neither of us spoke Spanish well; somebody went to the pilot and got the message through . . . we managed to get back to base, sat on the ground for an hour and a half, waited for the sun to burn off the clouds. Kris said, 'Now we're safe.' "

Some of the places the pair flew over were active war zones and Willson was aware of the very real dangers. "The Contras had shoulder-to-air missiles, which they regularly used to shoot down Sandinista aircraft. Our helicopter had heat-emitting devices to draw the missiles to an extended high-heat air zone 30 feet away from the body of the helicopter. But they didn't always work properly . . . Kris did not appear unduly fazed . . . he was only concerned that since the helicopters flew by sight rather than instrumentation, the pilot had a clear view of the air space ahead of us."

During one Nicaraguan trip, Kristofferson met Eugene Hasenfus, a US cargo handler who parachuted from a plane that was shot down while trying to resupply the Contras. When the Sandinistas first asked Kristofferson if he wanted to talk to Hasenfus, he was unsure, feeling more empathy with the Sandinistas than with the Americans. However, since he had served time with the American military, Kris had sympathy for Hasenfus's situation. The day before the visit, President Ortega told Kristofferson that Hasenfus faced a maximum 30-year prison sentence.

Hasenfus felt he'd been neglected by the Reagan administration, later saying that Kristofferson was the only American who visited him while captured. As a form of solace, Kris told Hasenfus of his daughter Tracy's near-fatal accident and relayed the idea of praying for something that seemed impossible but just might come true. Kris agreed to meet Hasenfus's wife at the US Embassy. He again relayed the story about his daughter but worried that he was offering false hope. (Hasenfus ended up receiving a 25-year sentence.)

Before leaving Nicaragua, Kristofferson appealed to the warden of the prison where Hasenfus was being held, telling her about his visit to a Saudi Arabian jail to visit an American who had worked for the same company as his father and who'd suffered a nervous breakdown. Kristofferson said Hasenfus was showing similar signs and that it would be tragic if he submitted under the same pressure. The Sandinistas prided themselves on prison reforms they had introduced since the revolution and soon afterwards, Hasenfus was released and sent home to America.

Kristofferson tracked him down and said, "I don't know if this has done anything for your faith but it's done something for mine." In fact,

Hasenfus was released as part of an exchange of prisoners deal, so it would be hard to sustain the claim that divine or any other intervention had helped him.*

Kristofferson believed what he was uncovering on American foreign policy – in Nicaragua and other trouble spots – was not widely disseminated in America and felt that he had a duty in using his gift as a singer-songwriter to help effect a change. "I think that songs can be a terrific weapon. If you can write something that is popular, that strikes a chord with other people, you become part of their life and every time they hear the song they'll get the emotion that you give them about something you believe in."

However, it doesn't appear to have occurred to him that many Americans might have been aware of what was happening overseas in the name of their country but were either untroubled by or supportive of what they perceived to be initiatives to protect American interests.

After several years of conflict in Nicaragua, events moved the opposing sides towards negotiations. Kristofferson and Willson were present at Sapoa on the border with Costa Rica to witness the Sandinista leaders meeting directly for the first time with the Contra leaders.† "It was kind of a historic moment . . ." Willson recalls. "Kris sat next to me at a press conference. I don't remember him ever being asked any questions, or asking any . . . he always seemed relaxed, but fully present. He was listening to what very few Americans experienced in person about the counterrevolutionary use of terror and how demonic it really is. I know he was very troubled by what he was hearing, but I don't think he was surprised, just viscerally affected."

Although they have not worked together since, Kristofferson has regularly met up with Willson at concerts and fund-raising events for solidarity movements in Latin America. Kristofferson has remained steadfast in his admiration of the political activist despite his unpopularity in many mainstream circles. As recently as 2007, he dedicated a song to Willson and the Sandinistas at a concert in northern California. "There's a guy in the

---

* Hasenfus did not become part of the anti-war movement; Kristofferson claims that the CIA got involved and gagged him; whether this was true or a case of left-wing paranoia remains unclear.
† The Sandinistas were democratically removed from office in 1990.

audience who is a friend of mine whom I respect – he's a hero to me."

Willson was amused at Kristofferson's anti-war comments against the Bush administration, when the audience was "a very conservative crowd, fundamentalist right-wing Christians." When he pointed this out to Kristofferson's wife, Lisa, she joked, "Well I guess we probably won't be invited back here again . . . but so what? We gave them a taste of what we believe." When they parted that night, Kristofferson told Willson, "Let's continue telling the truth."

At the same time as he was pursuing his political interests, Kristofferson continued to appear in a succession of films that were little better than mediocre. A 1988 article about a Kristofferson film in a local Nashville newspaper almost had the feel of an obituary: "Editor's note: Kris Kristofferson may best be remembered as a leading man of the 70s [*A Star Is Born,* 1976] and a country singer and musician ['Me And Bobby McGee']. So audiences may not recognise the 52-year-old actor in his forthcoming movie . . ."

In the television movie *The Tracker*, Kristofferson played Sheriff Noble Adams, a once great Indian tracker and fighter, who is called out of retirement to hunt down a murderous religious fanatic and his gang after they break out of jail. Kristofferson invariably relished such a role, jokingly telling an interviewer, "Every time I read about a western being made and I'm not in it, I feel a keen sense of personal loss."

Kristofferson was called upon to display the kind of understated gravitas and wisdom that comes with age. The role also required him to address a difficult relationship with his estranged son – a neat reversal of his own father-son experience that helped him to imbue the character with greater depth.

Whereas he could act naturally as part of a western, Kristofferson was completely miscast in the bizarre comedy *Big Top Pee-Wee*, a vehicle for idiosyncratic children's comedian Paul Reubens in his surreal persona of Pee-wee Herman. The slim storyline concerned attempts by Pee-wee and the circus folk to come up with a show that the townsfolk will like. It was hard to fathom how Kristofferson could have been regarded as right for the part of ringmaster and manager of a travelling circus troupe that fetches up on Pee-wee's doorstep during a violent storm – with a wife who is three inches tall and lives in his shirt pocket.

Despite the presence of big names including director Randal Kleiser (*Grease*) and future Oscar winner Benicio Del Toro, who was making his cinema debut, the film totally misfired. One critic said of Kristofferson, "He leads his troupe with undisguised shame," while another charged, "Kris Kristofferson has never been a kitsch object, but playing opposite Pee-wee he suddenly ascends to a place in the pantheon of show-biz awfulness."

Ironically, during an interview that touched on the state of the film industry, Kristofferson commented, "It's depressing to see so many stupid movies get a lot of money." *Big Top Pee-Wee* lost around $8 million and only the most fervent of Kristofferson completists would want to investigate this forgettable oddity.

In 1989 Kristofferson dipped into the world of science fiction for *Millennium*, a low-budget piece of hokum in which he played air accident investigator Bill Smith. In the course of investigating a mid-air collision, he discovers a futuristic stun gun and later meets Louise, played by former *Charlie's Angels* actress Cheryl Ladd, the leader of a commando team from a thousand years in the future on a mission to save a race of dying humanoids. A romance develops but Kristofferson, looking every grizzled inch his 53 years, was a different proposition from the manly hunk of *A Star Is Born*. Apart from an unconvincing script involving clunky dialogue that sought, laboriously, to explain the science behind the story, the film was compromised by unconvincing, cheap-looking sets as a reviewer remarked, "When the time travellers enter and leave a scene, they step in and out of an animated blue-and-white funnel of the sort one might expect to see in a cleanser ad."

That same year, Kristofferson had been invited to perform at a concert in Nicaragua celebrating the 10th anniversary of the Sandinista revolution. Daniel Ortega asked him to sing just after Oliver Tambo of the African National Congress spoke. Before he started, Kris said, "This is in honour of the spirit of the people who overthrew the oppressive US-supported Somoza dictatorship." On his return to America, some people picketed his concerts. For the less politically vocal, it was doubtless unsettling to hear anti-American diatribes when the concertgoer had anticipated a pleasant evening listening to old favourites such as 'For The Good Times' and 'Help Me Make It Through The Night'. At one show in Atlanta, around 300 people asked for their money back.

Kristofferson had often complained about a lack of record company support but his political stances undoubtedly affected his bankability. During much of the Reagan era, it seemed that simply attending a Kris Kristofferson gig was a political statement. Though there was still a demand, he now played "two shows a night in these little honky-tonks" as Kristofferson described them. Without Rita Coolidge, he was considered less of a draw though he continued to maintain a loyal following.

Touring with The Borderlords increased his financial pressures, as Billy Swan confirmed: "[Kris] couldn't afford to pay a lot. It's just so damned expensive on the road with a bus and hotel rooms. And there was a light man, a sound man for the house and a sound man for the stage, so there were quite a few people working with Kris, apart from the road manager."

There was insufficient work to keep the band on a retainer so members worked on other artists' tours until Kristofferson eventually disbanded The Borderlords around 1990, though he continued to work with the individuals on an *ad hoc* basis for live and studio work.

On July 2, 1989, Kristofferson was among a number of performers including Neil Young, Willie Nelson and John Denver who performed in front of an audience of 6,000 at the Paha Sapa Festival in Rapid City, South Dakota, in aid of various causes, including an alcohol and family counselling centre supportive of Native Americans. Some referred to the event as the Woodstock of Indian country. Kris had appeared at a similar benefit two years earlier entitled Cowboys for Indians on a bill that included David Crosby, Stephen Stills and Jerry Jeff Walker.

In 1990, Kristofferson joined around 14,000 well-wishers at a party in Austin, Texas, for Democratic governor-elect Ann Richards, who claimed she would return government to the people.

Kristofferson also opened a number of shows for Johnny Cash, creating a stir in Philadelphia when he dedicated a song to Mumia Abu-Jamal, who was on death row for the murder of a policeman; his supporters argued that he had not received a fair trial. Members of the police who were supervising crowd control were furious and demanded that Kristofferson go back out and apologise. Cash told him he did not have to apologise for anything he believed in and by way of support, he invited Kristofferson back out onstage for the final number.

Kristofferson and Cash were reunited – with Willie Nelson and Waylon

Jennings – for the follow-up to *Highwayman*, the unimaginatively titled *Highwayman II*. When released in early 1990, the album performed reasonably well, spending over 40 weeks in the country chart and peaking at number four, but it did not repeat the spectacular success of the first collaboration. Chips Moman produced in such a fashion – prominent drums, electric guitars and organs – as to bring rock values to songs that, with a different approach, could just as easily have been pure country. There were more writing contributions from the members – Kristofferson recycled two songs, 'Anthem '84', from *Repossessed*, while 'Living Legend' had first appeared on 1978's *Easter Island*, but once more, with a view to variety, songs by outside writers were used.

The inclusion of 'American Remains', which bore a striking resemblance to 'Highwayman', kick-started the career of an aspiring writer called Rivers Rutherford. With faint echoes of Kristofferson's dramatic effort to grab Cash's attention in 1969, Rutherford invaded Moman's house after leaping his security fence. The guard dogs and police were aroused but the producer was in a forgiving mood. Much to his surprise and delight, after Rutherford played him the song, Moman decided to include it and the writer got to sing background vocals.

As with 'Highwayman', each singer was allotted the role of a character – a shotgun rider, a Midwest farmer, an American Indian and a river gambler – whose life has hit problems, with the chorus reading like an epitaph for the four principals. Kristofferson described the real-life characters in his own inimitable way: "Willie's the old coyote, Waylon's the riverboat gambler, I'm the radical revolutionary and Johnny's the father of our country."

To promote the album, the Highwaymen's first full-scale tour started in March, soon after the extraction of a single, 'Silver Stallion'. Over 55,000 fans turned up for the opening show at the Houston Livestock Show and Rodeo, breaking all previous attendance records, and the rest of the tour attracted near sell-out audiences. It was a wonder the tour happened at all – Cash had suffered a broken jaw that had been misdiagnosed as toothache, but a combination of painkillers and adrenalin helped to ensure that the show went on.

In June, the Highwaymen fulfilled a week-long engagement at the ostentatiously lavish Mirage hotel in Las Vegas (returning for another week towards the end of the year after a short US tour) and again played at

Willie's Fourth of July picnic. In 1991, the troupe left America for a short tour of Australia and New Zealand, playing to almost full houses. Unlike the albums, The Highwaymen went in for unashamed crowd pleasing, playing individual hits such as 'Me And Bobby McGee', 'Good Hearted Woman', 'Folsom Prison Blues' and 'Crazy', but with new arrangements for some – perhaps to make the songs more interesting for the players – though an uptempo 'Help Me Make It Through The Night' lost much of its emotional intensity in translation.

Inevitably, there were occasional flare-ups. On one occasion in Australia, some wires on stage got mixed up as Kristofferson later recalled, "Willie was getting my guitar and I was getting his. He didn't want his monitor so I wasn't getting anything, so I'm yelling at the monitor guy through the whole show to raise my volume because I can't hear it and he's making it louder but it's on Willie's monitor . . . Willie hates the way I play guitar. Finally he walked forward and just ripped the wires out." For his part, Nelson was quick to compliment Kristofferson. "He shows more soul when he blows his nose than the ordinary person does at his honeymoon dance."

Not every venue was large scale. On one occasion, Cash's manager, Lou Robin, having been unable to set up an intended show in Hong Kong, arranged a private performance for some American businessmen. It was strange indeed for The Highwaymen to be playing to around 200 people but as Robin explained with some understatement, "The show was not typical but it made financial sense."

While Kristofferson was honoured to be among The Highwaymen's ranks, he didn't shy away from expressing his political views on occasion – even though this risked displeasing the audience, not to mention members of the band and crew who reputedly held up signs saying, "That doesn't go for me."

Journalist Stacy Harris recalls covering a Highwaymen press conference in Nashville. "I asked him something about his political stuff; being Kris he didn't just give the usual pat answers but went into quite a lot of detail about his opinions and why he felt he had to speak out. Afterwards Waylon stopped me, he was really irritated, and said I shouldn't have asked Kris about politics. I justified the question on the basis that Kris was making political records and political statements. Waylon's concern was that it would be bad publicity for the band because a lot of people did not approve of what he was saying and doing. He said, 'We've been trying to get him to shut up about that stuff.' I think Waylon's view was that if Kris wanted to take away from his own record sales that's fine, but not The Highwaymen."

Jennings was also annoyed when Kristofferson made a negative comment about American foreign policy during a concert. It turned out that Colin Powell, then Chairman of the Joint Chiefs of Staff, was in the audience – though Kristofferson was not aware of this at the time.

Unlike Jennings, Cash didn't show any undue concern over his band-mate's views. Indeed he wrote to *Country Music* expressing strong support for Kristofferson's right to express his opinions after the magazine had printed some adverse comment – pointing out that unlike some of his critics, Kristofferson had actually served in the army.

While most of the songs The Highwaymen played in concert were not in any way political, there were exceptions that created a jarring effect. Kristofferson's 'They Killed Him' and Cash's 'Ragged Old Flag' were not so contradictory – both concerned patriotism, conflict and a struggle for freedom – but their respective emphases were completely different.

Cash's delivery of his highly sentimental 'Ragged Old Flag' was charged with extra emotion following the 1989 Supreme Court ruling in *Texas -v-Johnson*, which held that a statute that criminalises the desecration of the American flag violates the First Amendment – in other words it was not against the law to burn the American flag.

A week after the release of *Highwayman II* came Kristofferson's second Mercury album, the grimly militant *Third World Warrior*, in which he once more sought to tell the truth as he saw it. The mood was set by the cover photograph, which captured Kris staring with intense and frowning con-centration, like a gunslinger about to draw. Backed by The Borderlords, the music had a harsh and aggressively choppy rock sound – far away from Kristofferson's country origins – in line with the austere, manifesto-like quality of the songs. The mood was lightened slightly by the presence of some Latin rhythms that he'd soaked up at some of the music events he attended during his trips to Nicaragua.

For the title track, in a specific reference to El Salvador, Kristofferson described the indomitable spirit of those who fought for their freedom against the forces of oppression. 'Aguila Del Norte' was a full-frontal assault on the actions of the Contras in Nicaragua, as supported by Reagan. 'Don't Let The Bastards Get You Down' contained more in a similar vein but in the chorus, Kristofferson identified with his late father, making it clear that recent American administrations had betrayed the ideals earlier generations had believed in and felt the right to fight and die for.

Kristofferson was one of a number of celebrities who had endorsed Jesse Jackson when he unsuccessfully ran for the Democratic presidential nomination in 1988. He admired Jackson because he was prepared to take political risks, such as meeting Castro and Ortega, and considered there would have been far greater communication with the Third World with Jackson as president. The "his brother" reference in the hopeful 'Jesse Jackson' (featuring a guest appearance from Willie Nelson) was to Martin Luther King.

At the time, Kristofferson brushed away accusations that the album's songs were sermons with the patronising defence that he had a duty to tell people what was going on because so many were unaware of the situation. But it was a fair criticism. 'Sandinista' acted as a biased platform on the total worthiness of the Nicaraguan government's case, while 'Third World War' was similarly reductive over the divisions of good and evil. 'The Eagle And The Bear' functioned as another declaration of righteous intent, again evoking the spirit of Henry Kristofferson, with references to the problems in Nicaragua and El Salvador and the imprisonment of Nelson Mandela. The song's message was blunted, however, by Mandela's release from prison the month before the record hit the shops.*

The emotion and subtlety that Kristofferson was able to express in his earlier love and relationship songs was eradicated by the grating anger of his delivery; however, the strength of these feelings skewed his artistic judgement. In effect, *Third World Warrior* was a series of preachy and simplistic political soundbites – in many ways similar to John Lennon's 1972 reportage journal, *Some Time In New York City*, which many considered damaging to Lennon's post-Beatles solo career. Kristofferson later conceded as much when he said he would never play a concert that only included political material.

---

* Kristofferson was invited to sing 'The Eagle And The Bear' at an event celebrating Mandela's release at the Los Angeles Coliseum in March 1990.

There was praise for *Third World Warrior* from some quarters, predictably from such like-minded liberals as Jackson Browne who claimed, "It has brought me to tears and it has strengthened my resolve."

Not surprisingly those with opposing political views loathed everything about it and the general consensus was summed up by one critic who said, "This is neither a rallying cry nor an emotional spur, merely a bore."

At a time when the Republicans were still in office, Kristofferson's detractors were many. One wrote, "In the late Sixties and early Seventies, Kris Kristofferson was the voice of his generation. Today he is more the conscience of his generation. Unfortunately nobody pays much attention to his conscience any more." Another accused him of "chloroforming millions [how Kristofferson must have wished the numbers listening to his music could be counted in millions] with new songs about freedom fighters, Latin American rebels and other leftist causes."

What some saw as honest and courageous, others dismissed as irrelevant. Kristofferson's right-wing detractors argued, for example, that Reagan's call to "tear down that wall, Mr Gorbachev" resulted in personal freedom for millions who had long been subjugated by communism. While artists like Kristofferson preached about freedom to the converted, tough conservative policies had actually achieved it.

# Chapter 20

IN the late Seventies, to exploit his high public profile following *A Star Is Born*, the first Kristofferson compilation album had appeared. Another followed in the Eighties before a minor flood from the early Nineties onwards. Most contained some or all of the best-known hits plus a sample of lesser known songs from Kristofferson's sizeable back catalogue. In 1991, Columbia-Legacy released the compilation *Singer/Songwriter*, a double-CD set containing both Kristofferson's original versions and the best-known covers by people like Janis Joplin and Ray Price.

In 1992, a more interesting Kristofferson archival release saw the light of day. *Live At The Philharmonic* was recorded at a December 1972 New York show in support of *Jesus Was A Capricorn* but remained in the vaults, probably due to the amount of Kristofferson product released at the time. Two decades on, it was a timely reminder of Kristofferson's writing talent and his remarkably fecund period of creativity in a short space of time – of the 23 songs, the set list even omitted two of his most well-known songs, 'Why Me' and 'Help Me Make It Through The Night'.

Apart from major hits such as 'Sunday Morning Coming Down' and 'Me And Bobby McGee' (one of three songs on which Kris duetted with Rita Coolidge, whom he would marry eight months later), the album included John Prine's 'Late John Garfield Blues' and 'Whisky Whisky' by Tom Ghent, a song that Kristofferson later recorded for 1979's *Shake Hands With The Devil*. Willie Nelson, then a largely unknown quantity on the East Coast, performed a few of his own songs and Larry Gatlin joined Kristofferson for 'Help Me'.

*Live At The Philharmonic* captured Kristofferson at the top of his game. Backed by some of the musicians – Donnie Fritts, Stephen Bruton, Mike Utley and Sammy Creason – who became his loyal sidemen, Kristofferson's vocals were on the mark, evidently inspired by the band's tasteful countrified backing. For those used to the jarring attack of his politicised albums and some of the banal films he was appearing in, the recording was a revelation, capturing the subtler, softer side of the man and his music. It still stands as a minor classic.

At the turn of the Nineties, Kristofferson was as busy as ever with his acting career. Though by no means a masterpiece, *Welcome Home* was a film that deserved to be taken more seriously than Kristofferson's usual output from this time. He played the part of Jake Robbins, thought to have been killed in Vietnam 17 years previously, who returns to America having married a Vietnamese woman with whom he has fathered two children. His move is precipitated by ill health rather than a desire to resume life in his homeland, which causes emotional upheavals for his father, his American wife – who has since remarried – and their son. The authorities pressure Jake into keeping quiet about his experience and the uneasy feeling that permeates the story is that it would probably have been better if Jake had stayed "lost" in Asia.

*Welcome Home* raised issues associated with the aftermath of the Vietnam war, and awkward questions were directed towards the covert military authorities about missing servicemen who might still be alive and, like Jake, living in Vietnam by choice. Although spoiled by an overly sentimental ending (intensified by a soppy Henry Mancini score) that resolved all the issues too neatly, the movie's strength lay in the fact that there were no obvious heroes or villains. As in real life, events conspired to create difficult choices and challenges that ordinary people have to struggle with knowing that whatever choices they make, they will be left with lingering doubts.

Kristofferson's reserved acting, conveying the impression of a decent man suffering inner turmoil, suited the part well – "convincingly weary and ravaged", as one critic put it. Less convincing were his forced attempts to express strong emotion in an overt way in the latter stages of the film. Keeping it in the family musically, Willie Nelson sang the title song.

In 1990's *Perfume Of The Cyclone* (aka *Night Of The Cyclone*), set in the Comoro Islands, Kristofferson played Stan Wozniak, a police officer searching for his daughter after she fails to return from a modelling assignment. Along the way he has a dangerous liaison with a French beauty, Francoise (played by Marisa Berenson), and survives a hurricane. For what was essentially the kind of routine fare that featured on American daytime television, the movie included quite a lot of sex and violence. Tracy Kristofferson had a small part as an "arty lady".\*

Also in 1990, for *Sandino*, Kristofferson played the part of an American journalist in the early part of the 20th century following the exploits of Nicaraguan revolutionary Augusto C. Sandino. Given his great interest in the subject, the part was a natural for him. Sandino, who was assassinated in 1934, led a rebellion against the US military presence in Nicaragua between 1927 and 1933. Sandino, who identified strongly with the indigenous peoples, was a hero to many in Latin America, being the archetypal revolutionary guerrilla and the inspiration for the Sandinistas, whereas to the Americans he was a bandit.

In 1992, by complete contrast, Kristofferson starred in the television film *Miracle In The Wilderness*, which the press described as a "holiday drama". Based on a novella by Paul Gallico, Kristofferson played Jericho Adams, a former US cavalryman trying to establish a new life in the country with his city-bred wife and baby. The family's new-found idyll is shattered when they are captured by a tribe of Blackfoot Indians whose leader holds Jericho Adams responsible for the killing of his child – and wants revenge. Salvation comes in the form of Jericho's wife who, by the somewhat incongruous expedient of relating the story of the birth of Christ, somehow manages to change the tribal chief's point of view. Kris rather stretched the point when relating the film to his political views, saying he regarded *Miracle In the Wilderness* as "a strong argument against violence . . . I think the message could be taken by the people who are running our government today".

In 1992, Kristofferson put his support behind maverick billionaire businessman Ross Perot's Reform Party in its election battle with Bill Clinton and George Bush Snr. Perot struck a chord with many Americans who were disillusioned with mainstream politicians and their apparent inability to steer the economy away from recessionary threats. Perot had never held an elected office; initially, at least, his common-sense approach to reducing the American deficit – measured in trillions – boosted his ratings in the opinion polls to the extent that he earned the right to take part in three-way television debates with the other candidates.

---

\* Tracy worked as an assistant producer on a number of Kristofferson's films and also assisted Lisa with some management duties in connection with Kris' tours.

Perot was certainly not perceived as a liberal, favouring tougher law enforcement and stronger national defence. By way of explanation, Kristofferson said, "I'm sure a lot of my views are to the left of Ross Perot but for me the old labels just don't work any more. I think there's a point where people who just believe in respect for human life on this planet can agree." In the event, though Perot won 19 million votes, about 20 per cent of the popular vote, he did not win a single state.

In October, Kristofferson was honoured to be among the artists chosen to appear at a concert marking and celebrating Bob Dylan's 30 years as a recording and performing artist. The event, which featured only songs written by Dylan, was staged at New York's Madison Square Garden in front of 18,000 fans. The concert – which included Stevie Wonder, Lou Reed, Tracy Chapman, Johnny Cash, Willie Nelson, The Clancy Brothers, Shawn Colvin, The Band, George Harrison, Eric Clapton, Roger McGuinn, Neil Young (who dubbed the star gathering "Bobfest") and Mary Chapin Carpenter – was recorded and later released as a double CD and eventually achieved gold status.

Kristofferson sang 'I'll Be Your Baby Tonight' but this was over-shadowed by his instinct to defend a fellow radical during the evening's most controversial moment. Sinead O'Connor had recently appeared on the popular NBC show, *Saturday Night Live*, during which she unexpectedly tore up a picture of the Pope, to a subsequent stream of outrage. Having been introduced, sections of the crowd at the Dylan event booed and hissed while O'Connor defiantly stood her ground.

"The atmosphere was great, everybody was there for the right reasons, respect for Dylan . . ." Kristofferson later said. "A stage manager came up to me because I was one of the MCs and said, 'Get her off the stage.' I was so pissed off . . . I wasn't about to tell her to get off the stage so I walked out and said to her, 'Don't let the bastards get you down,' and of course the mike was on. She's such a good example of good intentions that just get you into trouble. She's talking about human rights and she's not a bad guy; the bad guys are the guys who are against human rights."

O'Connor eventually broke down in tears and was escorted offstage with words of comfort by Kristofferson.

To end the year, Kristofferson appeared in *Christmas In Connecticut*, a lightweight comedy co-starring Dyan Cannon, Richard Roundtree and Tony Curtis, with Arnold Schwarzenegger as the rather surprising choice of director. Kristofferson played Jefferson Jones, a forest ranger and a national hero after saving a young child – but who has lost his log cabin in the fire that engulfed it. The producer of a successful television cookery show hosted by Elizabeth Blane (Dyan Cannon) comes up with the idea of a live show in which Elizabeth prepares a Christmas dinner for Jefferson. The problem is that she is only acting the part; she can't cook at all and is a lonely widow living in New York.

Most of the film is taken up with Elizabeth's attempts, and those of the various people roped in to act as her happy family, to keep this a secret from Jefferson and the TV audience. Kristofferson admirers were doubtless surprised to see him engaging in such slapstick comedy routines as checking out Elizabeth's behind as he follows her up a ladder or trying to deal with an overflowing coffee pot and the subsequent mess.

*Christmas In Connecticut* had enough clean-cut humour to make it popular family viewing but far too many clichés to make it a good film. As one critic drily stated, "You'll be hungry for a better movie after suffering through this film." When talking about his recurrent self-doubts, Kris said – with characteristic candour – that he had "no business" in films and performing music – he had only got into them because of his songwriting gift. "Between my family life and my unpopular politics, I'm fairly limited in what I'm offered."

However, it seemed that so long as Kristofferson was prepared to earn a significant part of his income from the cinema he would have little option but to accept roles that were rarely better than routine television fodder. He had made so many by now that he was comfortable with the process, which was familiar and manageable.

In 1992, Kris accepted work as a performer on the cruise ship QE2; by doing so he was following a path trodden by the likes of such MOR artists as Petula Clark and Neil Sedaka. As if this didn't raise a few eyebrows, his good friend Johnny Cash accepted a gig at Butlin's holiday camp in the south of England, around the same time.

John Hedley, a fellow musician, recalls seeing Kristofferson during a country and western themed cruise up America's East Coast, in which they both appeared. Hedley found Kristofferson to be a "gentle and polite man" and was struck by the fact that in contrast to the formally attired audience, Kris was very casually dressed in black T-shirt, jeans and a cowboy hat. Even in the presence of a self-evidently conservative crowd, Kristofferson could not restrain himself from bringing up politics – to his cost, as Hedley recalled, "When he declared his backing for Bill Clinton in the upcoming presidential contest, half the audience walked out." As a quote, attributed to Paul Newman but which Kristofferson admired, said, "If you're not pissing somebody off, you're not doing anything."

Kristofferson was on board for a week or so, playing two shows an evening as top of the bill, backed by a 10-man band. He was fortunate to disembark at Martha's Vineyard because, two hours later, the QE2 hit a granite outcrop in the Nantucket Shoals, which cut an 85 foot gash into the hull and put the ship in danger.

In 1993 Kristofferson was the subject of a lengthy documentary on his career: *Kris Kristofferson: Pilgrim. His Life And Work*. Generally uncritical in its honour, it nonetheless benefited from Kristofferson's co-operation with many of the major players he'd worked with in music, films and political activism. Contributors included Johnny Cash, Billy Swan, Fred Foster, Willie Nelson, John Prine, Joan Baez, Vernon White and Cesar Chavez, President of the United Farm Workers.

Kristofferson's early life was examined with rare photographs from his school and army days. Naturally Kristofferson's songwriting was discussed; Nelson said there had always been sex in country music but up until Kris achieved recognition, it had never been described so directly. "It raised some eyebrows and sold some records." Cash praised Kris for the spiritual nature of his celebration of love and sex and beauty, stating Kristofferson had made other writers work at their art rather than just "rhyming words and using catchphrases and clichés".

Don Was considered Kristofferson's varied use of imagery relating to personal freedom, "the sorts of things that all men aspire to . . . I think he represents a certain ideal; he's really got it all covered, boxer, helicopter pilot, all these romantic images. Freedom, isn't that at the core of what everybody wants – to live the life that they choose?"

It wasn't all sweetness and light. Kristofferson reflected on his drink problem which had led him to "the darker side". He also revealed that the only time he felt despair "in such a way as to consider checking out" had been when he was drinking heavily. Michael Cimino talked of Kristofferson's descent into "Lincolnesque black moods" during *Heaven's*

*Gate* – a time when, among other troubles, his marriage had broken up and he feared he might lose contact with his daughter.

Acknowledging the vicissitudes of his lengthy exploration of the wild side of life, Kristofferson appeared truly grateful that he had come through the other side and learnt to appreciate the supreme value of the relationships he enjoyed with his wife and children. "My life's damn near normal now."

The sheer number of films he continued to appear in – four in 1993 alone – was striking. *Paper Hearts* was an occasionally touching family drama about the effects of a marriage break-up. Kristofferson's task was to portray a virile yet sensitive man willing to accept women on their own terms. In *No Place To Hide,* he played a detective who forms a bond with a 14-year-old girl whose sister, a ballerina, was murdered during a performance. After a moderately intriguing start, the film descended into formulaic sentimentality.

A few phrases extracted from a review of *Trouble Shooters: Trapped Beneath The Earth* pretty much sums up Kristofferson's cinematic output from this period: "Pure TV pap . . . every cliché thrown in . . . killed by a small budget . . . no tension." For his final 1993 movie, *Knights*, Kristofferson entered the realm of science fiction as an android, Gabriel, but the plot was a galaxy removed from Wells and Asimov.

Away from the media and his active political escapades, Kristofferson had an ever growing family to support. His and Lisa's first child, Jesse Turner, was born in October 1983, and the couple went on to have four more, one of whom, Johnny, was named after Cash, and the last, Blake, born in 1994, after the artist who had been such an important inspiration to Kristofferson. In 1989, Kris and Lisa had been named joint guardians of the three young children belonging to their nanny-housekeeper, Maria Juana Aguilar, who had died in a shooting incident.

Maria worked for Kristofferson for approximately 10 years and had asked him if he would take care of her children should anything happen to her. He was originally granted temporary guardianship but his subsequent petition for full guardianship was opposed. After listening to legal submissions, the court granted co-guardianship to Kristofferson and Maria's sister, with whom the children lived on a day-to-day basis. A further petition on behalf of the children's father was rejected.

Kris and Lisa did not want to raise the children in the city. Having enjoyed holidays in Hawaii since the mid-Seventies, Kris decided to relocate to the idyllic island of Maui, where he and Lisa acquired a secluded ranch-style property in grounds of around 50 acres. The house was in the town of Hana, on the undeveloped side of the island, away from the tourist areas. Another benefit was that Willie Nelson owned a property nearby.

Hana is sometimes referred to as the last tropical paradise on Maui and the outdoor lifestyle reminded Kristofferson of where he grew up. Tropical fruit including bananas and a variety of citrus fruits are grown – as was the case in Brownsville and there were beautiful beaches and spectacular waterfalls. While the locals all knew each other – some of the local children called Kris "uncle" – he could also get away from it all if he wanted to. "Sometimes I'll go off for three days at a time or I'll go and clear the land with a chainsaw and be gone by myself for 12 hours at a time."

He was now much healthier and regularly ran for miles along the beach. "It's easier for me to work now . . . after I hit 40 and got off the chemicals, my life was much better and happier." It was a message Kristofferson hammered home in many interviews; he stressed that having to be responsible for his daughter Casey was a major factor in helping to get himself "straightened out". Kris had taken major strides towards curbing his indulgences but there was no permanent clean break in 1976 as has often been reported. It seems clear, however, that he never returned to the major excesses of earlier years.

He was well aware of the danger of backsliding. Interviewed in 1988, he said, "I could end up a drunk tomorrow, but I doubt it. I think I have all the chemistry to be a full-fledged alcoholic or drug addict because I welcome oblivion like an old friend sometimes."

He talked openly that year to journalist Candace Burke-Block about his past vices. "I drank like a fish for a long time. I had a drinking problem until I was almost 40 . . . I cleaned up. I still smoked grass after that but I found out at Alcoholics Anonymous that grass counts too, so I quit that as well."

One particular reason for Kristofferson wanting to get clean was to appear credible when pushing political issues; he believed it might weaken the strength of his arguments, at a time when he was "fixing to get controversial", if he was perceived to be someone with a heavy drinking habit. He wanted to appear "unbustable".

Though clearly a highly personal area, he has nonetheless endeavoured to give reasonably straight answers to questions on the subject. When interviewed by Diane Baroni in 1998, Kris confessed, "I've been through everything, all the rehabs in California."

By the mid-Nineties a new brand of commercial country was sweeping America with platinum sales for two of its main players, Garth Brooks and Billy Ray Cyrus. Up against an artist like Brooks – with a degree in advertising and a stadium-rock attitude in the presentation of his live shows – four ageing icons had little chance of competing on equal terms. The Highwaymen had endured as a semi-active brand for a decade, providing Kristofferson with a degree of commercial success right when he needed it. However, audience numbers had gradually diminished and though they found substantial support from a new breed of country purists like Dale Watson, who berated country DJs for not supporting the old brigade, the writing was on the wall.

"Watching the four of them is like watching Rushmore. It was great, very poignant and inspirational . . ." observed eccentric singer-songwriter Kinky Friedman, who attended one of The Highwaymen's final concerts, "but these guys can't keep jumping through their assholes for America. They're getting OLD."

The final throw of the dice came in 1995 with a third album, *The Road Goes On Forever* – an accomplished and pleasing album even if not one single track hit the heights each member of the band had proved capable of individually. It stands as a fitting tribute to a worthwhile venture that enriched the careers of all four artists and delighted audiences around the world. Kristofferson regards it as the best album The Highwaymen produced; up until this point he felt their live performances were more impressive than their studio output.

Recorded in California, the album was produced by Don Was, with whom all the members, apart from Cash, had worked before. A polished bass player, he started his own band, Was (Not Was), who released a number of moderately successful albums in the Eighties, before finding his real metier in production. Over the years, Was produced albums by some of the biggest names in the business including Bob Dylan and Elton John, acquiring something of a reputation for reinvigorating the stalled recording careers of major artists. "[Was] orchestrates his sessions with the skill of a master conductor . . ." Waylon Jennings said. "Some complex jug-gling was required. Don was at his ease moving everything forward, keeping everybody loose and alert and letting nothing faze him."

The album was imbued with a country essence yet managed to incorporate elements of AOR and affecting balladry; it also allowed the individual qualities of each member to emerge from the overall loose and relaxed band sound, even if the production might have benefited from being a little rougher around the edges. Each artist contributed a song; Kristofferson's being a new version of 'Here Comes That Rainbow Again'. Inspired by an incident in *The Grapes Of Wrath*, Kristofferson said John Steinbeck should have been credited as co-author. Cash had previ-ously recorded the song, describing it as one of his favourites, although interestingly, Kris apparently only found this out when reading it in Cash's autobiography.

The opening track, 'The Devil's Right Hand,' written by Steve Earle, was custom-made for the gnarled features and attitudes of The Highway-men in its evocation of the Old West, while 'The Road Goes On Forever', written by Robert Earl Keen Jr, was a fitting end to the album. With its understated but insistent rhythm, it related the kind of doomed romance-and-crime story, about Sherry and a loner she chances upon, that was meat and drink to The Highwaymen in general and Kristofferson in particular. It also carried the message that, regardless of what the future held, the music of four remarkable individuals would last well beyond their own lives.

The album received a positive reception from critics, many of whom greatly preferred the authenticity of four irreplaceable originals to the manufactured cookie-cutter acts that were being turned out with a cool image, a hip video and a distinct lack of any country music heritage. One was inspired to end his full stars review with the words, "God bless you boys for keeping the true spirit of country music alive." There was even a collective swipe at the increasingly commercialised world of modern country with its short-lived pretty boy hat acts in the album's sleeve notes. "This is not country music as an image accessory or a corporate game plan."

The predictable weak spot was Kristofferson's vocals. As one reviewer put it, "He's required to sing once in a while. He stumbles in barely on key, and he doesn't project much vocal character . . . a curious failing for a guy who has lived a lot of life. Everything on *The Road Goes On Forever* flattens out until his turn ends."

Despite the album's undoubted quality and high-profile promotional appearances on the television shows of David Letterman and Jay Leno, it did not fare well commercially. There were further releases including a video, a compilation and a new version of *The Road Goes On Forever* with six bonus tracks, but The Highwaymen effectively disbanded in 1995 amid disagreements over plans for another tour.

For years Kristofferson had found it hard to win over critics with his recorded output. However, the tide unexpectedly changed with a well-balanced collection, *A Moment Of Forever*, released in 1995, which elicited widespread approval from reviewers. Typical was the response from *Q* magazine: "Excellent . . . his best work in donkey's years . . . nothing less than the sound of a man suddenly rejuvenated."

The album had been recorded, with Don Was producing, several years previously, and intended for release on Was' own imprint, Karambolage (supported by MCA). However, these plans were shelved after the label lost its distribution deal and the album was eventually released on a small independent, Justice Records.

In the stark cover shot, Kristofferson, looking ravaged but defiant, world-weary but wise, stared intently at the camera as if to say, "This is me, you wanna make something of it?" With his short grey hair, moustache and desiccated skin, he looks every bit of his near six decades.

*A Moment Of Forever* was a different proposition from the blinkered raucousness of *Third World Warrior*. The album's strengths were those that had helped launch Kristofferson in the early Seventies – powerful succinct lyrics and evocative imagery exploring themes of enduring love, freedom (the artwork for the sleeve incorporated a dictionary definition of the word) and escape, among other well-worn Kristofferson trademarks. Thanks in part to Was' ability to sort the wheat from the chaff, there were far more hits than misses.

Allied to this, Kristofferson had evidently gone through some sort of mellowing process since the rhetorical onslaught of *Third World Warrior*. Passion and insight were still very much in evidence, as was angry denunciation of minority oppression, but the songs were delivered with a lightness of touch enhanced by a pleasingly loose rock sound that swung, making listening a pleasure rather than an ordeal.

Thanks to Was' connections, the cream of L.A.'s session players including drummer Jim Keltner, keyboard player Benmont Tench and guitarist Waddy Wachtel provided top-notch support, being impressive without detracting from the main attraction. Long-time Kristofferson allies Billy Swan and Danny Timms contributed to the informal backing vocals; Timms also played keyboards and co-wrote three of the songs including the title track.

*A Moment Of Forever* featured several songs of great sensitivity and poignancy, celebrating the life-enhancing joys of human relationships, such as the title track and 'New Game Now', with its breathlessly grandiose language, presumably inspired by Kristofferson's love for his wife, who had been a stabilising influence on him for over 12 years by the time the album appeared.

In 'The Promise', Kris expressed the pleasure and pain of rearing a child. Talking about the genesis of the song, he said, "What may be happening to me is through the love of my children, I'm learning how to love older people too. You know 'The Promise' . . . to begin with it was just for the kids but now it's for their mamas too and it's anything that you love with absolutely no strings . . . my kids can do whatever they want to; they're absolutely free because my love's unconditional."

Kristofferson may have been showing his sentimental side but in 'Johnny Lobo', he was on the warpath once more. The song was inspired by the true story of John Trudell – a half Sioux, half Mexican poet – who lived on a reservation in Omaha and served in Vietnam. After completing two tours of duty, he became an outspoken activist in the American Indian Movement. In 1979, a fire claimed the lives of his pregnant wife, his three children and his mother-in-law and there were suspicions in some quarters that government agents may have had a hand in the tragedy.

In a similar though rather more personal vein, 'Sam's Song (Ask Any Working Girl)' was a vehicle for Kristofferson to express his anger at the way the film industry had turned its back on Sam Peckinpah. Kris showed that the flame of freedom, the desire to strike out and escape the humdrum, still burned brightly in his spirit and 'Worth Fighting For' mined the same rich seam that had produced 'Me And Bobby McGee'.

The album also featured worthwhile revisits to some of Kris' older songs, namely 'Shipwrecked In The Eighties', 'Casey's Last Ride', 'Under The Gun' and a swaggering version of 'Good Love (Shouldn't Feel So Bad)'.

*A Moment Of Forever* stands out in Kristofferson's catalogue as a mature album containing an excellent representation of the man, his intellectual approach to writing, and his personal credo in respect of internal and external concerns and philosophies. The fact that he had written or co-written all of the songs served to confirm his status as a writer still able to come up with strong material.

The critical acclaim did not translate into commercial success as Was remarked, "Kris' record might be the favourite record I've ever worked on . . . but hardly anyone noticed it was out there."

Released on a small label with little promotion, Kristofferson's low commercial profile and the acquired taste that was his voice were all factors that acted against the album. Willie Nelson could make a mediocre album that lots of people would still buy just to hear new product from him. Kristofferson did not have that luxury. However, he still had a way with words that few could match. Talking about Willie in 1995, Kris described him as "A carved-in-granite Samurai poet warrior gypsy guitar pickin' wild man with a heart as big as Texas."*

It would have been interesting if some of the major country stars of the day had covered some of the album's more accessible songs – as they used to do in the early Seventies. Garth Brooks hamming up 'The Promise' would surely have been a number one hit that would have thrust Kristofferson's songwriting forte back into prominence once more.

There were people out there who still appreciated Kristofferson's message but to reach larger numbers he would have to go out on the road. While this was something he loved, the question over the economics of taking a band on tour continued to rankle. It was an issue that had to be addressed and in due course, Kristofferson was to discover that less was more.

---

* In 1996, Kristofferson contributed a track to *Twisted Willie*, a Willie Nelson tribute album. He shared vocals with Kelley Deal (guitarist/singer in American alternative band The Breeders) on 'Angel Flying Too Close To The Ground'. Instead of a drummer, the producer sampled a sewing machine for the rhythm and had Kristofferson sing through a distortion pedal. One reviewer described the track as "a smoky Sonic Youth kind of dissipation wrung tired and spent through a song that feels like that anyway".

# Chapter 21

THOUGH usually respectful when talking about other artists, Kristofferson found it hard to get enthusiastic about modern country or rock – dismissively referring to various newcomers as "Stepford musicians". Despite his forward-thinking political views, musically, he preferred the established perennials, especially the singer-songwriters who broke new ground and took risks. In one interview, Kristofferson professed admiration for a song by Garth Brooks when in fact it was by Vince Gill. "I'm not hip enough . . . I'm the most out of touch guy in the room. My kids have to tell me who is singing."

Against this background it was perhaps surprising that Kristofferson agreed to take part in a video with Lorrie Morgan, one of the modern stars of country music. Kristofferson intriguingly compared her to Edith Piaf in that Morgan combined the old traditional music with the new. The two had met at the Association of Country Music awards in 1992 and Morgan thought that, despite an age difference of 23 years, Kristofferson might be suitable for the part of her estranged husband in the promo for 'I Guess You Had To Be There'. For the video, shot in New York's Central Park, the pair meet and reminisce about their time together.

Like Elvis Presley before him, Kristofferson continued to ply his trade in a series of forgettable films. A spoof western, *Sodbusters* (1994), had the bones of something potentially amusing but the jokes that needed to contain some irony far too often lacked the necessary sharpness. The whole dismal affair was neither one thing nor the other and made for tedious viewing. Comparisons with *Blazing Saddles* by a few critics were an insult to Mel Brooks and Gene Wilder. Kristofferson also accepted a fairly minor role, as a preacher, in the Civil War film *Pharoah's Army*. Despite this, his was the face that occupied most space on the promotional poster.

In 1995 he played the part of Abraham Lincoln in *Tad*, a television film for children about the president's youngest son, and how the White House looked through the seven-year-old's eyes. Kristofferson initially turned the role down because he felt he was neither tall nor thin enough to play Lincoln convincingly. At around five feet ten inches tall Kris was more than four inches shorter than his intended character. (As had also been the case with his father, many people assumed that Kris must have been at least six feet tall.) However, he regretted turning down the role of Woody Guthrie in the 1976 biographical film, *Bound For Glory*, so he quickly changed his mind.

While he could not change his physical size, he got closer to his character's appearance by having his grey hair dyed black. His beard was shaved off and replaced with an artificial one; the whole make-up process took up two-and-a-half-hours.

While it was understandable that Kristofferson needed the work, it seems hard to believe he was artistically fulfilled. This was after all an artist who professed great admiration for Ingmar Bergman, whose imagination had been stimulated by the greatest writers of English literature and who had found inspiration in the wild lives of intellectuals such as Ernest Hemingway and Paris in the Twenties. In an interview on the subject of public funding for the arts, Kristofferson said, "I think that a society lives or dies according to its respect for its art." He surely had in mind Shakespeare and Blake rather than portraying a circus ringmaster or an android.

Salvation of a sort came in 1995 when he was offered the part of the violent and corrupt sheriff Charlie Wade in *Lone Star*, written and directed by John Sayles, a man with a formidable reputation as an independent thinker in the movie world. Sayles had worked as a screenwriter on major Hollywood films such as *Apollo 13* and subsequently made a string of thoughtful films that examined in depth the historical complexities of race, politics, power and human frailty on personal relationships and communities.

Kristofferson had caught Sayles' attention early in his career with films such as *Blume In Love* and *Alice Doesn't Live Here Any More*. "[Kris] played them as a kind of alternative to Hollywood . . . to the kind of people in the movies, and there seemed to be something genuine about the character; it was not played as an ironic wild hippy guy . . . there's no pretence about him."

In line with his usual practice, Sayles personally cast Kristofferson. "I was thinking this is a character you have to buy as a Texan and a sheriff. It's a flashback to 1957, so he can't seem too contemporary; not educated but with a kind of shrewdness, a kind of natural but cruel intelligence . . . I thought about who were western iconic actors and thought of Kris."

Though aware of Kristofferson's formal schooling, it was the education he had received outside academia that Sayles felt matched what he was looking for. "In some ways Kris is like actors of the Thirties and Forties such as Robert Mitchum. What he brings . . . he's done other things besides being an actor – and it's very rare to get that any more . . .

"When directing him I might say, 'This time let's do it but be mad but don't show it,' or 'You're acting angrier than you really are to make a point, or you're doing it to intimidate the guy and this time push him a little bit more.' These sorts of things he does very well and it's usually just an increase or a decrease of a level of something that he's already doing."

Sayles described Kristofferson's presence on the set. "He is fun to have around the place . . . he's gone through a lot, some ups and downs . . . he's a very good storyteller."

*Lone Star* is set in a town on the Texas–Mexico border, another reminder for Kristofferson of his early years in Brownsville. The main plot concerned the discovery of the skeleton of Sheriff Charlie Wade who had mysteriously gone missing a generation before, and the efforts of the current sheriff to find out who killed him. A labyrinthine tale gradually unfolds, enriched by an adroit use of flashbacks, enhanced by some excellent musical touches. Tensions caused by the perceived rewriting of history, immigration, race, family breakdown, small town politics and – an overarching theme – breaching boundaries, underlie what is a compelling screen novel.

Though overly long and with at least one subplot too many, *Lone Star* was undoubtedly a top-notch film, winning a Golden Globe award for best screenplay. Kristofferson gave one of the best performances of his acting career, generating a credible air of psychopathic menace, which made his scenes among the film's high points. Even though he was only seen in a few flashbacks, the persona he created was a constant malicious presence hanging over the drama.

Kristofferson went on to have parts in two other Sayles' films, *Limbo* (1999) and *Silver City* (2004). The director hired a bus for a tour to help generate interest in the latter, and Kris, Lisa, Steve Earle and Darryl Hannah among others came along for the ride. "He was really nice to hang out with," said Sayles, "a good co-conspirator . . . we try to make a good movie and we try to have people who take the attitude, 'How can I help?' Kris is one of those guys."

Sayles was also struck by Kristofferson's lack of airs and graces and, unlike many other stars, his apparent contentment with his own company – a rather different picture from his extravagant social excesses of the Seventies. "Sometimes he comes with family, sometimes not; he never seemed like a guy who has to have a posse. On his days off he's just as likely to go out on his own and check out the town. He's a thoughtful person who needs time to think. On the movie set you are surrounded by people – fussing with your hair or make-up, people putting light meters in your face. Some people thrive on that, and the minute they finish work they are down in the bar or organising parties, keeping the social thing going. Kris is fine with it all – he understands and likes the job but does not need to have an entourage, as some do."

Sayles modestly dismissed the claim by one film critic that he was the "agent of Kris' re-birth as an actor." Acknowledging the poor quality of many of the parts Kristofferson accepted over the years, Sayles felt this was more a consequence of the negative effect of those cinematic flops than Kristofferson's limited abilities as an actor. Sayles also attributes an unwillingness to get involved in the Hollywood schmoozing scene as another contributory factor. Sayles also believed Kristofferson could have been successful on the other side of the camera.

"Movies are part of the American conversation; they say a lot about the culture of the country good and bad. Kris would have followed and been interested in that conversation from an early age as an intellectual observer and also an enthusiastic contributor. It would really have been interesting to see him in the director's chair."

While this has not happened, in 1999, Kristofferson said that he had written a 40-page treatment of a story that would be suitable for a screenplay. The difficulty with such a proposition is that it would mean collaborating and Kristofferson is not much of a team player.

John Sayles was not alone in admiring the quality of Kristofferson's rich southern drawl with its engaging, lived-in timbre to which a lifetime of smoking had added a hint of crackle and wheeze; "smoke-cured" as a journalist described it. Throughout the Nineties and beyond, he came to be an in-demand narrator for television programmes, films, cartoons and video games.

In 1992, he hosted a PBS (Public Broadcasting Service) programme, *In Country: Folk Songs Of Americans In The Vietnam War,* a special Veteran's Day presentation by *Austin City Limits.* In 1994, again for PBS, he hosted *The Songs Of Six Families,* which profiled folk artists and their families. Included was the kind of authentic, earthy roots music Kristofferson was happy to be associated with, including an Eskimo wolf dance, an Irish ceilidh, a Cajun Saturday night, the New Orleans Mardi Gras Indians, and a visit to a mariachi festival featuring an interview with Linda Ronstadt.*

Kristofferson also played his part in honouring more mainstream country singers. Along with Chet Atkins and Loretta Lynn, he participated in *Big Dreams And Broken Hearts: The Dottie West Story,* one of the highest-rated television movies ever to air on CBS, on January 22, 1995.

His laconic eloquence also made him a particularly valued talking head in features about country music and its characters. *Adventures Of The Old West* was the title given to a series of excellent documentaries vividly bringing to life many aspects of the Old West and the struggles and challenges facing the pioneers, aided by faded photographs and early moving film, official documents, personal diaries, reconstructions and narration by Kristofferson.†

The only weakness came when he sang songs about the Old West – these would surely have been done better by somebody else. In marked contrast to his singing voice, Kristofferson's narration found immediate favour with viewers of all tastes, perfectly matching the subject matter. His rich delivery did full justice to some of the florid lines he had to deliver: "The land was so fertile that even the fence posts sprouted roots in it." Kris was doubtless moved by some of the pioneers' tales; his paternal

---

* In 2001, Kristofferson's voice-of-experience also added value to *American Roots Music,* a high quality four-hour PBS historical documentary, which explored the origins and development of folk, country, blues, gospel and bluegrass among others.

† The self-explanatory titles of each programme provided a strong flavour of the series: *Texas Cowboys And The Trail Drives, Frontier Justice: The Law And The Lawless, Great Chiefs At The Crossroads, Texas Cowboys And The Trail Drivers, The 49ers And The California Goldrush, Pioneers And The Promised Land* and *Scouts In The Wilderness.*

grandparents' experience of arriving from Sweden and starting a new life in America were within living memory.

Between 1997 and 1999, Kristofferson narrated 41 episodes of the television programme *Dead Man's Gun*, produced by Henry Winkler ("The Fonz" from the Seventies TV sitcom *Happy Days*), a series of stories about the misfortunes, often death, that befall people who come into possession of a gun made in hell and thus "touched by evil".

In the wake of *Lone Star*, Kristofferson was offered parts in a variety of films of differing quality. He was typecast as a senior figure with experience and worldly wisdom – the sort turned to in times of crisis – or the head of an organisation – just as likely to be an amoral criminal Mr Big as a benevolent figure – who might only make a brief cameo.

One inspired casting came in 1997 when Kristofferson took on the role of Abraham Whistler in *Blade*. One of the first black super-heroes, Blade was first introduced to comic-book fans in 1973 as a supporting character in Marvel Comics' *Tomb Of Dracula*. In the film adaptation, Blade, played with menacing zest and a touch of humanity by Wesley Snipes, is on a mission to rid the world of the evil of vampires. His mother had been bitten by a vampire when she was pregnant with him and through a genetic aberration Blade is born with positive vampire attributes in combination with superhuman skills – a so-called dhampir. Unlike other vampires he is unaffected by daylight. He is, though, hunted as well as hunter; his special blood is required by the vampires in order to summon La Magra, the blood god, to enable them to achieve dominance over humans.

The character of Abraham Whistler first appeared on screen in a 1996 episode of *Spiderman: The Animated Series*, sharing his first name with both Abraham "Bram" Stoker, creator of *Dracula*, and Stoker's fictitious hero, Abraham Van Helsing. In the film, Abraham is a long-time friend and mentor to Blade. His wife and two daughters were killed by a vampire after he was tortured and forced to choose which of his family died first. An expert in weapons and martial arts, he comes across Blade as a teenage delinquent and soon discovers his rare qualities and takes him under his wing. Abraham has a limp caused by the rebellious teenage Blade breaking his leg. This was an easy affectation for Kristofferson, whose asymmetrical gait was close to what the role required.

The film was a spectacle of carefully choreographed violence, at times having the feel of a computer game. One reviewer summed it up: "The recipe for *Blade* is quite simple; you take one part *Batman*, one part horror flick, and two parts kung fu, and frost it all over with some truly camp acting. What do you get? An action flick that will reaffirm your belief that the superhero action genre will never die."

The generally favourable reviews and box-office takings meant there were two sequels, *Blade II* in 2002 and *Blade: Trinity* in 2004. Both followed the general pattern of the first, though the special effects and graphic violence became more sensational and shocking, with an ambiguous ending in *Trinity* ensuring that a fourth film remains a possibility. Merchandising for *Blade* resulted in another unusual accolade; for the first time it was possible to buy a Kris Kristofferson action figure – in his role of Whistler.

Kristofferson might have had some doubts about participating in the kinds of films that some accuse of helping to desensitise young people to violence by turning it into light entertainment. Would he allow his own children to watch such films? The reality is that professional actors take the best jobs offered – and from a career point of view, the success of *Blade* did a very good job in reactivating the 62-year-old's celluloid career.

Since Kristofferson now only appeared in minor supporting roles, the overall quality of a film could no longer be attributed to his performance. In 1998's *Dance With Me* he played the proprietor of a Texas dance studio, while in Merchant Ivory's *A Soldier's Daughter Never Cries* he took on the role of writer Bill Willis (based on the American novelist James Jones), earning praise from one critic for his "wizened machismo". Kris found it easy to identify with his character's love-hate relationship with the military, his devotion to his children and his need to fulfil his destiny as a writer. The film was later shown at The Overlooked Film Festival, founded by esteemed critic Roger Ebert.

In 1999 he appeared in what was billed as Tom Clancy's *Netforce*, although Clancy was executive producer rather than writer. The film, clichéd, unconvincing and overflowing with internet language, hypothesised on the dangers of the internet being manipulated by malevolent forces. Kristofferson was cast as Steve Day, an FBI agent whose early demise is not all that it seems.

Kris appeared as Mr Big in *Payback* – a stylish, fast-moving and beautifully shot remake of the 1967 film noir classic *Point Blank*. A compulsive, action-packed tale of revenge, starring Mel Gibson, the film reunited

Kristofferson with James Coburn, his nemesis in *Pat Garrett And Billy The Kid*, and was a satisfying cinematic vehicle for Kristofferson to end the millennium on.

While Kristofferson had managed to get a grip on his drink and drug intake around the time of *A Star Is Born*, he had not managed to curb his heavy smoking habit. He was aware that he needed to address the situation because by his early sixties, he could no longer run more than a hundred yards or so without suffering angina pains. An angiogram revealed significant impairment to his coronary arteries. Initially Kris' medical advisers put him on cholesterol-lowering drugs and told him to stop smoking and eat less red meat.

He was monitored for approximately 18 months and then had a further angiogram. While hoping that he might get away with angioplasty, a much less intrusive procedure, Kristofferson was told that he required a triple heart bypass operation. Afterwards Kris said he felt as though he had been "hit by a truck" and was so weak, he seriously doubted whether he had done the right thing, complaining that "they carve you up like a turkey". However, he soon regained some strength and within a few months was able to start running reasonable distances again and undertaking gardening work at his Maui home. At last he understood the importance of looking after himself if he was to enjoy a productive and fulfilling old age. "I feel like I've got to keep the pipes clean now that they're working."

Not surprisingly he reflected a lot on mortality at this time; a lot of the people he had known for years were succumbing to a variety of ailments. Shel Silverstein died in May 1999 – the same month as Kristofferson's operation – as a result of similar pathology, having apparently not sought medical assistance. Although he claimed always to have regarded life as precious, his brush with death helped to reinforce the message and made him spend more time with his family while still maintaining professional duties.

Despite his health worries, Kris was not prepared to miss what was being hyped in the media as "the music event of 1999" – *An All-Star Tribute To Johnny Cash*, a concert of (mainly) Cash songs performed by an eclectic mix of artists at Manhattan's Hammerstein Ballroom, later screened on the TNT channel. Most of the artists – including Lyle Lovett,

Mary Chapin Carpenter, Sheryl Crow and Brooks and Dunn dressed in black for the occasion. Bruce Springsteen, Bob Dylan and U2 could not be present but recorded video tributes. Kristofferson performed 'The Ballad Of Ira Hayes' and 'Sunday Morning Coming Down', the latter with Trisha Yearwood.

After the commercial failure of *A Moment Of Forever*, Kristofferson spent more time at home and did little in the way of recording or performing. He felt disillusioned by the commercial failure of the album he described as "my best work". 1999 saw the release of *The Austin Sessions* – recorded two years earlier but held up by label problems before its release on Atlantic. The project was the brainchild of producer Fred Mollin, who conceived a series of albums featuring new recordings of the best work of various songwriters. The first, Jimmy Webb's *Ten Easy Pieces*, was a critical success and Mollin was keen to follow it up with the work of another exceptional songwriter.

Mollin and Kristofferson agreed a representative selection – though none of Kristofferson's recent material was among the dozen songs chosen. The tracks were recorded in under a week at Willie Nelson's Arlyn studios, described by Mollin as "a ramshackle little 24 track studio that had seen better days". Fred arranged for the musical backing to be added later using sessionmen he regarded as "emotionally suitable" for the task. They came from an eclectic background from pop to Cajun. *The Austin Sessions* combined spontaneity with uncluttered delicate instrumental work of the highest calibre. As Mollin put it, "It was about serving [Kris]."

In an arrangement that suited both camps, Kristofferson was able to reach new listeners by revisiting some of his best-known songs – including 'Sunday Morning Coming Down', 'Me And Bobby McGee', 'For The Good Times', 'Help Me Make It Through The Night', 'The Pilgrim – Chapter 33', 'The Silver Tongued Devil And I' and 'To Beat the Devil' – in the company of a stellar posse of artists including Steve Earle, Jackson Browne, Vince Gill, Alison Krauss and Mark Knopfler. The guests bene-fited by associating themselves with a songwriter who was rapidly gaining living legend status – Johnny Cash modestly opined that this status was conferred on those who "stuck around long enough".

Mollin described the album as "a labour of love". The idea of duets was soon dismissed – this was to be Kristofferson's album and nothing should detract from that. As with the Jimmy Webb project, Fred wanted Kris to be heard, "for the first time ever doing the songs his own autonomous way and in the proper way . . . a way that would stand the test of time". Mollin suggested that the songs be done in the way that Dylan cut his songs during the *Blonde On Blonde* sessions. "[Kris] loved the idea of that . . . he always wanted to be produced like Dylan . . . he loved that free rootsy feel."

The songs were recorded almost as if they were live, with a minimum of preparation. Kristofferson was with the musicians for part of the time and though he had not worked with them previously – apart from Stephen Bruton – Mollin was keen to create a sense of camaraderie of the kind Kris had enjoyed with The Borderlords.

Kristofferson's voice had not improved with age but his warm and sensitive delivery, aided by light and sympathetic production, helped to bring out the timeless quality of the songs. At a time when the influence of rock music was pervasive in the world of country, traditional fans could justifiably describe the album as the real deal. One reviewer described Kristofferson as an "American original".

A note on the sleeve said, "I will carry these versions of these songs as my artistic ID into the hereafter", and Mollin said that Kristofferson later told him that *The Austin Sessions* was his favoured choice among his own recordings. Mollin has nothing but happy memories of the experience. "I got to work with Kris and 12 of the best songs ever of this style of songwriting. It was like the handbook – I wasn't present at the creation but I certainly was present at the re-creation."

*The Austin Sessions* sold around 140,000 copies in its first year – not bad going for an artist of Kristofferson's stature but not enough to persuade Atlantic to consider a follow-up of more recent material. To promote the album, Kristofferson appeared on a double bill with fellow legend Merle Haggard. The two had talked about performing together 30 years previously but Haggard's manager at the time said Kristofferson would have to shave off his beard and was genuinely shocked when Haggard said he was thinking of sporting one himself – which, for a time, he did.

On the face of it, the two might not have worked together given that Kristofferson's political opinions clashed with the conservative views expressed by Haggard in his early populist hits like 'Okie From Muskogee' and 'The Fightin' Side of Me'. The reality was that Kristofferson recognised a great artist who, he said, had written some of the best folk songs ever ("the closest thing to Hank Williams walking the streets") and has always defended the right – even encouraged it – of people to express views in opposition to his own. Though naturally drawn to those whose philosophies chimed with his, a difference of political opinion was not a bar to friendship.

In 2000, Kristofferson contributed 'Shipwrecked In The Eighties' to *Concerts For A Landmine Free World* – drawn from 1999 and 2000 benefit concerts held in California and Canada and instigated by Emmylou Harris, a fervent advocate of the cause. Other artists appearing at the acoustic-only concerts included John Prine, Guy Clark and Terry Allen.

Also that year, a partial Highwaymen reunion (without Cash) occurred on *Honky Tonk Heroes*, a collection of songs by Billy Joe Shaver. The songs, including 'I'm Just An Old Chunk Of Coal', 'Ain't No God In Mexico' and 'We Are The Cowboys', had been recorded over several years at Willie Nelson's Pedernales Studio and while not necessarily the best versions of Shaver's songs, they were nonetheless delivered with exuberance and charm.

The follow-up to *The Austin Sessions* became *Broken Freedom Song: Live From San Francisco*, recorded in the summer of 2002 at the Gershwin Theater, San Francisco State University, though at the time there was no thought of a live album. Producer Alan Abrahams was putting together a CD honouring the work of Mimi Fariña, who died in 2001, and asked Kristofferson to contribute a track. Kristofferson allowed Abrahams to tape the Gershwin Theater show on the understanding that he would select one track for the album.

After Kristofferson heard the recording he decided it was good enough to release as a live album. As Abrahams recalled there was no soundcheck for the concert, "We were all winging it . . . we caught a moment in history." The musical backing was minimalist in nature; Kristofferson's own rudimentary guitar and harmonica work was supported by Stephen Bruton on guitar and mandolin and Keith Carper on bass; the two also provided backing vocals.

Unlike *The Austin Sessions*, the show did not include many of Kristofferson's best-known songs but rather an intriguing mix ranging from minor gems such as 'Darby's Castle', 'Here Comes That Rainbow Again,' 'Nobody Wins' and 'A Moment of Forever' to overtly political songs like 'Sandinista' and 'Don't Let The Bastards Get You Down'.

Unusual choices were 'Sky King', Kristofferson's adaptation of 'Big Bad John' from his army days – a song he regularly featured in concerts over the years but had never recorded – and 'The Race', a humorous effort that parodied 'The Wind Beneath My Wings'. Recent events inspired 'The Circle (Song for Layla Al-Attar And Los Olividados)'. In 1993 President Clinton had ordered an attack on Iraq in which the well-known artist Layla Al-Attar and members of her family were killed or injured. Kristofferson linked the fact that the victims were virtually invisible in the American press to the "disappeared ones" (*los olividados*) of Argentina's military junta.

Reviews were favourable despite Kristofferson's voice being described as "unvarnished", although one reviewer went overboard when describing Kris as "a great singer". One commentator summed *Broken Freedom Song* up thus: "It's the way a songwriter's album should be done – full of unpretentious songs that offer wisdom, a sense of community and empathy, and a performance that is as soulful and humorous and humble as they come."

Again the album did not sell in significant numbers – as with all such small independent label projects, it failed to receive extensive promotion. However, both *The Austin Sessions* and *Broken Freedom Song* demonstrated that though great singers were capable of raising Kristofferson songs to great heights, given the right musical context, his own versions were capable of delivering an emotional intensity and intimacy few could match.

# Chapter 22

FROM an early age, Kristofferson had experienced losing people he'd worked with in music and films; it went with the territory. However, in the early part of the new millennium, he received a particularly harsh reminder of the passing of time with the loss of some of his closest friends. On February 13, 2002, Waylon Jennings died. Although the two sometimes fought, it was never in a way that threatened their strong friendship. "[Waylon] fought with everyone a lot . . . he was like a brother. He was an American archetype, the bad guy with a big heart."

Kristofferson admired Jennings' tough exterior, in particular the fact that he was able to kick a particularly heavy drug habit "without any of those self-help programmes". Kris also appreciated the fact that Waylon was good with his children and phoned Waylon's son Shooter on Father's Day to see how he was; he has also remained in touch with Jennings' widow, Jessi Colter.

That September, Mickey Newbury succumbed to a long illness, but the hardest loss for Kristofferson to bear came exactly a year later with the death of Johnny Cash, not long after the passing of June Carter, Cash's wife of 35 years and the love of his life. Kris was quick to acknowledge the vital contribution Cash had made both to the development of his social consciousness and his recording and performing careers – though the respect had been mutual; Johnny rarely played a show that did not include a Kristofferson song and had great respect for his integrity.

Though Johnny and Kris enjoyed a rare bond based on shared attitudes in politics, music, individual freedom and the paramount importance of love – not to mention a well-developed sense of humour – Kristofferson struggled to feel that he was Cash's equal. "I never got over the feeling that he was larger than life. He was just one of the giants . . . he was such a powerful presence."

Kris talked to Johnny every day in hospital; despite his rapidly deteriorating health, Cash had spent most of his waking hours in the studio desperately pushing himself to lay down more material, to remain creative to the end – an example that Kristofferson will doubtless seek to emulate.

Kristofferson spoke eloquently at Cash's funeral service held at the First Baptist Church, Hendersonville, in September 2003. "Thank you Father for blessing us with the presence of this wonderful man whose life and work has been an inspiration and salvation for so many all over the world . . ." He went on to describe his mentor as "a deeply spiritual, compassionate man, willing and able to champion the voiceless, the downtrodden, the underdogs, who was also something of a holy terror. Abe Lincoln with a wild side. He was a dark, dangerous force of nature that somehow seemed to stand for freedom and justice, and mercy for his fellow man." After his eulogy, Kris sang 'A Moment Of Forever'.

In his public comments after Cash's death, Kristofferson revealed Johnny's razor-sharp sense of humour, evident even when in poor health. Among the mourners visiting the funeral home where June had been taken to say a final farewell, a stranger had come up to Kristofferson and said how much he admired his singing. After the man was out of earshot, Johnny had leaned over and said, "Well that's *one*." Not long after Cash's death, Kristofferson met Willie Nelson and told his fellow surviving Highwayman, "Man don't get sick, there ain't many of us left." On another occasion, Kris reflected on his own survival. "Sometimes I'm amazed I'm still above ground."

Cash just missed out on seeing his friend pick up the 2003 Spirit of Americana Free Speech Award presented by the First Amendment Center and the American Music Association. The previous month he had been inducted into the Texas Country Music Hall of Fame and Willie was on hand to do the honours. Kris was greatly amused when one of his daughters quipped, "Don't you old guys have something better to do than give each other awards all the time?"

The following year Kristofferson was selected for country music's top honour – induction into the Country Music Hall of Fame. The ceremony, held at the CMA's 2004 awards night, retrospectively acknowledged the surprising fact that the Association had never bestowed recognition for Kris having written some of the genre's most covered standards.

Assisting with the formalities were Willie Nelson and Faith Hill, representatives of country music old and new. Kris was inducted along with music executive Jim Foglesong. CMA executive director Ed Benson said it had proved difficult to summarise the "lifetime of contributions" Kristofferson had made to the industry in the time available. In contrast to the hostility his first appearance at the CMA awards generated, Kris had become one of the Association's more revered figureheads.*

An award that gave Kristofferson particular pleasure came in 2002 when the American Veteran Awards named him Veteran of the Year. This was a bittersweet moment for Kris; over the years many had equated his attacks on American foreign policy with a lack of patriotism. The Veteran of the Year Award is given to a person "all Americans can look up to as an example of the very best virtues embodied by our proud military traditions of service and sacrifice". In terms of the organisation's constitution, an award recipient is "chosen by a select directorship of corporate, entertainment and military leaders and recognised by the President of the United States each year; the Veteran of the Year is a shining beacon for America, lighting the path of Vision, Fortitude and Integrity."†

Kristofferson had become disillusioned with mainstream politics by the late Nineties. He supported Bill Clinton but only in the negative sense that he regarded him as less unacceptable than the Republicans. "What's depressing is that there is really no 'our side' any more." He was fiercely opposed to the invasion of Iraq led by America in March 2003 and was one of nearly 1,000 signatories to a letter sent by US war veterans group Veterans for Common Sense to President Bush questioning the wisdom of the pursuit of war. Whether the operation was successful or not was irrelevant to Kris; it was simply wrong and morally indefensible. "To attack another country because you don't like their leader. My God, how many people would be attacking us, and probably will be?"

Quite apart from foreign policy, Kristofferson nostalgically yearned for the days when American citizens elected John F. Kennedy, a man capable

* In 1996 Kristofferson had helped to induct Ray Price (despite the latter's substantial output, 'For The Good Times' remains among the songs most closely associated with Price) and in 2006 he introduced that year's inductees to the Hall of Fame, including Sonny James and George Strait.
† Kris was happy to contribute to projects with military connections. In 2006, he narrated a documentary music video about the events of November 8, 1965 when the 173rd Airborne Brigade was ambushed by over 1,200 Viet Cong; 48 American soldiers lost their lives. The song about the incident was performed by Big and Rich. The video was nominated for the Grammys and the 2006 CMA Video of the Year.

of the Blakean assertion that "If art is to nourish the roots of our culture society must set the artist free to follow his vision wherever it takes him." Kristofferson once had the naïve idea of the government being made up entirely of writers. "Kurt Vonnegut was the president because of his passion. I think J. D. Salinger was the secretary of state because he'd never go anywhere and never talk to anybody, and we wouldn't get in trouble."

In 2004, the Oh Boy label, part owned by John Prine, put out an hour-long Kristofferson concert documentary DVD, *Breakthrough*, featuring the usual classics as well as some of his more politically inspired songs. There was considerable emphasis on Kristofferson's support for social causes and the songs, backed by The Borderlords, were interspersed with interviews and film clips of iconic people and events such as Gandhi, Martin Luther King, the Kennedys and Tiananmen Square. The album's release came around the same time *Repossessed* and *Third World Warrior* were reissued as a double package. With the unpopularity of Bush, it was thought that Kristofferson's radical agenda would receive a more favourable response than when the albums originally came out.

That year, Kristofferson was one of the subjects in an unusual exhibition by photographic artist Sam Taylor-Wood entitled *Crying Men*, featuring photographs of 28 well-known actors including Sir Michael Gambon, Tim Roth, Paul Newman, Jude Law, Robert Downey Jr and Ray Winstone. Taylor-Wood asked each man to adopt a role that would enable them to cry for the camera. Her photographs were not passive portraits; they displayed an extraordinary range of expressions of grief from mild to cathartic. Thoughts of Johnny Cash, not far below the surface, helped Kris to express dignified sorrow.

He also contributed to a documentary *Be Here To Love Me*, about another departed friend, Townes Van Zandt. Kristofferson recalled that when filming a musical scene for *Songwriter*, an audience was brought in that included Van Zandt. Kris interrupted proceedings and introduced him, informing those present what a great songwriter the native Texan was. Like Kristofferson, Van Zandt experienced a comfortable and conventional upbringing that he rebelled against.

In 2005, Kristofferson was one of the guests at the gala opening of the Muhammad Ali Center, a museum and cultural complex in Louisville, Kentucky. Though debilitated by Parkinson's Disease, Ali was present along with a galaxy of celebrities including Bill Clinton, Brad Pitt, James Taylor and Attallah Shabazz, the eldest daughter of Malcolm X. There were performances from some of the guests and Kristofferson sang 'Here Comes That Rainbow Again'. By complete contrast, he was one of the voices (Ned White) for a violent Wild West video game called *Gun*.

In 2006, Kristofferson, along with Waylon Jennings, was inducted into Hollywood's Rock Walk in Sunset Boulevard. His exceptional song-writing gained further recognition at the highest level on June 15 when he was presented with the prestigious Johnny Mercer Award, an accolade given each year to writers of popular music who have already been inducted into the Songwriter's Hall of Fame (Kris was inducted in 1987) and whose body of work is considered to be of such outstanding quality that it maintains the gold standard set by Mercer, co-writer of 'Jeepers Creepers' and 'You Must Have Been A Beautiful Baby'. The award put Kristofferson in the company of such greats as Stevie Wonder, Burt Bacharach, Hal David and Stephen Sondheim.

In the wake of *Lone Star*, Kristofferson enjoyed a new influx of movie offers. He was invariably willing to accept a strikingly wide variety of characters as brief details of a sample of his more recent films demonstrate.

For *The Life And Hard Times Of Guy Terrifico* (2005) he played himself in a wickedly funny spoof documentary – variously referred to as a "honky-tonkumentary" and a "mockumentary" – about the rise and fall of a fictional country singer. In many ways it was to country what *Spinal Tap* had been to rock. As Terrifico's story unfolded, a number of singers, including Merle Haggard and Ronnie Hawkins, are filmed passing comment on him. In admiration, and deadly earnest, Kristofferson says at one point, "He was the only person I knew who drank more than I did." It is even suggested that 'The Pilgrim – Chapter 33' ("He's a walking contradiction partly truth partly fiction . . .") was written about Terrifico.

*The Jacket* (2005) further demonstrated Kristofferson's aptitude for por-traying unpleasant characters. The film made for a gruelling and unpleasant experience, not helped by a plot that was, to say the least, complex. Kris played Dr Becker, who employs brutal experimental treatments on his patients at an institution for the criminally insane. The central character, Jack Starks (played by Adrien Brody), is injected with mind-altering drugs, trussed up in a straitjacket and left for hours on end in a corpse drawer in a mortuary; in his mind the future merges with the present and past. For the sequences filmed in Scotland, Kris brought some of his younger children with him and they briefly attended school in Glasgow. If possible, he liked to have the company of family members when away from home.

Far more grounded in reality was *Fast Food Nation* (2006), a fictional film loosely based on the book by Eric Schlosser that exposed some of the horrors and gross excesses of the worldwide junk food industry. Kris had a small cameo role as eco-rancher Rudy Martin, the kind of role he warmed to.

Despite having appeared in over 100 films, Kristofferson had won few awards for his acting. In recognition of his work for over 35 years, he was given what amounted to a long-service medal when inducted into the Texas Film Hall of Fame in 2006.

The flow of work has diminished but his distinguished, careworn appearance and lengthy track record mean that offers still come his way. As of writing, there are several films in post-production including *Powder Blue*, in which Kristofferson portrays the head of a corporate crime organisation, and *He's Just Not Into You*, starring Scarlett Johansson and Jennifer Aniston. As with other areas of creative output, he intends to continue in films for as long as physically possible even though he says he still feels vulnerable in front of the camera.

In recognition of his living legend status, Kristofferson has regularly been invited to contribute alongside other artists to a variety of projects. Along with many country stars, he put in an appearance singing 'Why Me' at a 2004 concert (later released as a double CD) held to mark George Jones' 50 years in the business. In 2005 he duetted with Dolly Parton on 'Me And Bobby McGee' for her covers album, *Those Were The Days*.

Kris was an obvious choice for a major CBS television special on Johnny Cash, *I Walk The Line – A Night For Johnny Cash*, aired November 16, 2005, which featured film footage of the great man as well as musical contributions from a diverse range of artists including Kid Rock, Sheryl Crow and Norah Jones. 2006 saw the CD and DVD release of *Live From Austin TX: Outlaw Country*, taped in September 1996, featuring Kristofferson, Waylon Jennings, Willie Nelson, Billy Joe Shaver and Kimmie Rhodes in an Austin City Limits' Songwriter's Special guitar pull.

Appropriately enough the album ended with Nelson's 'On The Road Again'.*

Kristofferson continued to be a first choice for a variety of narration work: in 2006 alone he provided the off-screen voice of Billy for the film *Requiem For Billy The Kid*; narrated *Sacred Tibet – The Path To Mount Kailash*, a pilgrimage by flautist Paul Horn and Maui resident Lama Tenzin to "the roof of the world" in Chinese-occupied Tibet; and fittingly, he added a voice of gravitas to the remarkable biopic about Bob Dylan, *I'm Not There*.† More recently, he has been heard on *Snow Buddies*, a Disney cartoon in which five puppies compete in a sled race in the Alaskan wilderness.

To mark Kris' 70th birthday, friends and admirers contributed to a lovingly compiled album, *The Pilgrim: A Celebration Of Kris Kristofferson*, featuring cover versions of songs from all periods of his career as well as a 1970 demo of Kristofferson singing 'Please Don't Tell Me How The Story Ends' – an apposite finale. The diverse cast – including Rosanne Cash and Shooter Jennings, Emmylou Harris and Randy Scruggs, Patty Griffin and Russell Crowe, and Willie Nelson and Jessi Colter – told its own story: Kristofferson's influence reached into numerous areas of the world of music. Kris said he was "humbled and blown away" by it. The album included lengthy and erudite notes by journalist and musician Peter Cooper. While fulsome in his admiration for Kristofferson's life and work, Cooper did not shy away from the dark side, saying that Kris "remains given to fits of bleak depression".

In 2007 Kristofferson was honoured with the Johnny Cash Visionary Award by Country Music Television. Appropriately enough the award was presented, in what turned out to be an emotional exchange, by Rosanne Cash (who had played several dates with Kris the previous year). Rosanne remarked that Kristofferson was "the living artistic link to my dad . . . he and my dad were closer than brothers". In his acceptance speech, Kristofferson announced, "Bob Dylan said it the best. He said that John was like the North Star: you could guide your ship by him." Tributes

---

* In 2007 Kristofferson also narrated a radio documentary about Willie Nelson for BBC Radio 2.
† In 2002, Kristofferson was one of over a hundred artists asked by *Uncut* magazine to vote for the 40 best songs by the songwriter and artist Kristofferson admired above all others. The top three Dylan choices were 'Like A Rolling Stone', 'Tangled Up In Blue' and 'Visions Of Johanna'.

were paid by other artists including Martin Scorsese, Don Was, Keith Urban and Gretchen Wilson and there was a video collage of Kristofferson's career.

That year, Kristofferson appeared at the Fillmore in San Francisco, on a bill including Taj Mahal and Peter Coyote, to raise funds for The Longest Walk, from San Francisco to Washington DC, planned for 2008.\*

Yet another honour came Kristofferson's way when he was offered the position of artist-in-residence at the Country Music Hall of Fame and Museum in Nashville. His main duty was to play two shows at the Ford Theater in front of full houses of around 250 people including many country music insiders. "It's just one of those nights where you want to be so good so bad," Kris said. In the course of the two performances, he played an impressive total of 69 songs – only repeating two, 'Sunday Morning Coming Down' and 'Me And Bobby McGee' – featuring some he had never performed in public before. Kris was the fifth artist-in-residence; the first being Jack Clement who was in the audience.

Kristofferson received a highly enthusiastic reception and was greatly honoured to have been chosen. However, some more cynical Nashville insiders regarded the artist-in-residence idea as essentially self-promotion for the Country Music Foundation. As one writer puts it, "Every mention in *The Tennessean* theoretically puts the Hall of Fame in the forefront of not-for-profits organisations vying for city council-awarded subsidies; and the artist-in-residence has another 'prestigious honour' to add to his or her resumé."

Kristofferson's appearances in the new millennium have not been restricted to appearing at self-congratulatory tribute events. During the filming of *The Jacket* in Scotland he received an offer to play in Ireland but had insufficient time to put together a backing band. So, in what was the logical conclusion to his moves towards a more stripped-down unit, Kris decided to play the gigs solo, playing songs from all periods of his career. Over 6,000 people attended each of three sold-out shows at The Point in Dublin and as he later said, "You could hear a pin drop."

---

\* The 2008 event was planned to commemorate the original 1978 walk, whose mission was to clean up the planet and to raise awareness of the environmental damage caused by human activities. Since that time there have been associated runs and walks in many parts of the world.

The favourable response helped to ease his nerves, especially without the cover provided by a band. If something went amiss, he could shrug it off. "I don't have to worry about causing a train wreck. I can correct it myself." On a more mundane level, a one-man show kept the costs down.

Kristofferson took his intimate and politicised shows all over America, Europe and Australia, with time off for rest and recuperation as befitting a man now into his seventies. In 2006, he performed a double bill with George Jones at the Carnegie Hall and his spring tour of Europe in 2008 took in 12 concerts in 19 days in Holland, Ireland and Great Britain.

One reason for Kristofferson's current popularity has been the increasing receptiveness of audiences to his political message – which he hammers home with between-song diatribes against George. W. Bush's foreign policy that are well received by large sections of his politically like-minded audiences. Since the plummeting approval ratings for Bush, Kristofferson has found favour not just with long-time fans but also a younger audience who express solidarity with his anti-war views. They somehow recognise an icon who has stuck to his guns despite the opprobrium his stances attracted in the past and who now has the satisfaction of seeing the preponderant political mood moving in his direction.

For his part, Kristofferson likes to see comparisons with an old-style itinerant blues player laying down his message in town after town. The message does not appeal to everyone as he self-disparagingly conceded to one interviewer. "God knows there's people I'd rather hear sing my songs than me." Given the lack of variety in his shows – two hours of basic guitar and harmonica with little between-song dialogue – some concertgoers inevitably find a Kristofferson show heavy going. James Blundell, who was support act on Kristofferson's Australian tour, said, "It was a case of two hours in a blackened environment with a white spotlight – no colour washes or mood changes or lighting; and Kris was putting over his political message. People [in Australia] were not really expecting that."

However, Blundell feels that only a minority did not like the shows and that if Kristofferson were to return to Australia he might well double his audiences, to around 3,000 per show. To some extent Kris has now joined the lucrative circuit of ageing stars, The Eagles, The Rolling Stones, Crosby, Stills, Nash & Young, among others – what some might sneeringly refer to as heritage acts – who pull in large crowds keen to be able to say, "I saw Kris Kristofferson."

Kristofferson's first album of (mostly) new material since 1995's *A Moment Of Forever* appeared in 2006. Produced by Don Was for a small independent label (New West), *This Old Road* had the feel of a self-written epitaph in which the artist took stock of his life, while revisiting familiar themes along the way. "Freedom and redemption are at the core of just about every album I've ever done . . . I guess it's just the same thing only from an older perspective." Perhaps a sign of mellowing with age, generous helpings of sentimentality, nostalgia and an awareness of mortality competed with Kristofferson's philosophical and political credos.

While watching Kris play at Austin's South by Southwest festival, Was formulated the idea of focussing solely on the vocals with a minimal amount of backing. The two men laid down about 50 songs at Kristofferson's house in Maui and 11 were then picked to be recorded in Los Angeles. The original plan was to use an experimental five microphone set-up for easy translation into surround sound, but this was dropped as being overly complicated. Following the less-is-more principle, Was' uncluttered production starkly exposed Kristofferson's emotionally charged delivery, and allowed him to commune intimately with the listener; through headphones, it sounded like a supplicant in the confessional.

The songs were mainly slow-paced to fit the meditative mood of the album with the only additions to Kristofferson's guitar and harmonica being unobtrusive contributions from Stephen Bruton (guitar and mandolin), Jim Keltner (drums) and Was on piano and bass.

Kristofferson's voice sounded older and weaker, though his phrasing had improved. For 'Pilgrim's Progress', which had first appeared on *Repossessed* back in 1986, his low growling vocal bore a passing resemblance to Tom Waits. In 'Wild American', Kris paid tribute to the men he regarded as genuine American heroes giving name-checks along the way to John Trudell, Steve Earle (someone Kris described as a "great artist and a concerned American"), Merle Haggard and Willie Nelson.

The idea for the song, which some might consider to have more than a hint of left-wing paranoia, came to Kristofferson while on horseback with some Native Americans waiting to shoot a scene for a movie. "I got to

thinking I had more in common with these guys than the so-called civilised people . . . I got the notion that maybe there were wild Americans and
civilised Americans; one lot loves freedom and the other ones don't
necessarily love it."

'In The News' made a link between a particularly brutal murder, the
damage inflicted on the environment by man-made exploitation and
religious conflict and war. "It seemed to me the cold-bloodedness of the
Laci Peterson [murder] was like the cold-blooded way they bombed
civilians unprovoked in Baghdad – a lack of conscience or morality; I was
as repulsed by one as the other." An accompanying video, though containing clips of the 9/11 attacks and photographs of American victims, left
little doubt that Bush and his administration were the principal villains of
the piece.

'Burden Of Freedom' (from 1972's *Border Lord*), took the form of a
prayer in which Kristofferson strove to find ways to pardon his detractors.
When originally written, he may well have had in mind those family
members who rejected him. The song had more up-to-date relevance for
Kristofferson in reaching out to people. His somewhat naïve view was that
the kind of unconditional love people showed to their children could
somehow be used to embrace others with radically divergent opinions.
The spirit of such an ideal might be superficially appealing but was surely
disingenuous – taking a personal hypothesis, could Kristofferson ever
seriously evince such feelings towards George W. Bush? His conciliatory
approach had less to do with compromise or pragmatism but rather a biblical forgiveness of the type expressed by Jesus on the cross.

At the time, Kristofferson stated that the older he got the more spiritual
he became. However, apart from a brief foray in the early Seventies –
around the time of 'Why Me' – he never openly embraced religion. In the
same interview, he admitted he'd probably been to church about six times
in his life, though somewhat patronisingly added that some of the finest
people he knew attended mass regularly. In 'Holy Creation' Kris alluded
to a religious dimension in his love for his children, while in 'Thank You
For A Life', Kris paid tribute to his marriage while acknowledging the
difficulties and stresses he created. The thanks he gives is to his wife but
also, ultimately, to God.

For the last cut, aptly named 'The Final Attraction', Kristofferson ana-
lysed the alchemy between the best artists and their audience – naming

some of those he regarded as being able to commune most effectively with their fans such as Hank Williams, John Lennon, Lefty Frizzell, Jimi Hendrix and Janis Joplin. The original inspiration came around 1984, at the time of the film *Songwriter*, after Kristofferson watched Willie Nelson close a performance, but it was only completed for *This Old Road*.* The song also exhorted aspirant singer-songwriters to embark on the journey; the line "Go break a heart" came from Guy Clark by way of encouragement as Kris was about to go onstage one time.

Reviewers from various music journals queued up to pay homage; it was as if the countless unkind words their predecessors had aimed at Kristofferson had never been written. "Kristofferson lays a chunk of his own soul on every track . . . the album is so intimate it makes the listener feel as if they are sitting in Kristofferson's living room while he picks and sings just for them"; "Welcome back to the music world, Kris. We've sorely missed you!"; "Razor-sharp, economical in his language and to the bone in his insight"; "Kristofferson has made an album to help us through our own dark times."

Comparisons were made with Johnny Cash's superb *American Recordings* album – what Rick Rubin had done for Cash, Don Was had achieved for Kristofferson. Both producers played an important part in contributing to a late resurgence in each artist's career by simply letting them play the songs in a style that did them full justice.

In the eyes of the tastemakers occupying the more intellectual spectrum of the music world, Kristofferson was now officially established as a grand old man of the liberal left who had been right all along. Kris appreciates the widespread respect he now receives; he feels he has earned it. Reaching 70 has meant for him a time of self-assessment, "more reflective than looking forward . . . looking forward ain't that great."

* Willie later phoned Kris to say he'd been very moved by the song.

# Endword

KRISTOFFERSON continues to juggle his professional activities; the difference being that the demands he allows to be placed on his time are commensurate with advancing years and declining physical energy. His knees are now weak and so consequently he has had to give up running. Kris is still drawn to the road. As with many other performers, Kris loves the adulation and is grateful that after many lean years, people are once more flocking to his concerts in large numbers – to his admitted surprise.

Kristofferson has never had any regrets about speaking out on political issues despite the adverse affect on his career. "I was telling the truth as I saw it; never have considered doing it any other way." Since the Eighties he has been vocal in his criticism of what he sees as the misguided foreign policy of successive US administrations, especially those of the right. Therefore it's no surprise that he intends backing Barack Obama, with his left-leaning idealism, as the Democratic presidential candidate for 2008. "I believe in Barack Obama like I believed in the Kennedys . . . It's this spirit of finding common ground and working things out through dialogue and diplomacy that the world needs so desperately today at this critical point in our history. This is the hope that Obama inspires."

However, Kristofferson supported singer Toby Keith's right to express his right-of-centre views no matter how repugnant he found them and also spoke approvingly of Merle Haggard coming to the defence of the Dixie Chicks, who caused a furore when lead singer Natalie Maines made disparaging remarks about George W. Bush. Kristofferson's philosophy remains "Share the information you have and tell the truth as you see it."

As an entertainment figure, Kris is well-respected by his peers as both a musician and a friend. Early in 2008, he made a guest appearance (with Brian Wilson among others) at the second annual Valentine's Day reunion concert by Was (Not Was) in Los Angeles. For the induction of Donnie Fritts into the Alabama Music Hall of Fame, Kris performed a couple of songs and gave a speech honouring his old pal of 40 years. Though it meant losing a small role in a film, it was a case of friendship coming before work.

Kristofferson continues to grapple with the dark side that has dogged him throughout most of his adult life and that he sought to obliterate in one way or another during the Sixties and Seventies. Though it can only be a matter for speculation, Kris' problems might have been worse if he hadn't followed the path his inner voice said was right for him. However, he has, as one writer advised others in similar situations, "felt the fear and done it anyway". Apart from anything else, it helped with addressing his personal struggles. "It's the way us singer-songwriters make sense of our lives."

Like all artists Kristofferson has his creative frustrations. His principal output has been limited to poetic lyrics; given the standards he has set with his best work, many might say his achievements should satisfy any artistic yearnings. Kris has regularly said he would like to tackle longer works, including his memoirs, for which he signed a contract several years ago, but he openly admits having problems disciplining himself. However, as a colleague of his pointed out, "You might not have written the great novel but you sure have lived it."

Kristofferson has also expressed an interest in painting, which he may have in mind as a fallback when the demands of the entertainment business become too much. Nowadays Kris gets pleasure from the simpler things, like tending his garden in Maui and spending a considerable amount of time with his extended family of eight children and a posse of grand-children. With the older ones, there was some ground to make up since the days when his main focus in life was elsewhere, which led to inevitable tensions in their relationships. Kris expresses delight that all of his children now mix well, though he's not sure how seriously the younger ones take him. "God knows, in my house I'm just the old guy they laugh at every now and then."

Perhaps one of the most fortunate occurrences in Kristofferson's life was meeting Lisa Meyers, to whom he has now been married for 25 years. Not only was she prepared to dedicate a large part of her life to raising their children and providing order and stability, but her legal experience also enabled her to take charge of the various business aspects of her husband's career. One friend describes Lisa as a one-woman entourage who "drives the van".

Kris is proud his passport states his occupation as "writer". Writing is for him, "Where the stuff you feel in your heart is expressed . . . it's the closest thing to your soul." He will continue to write words until, as he puts it, "They throw dirt on me." One of his closest friends, Willie Nelson, paid a powerful tribute when he said of Kristofferson's lyrics, "They are words to live by and that's about as much praise as you can say about any writer." In considering his legacy, Kristofferson concluded, "I will probably be remembered for my songs and my children. I think they are the best things that I have left behind me on the planet."

It remains a blessing for Kris to hear one of his songs on the radio or being hummed by a stranger. As he reflected, "It's nice to know you made a mark that will outlive you."

# Discography

## *(ALBUMS)*

### KRISTOFFERSON

1970 (Monument) Re-released in 1971 as *Me And Bobby McGee*
Blame It On The Stones/ To Beat The Devil/ Me And Bobby McGee/ The Best
Of All Possible Worlds/ Help Me Make It Through The Night/ The Law Is For
The Protection Of The People/ Casey's Last Ride/ Just The Other Side Of
Nowhere/ Darby's Castle/ For The Good Times/ Duvalier's Dream/ Sunday
Mornin' Comin' Down

### THE SILVER TONGUED DEVIL AND I

1971 (Monument)
The Silver Tongued Devil And I/ Jody And The Kid/ Billy Dee/ Good Christian
Soldier/ Breakdown (A Long Way From Home)/ Loving Her Was Easier (Than
Anything I'll Ever Do Again)/ The Taker/ When I Loved Her/ The
Pilgrim-Chapter 33/ Epitaph (Black And Blue)

### BORDER LORD

1972 (Monument)
Josie/Burden Of Freedom/ Stagger Mountain Tragedy/ Border Lord/ Somebody
Nobody Knows/ Little Girl Lost/ Smokey Put The Sweat On Me/ When She's
Wrong/ Gettin' By, High and Strange/ Kiss The World Goodbye

### JESUS WAS A CAPRICORN

1972 (Monument)
Jesus Was A Capricorn (Owed To John Prine)/ Nobody Wins/ It Sure Was
(Love)/ Enough For You/ Help Me/ Jesse Younger/ Give It Time To Be
Tender/ Out of Mind, Out Of Sight/ Sugar Man/ Why Me

### FULL MOON (with Rita Coolidge)

1973 (A&M)
Hard To Be Friends/ Its All Over (All Over Again)/ I Never Had It So Good/
From The Bottle To The Bottom/ Take Time To Love/ Tennessee Blues/ Part

Of Your Life/ I'm Down (But I Keep Falling)/ I Heard The Bluebird Sing/
After The Fact/ Loving Arms/A Song I'd Like To Sing

## SPOOKY LADY'S SIDESHOW
1974 (Monument)
Same Old Song/ Broken Freedom Song/ Shandy (The Perfect Disguise)/
Star-Spangled Bummer/ Lights of Magdala/ I May Smoke Too Much/ One For
The Money/ Late Again (Gettin' Over You)/ Stairway To The Bottom/
Rescue Mission/ Smile At Me Again/ Rock And Roll Time

## BREAKAWAY (with Rita Coolidge)
1974 (Monument)
Lover Please/ We Must Have Been Out Of Our Minds/ Dakota (The Dancing
Bear)/ Watcha Gonna Do/ The Things I Might Have Been/ Slow Down/
Rain/Sweet Susannah/ I've Got To Have You/ I'd Rather Be Sorry/
Crippled Crow

## WHO'S TO BLESS AND WHO'S TO BLAME
1975 (Monument)
The Year 2000 Minus 25/ If It's All The Same To You/ Easy, Come On/
Stallion/ Rocket To Stardom/ Stranger/ Who's To Bless And Who's To Blame/
Don't Cuss The Fiddle/ Silver (The Hunger)

## SURREAL THING
1976 (Monument)
You Show Me Yours ( And I'll Show You Mine)/ Killing Time/ The Prisoner/
Eddie The Eunuch/ It's Never Gonna Be The Same Again/ I Got A Life Of My
Own/ The Stranger I Love/ The Golden Idol/ Bad Love Story/ If You Don't
Like Hank Williams

## A STAR IS BORN (Soundtrack)
1977 (Monument)
Watch Closely Now/ Queen Bee/ Everything/ Lost Inside Of You/ Hellacious
Acres/ Evergreen (Love Theme From A Star Is Born)/ The Woman In The
Moon/ I Believe In Love/ Crippled Crow/ With One More Look At You/
Watch Closely Now/ Evergreen Reprise (Love Theme From A Star Is Born)

## EASTER ISLAND
1978 (Monument)
Risky Bizness/ How Do You Feel (About Foolin' Around)/ Forever In Your
Love/ The Sabre And The Rose/ Spooky Lady's Revenge/ Easter Island/ The

Bigger The Fool (The Harder The Fall)/ Lay Me Down (And Love The World Away)/ The Fighter/ Living Legend

## NATURAL ACT (with Rita Coolidge)
1979 (A&M)
Blue As I Do/ Not Everyone Knows/ I Fought The Law/ Number One/ You're Gonna Love Yourself (In The Morning)/ Loving You Was Easier (Than Anything I'll Ever Do Again)/ Back In My Baby's Arms Again/ Please Don't Tell Me How The Story Ends/ Hoola Hoop/ Love Don't Live Here Anymore/ Silver Mantis

## SHAKE HANDS WITH THE DEVIL
1979 (Monument)
Shake Hands With the Devil/ Prove It To You One More Time Again/ Whiskey, Whiskey/ Lucky in Love/ Seadream/ Killer Barracuda/ Come Sundown/ Michoacan/ Once More With Feeling/ Fallen Angel

## TO THE BONE
1981 (Monument)
Magdalene/ Star-Crossed/ Blessing In Disguise/ The Devil To Pay/ Daddy's Song/ Snakebit/ Nobody Loves Anybody Anymore/ Maybe You Heard/ The Last Time/ I'll Take Any Chance I Can With You

## SINGER/SONGWRITER
1981 (Sony)
Jody And The Kid/ From The Bottle To The Bottom/ Me And Bobby McGee/ Sunday Morning Coming Down/ The Taker/ For The Good Times/ Help Me Make It Through The Night/ Once More With Feeling/ Come Sundown/ I'd Rather Be Sorry/ Nobody Wins/ Stranger/ Loving Her Was Easier (Than Anything I'll Ever Do Again)/ If You Don't Like Hank Williams/ Josie/ Why Me/ They Killed Him/ Vietnam Blues (Dave Dudley)/ Jody And The Kid (Roy Drusky)/ From The Bottle To The Bottom (Billy Walker)/ Sunday Morning Coming Down (Johnny Cash)/ Me And Bobby McGee (Roger Miller)/ The Taker (Waylon Jennings)/ For The Good Times (Ray Price)/ Help Me Make It Through The Night (Sammi Smith)/ Once More With Feeling (Jerry Lee Lewis)/ Come Sundown (Bobby Bare)/ I'd Rather Be Sorry (Ray Price)/ Nobody Wins (Brenda Lee)/ Please Don't Tell Me How The Story Ends (Ronnie Milsap)/ Stranger (Johnny Duncan)/ Help Me Make It Through The Night (Willie Nelson)/ Loving Her Was Easier (Than Anything I'll Ever Do Again) (Tompall and The Glaser Brothers)/ If You Don't Like Hank Williams (Hank Williams Jr)/ Me And Bobby McGee (Janis Joplin)/ They Killed Him (Bob Dylan)

## THE WINNING HAND (with Willie Nelson, Dolly Parton and Brenda Lee)

1982 (Monument)

You're Gonna Love Yourself In The Morning (Nelson and Lee)/ Ping Pong (Kristofferson and Parton)/ You'll Always Have Someone (Nelson)/ Here Comes That Rainbow Again (Kristofferson)/ The Bigger The Fool The Harder The Fall (Kristofferson and Lee)/ Help Me Make It Through The Night (Kristofferson and Lee)/ Happy, Happy Birthday Baby (Parton and Nelson)/ You Left Me A Long, Long Time Ago (Nelson and Lee)/ To Make A Long Story Short, She's Gone (Nelson and Kristofferson)/ Someone Loves You Honey (Lee)/ Everything's Beautiful (In Its Own Way) (Parton and Nelson)/ Bring On The Sunshine (Lee)/ Put It Off Until Tomorrow (Parton and Kristofferson)/ I Never Cared For You (Nelson)/ Casey's Last Ride (Kristofferson and Nelson)/ King Of A Lonely Castle (Nelson)/ The Little Things (Parton)/ The Bandits Of Beverly Hills (Kristofferson)/ What Do You Think About Love? (Parton and Lee)/ Born To Love Me (Lee and Kristofferson)

## MUSIC FROM *SONGWRITER* (with Willie Nelson)

1984 (Columbia)

How Do You Feel About Foolin'Around/ Songwriter/ Who'll Buy My Memories?/ Write Your Own Songs/ Nobody Said It Was Going To Be Easy/ Good Times/ Eye Of The Storm/ Crossing The Border/ Down To Her Socks/ Under The Gun/ Final Attraction

## HIGHWAYMAN (with Johnny Cash, Waylon Jennings and Willie Nelson) 1985 (Columbia)

Highwayman/The Last Cowboy Song/ Jim, I Wore A Tie Today/ Big River/ Committed To Parkview/ Desperados Waiting For A Train/ Deportee (Plane Wreck At Los Gatos)/ Welfare Line/ Against The Wind/ The Twentieth Century Is Almost Over

## REPOSSESSED

1986 (Mercury)

Mean Old Man/ Shipwrecked In The Eighties/ They Killed Him/ What About Me/ El Gavilan (The Hawk)/ El Coyote/ Anthem '84/ The Heart/ This Old Road/Love Is The Way

## THIRD WORLD WARRIOR

1990 (Mercury)

The Eagle And The Bear/ Third World Warrior/ Aguila Del Norte/ The Hero/ Don't Let the Bastards (Get You Down)/ Love Of Money/ Third World War/ Jesse Jackson/ Mal Sacate/ Sandinista

## HIGHWAYMAN 2 (with Johnny Cash, Waylon Jennings and Willie Nelson)

1990 (Columbia)

Silver Stallion/ Born And Raised In Black And White/ Two Stories Wide/ We're All In Your Corner Tonight/ American Remains/ Anthem '84/ Angels Love Bad Men/ Songs That Make A Difference/ Living Legend/ Texas

## LIVE AT THE PHILHARMONIC

1992 (Monument) (Recorded live in 1972)

Late John Garfield Blues/ Jesus Was A Capricorn (Owed To John Prine)/ Nobody Wins/ Jesse Younger/ Loving Her Was Easier (Than Anything I'll Ever Do Again)/ Late Again (Gettin' Over You)/ Out Of Mind, Out Of Sight/ Sugar Man/ Billy Dee/ The Law Is For The Protection Of The People/ For The Good Times/ Sunday Mornin' Comin' Down/Okie From Muskogee/ Border Lord/ Funny How Time Slips Away / Me And Paul/ Mountain Dew/ The Pilgrim – Chapter 33/ Rainbow Road/ It Sure Was (Love)/ Help Me/ Me And Bobby McGee/ Whiskey, Whiskey

## THE ROAD GOES ON FOREVER (Highwaymen with Johnny Cash, Waylon Jennings and Willie Nelson)

1995 (Capitol/EMI)

The Devil's Right Hand/ Live Forever/ Everyone Gets Crazy/ It Is What It Is/ I Do Believe/ The End Of Understanding/ True Love Travels On A Gravel Road/ Death And Hell/ Waiting For A Long Time/ Here Comes That Rainbow Again/ The Road Goes On Forever

## A MOMENT OF FOREVER

1995 (Justice Records)

A Moment Of Forever/ Worth Fighting For/ Johnny Lobo/ The Promise/ Shipwrecked In The Eighties/ Slouching Toward The Millennium/ Between Heaven And Here/ Casey's Last Ride/ Good Love (Shouldn't Feel So Bad)/ New Game Now/ New Mister Me/ Under The Gun/ Road Warrior's Lament Sam's Song (Ask Any Working Girl)

## THE AUSTIN SESSIONS

1999 (Atlantic)

Me And Bobby McGee/ Sunday Morning Coming Down/ For The Good Times/ The Silver Tongued Devil And I/ Help Me Make It Through The Night/ Loving Her Was Easier (Than Anything I'll Ever Do Again)/ To Beat The Devil/ Who's To Bless And Who's To Blame/ Why Me/ Nobody Wins/ The Pilgrim – Chapter 33/ Please Don't Tell Me How The Story Ends

## HONKY TONK HEROES (with Waylon Jennings, Willie Nelson and Billy Joe Shaver)
2000 (Free Falls Entertainment)
Honky Tonk Heroes (Like Me)/ Willie The Wandering Gypsy And Me/ I'm Just An Old Chunk Of Coal/ Ain't No God In Mexico/ You Asked Me To/ Oklahoma Wind/ I Couldn't Be Me Without You/ Tramp On Your Street/ Easy Come Easy Go/ We Are The Cowboys

## BROKEN FREEDOM SONG: LIVE FROM SAN FRANCISCO
2003 (Oh Boy Records)
Shipwrecked In The Eighties/ Darby's Castle/ Broken Freedom Song/ Shandy (The Perfect Disguise)/ What About Me/ Here Comes That Rainbow Again/ Nobody Wins/ The Race/ The Captive/ The Circle (Song For Layla Al-Attar and Los Olividados)/ Sky King/ Sandinista/ Moment Of Forever/ Don't Let The Bastards Get You Down/ Road Warrior's Lament

## THE ESSENTIAL KRIS KRISTOFFERSON
2004 (Sony)
Sunday Mornin' Comin' Down/ To Beat The Devil/ Just The Other Side Of Nowhere/ Me And Bobby McGee/ The Best Of All Possible Worlds/ Casey's Last Ride/ Help Me Make It Through The Night/ Darby's Castle/ Jody And The Kid/ Loving Her Was Easier (Than Anything I'll Ever Do Again)/ For The Good Times/ Come Sundown/ From The Bottle To The Bottom/ Billy Dee/ Breakdown (A Long Way From Home)/ The Silver Tongued Devil And I/ The Taker/ The Pilgrim: Chapter 33 (Live)/ Border Lord/ The Sabre And The Rose/ Broken Freedom Song/ Jesus Was A Capricorn (Owed To John Prine)/ Shandy (The Perfect Disguise)/ Sugar Man/ The Last Time/ Nobody Wins/ I'd Rather Be Sorry (with Rita Coolidge)/ Highwayman/ Don't Cuss The Fiddle/ The Bigger The Fool, The Harder The Fall/ Stranger/ If You Don't Like Hank Williams/ Here Comes That Rainbow Again/ Once More With Feeling/ How Do You Feel About Fooling Around (with Willie Nelson)/ Why Me/ Please Don't Tell Me How The Story Ends

## THIS OLD ROAD
2006 (New West Records)
This Old Road/ Pilgrim's Progress/ Last Thing To Go/ Wild American/ In The News/ Burden Of Freedom/ Chase The Feeling/ Holy Creation/ Show Goes On/ Thank You For A Life/ Final Attraction

## LIVE FROM AUSTIN, TEXAS
2006 (New West Records)
Star Crossed/ You Show Me Yours (And I'll Show You Mine)/ Here Comes

That Rainbow Again/ Help Me Make It Through The Night/ Me And Bobby
McGee/ Magdalene/ Nobody Loves Anybody Anymore/ Darby's Castle/
Casey's Last Ride/ Pilgrim/ For The Good Times/ Loving Her Was Easier (Than
Anything I'll Ever Do Again)/ Sunday Mornin' Comin' Down/ The Silver
Tongued Devil And I/ Smile At Me Again/ Why Me

## LIVE FROM AUSTIN TX: OUTLAW COUNTRY (with Willie Nelson, Waylon Jennings, Kimmie Rhodes and Billy Joe Shaver)
2006 (New West Records) (recorded in 1996)
Fighter (Kristofferson)/ I'd Have Been Out Of Jail (Jennings)/ Just One Love
(Rhodes)/ First And Last Time (Shaver)/ We Don't Run (Nelson and
Kristofferson)/ Promise (Kristofferson)/ I Do Believe (Jennings)/ Espiratu Santo
Bay (Rhodes)/ You Just Can't Beat Jesus Christ (Shaver)/ Too Sick To Pray
(Nelson)/ Pilgrim's Progress (Kristofferson)/ Just Watch Your Mama And Me
(Jennings)/ Lines (Rhodes)/ On The Road Again (Nelson and Jennings)

## THE PILGRIM: A CELEBRATION OF KRIS KRISTOFFERSON
2006 (American Roots Publishing)
The Pilgrim-Chapter 33 – Emmylou Harris & Friends (Sam Bush, Jon Randall,
Byron House, Randy Scruggs)/ Maybe You Heard – Todd Snider/ The Circle –
Marta Gómez/ Loving Him Was Easier (Than Anything I'll Ever Do Again) –
Rosanne Cash/ Come Sundown – Rodney Crowell/ For The Good Times –
Lloyd Cole & Jill Sobule/ Jesus Was A Capricorn (Owed To John Prine) –
Marshall Chapman/ The Silver Tongued Devil And I – Shooter Jennings/
Sunday Morning Coming Down – Gretchen Wilson/ Sandinista – Patty Griffin &
Charanga Cakewalk/ Darby's Castle – Russell Crowe and The Ordinary Fear of
God/ Me And Bobby McGee – Brian McKnight/ Smile At Me Again
(instrumental) – Randy Scruggs/ The Captive – Jessi Colter w/special guest
Vance Haines/ Help Me Make It Through The Night – Bruce Robison & Kelly
Willis/ Why Me – Shawn Camp/ The Legend – Willie Nelson/ Coda: Please
Don't Tell Me How The Story Ends – Kris Kristofferson (demo recording,
circa 1970)

# Filmography

Over nearly four decades of acting work, Kris Kristofferson has appeared in big-screen movies, television films and mini-series, documentaries, talk shows, music videos, public service broadcasts, awards and variety shows (for which he has sometimes been the master of ceremonies). There have also been many musical concerts filmed for later release on video or DVD as well as movies, television or radio shows and even computer games for which he has provided narration or voice-over. His songs, mainly the early classics, have been featured on the soundtracks of countless screen offerings.

What follows is a list of his main films for the big screen and television. As his celluloid career shows no signs of abating, it remains a case of "to be continued".

*The Last Movie* (1971)
*Cisco Pike* (1972)
*Pat Garrett And Billy The Kid* (1973)
*Blume In Love* (1973)
*Bring Me The Head Of Alfredo Garcia* (1974)
*Alice Doesn't Live Here Anymore* (1974)
*The Sailor Who Fell From Grace With The Sea* (1976)
*Vigilante Force* (1976)
*A Star Is Born* (1976)
*Semi-Tough* (1977)
*Convoy* (1978)
*Freedom Road* (1979) (TV)
*Heaven's Gate* (1980)
*Rollover* (1981)
*The Lost Honor Of Kathryn Beck* (1984)
*Flashpoint* (1984)
*Songwriter* (1984)

*Trouble In Mind* (1985)
*The Last Days Of Frank And Jesse James* (1986) (TV)
*Blood And Orchids* (1986) (TV)
*Stagecoach* (1986) (TV)
*Amerika* (1987) (TV)
*The Tracker* (1988) (TV)
*Big Top Pee-wee* (1988)
*Millennium* (1989)
*Welcome Home* (1989)
*Sandino* (1990)
*Perfume Of The Cyclone (aka Night Of The Cyclone)* (1990)
*Pair Of Aces* (1990) (TV)
*Another Pair Of Aces: Three Of A Kind* (1991) (TV)
*Original Intent* (1992)
*Miracle In The Wilderness* (1992) (TV)
*Christmas In Connecticut* (1992) (TV)

*Paper Hearts* (1993)
*No Place To Hide* (1993)
*Trouble Shooters: Trapped Beneath The Earth* (1993) (TV)
*Knights* (1993)
*Sodbusters* (1994)
*Pharaoh's Army* (1995)
*Brothers' Destiny* (1995)
*Tad* (1995) (TV)
*Inflammable* (1995) (TV)
*Lone Star* (1996)
*Blue Rodeo* (1996) (TV)
*Fire Down Below* (1997)
*Two For Texas* (1998) (TV)
*Girls' Night* (1998)
*Blade* (1998)
*Dance With Me* (1998)
*A Soldier's Daughter Never Cries* (1998)
*Outlaw Justice* (1999) (TV)
*NetForce* (1999) (TV)
*Payback* (1999)
*Molokai: The Story of Father Damien* (1999)
*Limbo* (1999)
*The Joyriders* (1999)

*Comanche* (2000)
*Perfect Murder, Perfect Town: JonBenét And The City Of Boulder* (2000) (TV)
*Planet Of The Apes* (2001)
*Chelsea Walls* (2001)
*Wooly Boys* (2001)
*D-Tox* (2002)
*Blade II* (2002)
*The Break* (2003) (TV)
*Where The Red Fern Grows* (2003)
*Silver City* (2004)
*Lives Of The Saints* (2004) (TV)
*Blade: Trinity* (2004)
*The Jacket* (2005)
*The Wendell Baker Story* (2005)
*14 Hours* (2005) (TV)
*Dreamer: Inspired By A True Story* (2005)
*Disappearances* (2006)
*Fast Food Nation* (2006)
*Room 10* (2006)
*Crossing The Heart* (2007)
*Jump Out Boys* (2008)
*Powder Blue* (2008)
*For Sale By Owner* (2008)
*He's Just Not That Into You* (2008)

# Bibliography

## *Magazines and Newspapers*

I consulted a very large number of newspapers and magazines. Thanks to the wonderful world of the internet I was able access newspaper articles going back to the Thirties, which would have been extremely hard to get hold of any other way. These were of particular assistance in giving an insight into the privileged world Kristofferson was brought up in. One website in particular – www.newspaperarchive.com – was invaluable. It allowed me to search through countless old newspapers with a series of clicks of the mouse from the comfort of my study. Some of the articles I read provided valuable factual information and original insights; others simply contained useful snippets. The following were of particular interest:

Bowman, David. "My Lunch With Kris Kristofferson", *Salon People*. http://www.salon.com/people/lunch/1999/09/24/kristofferson/index2.html September 4, 1999.

Burke, Tom. "Kristofferson's Talking Blues", *Country Music Review*, October 1974.

Burke, Tom. "Kristofferson's Talking Blues Part 2", *Country Music Review*, November 1974.

Cackett, Alan. "A Man Repossessed", *Maverick*, March 2007.

Denton, Andrew. Transcript of interview on ABC's *Enough Rope*. http://www.abc.net.au/tv/enoughrope/transcripts/s1422317.htm July 25, 2005.

Ditlea, Steve. "Kris Kristofferson Stars As 'Billy The Kid' ", *Country Music*, July 1973.

Flippo, Chet. "Kris Kristofferson Talks Songwriting", interview for CMT (Country Music Television) http://www.cmt.com/artists/news/1564469/20070710/hall_tom_t_.jhtml July 10 and 11, 2007.

Friskics-Warren, Bill. "To Beat The Devil – Intimations of Immortality", *No Depression*, March–April 2006.

Hedy, Judy. "Kristofferson . . . 1980" *Country Song Roundup*, September 1980.

Langer, Andy. "Q & A With Kris Kristofferson", *Esquire*, February 27, 2006.

Leigh, Spencer. "The Films Of Kris Kristofferson", *Country Music People*, February and March 1984.

Leigh, Spencer. "Rita Coolidge", *Country Music People*, October 2006.

McPherson, Douglas. "Kris Kristofferson The Last American Hero", *Country Music People*, April 2004.

Nickerson, Marina. "Kris Kristofferson Talks About Willie Nelson – And Much More", *Country Music Scene*, summer 1980.

Patterson, John. "I Was Killing Myself", *The Guardian*, March 4, 2008.

Redshaw, David. "Kristofferson: Now Leader Of The Pack", *Country Music People*, July 1978.

Rensin, David. "King Kristofferson", *Country Music*, September 1974.

Robertson, Peter. "King Of The Road", *Country Music International*, June 1995.

Tobler, John. "Billy Swan", *Country Music People*, April 1995.

Unattributed. "Kris Kristofferson. Lone Star Loner", *Country Style*, April 1981.

The complete list of newspapers and magazines consulted – some via the internet – is as follows:

*Amarillo Globe-Times* (Texas)
*Anniston Star* (Alabama)
*Austin Chronicle* (Texas)
*Bridgeport Telegram* (Connecticut)
*CBS News*
*Country Music*
*Country Music International*
*Country Music People*
*Country Music Review*
*Country Music Scene*
*Country Rhythms*
*Country Song Roundup*
*Country Style*
*Daily Herald* (Chicago)
*Daily Intelligencer/Montgomery County Record*
*Daily Kennebec Journal* (Augusta, Maine)
*Daily Telegraph*
*Des Moines Register*
*Esquire*
*European Stars and Stripes* (Darmstadt, Germany)
*Fond Du Lac Reporter* (Wisconsin)
*Hillsboro Press Gazette* (Ohio)
*Independent* (Long Beach, California)
*Indie News*
*Lincoln Star* (Nebraska)
*Look*
*Marysville Journal-Tribune* (Ohio)
*Maverick*
*Modern Screen's Country Music Special*

*Moviecrazed*
*Nevada State Journal*
*New Castle News* (Pennsylvania)
*No Depression*
*Pacific Stars and Stripes* (Tokyo)
*Playboy*
*Pomona College Magazine*
*Press-Telegram* (California)
*Rolling Stone*
*Salon People*
*San Antonio Express*
*San Mateo Times* (California)
*Star-News* (Pasadena)
*Stevens Point Daily Journal* (Wisconsin)
*Sunday Freeman* (Kingston, New York)
*Syracuse Herald Journal*
*The Argus* (Fremont, California)
*The Brandon Sun*
*The Bridgeport Post* (Connecticut)
*The Brownsville Herald*
*The Capital* (Annapolis, Maryland)
*The Chronicle Telegram* (Elyria, Ohio)
*The Daily Intelligencer* (Doylestown, Pennsylvania)
*The Daily Times – News* (Burlington, North Carolina)
*The Gallup Independent* (New Mexico)
*The Gastonia Gazette* (North Carolina)
*The Gleaner* (Kingston, Jamaica)
*The Guardian*
*The Lima News* (Ohio)
*The Nashville Banner*
*The News* (Port Arthur, Texas)
*The News and Tribune* (Jefferson City, Missouri)

*The Observer*
*The Oakland Tribune* (California)
*The Pocono Record* (Stroudsburg, Pennsylvania)
*The Post Crescent* (Appleton, Wisconsin)
*The Post-Standard* (Syracuse, New York)
*The Salina Journal* (Kansas)
*The Salt Lake Tribune* (Salt Lake City)
*The Sunday Oakland Tribune* (California)
*The Tennessean* (Nashville)
*The Times*
*The Times* (San Mateo)
*The Times-Picayune* (New Orleans)
*The Times Recorder* (Zanesville, Ohio)
*The Times Record* (Troy, New York)
*The Valley Independent* (Monessen, Pennsylvania)
*The Valley Morning Star* (Harlingen, Texas)
*The Valley News* (California)
*The Valley Star – Monitor – Herald* (Brownsville)
*The Valley Sunday Star – Monitor – Herald* (Brownsville)
*Time*
*Troy Record* (New York)
*Tucson Daily Citizen* (Arizona)
*Van Wert Times-Bulletin* (Ohio)
*Walla Walla Union-Bulletin* (Washington)
*Waterloo Courier* (Iowa)
*Weekend*

# *Books*

Allen, Bob. (Editor). *The Blackwell Guide To Recorded Country Music*. Blackwell Publishing, Oxford. 1994.

Baggelaar, Kristin and Donald Milton. *The Folk Music Encyclopaedia*. Omnibus Press, London 1977.

Bane, Michael. *Willie*. Dell Publishing Co, New York. 1984.

Blake, Mark (Editor in Chief). *Dylan. Visions, Portraits And Back Pages*. Dorling Kindersley, London. 2005.

Bockris, Victor. *Patti Smith*. Fourth Estate, London. 1998.

Bogdanov, Vladimir, Chris Woodstra, and Stephen Thomas Erlewine, (Editors). *All Music Guide To Country: The Definitive Guide To Country Music*. 2nd edition. Backbeat Books, San Francisco. 2003.

Brown, Jim. *Willie Nelson. Red Headed Stranger*. Quarry Music Books, Ontario. 2001.

Bufwack, Mary A, and Robert K Oermann. *Finding Her Voice. The Illustrated History Of Women In Country Music*. Henry Holt and Company, New York. 1993.

Byworth, Tony. *Giants Of Country Music*. Hamlyn, London. 1984.

Cantwell, David and Bill Friskics-Warren. *Heartaches By The Number. Country Music's 500 Greatest Singles*. Vanderbilt University Press, Nashville. 2003.

Cash, Johnny, with Patrick Carr. *Cash. The Autobiography*. Harper Paperbacks, New York. 1997.

Dawidoff, Nicholas. *In The Country Of Country. People And Places In American Music*. Pantheon Books, New York. 1997.

Doggett, Peter. *Are You Ready For The Country?* Penguin, London. 2001.

Dolan, Sean. *Johnny Cash*. Chelsea House Publishers, New York. 1995.

Dylan, Bob. *Chronicles Volume 1*. Simon and Schuster, London. 2004.

Eggar, Robin. *Shania Twain. The Biography*. Headline, London. 2001.

Emery, Ralph, with Tom Carter. *Memories: The Autobiography Of Ralph Emery*. Macmillan, New York. 1992.

Emery, Ralph, with Tom Carter. *More Memories*. GP Putnam's Sons. New York. 1993.

Escott, Colin. *The Story Of Country Music*. BBC Worldwide Ltd, London. 2003.

Friary, Ned, and Glenda Bendure. *Hawaii*. Lonely Planet Publications, Victoria. 2000.

Friedman, Myra. Janis Joplin. *Buried Alive. The Biography*. Harmony Books, New York. 1992.

Gatlin, Larry, with Jeff Lenburg. *All The Gold In California And Other People, Places And Things*. Thomas Nelson, Nashville. 1998.

Hall, Tom T. *The Storyteller's Nashville*. Doubleday and Company, Inc, New York. 1979.

Hefley, James C. *Country Music Comin' Home*. Hannibal Books, Garland, Texas. 1992.

Heylin, Clinton. *Bob Dylan. Behind The Shades. The Biography – Take 2*. Penguin Books Limited, Harmondsworth. 2000.

Horstman, Dorothy. *Sing Your Heart Out, Country Boy*. Country Music Foundation Press, Nashville. 1996.

Jennings, Waylon, with Lenny Kaye. *Waylon*. Warner Books, New York. 1996.

Kalet, Beth. *Kris Kristofferson*. Quick Fox, New York. 1979.

Larkin, Colin (General Editor). *The Guinness Who's Who Of Country Music*. Guinness Publishing, Enfield, Middlesex. 1993.

Leamer, Laurence. *Three Chords And The Truth. Hope, Heartbreak, and Changing Fortunes In Nashville*. HarperCollins, New York. 1997.

Lewry, Peter. *Johnny Cash Chronicle. I've Been Everywhere*. Helter Skelter Publishing, London. 2001.

Lindwall, Bo (Editor). *24 Famous Swedish Americans And Their Ancestors*. The Federation Of Swedish Genealogical Societies, Stockholm. 1996.

Logan, Nick, with Bob Woffinden. *The New Musical Express Book Of Rock 2*. Star, London. 1973.

Lomax III, John. *Nashville: Music City USA*. Harry N Abrams, Inc., Publishers, New York. 1985.

Lynn Loretta, with George Vecsey. *Coal Miner's Daughter*. Warner Books, New York. 1976.

McCloud, Barry (Editor). *Definitive Country. The Ultimate Encyclopedia Of Country Music And Its Performers*. Perigree Books, New York. 1995.

Malone, Bill C, and Judith McCulloh (Editors). *Stars Of Country Music*. University of Illinois Press. Urbana. Chicago and London. 1975.

Marschall, Rich. *The Encyclopaedia Of Country And Western Music*. Bison Books, London. 1985.

Mattson, Hans. *Reminiscences. The Story Of An Emigrant.* St. Paul, Minnesota, D. D. Merrill Co., 1891.

Medved, Harry, and Randy Dreyfuss. *The Fifty Worst Movies Of All Time (And How They Got That Way).* Warner Books, New York. 1978.

Medved, Michael, and Harry Medved. *The Golden Turkey Awards.* Putnam Publishing Group, New York. 1980.

Miller, Stephen. *Johnny Cash. The Life Of An American Icon.* Omnibus Press, London. 2003.

Miller, Stephen. *Smart Blonde. Dolly Parton A Biography* Omnibus Press, London. 2006.

Nelson, Willie, with Bud Shrake. *I Didn't Come Here And I Ain't Leaving.* Macmillan, London. 1988.

Obstfeld, Raymond and Shiela Burgener. *Twang! The Ultimate Book Of Country Music Quotations.* Henry Holt and Company, New York. 1997.

O'Brien, Karen. *Joni Mitchell. Shadows And Light. The Definitive Biography.* Virgin Books Limited, London. 2001.

Oermann, Robert K. *America's Music. The Roots Of Country Music.* Turner Publishing, Inc, Atlanta. 1996.

Parrish, James Robert, and Michael R Pitts. *Songsters: Singers Who Act And Actors Who Sing.* Taylor and Francis, New York. 2002.

Pugh, Ronnie. *Ernest Tubb: The Texas Troubadour.* Duke University Press, London. 1996.

Raine, Kathleen. *William Blake.* Oxford University Press, New York. 1970

Riese, Randall. *Nashville Babylon.* Guild Publishing. London, New York, Sydney, Toronto. 1989.

Seaborg, Glenn T, and Seaborg, Eric. *Adventures In The Atomic Age: From Watts To Washington.* Farrar, Straus and Giroux, New York. 2001.

Shelton, Robert. *No Direction Home. The Life And Music Of Bob Dylan.* Penguin, London. 1986.

Shipman, David. *The Great Movie Stars, 3 The Independent Years.* Warner Books, London. 1991.

Somma, Robert (Editor). *No One Waved Goodbye.* Charisma Books, London. 1973.

Sounes, Howard. *Down The Highway. The Life Of Bob Dylan.* Doubleday, London. 2001.

Streissguth, Michael. *Johnny Cash. The Biography*. Da Capo Press, Cambridge. 2006.

Turner, Steve. *The Man Called Cash. The Life, Love, And Faith Of An American Legend*. W Publishing Group, Nashville. 2004.

U2, with Neil McCormick. *U2*. HarperCollins, London. 2006.

Wacholtz, Larry E. *Inside Country Music*. (Revised Edition). Billboard Publications Inc, New York. 1986.

Willman, Chris. *Rednecks And Bluenecks: The Politics Of Country Music*. The New Press, New York. 2005.

Wootton, Richard. *The Illustrated Country Almanac. A Day-By-Day History Of Country Music*. Virgin Books, London. 1982.

Wren, Christopher S. *Johnny Cash. Winners Got Scars Too*. Abacus, London. 1974.

Wynette, Tammy, with Joan Dew. *Stand By Your Man*. Arrow Books, London. 1981.

Ziemer, Joe. *Mickey Newbury:Crystal And Stone*. Authorhouse, Indiana. 2004

Zmuda, Bob. *Andy Kaufman Revealed! Best Friend Tells All*. Little Brown and Company, New York. 1999.

Zwonitzer, Mark, with Charles Hirshberg. *Will You Miss Me When I'm Gone?: The Carter Family And Their Legacy In American Music*. Simon and Schuster, New York. 2002.

The liner notes to Kris' own albums contained a few gems. Of most interest though was the lengthy essay by Peter Cooper for the tribute album *The Pilgrim: A Celebration Of Kris Kristofferson*.